SO LONG, SHAKESPEARE

Tom Brown's two teenage obsessions were Shakespeare and *Star Wars*. To this day he remains uncertain whether *Hamlet* or *The Empire Strikes Back* is mankind's single greatest artistic achievement. In the 2000s, he worked at Shakespeare's Globe under the stewardship of the famous anti-Stratfordian Mark Rylance, becoming fascinated by the passion associated with discussion of 'Shakespeare's' true identity. At the same time, the *Star Wars* prequels were in cinemas, cheerfully wrecking a whole childhood's happy memories. One day, as if by magic, the two obsessions fused. *So Long, Shakespeare* is the result.

First published as an eBook in 2012.
This paperback edition printed 2013.

ISBN-13 978-1482091953
ISBN-10 148209195X

Copyright © 2012 Tom Brown
tombrownbooks.wordpress.com

Cover by Brian Edwards
brianedwards.co.uk

All rights reserved. This book may not be reproduced in any form, in whole or in part, without written permission from the author. This is a work of fiction. Names, characters, businesses, places, events and incidents are either the products of the author's imagination or used in a fictitious manner. 'Oscar ®,' 'Oscars ®,' 'Academy Award ®' and 'Academy Awards ®' are registered trademarks and service marks of the Academy of Motion Picture Arts and Sciences ('A.M.P.A.S.').

eBook edition available for Kindle, Nook, Kobo, Sony Reader and Apple devices.

So Long, Shakespeare

The Tortured Artist I

The room was cold, damp and dark. On every side, crumbling brickwork was held together by a thick smothering of black matt paint, illuminated by a shadeless 100 watt bulb that swung pendulously each time a train rumbled overhead – and since those disturbances came every five minutes, the shadows in the room were rarely at rest. The peak of the arched ceiling was directly above his desk, and it often felt like the walls were enveloping him; a sensation given depth and animation by the drugs.

He remembered little about his arrival. By the time they travelled, the initial dose had kicked in, and his mind was in the first of its now customary whirls, constantly shifting gear, refusing to fix on any one subject, at any one speed, for any period of time. The only thing he knew for certain was the name of the city he was in.

Worries were starting to mount. He was a fortnight in, and still had nothing to show. The daily doses came and went, rarely failing to deliver a surge that had him at least poised at his desk, ready to create. But the troughs quickly followed, while the headache – a terrible, pulsing, depressing thing – hadn't eased since day one, repeatedly deadening whatever liveliness he mustered. Throughout it all, he'd tirelessly mined memory and learning for inspiration, but had found little to ignite the explosive energy he was getting from the tablets. He was, after all, only young. 'Write what you know' could only carry him so far.

Still, he'd keep trying. He desperately wanted to do what was being asked of him, if only to alleviate the chaos inside, conjured by the multiplicity of ingredients going into the pills – a new one, sometimes even a new two, for every fruitless day. The morning before, he had tried suggesting a more settled regime – to see if a little stability mightn't catalyse things – but the old man wouldn't have it. If it wasn't working over one 24 hour span, he insisted, it needed changing for the next.

The young man sat at the piano and played a fragment of melody that had occurred to him the day before, sticking with him sufficiently to have popped into his head when he used the toilet overnight. It was a falling phrase, the end of something, though whether it was destined to resolve or collapse disharmoniously he wasn't sure. He could hear both outcomes, but when he tried to play them, the one cancelled the other out; his fingers wouldn't do as they were told.

He headed back to his desk, wondering if the old man's strategy – increasing the pills' complexity to unlock simplicity – was based on actual knowledge, or simply impatient guesswork. If the latter, as the young man increasingly suspected, then it was harder than ever to believe the assurances that this was collaboration, not incarceration.

He banished the thought. The only way he could survive what he was being asked to do, was to try to do it. His reward, he told himself, would be the one thing presently denied him: a coherent sense of why he was being asked to do it.

He looked around, watching the shadows sway on the armature, the easel, and across the dirty sheets on his bed. The rhythm of the room soothed his worries. Part of him wanted to sleep, but such moments of calm were precious. He needed to channel the peace.

Computers were banned – an enemy of clear-thinking – so he pulled up his notepad and raised his pen. Perhaps poetry, a little abstraction, might yet be the thing to transcend his present limitations.

He wrote an opening stanza, then a second, and a third. But before the fourth escaped his head, the sound of another train shattered the inspiration that, weakly and briefly, had connected the disparate parts of his creativity.

The poem went into the bin, and the young man went back to thinking.

Chapter 1

Seated snugly behind his desk, Joe Seabright couldn't help but look at his *Solix Chronicles* clock. Every few seconds, as if on a spring, his eyes snapped away from his screen and angled up at the far wall, squinting at the laser sword hands as they inched towards nine. He urged his eyes back to the business in hand, only to find his fingers wandering from the keypad, fiddling with action figures as his ears tuned in to the ticking and tocking. He stood and gathered himself – puffing out his cheeks, devouring a quick doughnut, air-punching the nerves from his body – before re-taking his seat and reprising the inexorable cycle one more time.

This pattern had been on repeat for at least an hour, during which he'd accomplished precisely zero, when a knock at the door confirmed what the clock suggested: the moment of truth had arrived.

'Yep.' He cast his eyes screenwards and pretended to type.

The door opened. 'It's starting,' said his visitor.

Refusing to look up, Joe shifted in his chair. 'I know.'

'Sure you don't wanna watch?'

Joe reached for an hour-old cup of coffee. 'Sure,' he replied, struggling not to retch as he swallowed the lukewarm liquid.

'Whatever you say, boss.'

He raised a hand to wave his producer away, only to realise it was shaking with nerves and swiftly remove it from view. Jerry gave a knowing chuckle.

'I'll be back in five to let you know.'

The door closed and Joe jumped up, jarring the desk with his belly and sending the action figures flying. Damn it all! He was a grown man, for Christ's sake: a grown man of fifty years, yet here he was, about to spew from anxiety like some stupid kid. And all because he couldn't help caring what others thought of him.

He yanked up his Levi's and tucked in his *Rise of the Glozbacks* t-shirt, grabbing another doughnut and focusing on some positives: on those gazillions of teenagers whose experience of the world was so much richer thanks to him; on how the saga had woven itself into the fabric of popular culture as a touchstone, a point of reference, a building block of youngsters' education; on the fact that literally everyone alive knew of the movies, and a great many, even the unfortunate few who'd never seen a frame, could recognise the characters, whistle the music, quote memorable lines.

As his guts rumbled with worry, that was all worth remembering. So what if there was one silly dream he had yet to realise? Fact was, people lived whole lives by snippets of his heroes' wisdom. In the space of two TV series and four movies, he'd forged a fiction so potent it mingled with reality itself. Not only that, he'd revolutionised Hollywood. Just what kind of fool was he to have attained so much and *still* want more?

He gobbled up his doughnut, becalmed by resurgent inner peace as he sat back down at his desk. Licking his lips clean of sugar, he was about to resume work when he caught sight of the shelf in the corner: his special, empty shelf, reserved for the one thing his world was lacking; the thing he craved above all else.

Oh Lord, how clearly he saw it there, standing handsomely in its immaculate posture, an object as admiring as it was admired, blessing him with acclaim. He imagined reaching out and caressing it, relishing the unfeasible weight as he wrapped his fingers round its golden slimness, holding it to his heart and feeling, finally, like he belonged: no longer derided as a moronic blockbusting brute, but acknowledged and embraced as the thing he knew he was – a genuine genius; an authentic *artist*.

'Boss?'

Joe tore his eyes off the shelf. Jerry was standing in the doorway.

'Well?!' He jumped up and grabbed his producer by the shoulders. 'Are we in?'

Jerry peeled off his boss's hands, and stepped away. A moment later, he shook his head.

Joe's mouth fell open.

'We're in,' said Jerry, 'but only for the usual. Visual Effects, Sound Design . . .' He gazed at the swimming pool that backed onto Joe's office. 'Music too.' He glanced back and smiled. 'Which is nice.'

Joe's stumpy legs felt like a pair of leaden weights, buried deep in the S and the C of a *Solix Chronicles* rug that felt more like quicksand than carpet. For all that he should have known better, a part of him really had believed this would be the one. *Rise of the Glozbacks* was the best picture yet, and by far the most popular with the franchise's fans who, in the six months since it premiered, had made it the highest-grossing movie of all time. As for the industry, Joe's PR people had assured him the traditional prejudice was dying; that people were accepting Joe as a visionary, the creator of grand stories, grandly told.

He looked again at his shelf. Emptier now than ever, it taunted him with its bareness. How could they have got it so wrong *again*? How could he have been so dumb to believe they might get it right?

He held his hands to his eyes as the tears worked their way out. Sure, it was silly, but the instinct was uncontrollable. Oscar glory had been his lifelong dream, and though the planetary dominance of his space epic swelled his heart with pride, it really only strengthened his craving for the ultimate vindication. Success had bred suspicion of his movies' true merits, making him ever more determined to show that a space opera like *Chronicles* was just as worthy as world-conquering masterpieces by Shakespeare or Wagner – and that its creator should be considered their imaginative and intellectual equal.

Nothing in the world could say that better than an Oscar. And though the franchise itself had already won heaps, awards for special effects, sound design and music were no consolation. Not when Joe's concern was with the whole: with the thing itself, the work of art. For him, there was only one Oscar that counted, and it was in the shadow of that elusive Best Picture statuette that all the other accolades languished as inconsequential footnotes.

'I can't believe it,' he croaked, mind and mouth drained of their accustomed vigour. 'Why can't they see me for what I am?'

Jerry embraced his boss. 'Come here, buddy.'

Joe started to sob. And as he sobbed, he looked over his producer's shoulder and caught sight of the five picture frames occupying the opposite wall. The first four were occupied by one-sheet posters for each movie to date – *Birth of a Hero, Tyron's Reign of Terror, Father and Son*, and *Rise of the Glozbacks* – while the fifth and final frame remained tantalisingly empty.

'Oh Lord,' he said, lifting his head.

'What is it?'

'I've only got one more movie, Jerry. One last chance to make it happen.'

He broke free and marched, zombie-like, back to the desk. His cushioned leather chair groaned as he settled.

'No time to waste. Gotta get working. Make this the best one yet.' He glanced up at his producer, sweat trickling down his brow as, pulse by painful pulse, a crushing headache took hold. 'I'll come find you later.'

Jerry nodded as Joe retrieved a bottle of painkillers from the drawer, slugged down half a dozen, and read the words on screen:

The Solix Chronicles V: Triumph of the Solix
by Joe Seabright

First Draft, 23rd February, 2022

He scrolled to the first page proper. Collecting himself, he closed his eyes and transported himself to that special place: the place where imagination was as infinite as the cosmos itself. He pictured the lights in the theatre darkening, the curtains opening, and the huge black screen filling with those familiar logos:

JoeCo Presents
A Joe Seabright Film

Then, out of the ghostly silence and star-speckled void, a glorious brass fanfare as the words THE SOLIX CHRONICLES swept into view, followed below by a mighty sea of text, parading upwards across the expanses of space.

He opened his eyes and read:

Triumph of the Solix

Sights set firmly on intergalactic domination, Nuranghy Tyron, High Lord of the Cafillians, has brainwashed his army of suppliant Glozbacks with a distorted version of the Spirit and dispatched them on a grievous mission to hunt down the Solix and turn them either to evil or slaughter them.

Back on Solus, the spiritual leader of the Solix, Greathan Earloser, is recovering after confronting his apprentice son Mark, who has rebelled against his father's training at every turn, ardent in his love for Regina, and blind to the importance of the arcane ways and mystical beliefs of the Solix.

Desperate to leave Solus and the Solix behind, Mark has eloped with Regina to a distant planet to live a life of peace and harmony, unaware of the horrific danger bearing down on his homeland, and threatening to destroy not only his fatally weakened father, but his entire race of people . . .

Joe skipped down to scene one, and swiftly sensed his headache receding. Hell yeah, he thought. The opening crawl was phenomenal; definitely his greatest achievement yet. Automatically, he rewarded himself with a giant doughnut – peanut butter, in celebration – only to spot that Jerry was still in the room: standing where Joe had left him, looking gravely concerned.

'What's up?'

There was no answer. The big man – six foot four, resolutely handsome in late middle age with studiously side-parted black hair – looked as disheartened as his boss had felt just before. Putting the rest of his doughnut to one side, Joe rose in sympathy.

'I'm sorry, Jerry,' he said. 'I know I took it bad just now, but it's ok. We'll do it next time. Sure, it's our last chance, but I just read the opening crawl, and seriously, never in my whole life have I read anything that gets the juices flowing like—'

But Jerry wasn't willing to listen. Holding up his hand, he turned his broad shoulders and walked away.

'I swear,' pressed Joe, 'the Academy have always *meant* to give us Best Picture. They know we deserve it. They're just saving it up to the last!'

'No,' said Jerry, spinning sharply on the spot.

A frosty silence stole across the room.

'Listen, boss,' Jerry continued, voice faltering with something like fear. 'Before I go on, you need to know that I do believe.'

'Believe?'

'Believe that *Chronicles* can win an Oscar. Believe in its credentials as great art: the mythic qualities, the universal relevance . . .' He smiled kindly. 'And of course I believe in *you* as a great artist.'

'You do?'

'You know I do. Always have done.'

'But?' Joe pressed. 'There's a *but*, right?'

Jerry rubbed his hands together as if trying to draw confidence out of himself. 'But there's a problem.'

'A problem?'

'Big problem.'
'*Big* problem?'
'Considerable.'
'What with?'
'The words.'
'Words?' echoed Joe. 'What words?'

'All of them. The words that come out of the actors' mouths, the words in the opening crawls . . .' Jerry shrugged. 'They're just no good.' He paused. 'In fact, they're pretty bad.' Another pause. 'Actually, they're worse than bad.'

Joe felt the sweat of shock bubbling through the pores in his skin. Overcome by instant nausea, he stepped forward, only to step back. He turned right, then turned back to his left. Trapped like a stunned insect, he dithered for several seconds until pushing past his producer and rolling towards the windows behind his desk, gazing down at his feet – or rather the blurred outer rim of his belly – as he went.

'I'm so sorry, boss,' sighed Jerry. 'I wish to God I didn't have to say it, but there's only one movie left. If I didn't speak now—'

'You don't think I can win with *Triumph*?'

'Not as things are. For the same reasons you were never going to win with any of the previous four – *Glozbacks* included.'

Joe let out a desperate laugh. Surely this was some kind of nightmare? The words he was hearing would have been hurtful from anyone. That they should be coming from Jerry, at such a sensitive moment, was as upsetting as it was inexplicable.

'Why have you never said?'

'Because I haven't wanted to upset you. And also . . .'

'Also what?'

'Also, because I hoped your writing might improve naturally. I hoped one day you might see it yourself and make it better without, y'know, *me* having to tell you.'

Joe paced round a figure-of-eight, trapped in a maze of confused, paranoid thoughts. A ferocious anger was boiling up inside, tempered only by the knowledge that Jerry – or so he thought – never acted without his best interests at heart.

'Ok,' he said, settling on the only reasonable comeback. 'That's your opinion. It's about taste, right? Mine says good, yours says bad.'

Jerry was frowning more deeply than ever. 'It's not just me.'

Joe stopped. 'Who else?'

'People I speak to.'

'People you *speak* to? Where?'

'Y'know . . .' Jerry threw up his hands. 'Around.'

'Around?' Yet again, Joe was disbelieving. 'Around *here*?!'

Jerry nodded.

'Oh, Jesus Christ . . .'

'But they only talk about it 'cos everything else is so perfect.' Jerry stepped forward with a hopeful smile. 'The same with the critics. It's their only complaint: that the dialogue is so clumsy, so awkward, so *drab*. Everything else, they love: pace, structure, special effects, music . . .' Smiling, he shook his head. 'They just marvel how all that can be so perfect, while the writing remains so unbelievably, so butt-clenchingly . . .'

'Ok,' cried Joe, 'enough already!'

He sank into an armchair and stared blankly ahead. Had the bubble around him really grown to such planetary proportions? Even though he'd always made a point of not reading reviews, surely hearsay alone should have alerted him to such pointed, persistent criticism by now? But no. Apparently, those closest to him in JoeTown had worked overtime to keep him from the truth, despite actually sharing the critics' gripes.

'Damn it, Jerry. You should have told me. I feel like the college idiot; everyone laughing behind my back.'

'Aw, come on boss. No-one's laughing at you. We all love you, and we all believe in you. We know you can win Best Picture. That you will, if only you can fix the writing.'

'But how, when I don't see the faults? To me, it's awesome. It kicks. It hits me right there.' Joe thumped his chest. 'Even then, as I sat reading the first goddamn draft of *Triumph of the Solix*, I felt a tingle in my spine. I saw the lights going down, the music, that *hush* of expectation—'

'Right!' exclaimed Jerry.

'Right what?'

'That's your problem, right there. Imagination overload. You're such a visionary, you blind yourself to the dialogue: like a big kid, swept away on this tidal wave, this *tsunami* of enthusiasm, so even when you're just reading, you're imagining the whole package.'

'Right,' nodded Joe, preferring this new line of analysis to the last. 'You're saying I *trick* myself?'

'Exactly. Your mind invests your words with a power they just don't have. Again, like a kid. Which is great, except that Oscars aren't given out by kids. They're awarded by cynical old grown-ups: people whose minds aren't as willing to cut loose, who get hung up on things your imagination bends to its will. Now sure, that's depressing, but it's also reality. And it means the only way to wow them is to see it from their perspective.'

Taking a deep breath, Joe stood and tightened his Levi's. His patience was slowly returning now he understood his weakness as the inevitable flipside of his peerless – damn it, his *dangerous* – imagination.

'So what do I do?'

'What do you do?' Jerry gave a cryptic, knowing grin. 'I'll tell you exactly what to do.' He headed to the corner of the room, into Joe's private movie theatre.

'What the . . . ?' Joe wandered through. 'Come on, Jerry. This is no time for games. I've got heaps of work to do.'

'This *is* work,' said Jerry. 'Pretty damn hard work, too.'

Joe looked at the blank screen.

'This afternoon, boss, you are going to watch all four *Chronicles* movies, back-to-back.'

'Already seen 'em,' said Joe.

'Not like this you haven't.' Jerry signalled to the booth to cue up the first in the series. 'These are special edits. I've had it all stripped back. No sound effects, no music, no visuals. Not even SolixScreen. Just green screen and the actors' basic performances.'

'Unbelievable,' said Joe. 'You had all this planned?'

Jerry shrugged. 'I had it on standby.'

'Garbage. You *knew* we weren't going to be nominated.'

'Alright, so I *knew*.' Jerry marched his boss to a central seat, midway back. 'Your challenge is to understand *why*.'

'I see what you're trying to do,' sighed Joe, sitting down. 'But I saw rough cuts in the edits.'

'Sure,' said Jerry, 'but in the edit more than ever you were thinking about the finished product, imagining it with the gaps filled in. What you're gonna do today is force yourself to forget all that. Be a grown-up. Tether your imagination. Don't think what's missing, just hear the words: the plain old, same old, *stale* old words.' He crouched down and looked Joe in the eye. 'Promise me you'll give it a shot?'

Knowing refusal was not an option – that Jerry, in this kind of mood, was not to be messed with – Joe lifted his feet onto the seat in front. With a mix of scepticism and trepidation, he signalled his cooperation to the booth.

'Enjoy!' chirped the producer, heading out as the opening crawl of *Birth of a Hero* appeared on screen. Concentrating hard, Joe dutifully leashed-up his imagination and – though he could recite them by heart – read the words as if for the first time, suppressing the stirring music in his mind, accepting the plainness of the text as it was, and forcing himself not to see the absent stars behind.

So the exhausting exercise in self-restraint began, and so it continued, with Joe not budging from his seat – except for the toilet, and to order more doughnuts, which he rationed to two per movie – until all four pictures were done. Once the final credits had disappeared from the screen on *Rise of the Glozbacks*, a full ten hours after starting, he heaved himself up and wandered onto the patio that backed onto his office, desperate to catch some air after his day-long solitary confinement.

A late-evening breeze was creating a ripple of disturbance in the clear blue water of his pool, atmospherically lit by the soothing floodlights, while the sky above was sprinkled with stars that clustered round the clearest of moons. On any other night, Joe would have gazed up and dreamed of thrilling new intergalactic adventures for his characters. Tonight, however, for the first time ever, it felt wrong to lift his eyes heavenwards. Instead, he cast his gaze dejectedly downwards: down to earth, or rather the bottom of his pool, where patterns of darkened tiling jumped around, contorted by the disorder on the surface.

His insides were all at sea, a stifling sickness overwhelming his body as he reflected on his day's viewing. How the hell had he got it so wrong? It wasn't like he'd never questioned the quality of his dialogue. Oftentimes he'd wondered if it did the job, and oftentimes he'd decided that yes, boy it did and *how*! But in the course of the day, having studied the bare-bones edits, fighting the temptation to flesh it all out, the certainties of the past sixteen years had shattered. His words had been exposed as not just weaker, but cataclysmically bad: clumsy, pretentious, relentlessly prosaic. It was like an optical illusion had resolved itself; the excellence he once perceived a mere mirage. Exchanges he thought fluent felt stilted. Speeches whose concision he adored rambled on. Phrases that once had him beaming with pride made his teeth itch with their terribleness.

As the day dragged on, the clouds of self-deception scattered so much that he'd have been happy to catch just the briefest glimmer of the genius he once perceived – but it was not to be. By the time *Glozbacks* rolled around, all hope was lost, and he knew Jerry was right. His Oscar dream was nothing more than a crazy, egomaniacal fantasy.

Captivated by the shapes in the water, mind numb with loneliness and despair, Joe's body began to sway in the breeze. He closed his eyes, strangely comforted, and soon his balance faltered. The sound of water licking against the rim drew him forward, and in his mind he saw a whirlpool, tempting him in with the promise of sweet oblivion.

'Boss?!'

Joe glimpsed Jerry running through his office.

'Don't do it!'

But it was too late. Before Joe knew it, dizziness took over and he toppled in. Gallons of water were displaced in an instant and he sank, like a stone, to the base of the pool.

***

It doesn't get much better than this, thought Wendy Preston, soaked gleefully to the bone after four hours of persistent London drizzle. Up on the wooden stage, inches from her face, Hamlet had just fallen, panting, to the floor, a great red blot of blood spreading across his white shirt. She felt his breath and spittle as he heaved in air. She could see the profundity in his eyes.

For a moment, everything was still. Then Laertes loomed up behind, sword at the ready, and Wendy implored the pitiful young Prince with her gaze, urging him to beware of the danger.

'Oooh!' she exclaimed, as Hamlet leapt to his feet and, in one perfect movement, spun round to slash his foe squarely across the ribs. The two men scuffled, exchanging rapiers, then Hamlet hit Laertes again, sending the hapless young fellow staggering back. He slumped against the marble pillar to Wendy's left, just as Gertrude collapsed by the one to her right, prompting mass confusion – instructions, confessions, revelations, apologies on all sides – which would have been impossible to untangle had Wendy not known the entire script as keenly as if she had written it herself.

It was difficult to tell which of the many gruesome bombshells hit Hamlet the hardest, but no matter: the breaking point had well and truly been reached. Strutting to the front of the stage, he puffed out his chest, and Wendy shivered as decisiveness seized him. At long last, the Prince of Denmark knew exactly what he needed to do – and by goodness, Wendy was behind him one hundred per cent of the way. She'd seen a lot of Claudiuses in her time, but this was comfortably the vilest: a *bona fide* psychopath whose charismatic scheming plumbed new depths of depravity.

The old rotter staggered past, and she was half-tempted to grab his shins and take him down herself. But this new, galvanised Hamlet needed no such assistance, retrieving the poisoned rapier and swiping unrestrainedly at his uncle, whose bleeding hulk he hurled on top of his mother's corpse – husband and wife, likewise condemned – before forcing poison down the dying brute's gullet.

It was wonderful, heartbreaking, filthy-gory stuff, and Wendy couldn't stop grinning, even as Hamlet tore back across the stage to try to save the dying Laertes. Never mind him, she felt like saying. Come back to the centre of the stage. Come back to me, and die right here.

Heeding her prayer, Hamlet stumbled away from Laertes and collapsed to his knees right in front of her, delivering his closing speeches so softly it felt like they were sharing a private moment, oblivious to the hundreds of others occupying the famous Wooden O. Even though Hamlet was talking to Horatio – and they were both addressing the audience – Wendy knew he was really speaking directly to her. As his face hit the ground, she reached out and held his hand, comforting him through his final words:

> 'But I do prophesy th'election lights
> On Fortinbras. He has my dying voice.
> So tell him, with th'occurrents, more and less,
> Which have solicited – the rest is silence.'

The Prince died, and Wendy mouthed along with Horatio's ineffably poignant tribute:

> 'Now cracks a noble heart. Good night, sweet Prince,
> And flights of angels sing thee to thy rest.'

She was crying freely now, wiping away tears and drizzle as Fortinbras arrived and Horatio brought him up to speed. The bodies were rounded up, the final words spoken, and the funereal thud of drums accompanied the departing procession.

For several moments, not a soul dared breathe. Only the soft patter of rain encroached on the dumbstruck scene, and again Wendy felt like the only one there: uniquely at one with the world of these plays, and all their extraordinary secrets.

The applause began to build. She deposited her programme on the edge of the stage, catching sight of the cover as the company reappeared:

Hamlet

Her eyes drifted down the page:

by William Shakespeare

Smiling to herself, she turned the programme over and cheered for all she was worth.

Chapter 2

'Seriously, boss. You must let me make amends.'

Jerry was in the hallway outside Joe's office.

'Amends for what?' shouted Joe, changing into a fresh set of clothes.

'It wasn't my intention to leave you so upset.'

'What?'

'I mean it. If I'd known you'd try to kill yourself, I'd have never made you watch those dialled-down edits.'

Joe pulled on a *Sense the Solix* t-shirt and opened the door.

'I wasn't trying to kill myself, Jerry.'

'No?'

'Of course not!'

'Then what the hell *were* you doing?'

'Just taking the air!' Joe headed back into his office. 'It was you, shrieking and shocking me, that sent me into the water.'

'Really? I thought you were trying to end it. I figured my little experiment had worked. That you'd gone suicidal in your despair.'

'Great, Jerry. And you say *I* have an overactive imagination?'

'So you didn't agree with me? You still think the writing kicks?'

Joe froze. His first, fearful instinct was to claim he'd learnt nothing; that he still reckoned his writing the stuff of genius. But Jerry was bound to see through such pride and, besides, he could only lose by continuing to deny the difficult truth. He knew that if he didn't come to terms with his failings, and fast, he could wave goodbye to the Oscar dream forever.

'I'm not a quitter, Jerry,' he said. 'Whatever it takes, I *will* improve.'

'You reckon?'

Joe stared at his producer. 'What the hell are you saying now? That I'm just crap, period? That I was born crap? That I'm never gonna win the Oscar and just need to grow old and deal with it?'

'Well surely if you had an Oscar-winning screenplay in you, you'd have produced it by now – and produced it *instinctively*. You wouldn't have deluded yourself for so long. You'd have seen the flaws yourself, and wouldn't have needed telling.'

Joe couldn't contain his anger any longer. 'God damn it, Jerry. I can't *believe* the lack of faith! All these years, and now, suddenly, this? How the hell do we make the last film together if you've stopped believing I can improve?'

'I don't believe you can't improve outright,' said Jerry, calmly and precisely. 'But I *do* believe you can't improve without – let's say – a change in your approach.'

Joe sat behind his desk. It was late at night. Exhausted and emotional, he didn't have a clue what Jerry was driving at, and lacked the energy to work it out.

'Let me ask you a question,' said Jerry, sitting opposite. 'What is my role here?'

'I'm starting to wonder.'

'Answer me.'

Joe took an action figure and fiddled with one of the arms, eventually raising it to point in Jerry's direction. 'You make it happen.'

'Right. You dream, I deliver. And have I ever failed you?'

Joe shook his head.

'Exactly. So why should now be any different? You have to trust me. The Oscar is your biggest dream of all – I know that – and yet there's only one more movie. I *can* deliver it, but only if you listen to what I'm saying; if you accept the reality of your own shortcomings.'

Joe looked into Jerry's capable, reassuring eyes.

'Well I guess . . .' he began uncertainly. 'I guess we *could* hire another writer to take a look.'

Jerry nodded. 'Maybe.'

'But no,' continued Joe, standing up. 'I need the credit: Written and Directed by Joe Seabright. That's the deal, right?'

'Right.'

Joe scratched his stubble. 'Of course, there is the option of getting someone in secretly.'

'Got it in two!'

'Got what?'

But Jerry, his straight white teeth exposed in a self-satisfied grin, wouldn't explain.

'Come into my office!' he commanded.

Intrigued, Joe grabbed a doughnut and set off. He took a couple of bites as he crossed the hallway, only to stop, open-mouthed, at the door to Jerry's office.

'Wow.'

Jerry's room, usually the model of tidiness, was in all kinds of chaos. No longer was there just a single glass desk and high-backed mesh chair. Instead, there were multiple steel trolleys, occupied by exotic scientific equipment: glass containers brimful with iridescent liquids, transparent plastic powder pots, rack upon rack of test tubes. On the desk itself, meanwhile, stood a white cuboid device that looked like an ancient CRT TV, beside which was some kind of mutant microscope. Most unexpected of all, however, was the woman standing smilingly beside the two devices: bedecked in a white lab coat, and looking for all the world like some kind of angel.

'Mr Seabright,' she said.

Joe detected a slight southern twang to her voice.

'What an honour to meet you at last.'

Joe shook her hand, unsure what to say. Unforgettable as she looked – slim, mid-40s, straight red hair, piercing brown eyes – he'd seen her around over the past few months, but had never got round to asking who she was.

'Joe, meet Grace Tremain,' said Jerry, shutting the door.

Dropping his doughnut in the wastepaper basket, Joe recalled the last thing Jerry said.

'You're a writer,' he said. 'Is that it? Summoned to help on *Chronicles V.*'

Grace smiled back. 'Kinda.'

'But if that's the case,' continued Joe. 'What's with all the equipment?'

'Grace has been based on the FX Campus for almost six months now,' said Jerry. 'She's the newest recruit to our special effects team.'

'Really?' The mystery was thickening by the second. 'What's your speciality? Visuals? Sound?'

'Neither.'

'Neither?' repeated Joe. 'What other kind is there?'

Grace chuckled, evidently charmed by Joe's befuddlement.

'We'll explain in a bit, boss,' said Jerry, retrieving a large rectangular object from the corner. 'First, there's something I want you to have.'

Taking the gift, Joe found himself looking at a plain grey picture frame. Inside was not so much a picture as a drawing. Not so much a drawing, even, as a scribble.

'I hope you like it,' beamed Jerry.

Joe looked up, puzzled. 'You did this?'

'Just a little something.'

Joe held the picture at arm's length, trying to decipher the abstract outlines and scattergun shading. It took him almost a minute to recognise the subject.

'It's the statue, right?'

'You got it,' grinned Jerry.

'Of Greathen Earloser. Outside my mansion?'

'Right.'

'Why, that's so very kind,' said Joe, marvelling not so much at Jerry's spontaneous kindness – though that was strange enough – as the fact that he thought his gift in any way passable. Ok, so maybe, as had just been demonstrated, his artistic judgment was prone to occasional lapses, but he knew for sure this sketch was total junk. 'Really, it's excellent. I never knew you could draw!'

'You really think I can?'

'Well . . .' Joe looked at the picture again. 'You've got *something*.'

Jerry frowned.

'I mean it,' said Joe, returning the picture, face-down, to the table. He glanced at Grace, who met his gaze with an inscrutable stare.

'My kids have been telling me lately how good I am at drawing,' said Jerry. 'So earlier on, when you were watching the movies, I thought I'd do this to say commiserations on not getting the nomination.' He picked up the picture and sighed. 'Now I look at it, though, I reckon they were just being kind – or sarcastic.'

'No way,' said Joe feebly.

'Well anyway, being the sort who can't let these things lie, I had another go.'

Perching the picture on the table, Jerry reached back and produced another.

'Here.' He handed the second frame to Joe. 'See what you think.'

The frame was identical to the first, but its contents were a universe removed from Jerry's original effort. This was a truly beautiful evocation, sensitively coloured and richly detailed.

'I'll be damned,' muttered Joe.

'You think it's better?' asked Jerry.

'Better?' Joe propped the picture alongside the first. 'Jerry, it's a whole different ball park. The first one, I admit, didn't blow me away. But this . . .'

He broke off, spotting something familiar.

'But this?'

'This is great,' said Joe, trying to place where he had seen the picture before. Seconds later, he realised: it wasn't the picture but the *style*; the style that unmistakably belonged to Larry Jones, Joe's Chief Conceptual Designer for *The Solix Chronicles*.

'Ok,' he laughed, 'I get it. Very good.'

'Get what?' asked Jerry.

'You got help from Larry.'

'Excuse me?!'

'Trust me. I know Larry's style when I see it.'

'Well, maybe I was inspired by Larry's designs but, swear to God, this is all my own work.'

Joe hesitated. He was struck by Jerry's sincerity but unable to accept what he claimed. Plainly, the two pictures were by completely different artists, one an amateur, the other a genius – *the* genius, no less, whose work he knew better than any other.

'Your producer speaks the truth, Mr Seabright,' announced Grace, heading to the door. 'Fact is, Larry knows nothing of the picture you're currently holding. Isn't that right?'

She opened the door, and in breezed the tall, bespectacled Larry Jones, long locks of sophisticated black hair flowing above his lanky, leather-jacketed frame.

'What's happening?' he asked, acknowledging his boss with a nod.

'Mr Seabright would like confirmation that this picture is not one of yours.'

Larry looked at the image. 'On my mother's life,' he declared, his rich, resonant baritone lending his words unimpeachable authority, 'I've never seen it before in my life.'

'Very good,' said Grace, turning to Jerry. 'But while it's true that this picture was all your own work, you would admit that Larry played a vital role in its composition?'

Jerry held up his hands. 'For sure. I couldn't have done it without him.'

'Would someone please cut to the chase?' asked Joe, beset in equal parts by intrigue and irritation.

The others swapped intrepid glances before Grace delved into the pocket of her lab coat to produce a small plastic bottle, which she handed to Joe. Inside was a tablet, no bigger than a pea.

'So that's it,' laughed Larry. 'That's what I've been reduced to.'

Joe's skin ran cold. Somehow he knew exactly what Larry had just insinuated but couldn't bring himself to believe it. Instead he just stared blankly at the bottle, only half noticing the touch of Jerry's hand as it landed on his back.

'This is your real gift, boss,' he whispered. 'In answer to the Academy snubbing you yet again, please make your acquaintance with the creative gene.'

Joe's grip on the bottle tightened. 'What did you say?'

'The creative gene,' said Grace. 'Imagination.'

Heart thumping ever quicker, knees turning to mush as the blood rushed to his brain, Joe closed his hand round the bottle and fell back against the wall.

'Are you telling me this pill contains Larry's . . .'

'His muse,' replied Grace. 'The essence of his creativity.'

'But creativity . . .' Joe drifted off as his thoughts short-circuited. 'Wait a second.' He massaged his brow with his spare hand, trying to settle the commotion within. 'The thing is, surely creativity is something learned? Not some kind of absolute, inbuilt and fixed?'

'Right,' said Jerry, standing beside his boss. 'And that's exactly what geneticist after geneticist told me: total insistence than my suggestion was nothing short of fantasy.' Jerry smiled at Grace. 'But then I got to Miss Tremain, Stanford's renegade genius: daring to believe the impossible, and doing all she could to prove it. A natural ally for JoeCo.'

Joe nodded. 'Damn right.'

'We met over a coffee, and my fancy turned out to be her conviction: there was simply no way creativity *wasn't* genetically programmed. This was her single biggest passion: proving that great artistry is the work of nature, not nurture.'

'Trouble was,' explained Grace, 'even my closest allies at Stanford would never entertain my suggestion – they were never gonna fund me looking into it.'

'Which only made it easier for me,' said Jerry. 'Come stay in JoeTown for six months, I said. You'll have whatever you need to attain that one, simple goal: finding the creative gene.'

'The best sabbatical ever,' smiled Grace.

'Six weeks in, she'd found it,' said Jerry. 'A gene, unidentified 'til now, dedicated to the brainwaves and nerve signals associated with imaginative endeavour.'

'Within two months we'd isolated and analysed it,' said Grace. 'A couple of weeks later, I'd deduced how to transfer its effects from one person to the next.'

Joe blinked, and blinked again. Surely this was a dream, some kind of deep-seated sci-fi fantasy? He looked again at Jerry's two paintings: the one so woeful, the other a masterpiece, executed precisely in Larry's style.

'Incredible,' he said. 'You just swallow the pill and—'

'Hey presto,' said Grace. 'Within a few minutes, your body starts emulating the muse of the person it's based on. Logically, you're still thinking for yourself, but thinking with their imagination. So Jerry could still draw whatever he wanted, but he did it with Larry's vision, Larry's style. His own creative characteristics entirely disappeared.'

'Disappeared?' repeated Joe. 'For good?'

'It lasts however long you like. Just depends on the dosage.'

'But the genius is,' pressed Jerry, 'it's still you. Still your original idea, still you, physically, doing the creating, being the artist. You just happen to be enlisting a little extra inspiration. All you need is the DNA of the person whose assistance you want to call on. Living or dead, it doesn't matter, as long as you've got the DNA.'

Joe nodded, but his mind was still reeling with shock.

'So come on boss,' said Larry. 'Who's it gonna be?'

'Who's what gonna be?'

'Who are you gonna choose?' asked Grace.

'Choose?'

'To collaborate,' urged Jerry. 'To help Joe Seabright win that Oscar.'

Joe wondered what the hell his Oscar hopes had to do with it, then caught sight again of Jerry's pictures. 'Oh boy,' he mouthed, scarcely able to speak as the day's events resolved themselves and he finally understood the relevance of Grace's gift – the greatest he had ever known. 'Oh my God.' He pulled the scientist towards him and hugged her tight in overflowing gratitude. 'This is unbelievable.'

'Isn't it just?' she smiled.

'We can't fail!'

'Well,' said Jerry, striking a note of caution, 'that all depends on who you choose.'

Joe started pacing, daunted as a universe of possibilities opened up like some portal to another dimension. Seconds later, he stopped dead, suddenly realising the choice wasn't difficult at all. On the contrary. This decision was just about the easiest he'd ever made.

He turned to the others and grinned.

'Let's go straight to the top.'

Chapter 3

'He'll be with us shortly.'

Joe and Grace were gazing at the snow-capped Pennsylvania mountains, towering over the scene like guards of the strange, secretive facility they'd come to visit.

'Thanks, Jerry,' smiled Joe, reaching inside his puffer jacket for a *Chronicles* handkerchief and mopping sweat from his brow. His stomach was churning ahead of the meeting that would seal or sink their masterplan.

'Have no fear,' said Grace. 'There's no way he'll refuse.'

'He's not gonna like it,' worried Joe.

'Maybe not at first. But let the idea stew and he'll bite in the end. This is progress. No one can resist it for long.'

She gave a wide, guileless smile, eyes glowing with a warmth that seemed both amused and charmed by Joe's fretfulness. Not for the first time, he sensed the symbiosis between them. In getting to know her over the past forty-eight hours, it had become apparent that, like him, her adult life had been defined by the pursuit of one, elusive dream: in her case, proving that even the most nebulous human qualities, of which artistry was the pinnacle, were attributable not to nurture but the DNA coding of nature. And, just like Joe, she had spent well over a decade achieving supposed success – helping to unlock revolutionary treatments for numerous mental illnesses – while remaining fundamentally unfulfilled, inviting scorn from her peers, and forsaking life's other great rewards – hobbies, relationships, kids – as she kept her eye on the ultimate prize.

'Over here, boss.'

Jerry was silhouetted against the windows at the opposite end of the narrow reception room. Setting off through the intervening gloom, Joe felt the goosebumps scurry across his skin. The high, imposing ceilings and wood-panelled walls were lent an almost religious quality by the few shaded lamps that illuminated them.

'One thing worries me,' he said as they walked. 'You're in this – at least partly – to prove a point.'

'I'm in it to win you that Oscar,' Grace said. 'That's why Jerry hired me.'

'But you need to be able to tell the world what you've discovered. And yet you must realise: this whole thing has to stay a secret. We're summoning assistance, but that's all it is. I'm still the author. If – *when* – we win the Oscar, I keep the credit.'

'I understand.'

'I mean, it would confuse things if I had to explain that I'd had – y'know, *help*.'

Grace laid a reassuring hand on his shoulder. 'Jerry said you'd want to keep the whole thing quiet, and that's fine with me. JoeCo has given me more resources in six months than I'd have had in a lifetime at Stanford. I can be patient in return. On leaving JoeTown I'll wait a couple of years, then re-make the discovery in my own time. Nobody will know it's linked to your Oscar.'

Joe smiled. It was a perfect plan. As Grace stroked his arm, he felt his heart beginning to melt. After decades of mutual frustration, their grandest dreams were coming true together.

'Boss?'

'Yep?' Joe turned abruptly to face his producer. 'What you got for me?'

'The bank's catalogue,' explained Jerry, who was inspecting a thick, leather-bound book, mounted on a stand. 'It lists every person whose DNA is stored here.'

Joe watched as Jerry leafed through the weighty pages. On each was a single entry, consisting of a picture of the artist together with dates of birth and death, details of how and when their DNA was acquired, plus the name of the owner. The entries were ordered by genre, and Jerry was currently at the back end of Classical Music, each page throwing up yet another composing legend: Tchaikovsky, Vivaldi, Wagner, every one a winner. Then it was on through Popular Music and Visual Arts, before finally reaching the section that housed their chosen prey: Literature, Theatre & Film.

Passing through the alphabetised names, what struck Joe the most was how quickly Lester Howells had amassed his astonishing collection. Almost every sample had been acquired in 2016 – within a year of Howells first imploring artists' descendents to assert ownership over their ancestors' DNA by letting him store it on their behalf.

By Howells' own admission, the whole thing served no real purpose beyond the symbolic. Certainly, there was never any talk of the DNA being used, not least because all available evidence argued that creativity was not genetic. But in a way, that very pointlessness helped the project's success. Already familiar with Howells as a benevolent, arts-adoring millionaire, folks were happy to regard his DNA Bank as one of those inexplicably appealing whimsies beloved by retiring financiers seeking an outlet for their time and wealth. For want of any practical application, people responded to the childlike innocence of Howells' plan, and it was no surprise when artists' estates rushed to sign up. Here, quite simply, was an altruist who wanted to spend his later years surrounded by the essence of the heroes he worshipped. Who could possibly begrudge him that?

'There he is,' said Jerry, turning the page to reveal their quarry: that familiar face, etched into the popular imagination with its receding hairline and neatly-trimmed beard, gazing out anonymously while his gold earring twinkled away, winking in mischievous acknowledgment of the genius that lurked behind those unprepossessing features.

'Well, well,' said a voice, its richly intellectual, east coast drawl gusting warmly across the room. 'If it isn't Mr *Solix Chronicles* himself.'

Joe turned to see Howells at the opposite end of the room. His tall, commanding figure was silhouetted against the mountainous backdrop.

'Thanks for seeing us at such short notice.'

'My pleasure,' said Howells. His spectacles glinted as he extended his arm outwards. 'Please, this way.'

Joe led them over, introducing his companions before their host turned cleanly on his heels and ushered them into his office. Joe's shoes squeaked on the varnished floor as he stepped over the threshold and took in the brilliant brightness. With windows on three sides and a glass ceiling, Howells' office was positively celestial.

'Mr Seabright?' came a voice, like Howells' but less deep. Joe dropped his gaze to see a young man, about his height, right in front of him.

'My son Casey,' explained Howells.

'A pleasure to meet you,' said Casey, wide-eyed with reverence.

'You too,' smiled Joe, shaking the kid's hand and guessing his age as maybe thirteen or fourteen, though it was hard to be sure. Certainly, he had an air of maturity about him, dressed in a smart pink shirt and corduroy trousers, topped off with brown, round glasses, and side-parted fair hair.

'You know I'm a huge *Chronicles* fan,' Casey blushed.

Joe felt a familiar pride swell up in his heart. In *lieu* of the real thing he took a near-paternal joy in the passions of his fans, which grew in line with his advancing years. Quite without realising it, he found himself smiling wistfully in Grace's direction. He was fairly certain she reddened in return, but she lowered her head so quickly it was hard to be sure.

'I write stories, you know,' the kid went on. '*Chronicles* stories.'

'You should send me some,' enthused Joe.

'Oh I will, sir,' replied Casey. 'You know I can't wait for part five. I can't believe it's a whole two years away!'

Joe laughed, looking up at Howells, whose face was once again silhouetted, punctuated only by spectacles in which Joe saw his own reflection.

'Do you have a title yet?' pressed Casey.

'That's enough, son,' said Howells.

'Oh, I don't mind,' said Joe, 'as long as Casey promises to keep it secret. He'll be the first outside JoeTown to know.'

Casey nodded. 'I understand.'

Joe leant forward and whispered the title in Casey's ear. The young man looked like he was about to burst with happiness.

'That's enough now, son,' said Howells. 'Time to get back to your studies.'

'Thank you so much, Mr Seabright,' said Casey, walking backwards and grinning. 'You don't know how much that means to me.'

'You're welcome.'

Joe waved as Casey left through a side-door which seemed to lead into Howells' living quarters.

'Take a seat,' said Howells without delay, directing his guests to a plush leather couch, situated beneath a row of pictures, each of which was identified by a small nameplate: a pair of Leonardo prints, the *Mona Lisa* and *Vitruvian Man*, a photo of Michelangelo's *David*, and a reproduction of the *School of Athens* by Raphael. To their right was a bookshelf devoted almost exclusively to histories of Renaissance art.

'Sweet kid,' said Jerry.

'Oh, I think you'd be surprised,' said Howells, his long, grave face just discernible amid the glare, shot through with wrinkles whose depth was exaggerated by the shadows cast from above. 'Never mind fan fiction, my boy's reading Goethe. In German.' He paused, the frown easing into a grin. 'But yes. He is, as you say, a very sweet kid.'

'You must have real high hopes for him,' enthused Joe.

'Sure I do,' replied Howells, perched on the edge of his desk. 'Course, you won't be offended that I sometimes wish he'd spend less time re-visiting your *oeuvre*. Casey reckons he's seen the first *Chronicles* film over twenty times. Now, I'm sure it's good fun. It's crap, but it's good crap – right?'

'Right,' murmured Joe.

- 37 -

'But still: *twenty times*?!'

Joe bit his tongue and nodded as understandingly as he could. 'Way too much,' he agreed, although Casey's OD-ing was nothing next to some stories he'd heard.

'There's just so much else to explore. Life-enhancing masterpieces of music, literature, art...' Howells sighed and shook his head. 'Ah, well, each to his own.'

Joe forced a smile. It really wasn't the time to argue back.

'But you didn't come for me to burden you with my parental problems,' said Howells. 'What is it I can do for you?'

Joe sat up and took a deep breath. 'We'd like to borrow one of your samples,' he said, as frankly as was humanly possible.

Howells removed his glasses to reveal a pair of deep-set eyes, glistening beneath a furrowed brow. 'Come again?'

'We'd like to borrow one of your samples,' said Grace.

The side of his mouth twitched. 'Are you for real?'

'Deadly serious,' said Joe.

Howells dropped his gaze to the floor. 'Well, I must say: this really is a first.'

'And your answer?' asked Jerry.

Howells replaced his glasses and peered down, over the rim, at each of them in turn. 'My answer's no. This is a storage facility, not a library. We don't lend DNA out. God forbid!'

Standing by their plan, the JoeCo delegation said nothing, trusting that Howells' curiosity would compel him to enquire further without their forcing it. Moments later, he picked himself up and wandered behind the desk.

'That said . . .' He eased himself into his high-backed chair. 'Even though there's really no way I can agree, I can only truly say no if you explain a bit more.' He folded his arms and reclined as far as the chair would allow. 'Who you want. Why you want them.'

'And we'll happily do so,' said Joe, stepping up to the desk. 'First, though, a deal: what's said in this room stays in this room.'

Howells considered for a moment, then shook Joe's hand. 'So

come on then. Whose DNA do you want?'

'William Shakespeare's.'

Howells gave a wry smile. 'Nice of you to choose one of our less high-profile samples.'

'I like to think big.'

'Quite right.' Howells angled his chair towards Grace, who was still seated on the couch. 'And what do you propose to do with it?'

Grace glanced doubtfully at Joe.

'Presumably you want to clone him?'

Grace frowned. 'How did you guess?'

'Joe said you were a geneticist. This being a DNA Bank, it follows that you wish to use your expertise to create a mini-Bard – hoping he'll turn out as talented as the man himself.'

'We just want to borrow his muse,' said Grace.

Howells' smile succumbed to straight-faced intrigue. 'His muse?'

'I've identified a new gene,' explained Grace, 'the one controlling a person's creativity. What's more, I've worked out how to emulate one person's creativity in another.'

Howells nodded. 'And you want to emulate Shakespeare's in . . . ?'

'Me,' said Joe, blood rushing to his cheeks. 'For the last *Chronicles* movie.'

'But why?' Howells removed his spectacles and chewed on one of the arms. 'Surely it's all fine as it is? The most lucrative franchise ever; all blocks already busted?'

'I want to win an Oscar,' blurted Joe.

Howells hesitated briefly, then threw back his head and roared with laughter.

'I'm serious,' protested Joe. 'Laugh as much you like, but that's all I've ever wanted, since first falling in love with the movies as a kid and pledging that one day, God willing, I'd win Best Picture for bringing my dreams to life.'

'But surely *The Solix Chronicles* is . . .' Howells tried, and failed, to stifle his amusement. 'Well it's not exactly what you'd

- 39 -

call Oscar material, is it?'

'You say that now,' answered Jerry, 'but that's only because the writing sucks. With a little Shakespearean polish . . .'

Jerry's enthusiastic contribution halted Howells' hilarity, and the big man lapsed into contemplative silence.

'Just think,' pressed Grace. 'Bringing Shakespeare's genius back; the greatest writer who ever lived, reborn. How can that not appeal to an arts-lover like you?'

Howells opened his mouth to reply, but hesitated, as if only now struck by the magnitude of the plan. He stood up and began pacing. Joe re-took his place on the couch.

'I'll be honest,' declared Howells. 'I think it's a fantastic idea.'

'You do?' Joe sat up.

'I really do.'

'That's great!'

'But I have two major problems.'

Joe slumped back down.

'First, I can't help feeling this technology would be more profitably employed on a more *substantial* project. Sure there's room for improvement in your films – and *then some* – but spaceships will only take you so far.' He stopped in front of them. 'Fact is, Shakespeare would be wasted on *The Solix Chronicles.*'

'I disagree,' returned Jerry. '*Chronicles* is right up his alley.'

'Really? You reckon if Shakespeare were alive today—'

'He'd be writing *The Solix Chronicles*?' Jerry nodded emphatically. 'Damn right I do. You of all people should know that theatre was the popular culture of Shakespeare's day. He wrote to make money, so he gave people what they wanted: big, passionate blockbusters about love and war. Universal stories, just like *Chronicles.*'

Howells was staring at his feet.

'I'm serious,' urged Jerry. 'If Shakespeare was alive today do you really think he'd squander his talent writing plays for audiences in the hundreds? Or would he write for the masses, for the millions: channel those talents to maximum effect?'

Howells turned away, hands clasped behind his back, thumbs twiddling. 'Maybe. But that still doesn't answer my other concern.'

'Which is?' asked Joe.

'That it's selfish. You want the great Bard of Avon on board, not because you adore his work, not because you have a high-minded desire to revive his talents for the enrichment of mankind – but simply because you, Joe *Rise of the Glozbacks* Seabright, want to win an Oscar.'

'That's not fair.'

'No? Then perhaps you'd tell me who, exactly, is going to benefit, other than you?'

Joe looked to Jerry, the producer's face as blank as his boss's mind. What on earth could they answer?

'Casey!' shouted Grace.

'What about him?' asked Howells.

'It'll benefit Casey,' said Grace, rosy cheeks rising above a triumphant grin. 'It'll make *The Solix Chronicles* a worthwhile passion. Rather than take Casey to Shakespeare, you bring Shakespeare to Casey. Suddenly, his tastes will be that much more sophisticated, and you'll have got your wish!'

Howells returned to his chair. He grabbed a rubber ball from the desk and squeezed it as he leaned back and gazed at the clouds. Seemingly, Grace's brilliant brainwave had had its desired effect. Joe reached out and held her hand to express his gratitude. To his delight, she laid her other hand on top of his.

Howells lowered his head and fixed his stare on the great Renaissance paintings above them.

'It's puzzling,' he said. 'My wife Ruth and I spent decades hoping high-art might one day make a resurgence. That people might yet be turned from trashy entertainment to something more profound.' There were tears glinting in his eyes. 'I've never admitted it before, but really the DNA Bank was a tribute to her. I founded it after she died, hoping to serve her memory by keeping alive, symbolically at least, the spirit of those great geniuses she worshipped. Just maybe, I thought, it might inspire living artists to raise their game, aspiring to one day have *their* DNA stored here, too.' He looked down at the ball in his hand. 'And yes, there was even a part of me which fantasised that some boffin might one day find a way of cloning Beethoven, or Picasso, or Dostoyevsky: that great new symphonies, paintings and novels would pour forth, redeeming the idiot masses.'

He leaned forward and looked at Joe. 'What never once occurred to me, was that that saviour would turn out to be such a phenomenal philistine. *The* philistine, indeed, whom I deplore above all others.'

Joe stared back, expressionless. He hadn't a clue where this was headed.

'Which makes it all the odder,' continued Howells, 'that the moment you explained what you wanted to do, the whole thing clicked into place.'

'It did?'

'Oh for sure. By having someone so utterly reprehensible come begging, I realised that this is *exactly* what we're here for. Not to do anything so crude as clone from scratch. Not to give up on the present by revivifying the past, but to use the dead, secretly, to heal the living. To take you, Joe Seabright, the lowest of the low, and enlist William Shakespeare, the highest of the high, to cure you of your ills. And to do this behind closed doors, so rather than perceive you as weak for seeking Shakespearean help, people celebrate you as self-improving: as having recognised your failings and worked to overcome them. For if Joe Seabright, of all God-forsaken so-called artists, is seen to have reformed himself, the future will be bright indeed. Standards of popular entertainment will rise such that nothing less than Shakespearean genius is tolerated!'

Peroration over, Howells set off once again, pacing with intense concentration. Joe looked to Jerry and Grace in ecstatic bewilderment.

'Of course,' resumed Howells, 'there is one minor problem. Strictly speaking, I'd have to ask the UK government for permission, since William Shakespeare's DNA is theirs, not mine, to lend out. Then again, given the plan's strength is its secrecy; given that it can only be truly effective if no one but us knows how you've achieved such extraordinary results . . .' He approached Joe, who rose from the couch. 'Given all that, I think we can probably overlook the Brits on this occasion. Agreed?'

Joe shook Howells' hand. 'You bet,' he said, insides lurching with disbelief as Howells turned to Jerry and Grace in turn, giving the latter a gigantic, celebratory hug.

'Shakespeare is the most securely stored of all our samples,' he explained, marching towards the door, fists clenched with purpose. 'So it'll take at least an hour to gain access. But fear not. I'll be back as soon as I can. Back, with the Bard in tow.'

Chapter 4

'Some place you've got here,' shouted Howells as they passed over the golf course, bathed in a warm golden sunset. Beyond, the rest of the settlement was popping up on the horizon like the most magnificent toy-town ever conceived.

'Not bad, huh?' yelled Joe, as modestly as was possible above the din of the chopper's blades. Truth was, the trip from the airfield to Jerry's office could just as easily have been made in a JoeTown taxi, but since Howells had insisted on guarding Shakespeare's DNA, Joe couldn't resist showing off his self-made civilisation from the best possible vantage point. Impressing high-fliers like Howells – men whose achievements rendered them hard to wow – was one of life's most dependable pleasures for Joe, and why the hell not? JoeTown was like nothing else that had ever been seen on Earth.

The town had grown out of a revolutionary philosophy that first took seed during the fraught early days of the TV series. Back then, frustrated by inflexible budgets, arcane shooting conditions and mindless network meddling, Joe's only escape had been to fantasise about the idyllic alternative. He dreamed of a haven where great things could be achieved and geniuses allowed to flourish, free from the constraints of time, travel and technology.

At first, the whole thing was a pipedream. But as Joe's experience grew, so did his conviction that this imagined oasis was pivotal to his saga's future: that only in such a cloistered environment could he attain the Oscar-winning greatness he craved.

So it was, when the franchise graduated to the big screen with *Birth of a Hero*, granting Joe unimaginable wealth through both the picture's success and the dissemination of SolixScreen – the immersive projection technique which reinvigorated movie-going – his priority was to treat himself to a new home.

Sixteen years on and, for those lucky enough to live and work within its 10,000 acres of untarnished beauty, JoeTown was Utopia itself. Located on the outskirts of Los Angeles, resplendent with its own airfield, school curriculum and currency, it was every bit the carefree paradise Joe had always dreamed of.

'The size is awesome,' said Howells, visibly humbled as they flew above the FX Campus, then on, over the residential district and city centre – town hall, leisure and shopping arcade, baseball stadium – until finally landing atop Joe's mansion.

Jerry led them down the stairs and into his office – which, for privacy's sake, was doubling as Grace's lab for the foreseeable future.

'Welcome to the home of MET,' he said.

'MET?' Howells donned his glasses and gazed round in fascination.

'Muse Enhancement Therapy,' explained Grace, closing the door. 'Mr Howells, do you have the Shakespeare sample ready?'

'Certainly do.' He placed his briefcase on the desk and removed a small transparent tube with a white screw cap.

Joe shivered. Even though all he was looking at was plain plastic containing an anonymous liquid, there was something ghostly about the overtones. Here, before them, was Shakespeare: not literally, but equally not something inanimate like a skull or a hair. This was altogether more spiritual, more profound: Shakespeare's essence, the genetic coding that had programmed the greatest writer who ever lived.

'Oh, Shakespeare,' he muttered. 'Boy, are you a sight for sore eyes.'

Grace took the tube and, grabbing a pipette, collected a tiny droplet of the liquid. She then deposited the sample on a glass plate beneath the probing silver eye of the strange-looking microscope.

'This is our MET Surveyor,' she explained. 'Its job is to isolate the creative gene.'

'Isolate?' repeated Howells. 'You actually detach the gene somehow?'

Grace shook her head. 'The sample itself is left well alone. This isn't a literal, *physical* transplant. They're only necessary with physical controllers: you know, primary genes, dictating hair and eye colour, where the effects are life-long, totally tied up with our growth. The joy of the muse is that it's not a physical but a *behavioural* controller. It affects us by altering our nervous system and, in turn, our brains and so our imagination, opinions, tastes: you name it, the muse dictates every aspect of our artistic selves.'

Grace flicked a switch. A red laser descended from the body of the machine, piercing the heart of the DNA. After counting to five, she turned off the device and removed the droplet from the glass.

'What I've been doing these past few months is studying how different muses alter different people's chemistry. Thanks to which, we can now infer those effects simply by analysing the gene itself. That's what the MET Surveyor has just done: looked at Shakespeare's muse and deduced what effects it had on his body so we can emulate them using potions of our own.'

Joe watched, spellbound, as Grace returned the droplet to the tube, which Howells placed back in his briefcase.

'The result,' continued Grace, grabbing a nearby print-out, 'we call the MET Prescription.' She handed it to Joe. 'Or in this case, the Shakespeare Prescription.'

Though he didn't understand a single detail of the formula, which just listed a load of different chemical agents and the quantities required, Joe was still wowed by what he was holding. Here, amazingly, was Shakespeare's genius, reduced to a chemical recipe.

'Incredible,' said Howells, peering over Joe's shoulder. 'Seriously, Miss Tremain. When the day comes for you to go public, you'll win the Nobel for sure.'

'Well, you know: a little vindication would be nice after all these years.' Grace retrieved the prescription and placed it beside the exotic powders and liquids. 'Something to go alongside Joe's Oscar.'

Enchanted, Joe folded his arms and watched as she began mixing the different substances.

'Today, I'm preparing two strengths,' she explained. 'One, lasting for just a few minutes to check against any allergic reactions. The second, to see Joe through 'til the screenplay is done.'

'What will I feel?' asked Joe.

'Not a whole lot. Except, of course, when you start noticing your extra imaginative potency. Jerry said that was a little disorienting.'

'Sure,' agreed the producer, 'but if you're anything like me, you'll be too busy relishing your new-found genius to care!'

'Will there be a come down?'

'Any psychological downturn will be countered by joy at what you've created,' said Grace. 'As for physical effects, the doses are structured to kick in and wear off gradually. There'll be plenty of time to adjust.'

Grace took the two tubes she had prepared and placed them on a tray which she inserted into the bright white cube. Thirty seconds later, after much whizzing and whirring, the door pinged open to reveal two perfectly formed pills in the tubes where, moments earlier, there had been liquid. Tipping the tablets, one white, one grey, onto a saucer, Grace grabbed a beaker of water and presented her handiwork to Joe.

'Voilà!'

Joe was salivating freely. He took the two pills in either hand. 'Shakespeare, eh? Looks delicious!'

'The grey lasts ten minutes,' instructed Grace. 'The white'll do you a month.'

'A month?' Joe looked up. 'What if I can't get the whole thing written in a month?'

'Oh please,' scoffed Howells. 'A month is ample. This is the

Bard we're talking about: the guy who used to knock off four-hour tragedies before breakfast! How long can he possibly take over a bit of stuff 'n' nonsense sci-fi?'

'Sure,' said Joe, refusing to rise to the bait. 'But what if there's some unexpected delay?'

'Either way it's not a problem,' said Jerry. 'We have the prescription here. We'll just make up another pill if needed.

'Actually,' said Howells, 'I'd rather you didn't hold on to anything. Not that I don't trust you. It's simply that Shakespeare is our most prized sample. Since I'm working without the UK government's consent—'

'Our security is the best there is,' protested Jerry.

'I know. But just for my peace of mind I need to know I'm witnessing the full extent of how you use the DNA.'

'So if we need to re-do this,' sighed Jerry, 'we have to repeat the whole process: you flying over with the DNA in hand?'

'Well, unless we compromise. Unless, say, I take the prescription away. Then, if you do need another pill, I can have it made up at my end and ship it safely across.'

'You have the facilities to do that?' asked Joe.

'You're not the only one with a boffin at your beck and call.' Howells smiled at Grace. 'Though I'll concede mine does rather pale alongside present company.'

'Alright,' sighed Jerry. 'Grace, get the prescription for Lester and delete all traces from our records.'

Grace obliged, tapping at her computer and handing the prescription to Howells.

'And so, the time has come,' said Joe, returning his attention to the pills and licking his lips at the power they contained: eager to take this one giant stride along the path to self-improvement. He picked up the beaker – 'Once more unto the breach' – and broke into a sweat as he popped the grey pill in his mouth and sent it swimming down his gullet, shuddering at the coolness of water as it sank. He closed his eyes and held his breath, hoping nothing abnormal happened as the miracle mixture took hold.

Moments later, he blinked his eyes open and assessed his state.

Sure enough, he felt fine: no nausea, no aches, no pains. Instead, there was just relief as the anxiety lifted and, in its place, an overwhelming elation eased itself around his body. Oh yeah, he thought: *this* was what it was all about. Damn it, he could virtually *feel* his imagination starting to expand!

'You ok?' asked Grace.

'Ok?' Joe strutted round the room in a state of mounting euphoria. '*Ok?* I'm William Shakespeare! How the hell do you think I feel? I feel goddamn unbelievable!'

'The energy's flowing?' enquired Jerry.

'Are you kidding me? The inspiration's flooding through me like never before!' He shook hands with Lester, then embraced Jerry and Grace as the genius juices cleansed the mediocrity in his veins. 'Seriously guys: I don't have the words to thank you.' He hesitated. 'Actually, maybe I do – maybe *I* don't, but *Shakespeare* does – but, hey, whatever. The point is, this is all new to me. I always believed I was a great artist, but only now, standing here, feeling this *life force* fizz through me – only *now*, people, do I really understand the difference between someone like me, your average Joe Seabright, and your solid gold genius like Shakespeare. Damn it, the inspiration's just bursting to get out of me. I feel so pumped!'

The exhilaration continued for a full ten minutes before the trial dosage began to wear off. Under Grace's watchful guidance, Joe slid into a steady comedown, his mind and muscles only fully relaxing from Shakespeare's spirit a whole hour after first popping the pill. Naturally, that was his cue to plead to go round again, this time with the full dosage to begin writing immediately, but Grace demanded the rest of the day be devoted to tests monitoring his return to ordinariness, and checking for any anomalies brought about by the pill.

It was only the following morning, when she confirmed that the trial had indeed gone safely, that the experiment proper began. After seeing Howells off at the airfield, Joe returned to his mansion and, itching to re-skin himself as Shakespeare, wasted no time in entering the purpose-built writing room where he was to spend the next month in solitary confinement.

'We didn't want to leave anything to chance,' explained Jerry. 'Even Shakespeare must have had his off days, when something blocked his inspiration. We can't afford that to happen. Being out of your study and putting your past behind you is one thing, but we thought we'd go even further: immerse you in the world you're creating.'

Joe was awestruck by the care that Jerry had lavished on his temporary abode. Aside from the essential conveniences – washroom, bed, kitchen, tonnes of food and drink – the place had been decorated à la *Chronicles*. The steel-grey walls and ceiling matched those of a Solix Transporter, with the windows giving on to a back-projected sea of stars, occasionally interrupted by the arc of some giant planet. The mood was further enhanced by strains of the saga's soundtrack, sounding periodically from concealed speakers, while the wardrobe mixed everyday outfits with costumes from the movies, so Joe could better enter the minds of his characters.

'Phenomenal,' he said, grabbing Emperor Tyron's regalia from the rail and pulling it over his t-shirt and jeans, determined to start *Triumph of the Solix* with the same portentousness that had concluded *Rise of the Glozbacks*. 'You're sure I'll be able to remember the crucial facts?' he asked, a familiar energy buzzing through his veins as the longer-lasting pill, taken moments earlier, kicked in. 'I won't forget the shape of the story. What's happened already; what needs to happen in *Triumph*?'

'Positive,' affirmed Grace. 'All your faculties, memory included, stay intact. As for the inspiration: just write from the heart and the genius will flow, sure as day follows night.'

Joe pulled on Tyron's jet-black military cap to complete the transformation. 'How do I look?'

'Fiendish,' laughed Jerry.

'Perfect! Then I'll see you in a month.'

'You bet,' said Jerry, hugging his boss before Grace stepped up and kissed him on the cheek.

'Go get yourself that Oscar!' she whispered.

'I will,' grinned Joe, heart skipping a beat as his two accomplices exited.

Left alone, he bounded to his desk, adrenalin coursing through his body as he settled at his computer. Without a second thought he typed the title line, then closed his eyes and transported himself to that special place: the place of infinite possibilities, where the lights dimmed, hush descended and those familiar logos appeared:

JoeCo Presents
A Joe Seabright Film

His eyes snapped open and focused on the screen, looking on captivated as his fingers began hammering away with a will of their own.

Chapter 5

With her introductory address concluded – key events earmarked, rules of engagement declared – Wendy was making way for the first speaker when Clive, their thickly-bearded, tweed-jacketed archivist, marched up the stairs and pushed her back towards the lectern.

'What's happening?'

Clive grinned at her. 'No need to blush.'

'Blush?' Wendy wasn't blushing. 'Why should I be blushing?'

Clive took his place at the microphone. Wendy started to blush.

'Ladies and gentlemen.'

Wendy spotted that he was holding a big, leather-bound volume under his arm.

'Despite Miss Preston's best efforts in the run-up to this year's conference, it can't have escaped anyone's notice that 2022 is a significant year for our jolly band of truth-seekers. We in the organising committee felt it only right that we commence the weekend's merriment by marking this momentous occasion.'

Clive winked at Wendy, who glared back in anger. She had expressly warned them not to make any fuss. Not that she didn't think the anniversary worth marking – heavens, twenty years was pretty bloody impressive in anyone's book. It was simply that the group, now as always, wasn't about her. It was about all of them, both what united them and what divided them. Democracy was paramount to the group's success, and it wouldn't do to have it undermined by pretending she was different from the rest.

'Of course, the group's success belongs to us all,' said Clive, 'but there is one woman to whom we are indebted above all others.'

And so it began. Inexorably, the spotlight fell on her, and Clive delivered the traditional account of Wendy's early epiphanies in the company of Jim Withers, followed by her pariahdom and subsequent fightback. She hung her head as he prattled on, embarrassed in the extreme, and was mightily relieved when he finally got to the point.

'And so, to say thanks . . .' Clive put his hand on his heart. 'To say *thanks Wendy, so much, for everything*, the organising committee has clubbed together for a special little something.'

Wendy took the big black book, kissing Clive on either cheek before reading the words embossed on the cover:

The Complete Works of Christopher Marlowe

For Wendy Preston, on the occasion of the
20th anniversary of the founding of the WAC

Becoming aware of its unusual weight – she'd held many complete Marlowes and none had been this heavy – she opened it to discover that this was a special edition indeed.

'Oh, my,' she whispered, dazzled by its beauty: everything from the typesetting to the paper stock. 'It's simply wonderful.' The tears were welling up at the back of her eyes, summoned by that familiar longing for a world where such a tome was as common as that other, better known Complete Works. 'It's a thing of perfect beauty.'

Answering requests from the floor, she held up the book so those at the front could see the cover. There was laughter – mingled with some good-natured booing – as details of the gift were relayed through the audience.

'Of course,' said Clive, into the microphone, 'this is in no way an endorsement of Wendy's views.'

Now it was Wendy's turn to laugh, her embarrassment momentarily suspended by the exquisiteness of the gift, and also the reminder that, for all her magnanimity, nothing quite beat those moments when she indulged the notion that she might be right, and so many of her colleagues *wrong*, about the issue which locked them together.

'It's traditional at this point to say "You shouldn't have",' she began, addressing the quietening crowd. 'But of course that would be quite wrong. They absolutely *should* have, and so should all the rest of you who haven't yet realised the truth of what us Marlovians have been trying to tell you!'

There was more laughter, together with more good-natured jeering.

'But seriously, charmed though I am, and deeply proud of our history to date, it is imperative that we retain our modesty. Twenty years is a fine landmark, but I didn't set up the WAC to tread water. Our distinguishing feature is not our determination to keep the issue alive, but to progress the debate: to believe that, against all odds, we *can* find a definitive answer to our questions.'

'So please: no more resting on laurels, and no more lauding me. Instead, let us use our anniversary conference to reinvigorate our discussions, and move us closer to what we all seek. For I do believe, more adamantly than ever, that an answer is just around the corner; that well before the next twenty years are up, we will finally learn what we all long to know. How it will happen I do not know. But I am certain that if we continue to work hard, and argue even harder, then discovery of the ultimate truth is not a case of *if* but *when*.'

***

Arms outstretched, the applause dying at last, Joe realised that Grace was standing alongside him. She'd obviously decided to join him on stage after all, and that was just fine by him. Though the movie was billed as having been 'Written and Directed by

Joe Seabright' – and no other – it was as much her mind as his that forged the masterpiece that was *Triumph of the Solix*. Besides which, it felt good, having her by his side. It made him feel whole.

'My Lords, Ladies and Gentlemen,' he proclaimed, drugged up on Shakespeare to preserve his verbal prowess. 'It is a surpassing honour to stand before you this evening to acknowledge your blessing, and accept—'

Out of nowhere, the fluency deserted him. He took a moment to clear his throat, then opened his mouth to resume. Try as he might, however – and even though he knew exactly what needed saying – the words weren't there.

He turned to Grace, but Grace had gone. Panicking, he looked back to the audience, only to see that they too had vanished, leaving a sea of empty seats which were themselves disappearing as the lights above faded. He went to grab his hard-won prize but the statuette, like everything else, was no longer there. Engulfed by darkness, he collapsed to his knees and roared in anguish. What the hell was happening?

'I've brought some doughnuts.'

Joe fell back and gazed into the void.

'And a little chocolate milkshake.'

An array of bright dots pricked the blackness above, gaining in number until finally he recognised the cosmic starscape painted on the ceiling of his writing room.

He turned over and saw Jerry perched on the edge of his bed.

'How long have I been out?'

Jerry looked uncomfortable. 'Twenty-four hours.'

Joe sat up in shock. 'You were meant to wake me after twelve!'

'I know. But you seemed so fast asleep, you clearly needed the extra rest.' Jerry shrugged. 'I dunno. Must've really exhausted you, channelling someone else's muse.'

Joe slurped some chocolate milk.

'So?'

'So what?'

'How'd I do?'

'Want to come see?'

Joe's heart jumped. Want to come *see*?!

'Follow me,' said Jerry blankly, chucking Joe his bathrobe, which he pulled on before following the producer through the mansion towards his office. Once there, instead of stopping for a debrief, Jerry pushed on, across the deep-pile *Chronicles* carpet, into Joe's private theatre.

'Morning, Joe.'

Grace's voice came from the projection booth. Up on screen was the familiar 'JoeCo Presents' logo, with the single word 'PAUSE' stamped across it.

'We've pre-vizzed the first and last reels,' revealed Jerry.

Joe felt a rush of teenage excitement. 'You've what?'

'We thought it best you see it.'

'That's incredible!' He darted down one of the middle rows and plonked himself in the centre. *Oh boy*! Even though he knew his FX team's pre-visualisation technology could, theoretically, ingest a screenplay and render it on screen, complete with computer-generated actors, within hours, this was the first time it had been deployed to maximum effect. 'Let's do it!'

The pounding fanfare erupted from the unbroken circle of speakers surrounding the auditorium. Joe watched as the great *Solix Chronicles* logo appeared, followed below by the opening crawl: an opening crawl written physically by him, but imaginatively and verbally conceived by his esteemed collaborator – the greatest writer who ever lived:

Triumph of the Solix

After making the scientific breakthrough required to achieve his dreams of galactic power, High Lord Tyron – still based, like last time, on Cafillia – has amassed an army of Glozbacks and injected them with a distorted, evil version of 'The Spirit,' which gives them all the miraculous powers of the Solix, but in a bad way.

A bead of sweat trickled down Joe's brow. Maybe it was a lingering drowsiness, a hangover from his day-long slumber, but the words weren't as gripping as he'd hoped.

> Meanwhile, Mark Earloser – after battling his father, Greathen Earloser, who instructed him to become less reckless and refute his love for the glamorous Regina – has gone into hiding from the Solix, leaving their home planet of Solua, and taking Regina with him. Mark was set to succeed his father as the Solix's spiritual leader, but now, in his insolence, it seems that he might not after all.

Joe itched his stubble. Stay calm, he told himself. Don't panic.

> With the brutal Glozbacks now embarked on their fiendish mission to hunt down the Solix – and then either kill them or transform their Solix powers into evil and force them to become Tyron's servants – the Solix, and Greathen in particular, find themselves facing an internal divide which leaves them not-very-well equipped to face the fight that none of them know are coming.

The words disappeared and the camera panned down to reveal the mellow orange glow of Solua. Joe glanced to his left, where Grace was sitting beside Jerry. Her eyes were cast down at the floor; his, up at the ceiling.

'Hey, that's only the crawl,' said Joe. 'No one ever said Shakespeare could write opening crawls. It's the dialogue where he excels: the fire and ice. The opening crawl I can see to myself.'

Spooked by the lack of response, Joe focused on the digitally-rendered figure of Greathen Earloser. As planned, he was at The Solix Temple, preparing to commune with the Solix Masters: spiritual leaders of yore who had successfully ascended to the Spirit Level.

'This pre-viz is stunning, Jerry,' enthused Joe. 'Won't be long before we can dispense with actors for good.'

> 'Oh, Solix Masters,' boomed Greathen. 'I seek your help. I come to you in my hour of need. I fear my son is lost. I have failed to prepare him for the future. He is not ready yet to succeed me. I tried telling him so, but we fought and now he's run off with Regina. I have no successor. The future of The Solix is fearsomely fragile.'

Joe repositioned his legs, from left over right to right over left. 'Come on Shakey, don't let me down.'

> 'But the worst bit,' continued Greathen, the ghosts of the Solix Masters flickering before him, 'is that by trying to help him, and ending up fighting, I'm weaker than I was. Mark has made my death come closer, but I'm still not prepared to progress. Worse, I don't think I've got the strength to learn anymore. I don't think I'll ever make it onto the Spirit Level. I face a cruel and nasty death. I'm going to be the first Solix leader to ever have failed.'

'Someone butt in!' yelled Joe, desperate for one of the Solix Masters to halt Greathen's dreary ramblings. But no: apparently, Shakespeare wasn't done yet.

> 'I don't know how this happened. I was always concerned at Mark's attitude. But so many Solix are like that when young: ambitious and arrogant. But as I fought him, the other day, I wondered: how had this come to pass? How could father and son go head to head like this?'

Sweet Jesus. Ok, so the interminability itself wasn't surprising. Everyone knew economy wasn't Shakespeare's strongest card. But where was the beauty, the flourish, the refinement? Where was the nourishment that justified the bloat?

'You come to us at a most momentous moment,' boomed
Devras, the most senior of the Solix Masters.

'Most momentous moment?' spluttered Joe. *To be or not to be, My kingdom for a horse, If music be the food of love* – and now, *You come to us at a most momentous moment*? Boy, Shakespeare's standards had slipped.

'Your relationship with your son,' said Youtron, Devras'
second-in-command, 'has been but a sign. A great evil
has been concealed from us. An unknown foe has discovered how to manipulate the Spirit. That is the root of
the problems you describe.'

This was the killer twist; the heart-stopping revelation that kick-started *Triumph of the Solix*. Even Joe would have been hard pressed to screw this up, yet Shakespeare simply threw the moment away.

'We know not how it happened,' said Devras. 'We know
only that evil has been simmering under the surface, beyond our vision, eluding our senses, these past twenty
years. And it is that evil which has caused the schism between you and your son.'

'Are you saying my son is evil?' shouted Greathen. 'Do
not!'

Joe dropped his eyes and simply listened. Maybe the pre-viz was distorting his judgment?

'Oh, that is not what we are saying,' replied Devras.
'Merely we are saying that the unifying power of The Solix
has been tarnished since this evil first appeared. Your
son misunderstands the power of The Solix for that power
is less powerful than it was before.'

'Kill it!' screamed Joe.

He marched out of the theatre, unable to endure another frame of the soul-crushing tedium he – or rather *Shakespeare* – had created.

'What the hell was that?' he screamed. 'That was even worse than me. Way worse!'

'I'm so sorry,' said Grace, as she and Jerry followed him into his office.

'You're sure there's no mistake?' Joe's eyes were filling with desperate tears.

'That's why we pre-vizzed it,' said Jerry. 'We read it and thought we might be missing something. Unfortunately, it seems—'

'But the *science*! You're sure everything went to plan?'

Grace nodded. 'We've been over and over your stats, checking there were no weird side-effects, nothing interfering with the MET. Everything indicates the experiment went smoothly. Your body behaved as expected.' She shook her head, overcome by a confusion Joe hadn't witnessed before. 'Everything was in place, yet the pill just didn't work.'

'The pill worked alright,' snapped Joe. 'It worked by making me even worse than usual!'

'Worse, and more unwieldy,' said Jerry. 'Based on the pre-viz, the whole script clocks in at four hours twenty.'

'But that was the thing!' exclaimed Joe. 'I was *digging it*. I was in the zone. I did exactly as you said: freed my mind, forgot about the Oscar, forgot about Shakespeare. I just let the words flow out of me.'

'And did they?' asked Grace.

'Hell yes! I could've gone on forever. I knew . . .' He thumped his breast, recalling the furious creative fission of his solitary confinement. 'I knew in *here*, the stuff I was writing was so damn *hot*.'

'You read it back?' asked Grace.

'I did.'

'And you thought it was good?'

'Sensational.'

'Extraordinary. Proof that creative and critical faculties are the same after all. As one changes, so does the other.'

'So?'

'So, critics and artists are actually flipsides of the same coin. Alter egos.'

'And that's supposed to cheer me up?!'

Joe stalked round the office, scratching his stubble and finding it longer than usual: an unwelcome reminder of how long he'd slaved away, only to discover that something had muddied Shakespeare's genius.

He looked at Grace, wondering if he wouldn't be better off ditching the drugs and just working harder to exceed his existing limitations. At least that way he'd regain some control. But seeing her so deadened by disappointment, bereft of her trademark against-the-odds optimism, reminded him that this was as much a disaster for her as for him: her greatest ambition in life, achieved one minute, annulled the next.

He wondered if he could shed any light on the experiment's failure. It seemed unlikely, since Grace herself couldn't fathom it, but maybe that in itself was a clue? Perhaps the source of the problem was simply too banal to have crossed her brilliant mind.

'A dead guy's DNA.' He clicked his fingers. 'That's gotta be it. MET won't work with a dead guy's DNA!'

Grace shook her head.

'But think about it. All your tests were on JoeCo workers. Living people.'

'Makes no difference.'

'What if his DNA has deteriorated?'

'Not possible.'

'What if we've evolved since Shakespeare's time? Maybe our genetic make-up has changed? Maybe things fit together differently now? We should at least *try* it. Get Shakespeare's DNA back, run some comparisons with modern-day DNA, then see if we can't adjust MET to make better sense of Shakespeare.'

'No point,' said Grace. 'We've known this for years. Fact is, dead DNA's as good as living, four hundred years is way too short a period for any significant change to happen, and Shakespeare's can't have deteriorated otherwise the Brits couldn't have isolated it in the first place!' She slumped into an armchair and drew her hands over her face. 'Trust me. I wish there was some logical explanation, but something's obviously gone wrong – and I just haven't got the first clue what!'

'Then there's only one thing it can be,' said Joe, his faith in Grace unshakeable. 'Somebody else's fault.'

He headed out of his office and into a nearby meeting room: an intimate space, whose deep-red walls were covered in *Chronicles* prints and paintings, a window at one end and a white screen at the other.

'What are you doing?' asked Jerry, as he and Grace joined him.

'Solving the mystery,' replied Joe, grabbing the handset that lay on the table and calling up the required number. Seconds later, a familiar face flashed up on screen.

'Good afternoon, Lester,' said Joe, pausing while the camera above the screen swivelled to focus on him. 'We have a problem.'

Howells leaned forward, his sage grey head filling the larger part of the screen. 'Go on.'

'Shakespeare's screenplay sucks. Even worse than my usual.'

Howells looked disconsolate, eyebrows angled inwards beneath a furrowed brow. 'I sure am sorry to hear that. Any ideas why?'

'Grace is beat, which left me wondering: is there any chance – I mean, by *mistake* – that you gave us the wrong sample?'

Howells' eyebrows rose. 'That DNA I gathered myself from the inner sanctum. I personally transferred it from one tube to another.'

'What Joe meant to ask,' said Jerry, prompting the voice-sensitive camera to turn to him, 'was if there's any reason to doubt that the Shakespeare DNA in your library does actually belong to William Shakespeare?'

Howells sat back a little. 'One can never say for sure. But you must remember when the Brits had the grave exhumed? The TV coverage was forensic: Shakespeare's remains extracted under the fiercest scrutiny. We all saw it. And even if we hadn't, surely the fact that the British government was happy should be proof enough?'

Joe sighed. 'I'm sorry, Lester. I don't mean to interrogate you. It's just that when you've ruled out all the possibilities—'

'Then whatever remains, however improbable . . .' Howells hesitated, the gruffness of his voice softening as his eyes strayed from the lens. 'Then whatever remains, however improbable, must be the truth.'

His face was a picture of glazed intensity, like his features were fighting to keep pace with his racing mind.

'What is it, sir?' asked Grace. 'What's wrong?'

Howells turned back to face them.

'I've just had the most incredible thought.'

The Tortured Artist II

Still, there was nothing. Nothing, at least, of scope or substance, to please the old man. Plenty of fragments and false starts, but most were scrapped immediately, and those that weren't elicited a groan of disappointment.

So it was, along with the intensifying mental and physical cramps – his stomach aching for change; his legs and back sore from stasis – a new barrier stood in his way. No longer was the challenge simply finding inspiration, but overcoming fear. Fear of the black door opening out of the black wall, and the old man entering full of hope, only to be let down again.

The one remaining solution was to make that fear his primary incentive, and his days had settled accordingly into a kind of routine: taking his pills, failing to find a prompt, fixing on the outline of the door, and then trying to alchemise the negative energy of dread into something constructive. It hadn't worked yet, but there was still hope. After all, if things kept on as they were, that dread would only increase.

The old man had tried to help. After a month, he had reached his own conclusion about the drugs, and stopped adding any more ingredients to the daily intake. He had also spent a fortnight making daily deliveries of materials to answer complaints about the lack of anything worth writing, composing, or painting about. The room was now piled high with prompts: maps, atlases, encyclopaedias, and biographies, as well as classic novels, poetry anthologies, full scores of symphonies, and prints of famous paintings.

Occasionally, when the glare of the overhead light was softened by delirium, it felt almost homely. But any comfort was countered by what the clutter symbolised. There were no more excuses. The old man had always said the drugs alone should suffice, but now he really had done all he could to assist. Henceforth, the onus was entirely on the young man to make the most of those rare times when his discordant internal energies achieved a coherent synergy.

The door opened. It was seven in the morning, according to his bedside clock. A train rattled over the arch, making the shadows dance as the old man flicked on the light. He was holding a brown paper bag, along with his usual plastic carrier.

'Good morning,' he whispered, placing the brown bag on the desk. 'I've brought breakfast.'

He didn't normally announce this. Usually, it was just a box of cereal bars, left for periodic consumption throughout the morning.

'Take a look, son.'

The young man rose and reached into the bag. He pulled out a plastic knife and fork, followed by a warm, yellow polystyrene container. Inside was a full cooked breakfast.

'Thank you,' he whispered, sitting down to eat.

The old man started making the bed.

'Why . . . ?'

'Just eat.'

The young man did as he was told. When he'd finished, the old man dispensed the day's pills, then placed a blank sheet of paper on the desk.

'Five sentences, son. What you had for breakfast this morning.'

'But why?'

'No why. Not yet. Just write.'

The young man wrote. It didn't take long.

'Very good.' The old man took the paper. 'I think you'll like what comes of this.' He collected the empty bags and headed

- 66 -

for the door. 'Get down to work, son. I'll stop by later.'

The old man shut the door; the young man went back to thinking.

Chapter 6

'Good afternoon,' began Jim Withers, 'and my warmest thanks to WP for her kind introduction.'

Taking her seat inches from Jim's feet, Wendy nodded politely as his bald round head, bordered by fluffy grey tufts, peered down in sarcastic gratitude. Oh, how she'd missed Mr Withers' withering grin: all wonky yellow teeth and flaky pale lips, upturned in a manner as unbecoming as the ear-ring he sported in his left ear, defiantly affixed in tribute to his hero.

'As ever,' continued Jim, 'it's an honour to put a case which needs no putting whatsoever: a privilege to explain such simple truths to a delegation so stubbornly blind to the facts.'

Wendy laughed, the condescension ringing in her ears as she marvelled how this sneering specimen could possibly be the same man she'd known at college and, for two years, genuinely believed she'd loved. Honest to goodness, they were like two different people. One, the faithful friend whose wit and dashing handsomeness enraptured her back at Cambridge; the other, an irreconcilable foe who had slid into a bitterness which Wendy proudly ascribed to her army of agitators – combined, of course, with Jim's continued failure to prove the point that, twenty years before, had driven such an almighty wedge between them.

'But seriously,' he went on, 'I'm as bored as anyone of stating the obvious, so this year I'm doing something different.'

He poured some water and Wendy, squinting through her round brown specs, spied his hand shaking. For all his scornful confidence, Jim was tense. Whatever he had planned, he knew it wouldn't be easy. He knew that of the thousand-plus gathered in the hall – the most he'd ever faced – every one was itching to disagree with him.

'This year, I'm not going to repeat why it's incontrovertibly the case that William Shakespeare, the glover's son from Stratford-upon-Avon, wrote that to which we ascribe the phrase "Written by William Shakespeare". I'm not going to bore you by noting that this "Stratford Man", as you disparage him, left gifts to London actors when he died, thus forging an unarguable link between William Shakespeare, the country bumpkin you love to hate, and the London theatre for which the *writer* Shakespeare wrote – a link reinforced by poems in the 1623 Folio referring *specifically* to the "Swan of Avon" and his "Stratford Monument". And I certainly shan't worry you with more general points, for instance wondering why Shakespeare's name appears on fourteen of the fifteen plays published in his lifetime, or why, for hundreds of years, nobody questioned his claim.'

'Get on with it!' shouted someone towards the back.

Jim looked sharply to Wendy, imploring her to admonish the heckler but surely knowing he'd get no such pleasure. As if she'd ever make his life easier! Besides, Jim knew better than anyone that the conference was a bear pit for those of his ilk. Surely *that* was part of the appeal – the challenge that kept bringing Stratfordians back, avid in the vainglorious belief that Wendy's pride of cynical beasts might one day be tamed.

'And the reason I shan't be wasting our time with these inconvenient truths?' resumed Jim. 'Because I know what you devils are like. I know, no matter how plain the truth of what I say, you will ingest it into your sordid little conspiracy theories, then spit it straight back at me. You will claim that the ubiquity of William Shakespeare's name is explained by the Earl of Oxford's audacious decision to use it as a pseudonym. You will merrily embrace the abundant evidence linking the Stratford Shakespeare with the London Shakespeare, arguing that this indicates the thoroughness with which the *actual* author orchestrated his – or her – *coup de théâtre*. And after neutralising my arguments, you will assault me with questions. Why do none of Shakespeare's letters survive? How could one of such lowly learning have displayed such expertise in foreign languages, science and the law? Why were eighteen of the plays unpublished at the time of his death? Why does the Stratford Man's will mention no plays, books or letters? You will ask, and at every turn my answer will be "I don't know". Which, to those of sound mind, would prove nothing, but to you would scientifically signal my wrongness.'

Jim's words were met by a burst of good-natured jeering, and Wendy rubbed her hands in gleeful anticipation. This was what it was all about: the climax of their big weekend – the grand denouement which would thrillingly reunite them in fervent anti-Stratfordianism after three days cooped up in combat, debating the alternative theories between themselves. For though that internecine warfare was compelling – and how Wendy adored arguing for Christopher Marlowe – there was no greater pleasure than battling a Stratfordian. The first-hand reminder of the injustice they were fighting strengthened their ambition for the year ahead, and doubly so when the Stratfordian was one so eminent and irritable as Withers.

As for Wendy herself, there was no denying that Jim's conference appearances were extra special, transporting her all the way back to her very own zero hour: that unforgettable moment when, in her third year at King's College, Cambridge, she sat with Jim by the banks of the Cam, reading sonnets one sunny spring afternoon, only to find herself seized by a compulsive desire to know more about the man whose words spoke to her so personally across four hundred years. Suddenly, it wasn't enough just to accept Shakespeare's anonymity and enjoy the poems and plays for themselves. Such was the intensity of her connection, this man – this Shakespeare, this *whoever* – couldn't remain a stranger any longer.

And that was it. The moment curiosity kicked in, she saw with breathtaking vividness that nothing – but *nothing* – in the Stratfordian orthodoxy made sense. From the dearth of biographical information to the vacuum between the Stratford Shakespeare and the London playwright, the illusion was shattered. Manifestly, the man Wendy worshipped was an impostor: a front for another who, for whatever reason, had elected to keep his identity secret.

For someone who had invested so much in Shakespeare – who had cherished every word since her first swoop through the Complete Works aged eleven – this was big news. But even more outrageous than the epiphany itself was the snobbery with which she was roundly attacked. First, she was unceremoniously dumped by Jim for making mention of her doubts. Then, when she voiced her concerns in an essay on Shakespeare's Latinate allusions – wondering how one of Shakespeare's education could possibly have filled his plays with such learned asides – she was ignominiously chucked off her course: thrown into the world jobless, penniless and degreeless, with no option nor desire but to fight back.

The solution came swiftly. Rather than join one of the existing campaigns, she would set up a shiny new authorship militia, more energised than its weary predecessors. Its unwavering aim would be to air the debate so widely that Shakespeare's true identity became a permissible talking point everywhere from the local pub, right up to the loftiest ivory towers of academia. In so doing, they would actually take the discussion forward, such that one day – by hook or by crook – the truth would be revealed.

'So instead of pursuing more traditional arguments,' continued Jim, 'today I'm forcing the spotlight back onto *your* theories. But I am not merely going to summon the leading spokesperson for each alternative theory and interrogate them with the same wilful suspicion you employ against me. Nor am I going to be so stupid as to list the evidential inconsistencies of your crackpot conspiracies, and demand explanations as thorough as those you expect of me. Why? Well, because, as you are all so very fond of reminding me—'

'The true author didn't want to be known!' exclaimed Wendy. 'No proof *is* proof!'

'QED. In view of which . . .' He glanced to his left, where a computer hummed away. 'We must resort to a rather more precise form of debate.' He gave a confident grin. 'That's right, ladies and gents. It's time for a little mathematics!'

A hearty cheer went up as Jim set about fiddling with his computer, the screen behind him turning white with anticipation. Of all the adversaries who addressed them on the final day of conferences, Withers was invariably the biggest draw: guaranteed box office in his combination of eccentricity, originality and futile determination – not to mention the added emotional charge conjured by his and Wendy's well-known history.

His debut had come just four years after they broke up. Devastated by her Damascene conversion, Jim had made it his life goal to prove her wrong. A mathematician by trade, he began day-jobbing in IT at the Stratford HQ of the Royal Shakespeare Company, using his spare time to seek definitive proof of the Stratford Man's claim. Such was his all-consuming passion, when Wendy issued her ultimatum that he either appear at their third annual conference or, by refusing, implicitly concede that Shakespeare wasn't the author, he quickly accepted her invitation – despite having got nowhere with his research.

And that was the joy of Jim: the fact that he kept coming back, no matter how calamitous his most recent presentation. Whether it was a hangover from his former entanglement with Wendy, or simply a pathological conviction that the Stratford Man wrote the plays, failure only made him more determined – making his supposed proofs ever more absurd, and serving only to damage the wider Stratfordian cause. Indeed, many of his comrades downright resented his persistence, since the more he was seen to try, the more he was seen to fail. Better not to engage with the WAC at all, they argued, than keep returning with increasingly foolish theories – like the most recent, which reduced the debate to a series of ludicrous probability ratios – that only seemed to vindicate the dissenters' claims.

'May I have a volunteer?' he asked.

A forest of hands shot up. Jim picked a doddery old fellow, spectacularly attired in double-denim, who Wendy immediately recognised as a Baconian.

'Name?' asked Jim.

'Derek.'

'Derek.' Jim was relishing the descent into magic-show cliché. 'Derek, name us a play – any play – by Christopher Marlowe.'

Derek's eyes darted around. '*Dr. Faustus?*'

Jim tapped away. 'Act and scene?'

'Three. Act three, scene three.'

'Lovely.' The screen filled with the beginning of Act Three, Scene Three of *Dr. Faustus*. 'Go on.' Jim gestured as he scrolled through the text. 'Pick a passage. Just say when.'

Derek waited a few seconds before shouting 'Stop!' as the text approached line 100. The following 50 lines turned black as Jim copied them, after which he switched into a new program, and deposited the chosen *Faustus* text into one of two adjacent windows.

'And some Shakespeare?'

Derek hesitated, trying to foresee the catch. '*Measure for Measure,*' he said tentatively. 'Act One Scene Two.'

Jim repeated the first process, pasting Derek's chosen 50 lines so they stood side-by-side with the Marlowe.

'What I'm about to do,' Jim declared, 'is an exercise we all did at school: namely, compare and contrast these two passages. But whereas we were compromised by subjectivity, this technique yields altogether more *precise* results.'

He navigated through a series of menus. Wendy felt a tingle of excitement as he reached the one called 'Compare'.

'Doesn't it matter that one's in prose, the other's in verse?' came a query from the floor.

Jim chuckled. 'Oh, this technique addresses subtler factors than such formal superficialities. All that matters is they're both in English, and both aspire to clear meaning.'

'And just what is that supposed to mean?' asked another, who Wendy instantly identified as Keith Cobley – not least because, as a fellow committee member, Keith was right beside her, his cream linen jacket complementing a pink shirt and bright white jeans.

'It means,' answered Jim, 'that the only thing which wouldn't work is the deliberately obtuse. Abstract poetry, say, where the writer wills it to make no sense. But as long as the intention is to be clear, this works with whatever you like: from discursive, academic prose, right through to drama.'

'Very well,' replied Keith, toying the finely-trimmed black goatee that answered the absence of hair on top. 'And the fact that both are written in character?'

'Again, not a problem. That's my big discovery, see? No matter how hard writers try to adapt or camouflage their innate authorial style, a part of it still remains.'

Keith tutted assuredly. 'Not with greats like Tom Cobley.'

'Cobley cobblers!' chorused the delegation, right on cue: their well-worn, affectionate riposte to Keith, who was pathologically incapable of going more than a minute without mentioning his little-known ancestor whom he, uniquely, believed wrote Shakespeare's plays.

'You only jest because you know I'm right!' shouted Keith, taking the banter in his usual good heart. 'But in any case, my point stands. After all, isn't that what makes Cobley – or *whomever* – so unique? His ability to convincingly create any number of characters?'

'Doesn't matter,' said Jim. 'This works on a much lower level, assessing patterns to which we're blinded: word and sound usage, sentence structure – things that automatically appear, however much the writer wishes them away, as soon as he writes more than one sentence. Think of it as the writer's DNA. The immutable crux of his creativity.'

Wendy pulled up the sleeves of her favourite baggy pullover and leaned forward, amused and intrigued, as Jim pressed 'Compare'. Seconds later, an ocean of numbers and ratios appeared, separated into two windows, 'Marlowe' and 'Shakespeare', each with three columns and rows too numerous to count.

'I've not yet labelled everything,' said Jim, grabbing his umbrella, 'but hopefully you'll get the gist.' He examined the hundreds of digits. 'So here . . .' He pointed the brolly to the three columns in the Marlowe window. 'You have the three different categories. The first are straightforward.' He moved the brolly down the screen, tapping each row in column one. 'Frequency of alliteration, onomatopoeia, similes, and so on. The higher the number, the denser the usage.' The brolly returned to the top of the screen, this time to column two. 'The second category analyses the writer's vocabulary: first, use of imagery, broken into animal, vegetable, mineral subsections, then use of synonyms, relative use of nouns, verbs, etcetera. Another subsection then dissects sentence structure: recurrent orders of words, rhythmic patterns, the extent to which grammar usage varies from one line to the next. Then, finally, we look at instances of rare, exotic or arcane words – arcane at the time of writing, that is.'

'How do you gauge that?' asked Wendy.

'The British Library database. I borrowed a copy and ran parts of this program on all its contents, compiling an accurate database of how language has evolved since Chaucer. Which also comes in handy since I can then express a writer's word usage in relation to other writing of the time. For this, I entered 1600 as the time of composition, so the program retrieves all the database entries from twenty years either side of that date, comparing our passages with the averages for that era, telling us how each writer is at variance from the norm.'

Jim paused for a moment, letting his words sink in, as a murmur – equal parts disapproval, bemusement and concern – rippled around the hall.

'But even in column two,' he picked up, 'we're still only considering superficial traits which could, theoretically, be faked.' He tapped the final column. 'Section three is where it gets tasty. That's where we go under the bonnet, taking the results from sections one and two and playing around with them, pinning down the writer's personal preferences in relation to my all-new probability engine: one which takes a sentence, processes its meaning, and then imagines the thousand different ways that sentiment could be expressed. By doing that, and then analysing the particular option the writer went with, one constructs a model of the writer's sub-conscious taste: everything he likes, from specific words to different syntactic formulations. For example, when synonyms are either available or necessary, I ask whether he tends to go for words with more consonants or vowels.'

'Oh, please!' hooted someone. 'As if writers ever fret about such things!'

'But they *do*,' insisted Jim. 'Sub-consciously.' He stepped to the front. 'What we're talking about here is taste: taste as an inherent part of our being; that which makes one man's meat another man's poison. You know it's true. Just as we all enjoy different music, we all have different favourite words. What appeals linguistically to you won't necessarily appeal to me. Who knows why? Perhaps it's genetic. Either way, that's the focus: deciphering writers' tastes such that one can compare the stylistic imprint of different authors.' He motioned proudly towards his handiwork. '*Quod erat demonstrandum.*'

A puzzled silence fell upon the hall. Apparently, Jim had nothing to add.

'Is that it?' asked Wendy.

'That is indeed it.' Jim tossed the brolly away. 'The two passages have been compared and, as you can see, the figures in each window aren't even close to matching. Ergo, the two passages were not written by the same individual. Ergo, the man who wrote *Doctor Faustus* didn't write *Measure for Measure*. Ergo, Shakespeare wasn't Marlowe.'

Jim's presentation had lurched from impenetrable complexity to suspicious simplicity in the blink of an eye.

'Still in doubt?' he went on. 'Then let's try some Bacon.'

He dropped his gaze to the front row, where the ten committee members sat side by side: Wendy, Clive, Pat, Keith, John, Felix, Leonard, Colin, Rob and Steve. Each was charged with a different administrative role but – more importantly – each also represented a different authorship candidate, so ensuring that the group was fundamentally unbiased in all its collective workings.

'Clive,' he said, picking out everyone's favourite Baconian, dressed in his faithful tweed jacket, 'name a passage.'

Clive rocked back in his seat, legs and arms crossed in thought. '"Knowledge is Power", from *Meditations*.'

Jim summoned Clive's choice, along with another random slice of Shakespeare. As before, he clicked 'Compare' and the screen filled with numbers. Once again, the numbers on either side were at variance.

'This isn't proof,' sniffed Clive. 'For all we know, the computer's just plucked those numbers out of thin air.'

'Very well.' Jim scanned the front row for a new victim, eventually settling on Wendy herself. 'Name me some Shakespeare.'

'*Henry V*,' suggested Wendy.

'Act, scene and line?' asked Jim.

'Act Four, Scene Two, line 24.'

Within seconds the passage was up on screen. 'And another?' Jim asked, pointing to their treasurer, Pat, bedecked in black from top to toe. 'More Shakespeare.'

'*Much Ado About Nothing*,' said Pat, his long grey hair quivering as he spoke. 'Act Five, Scene One, line 70.'

The second extract appeared, with the two results windows following moments later. Looking from one to the other, Wendy shivered. While by no means exact, the two passages had yielded remarkably similar figures.

'Do you see?' grinned Jim triumphantly. 'An extraordinary parity. Proof that the same individual wrote these two passages. Which isn't, of course, to say that the author *was* William Shakespeare. But it does provide a benchmark against which the divergences of the two prior comparisons all but eliminate Marlowe and Bacon, proving that neither the author of *Dr. Faustus* nor that of *Meditations* was also responsible for the Shakespeare plays.' He switched off the screen. 'And thus, ladies and gentlemen, two of your three leading theories are categorically debunked.'

A hush descended on the hall, the delegation dazed by what it had witnessed. Even Wendy herself was strangely speechless: not so much worried as bewildered – much as one feels when a conjuror, through sleight of hand and verbal ingenuity, leads one down blind alleyways of detail and digression, only to turn round and deliver a killer punch from nowhere. You know it's not for real, you know it's all a trick – and yet for a moment, before logic engages, the shock leaves you struck, almost to the point of believing, by the apparent truth of what you've just seen.

Jim was scrutinising the delegation intently, eyes darting round for signs of success. As the silence lingered, Wendy could just see his cheeks begin to rise above the most tentative of smiles – hopeful like that of a man daring to believe he's finally seen off an acute bout of hiccups.

'We don't believe you!' came a cry suddenly.

'It's a fix!' yelled another.

'Where are your workings?' shouted someone else.

'I'll show the workings if you like,' returned Jim, 'they won't make much sense . . .'

'It's tripe,' proclaimed a voice behind Wendy. 'The matches on the Shakespeare extracts aren't even exact.'

'Don't be so disingenuous,' protested Jim. 'The Shakespeare match is exact enough – compared to the others it's—'

'Never mind the numbers,' interrupted Clive. 'Surely the real problem here is that the whole thing is predicated on science fiction – ideas totally at odds with the accepted understanding of artistic endeavour as an act of imaginative skill which can be learnt, honed and nurtured. You talk about these fixed subconscious traits, but where's the proof?'

Jim opened his mouth to reply, but seemed suddenly lost. 'I . . .' he stuttered, sweat bubbling up on his brow as the hope fell from his features. 'The proof is here. This is what I've found. These are the facts.'

'No,' answered Clive, 'these are *symptoms*. Symptoms of something for which you've no proof; which runs against the very fabric of imagination as we know it.'

'Clive's right!' exclaimed Wendy, standing and striding onto the stage. 'Yes, these results are striking, but to infer any firm conclusions requires creativity to be some kind of bio-chemical absolute – such that no genius, however great, can disguise those innate characteristics.'

'That's what I seem to have discovered,' nodded Jim in mounting desperation.

'But you haven't discovered anything. There's no scientific grounding for the conclusions you're inferring. Nothing which stands up to the abundant evidence to the contrary: all those great artists who reinvented themselves time and again. Late Beethoven versus early Beethoven, say: proof that artistic identity is the slipperiest thing on earth; that artists change their creative skins at will.' She motioned to the audience. 'We need no reminding. It's that quicksilver quality we celebrate: the fact that someone, most likely Christopher Marlowe, was such a supreme shape-shifter they lived the most amazing double-life, writing both their own masterpieces and those we know as Shakespeare's, yet to this day defying all attempts to match the two – including your own!'

Jim shook his head. 'You can't fake the figures.'

'But you *can*. That's what's so exciting. Marlowe – or whoever – *did*.'

'Impossible.'

'But why? Where's the proof that such deception is impossible?'

Again, Jim set himself to reply, but this time there was not even a stutter. His expectant eyes sank down as if suddenly seeing his fatal flaw: the absence of any scientific proof supporting the supposition on which his numerical house of cards had been built.

'This is the truth of it,' pressed Wendy. 'You've nothing backing this up but faith. It seems like some big discovery to you because the results chime with your beliefs. But from our viewpoint, these figures only reinforce the true author's magnificence; expressing, with forensic precision, his astonishing ability to change from one guise to the next.'

Wendy's words hung in the air, daring Jim to come back at her. After a momentary silence, the hall echoed to the sound of clapping as the delegates, sensing the knockout blow had been landed, started applauding their leader. Moments later, after firing Wendy the bitterest scowl, Jim too accepted the game was up and began gathering his papers.

Head down, ignoring the victorious whoops from the floor, he stuffed his computer into his shoulder bag, grabbed his brolly, and made for the exit without another word.

Chapter 7

'Doubts about William Shakespeare's true identity first surfaced in the late 18th century, when James Wilmot, a scholarly clergyman from Warwickshire, grew obsessed by the lack of biographical evidence regarding the Bard, daring to ask the questions that more cowardly souls never ventured to address. Soon enough, others were on the case too, notably the American scholar Delia Bacon—'

'Damn this diversion!' exclaimed Joe, as Jerry continued reading. Ok, so he'd always known that there were some people who doubted Shakespeare wrote the plays, but surely they were just a bunch of cranks: scholars who'd never cut it at the top, or Shakespeare-worshippers so besotted they wanted to stake some kind of personal claim on his work.

Certainly, it had never once occurred to him that *this* would be the stumbling block that toppled their masterplan. After Jerry and Grace had overcome impossible odds to deliver the invention of a lifetime, it was infuriating to be screwed by something as simple as mistaken identity. One way or another, they had to solve the authorship puzzle, and solve it fast.

The question was: how? According to Jerry, dozens of candidates had been championed as the real author, right up to and including Queen Elizabeth I herself. Somehow, they needed to slice through the mesh of theories and strike straight at the truth.

'We use MET,' he declared, interrupting Jerry just as he listed the celebrity adherents – Sigmund Freud, Henry James, Mark

Twain – who had been attracted to the cause over the years: an elite club of which Joe was the latest, reluctant member.

'Never mind the history. We just need to get the DNA for all the alternative players.' He looked to Grace, seated at the opposite end of the meeting table. 'Agreed?'

'MET has destroyed Shakespeare's claim. Makes sense for it to identify his replacement.'

'Right,' said Joe. 'Which means digging.'

Half-smiling, Grace stared back. 'Are you serious?'

'Deadly. There must be people we can hire.'

'And keep it secret?' said Jerry. 'That's a lot of graves to dig, boss. And not all of them are low profile.'

'Then we do it in darkness! Either that, or act like it's legit. Invent a cover story and do it openly.'

'We could hide behind Lester,' suggested the producer. 'Pretend it's one of his projects.'

'Lester!'

Up on the conference screen, the great man lowered his eyes from the Pennsylvania sky, and Joe explained his plan – the only possible plan there was.

'Oh really,' chuckled Howells. 'I hardly think there's any need for such criminal rashness. Don't you realise all the necessary samples have already been obtained?'

'They have?'

'I should know. Really, it gave me the most enormous headache.' His eyes drifted off. 'Just think: if I'd known then what we know now.'

'Known when?'

'About six years ago. There's this organisation in the UK: a kind of fanatical self-help group called the Worldwide Authorship Circle. It's mainly made up of restless artistic types: writers, actors, directors, you name it. Spend their lives bickering over who really wrote Shakespeare's plays. All rather pointless, if you ask me, but they were undeniably determined. When I first approached the UK government to suggest storing Shakespeare's DNA, the WAC got wind of it and contacted me. If I was to have

William Shakespeare, they argued, I should have all the other possible authors too.' Howells smiled. 'Naturally, I told them where to go. My DNA bank was above such folly.'

'So what did they do?'

'Used it to their advantage. Went to the media, portraying me as a traitor to truth. And hey: you know how the Brits love an underdog. The pity poured forth, so much so they set up a campaign, raising cash to hunt down the remains of all the key authorship candidates.'

'And they succeeded?' asked Grace.

Howells nodded. 'They dug up the ten most likely, taking the best hair samples they could find. They couldn't afford to isolate the DNA, but still: the stunt worked wonders for their reputation.' He gave a rueful smile. 'I remember quietly admiring them – they fought a good fight, the lead woman especially. Unbelievable to think they were actually right.'

'So where are these clippings stored?' urged Joe.

'That I don't know.'

'I do,' declared Jerry, at his computer. 'They're kept at the WAC's HQ in London, near the Globe theatre.'

'Damn,' said Joe. 'Would've been easier elsewhere.'

'Easier?' asked Grace.

'To steal them. If they'd been in some storage facility, we could easily have gotten access. Someone could've just posed as a WAC member.'

'You don't think we should just ask them?'

Joe looked at her in amazement. 'But that would mean going public.'

'Well . . .' Grace smiled, a little nervously. 'It *is* a big discovery.'

'And? So was the creative gene. So was working out how to *transplant* the creative gene! Surely if you're happy to keep that secret, a trivial literary discovery shouldn't worry you.'

'But I'm only keeping my discoveries secret for *now*,' replied the scientist. 'What you're suggesting means that the truth about Shakespeare may never be known beyond the four of us. You talk, rightly, about winning the Oscar as an act of personal vindication, but what about vindicating the real author of Shakespeare's plays – whoever that may be?'

'It's not our problem,' asserted Jerry. 'This whole thing is about one thing only: delivering Joe his Oscar.'

'But can't we be honest and still achieve that?'

'Not given the practicalities. There's no way the Academy will let us win if we 'fess up. A genetically-enhanced screenplay? That's gotta be against the rules!'

'Oh, please. I doubt very much there *are* such rules.'

'But the *embarrassment*,' said Joe. 'I don't want to admit I needed the help.'

Grace studied him. Once again, something passed between them – a shared understanding of what these dreams meant; of the power that overwhelmed all peripheral concerns – and the passion in her eyes turned from anger to pity.

'Do whatever you feel is right,' she said at last.

'Here,' said Jerry, back at the computer. 'I've found some pics.'

Joe looked at the screen. The images indicated that the WAC's artefacts were stored in nothing more secure than a filing cabinet, each in a plastic bag with a label identifying the candidate to whom the sample belonged.

'All we need is to get someone into that room,' said Jerry.

'But how?' asked Joe.

Jerry looked up, drumming his fingers on the table, staring into the middle distance. 'Surely the how follows the who.'

'Ok. So who?'

Jerry nodded, and Joe realised he wasn't looking into space at all. In fact, his eyes were fixed on a framed photo to the right of the conference screen – a photo of a man whose villainy was ideally suited to the task in hand: Emperor Tyron, High Lord of the Cafillians.

Chapter 8

It was only her second glass, but Wendy was already wobbly with the wine. She hadn't eaten since breakfast, so was heading to the buffet needing to address the matter urgently or risk passing out, and that wouldn't have done at all. They liked to party, the WAC, and they liked to party – well, if not quite hard then as hard as was reasonable for academics of a certain age with similarly fragile constitutions.

So what was it to be? Surveying the handsome spread prepared by Clive, for whom archives were chiefly a means to enjoying cheese – his greatest passion in life, notwithstanding Bacon – Wendy settled on a generous slice of cranberry brie, and was munching joyfully away when someone tugged the back of her jumper.

'Thought you'd enjoy that.'

And there was Mr Cheese himself, dressed in the usual combo of threadbare tweed, baggy brown corduroys and unlaced brown shoes, topped off by his big, benevolent beard. Oh, Clive, she felt like saying: you're just so lovely. So exquisitely, incomparably lovely. One of those lovely souls for whom the word itself had been invented.

For years, the two of them had danced round each other, closer than friends, but stopping short of anything more. Whether it was a hangover from her experiences with Jim Withers, or the knowledge that she was a Marlovian, him a Baconian, and only one of them could be right, she couldn't tell. The only certainty was that, six months before, Clive had been the first to blink, finally getting engaged to an old librarian friend. Wendy was overjoyed for him – not jealous in the slightest – and frankly revelled in the knowledge that 'it' was never going to happen, either with him or anyone else. She had the group, and as long as the group stayed strong, that was all the family she needed.

'Best Withers takedown ever,' the cheese man declared. 'I really thought he had us for a moment. To have just batted it away would have been commendable, but to upend his theory such that it supported our *raison d'être*? Simply virtuosic!'

'Miss Preston?' said a voice from behind.

Recognising the warm, resonant tones, yet unable to place them, Wendy looked up at Clive, whose surprised eyes were directed back over her shoulder.

'Peter Heyward,' came the voice again.

Wendy froze. Surely not *the* Peter Heyward? *Sir* Peter Heyward?

Clive grinned. Yes, he was saying: *that* one.

'Sir Peter.' She turned and curtseyed. The man was much shorter than she expected.

'Delighted to meet you,' he whispered.

'Likewise,' smiled Wendy, shaking hands with the aged actor while trying to reconcile him with the fiendish Claudius she'd seen him give at the Globe a few weeks previously. It wasn't that he looked different. His weathered features, pronounced nose and silver grey hair were unmistakeable. He simply lacked a certain aura. He seemed humble, almost frightened.

'Just finished the matinee at the Globe,' he explained, rather frantically. 'On the way in I spied you all in session, and asked the company manager what was going on. Now I've always been fascinated by the authorship issue – *terribly* fascinated – so when I heard about this little shindig I thought I'd introduce myself.'

He smiled through straight, snow-white teeth.

'Good news, eh?' said Clive.

'Splendid,' agreed Wendy, delighted yet disconcerted. Sir Peter's interest was plainly marvellous, but how on earth could such a luminary be sympathetic to their cause and yet she not know a jot about it? Given their thoroughness in soliciting support, the only credible explanation was that Sir Peter preferred to keep his enthusiasm hush hush, lest it dent his credibility with the establishment. But if that was the case, why was now the right moment to approach the WAC? Had they truly worked their way so into the mainstream that even Sir Peter, steeped in old-school theatrical tradition, no longer felt embarrassed to be associated with them?

'Perhaps you should give our guest a tour?' suggested Clive.

'Yes,' nodded Wendy, adrenalin kicking in as she imagined what might arise if he could be persuaded to go public with his passion. 'We've been based here for almost six years,' she explained, stepping outside and surveying the building's brick exterior. 'Just next door we've got the remains of the Rose, the first Elizabethan Bankside theatre . . .' She checked herself, with a smile. 'But then I'm sure you already knew that.'

'Naturally,' said Sir Peter, with a bow of the head.

'Our building housed the Globe staff while the reconstruction was built round the corner. Then afterwards, it became their education base. For years, we lobbied them for a bit of office space – the authorship issue being fairly fundamental to Shakespearean education, if you ask me – but they wouldn't have it. It was only after our profile was raised by the rigmarole with Lester Howells that they finally granted our wish – realising the relationship might be mutually beneficial.'

'Splendid.'

'Oh, it was. Having the Globe's endorsement was an enormous breakthrough. People started seeing the authorship debate as an integral part of the whole Shakespeare thing, not just some loony sideshow.'

Sir Peter mopped his brow. Even though the mid-evening temperature was modest, the actor was perspiring heavily: unsettled, perhaps, by the heads being turned as he stepped out with the WAC for the first time.

They headed back indoors, where Wendy guided him through

the rabbit warren of corridors and stairs, commenting on the odd point of interest but for the most part listening to Sir Peter rage against the scandal of Shakespeare's claim – something he did with such eloquence she could scarcely suppress her excitement. Never mind the authority exuded by his lifelong association with Shakespeare's plays; Sir Peter's oratorical prowess alone would be a huge boon. The WAC's single greatest challenge, as long as a definitive solution eluded them, was to keep the argument alive as publicly as possible. For that they needed two things – money and members – and though they were highly proficient in acquiring both, neither appeared more prolifically than when a voice of authority spoke out in their favour.

'Truly,' he panted, climbing the spiral staircase that wound up to the attic. 'Truly, I should go so far as to argue it is not only the single greatest historical injustice in the history of art, but the whole history of mankind. We speak his words, think his thoughts day-in day-out, and yet we haven't even done him the dignity of finding out who he really was.'

'I couldn't agree more.' Wendy lent him a helping hand onto the landing. 'But tell me: who *do* you think wrote the plays?'

'Well . . .' Sir Peter's cheeks reddened. 'The honest truth is I don't subscribe to any one theory. All I know is that the Stratford halfwit could not possibly have been responsible.'

'Hear, hear.'

'I feel it deeply.'

'I'm sure you do.'

'In my bones.'

'Absolutely.'

'And my bones are worth listening to, are they not?'

'Indeed they are.'

'I've been on intimate terms with the plays for over fifty years. Truly, I feel closer to the author than any other man alive.'

'No question,' said Wendy, savouring the passion in Sir Peter's voice.

'I feel like I know him.' He thumped the fist of one hand into the palm of the other. 'I know what made him tick. What manner of man he was. A brilliant intellectual: not some second-rate glover's son from the provinces. There is simply no way—'

His eyes settled on a door leading off the landing.

'Tell me: why is there a lock on that door?'

'Oh, that's our archive. Centuries of research. Very valuable.'

He stepped forward. 'May I?'

Feeling wobbly once again – drunk, this time, on the great man's fervour – Wendy unlocked the door and flicked a switch to illuminate the WAC's treasure trove.

Sir Peter scoured the room. 'So is this where you store the samples?'

'Samples?'

'The bits of hair you collected six years ago.'

'Oh, yes. They're here.'

'Could I possibly . . . ?'

Wendy sifted through her keys, elation mounting as Sir Peter's secret fanaticism further revealed itself.

'I know it's a trifle odd,' he said as Wendy opened the cabinet where Clive stored the ten clippings. 'But just think . . .' He lifted out the bag containing one of Bacon's hairs and held it to the light. 'Just think what this hair has seen.'

'Absolutely,' agreed Wendy, watching him remove the other nine bags in turn.

'So courageous of you to stand up to Lester Howells,' he said. 'Although in a way his complacency was a blessing. Otherwise, he'd have got all these as well. As it is, he's left with the impostor Shakespeare, and you, somewhere, possess the actual author.'

Wendy couldn't help but laugh, delighted by the concrete conviction with which Sir Peter spoke of the authorship fraud. Genius actor that he was, it was like he *knew*, for absolute certain, that Shakespeare *didn't* write 'Shakespeare'.

'I'm sorry if I seem a little zealous,' he apologised, returning the clippings and closing the drawer. 'But truly, I'm a passionate man.'

'Of course, which is why we should talk. *You* should talk. Speak out for us.'

- 91 -

'And I'd be happy to – although I'd need to brush up on the detail. After all, my instinctive faith, while potent, would seem weak if not supported by knowledge of the facts.'

'Well, you know: anything we can do to help . . .'

'Most kind,' smiled Sir Peter. 'And as it happens, I do have the evening free. Perhaps I could start right away? Read through some of the stuff you have here?'

'Go for your life! Unless of course you fancy joining us downstairs, then maybe popping in some other time?'

He shook his head. 'I've had a busy day. I could do with some peace.'

'As you wish – although I really ought to head back down myself. Will you be ok on your own?'

'I'll be fine. I shall come down when I'm done.'

Leaving Sir Peter to his research, Wendy retreated downstairs and headed straight for the wine, pouring herself a large, calming glass of merlot.

'You seem tremendously jolly,' said Keith Cobley, wandering over at once.

'It's been a good day,' replied Wendy. 'Actually, no. It's been a *perfect* day. I can't imagine a better one.'

'Indeed.' Keith stroked his immaculate black goatee. 'And *so* exciting to see you with Sir Peter just now.'

Wendy smiled. 'It's promising: that's all.'

'I can't believe I missed him. You know he's my all-time acting idol?'

'Is that right?' sighed Wendy, glancing – quite despite herself – up the stairs.

'What's that?'

'I'm sorry?'

'You were looking upstairs.'

'No I wasn't.'

'You were.'

Wendy shrugged. 'No reason.'

'He's still here. Sir Peter's still upstairs!'

'Yes, but he doesn't want any fuss.'

- 92 -

'Oh, actors always say that,' said Keith, setting off. 'They invariably mean the reverse!'

'Just don't be pushy,' shouted Wendy, as Keith disappeared and lovely Clive came up to her side. 'What if he babbles on about Tom Cobley? If there's one theory which still makes us look cranky . . .' She reflected for a moment. 'Here, hold this.'

She handed her glass to Clive and set off up the winding staircase. But no sooner had she passed the first floor than she collided with a suited figure rushing the other way. Stepping aside, she spotted Keith further up, which meant the fleeing figure could only be Sir Peter himself.

'Where are you going?'

The aged actor turned to face her, his face moist with perspiration. 'My apologies, but I just realised I need to be elsewhere. I've an appointment which, in my enthusiasm, I'd quite forgotten.' He edged down the stairs, disappearing round the bend.

'We should have lunch.'

'Without doubt,' bellowed Sir Peter. 'Thanks for the tour!'

Wendy turned to Keith. 'When I left him he was fine.'

'I know.' Keith trudged back upstairs.

'What did you do?'

'He was like that when I arrived. Panicking, breathless: said he couldn't stay a moment longer.'

They stepped into the archive. What on earth had left Sir Peter so shaken up? Glancing around, everything looked in order, just as it had five minutes earlier. Whatever books he had examined had been carefully returned to their rightful place, even in his haste.

'Wait a second,' said Keith, striding to the filing cabinet. 'Did you show Sir Peter the hairs?'

'I did,' said Wendy. 'And?'

'You closed the drawer afterwards?'

'He shut it, yes,' said Wendy, turning cold as she saw it was only pushed to.

'And you locked it?'

Wendy shook her head.

There was a tense silence as Keith opened the drawer and flicked through. Moments later, he breathed a sigh of relief.

'Panic over,' he declared. 'They're all here.'

'What's going on?' cried Clive, stepping into his office. 'I just saw Sir Peter running away.'

'It's ok,' said Keith. 'For a moment we thought he might've stolen the hair clippings, but—'

'What?!' exclaimed Clive, shoving past to remove the bags one by one.

'It's fine,' Keith assured him. 'I've checked.'

But Clive wanted to be certain. He arranged the bags on his desk as Wendy described Sir Peter's interest in seeing the archive, and the hairs in particular.

'You didn't ask why?' demanded Clive.

'He asked, I agreed. He's a great Shakespearean, overflowing with enthusiasm for our project. The man gets what he wants!'

'Wait!' Clive pulled out a lock of hair and held it aloft. 'It's shrunk! This hair, Bacon's hair – a whole half centimetre, snipped off!' He went to the cabinet and produced photos of the samples, which he compared with the real things. 'Good grief. He's taken bits of each of them!'

Wendy's heart sank. 'What could he possibly want with them?' she asked, hoping the unanswerability of the question might excuse her negligence.

'Who knows?' Clive strode to the window and peered down at the street. 'Only one way to find out.'

'He's still here?' asked Wendy, following Clive out of the room.

'Just getting in a cab!'

They headed downstairs and scattered onto the pavement.

'There!' yelled Wendy, pointing to a black cab being held at a crossing at the easterly end of the street. She raced to catch up but failed to beat the lights, which turned green just as she got close enough to see Sir Peter's head in the back seat. The cab pulled away, towards London Bridge, as a car horn screeched in Wendy's ears. She leapt onto the pavement to make way, but instead of accelerating past the car rolled up beside her.

'Jump in,' shouted Clive, throwing open the passenger door.

Wendy leapt in and pointed him towards the cab. There were a few vehicles between them, providing a useful cushion in the late evening traffic as they followed Sir Peter over the river and on, through Whitechapel and Poplar.

'I reckon we're heading for Dover,' said Clive. 'He's making for the continent!'

Soon enough, however, Sir Peter's taxi strayed from the eastwards dual carriageway, manoeuvring its way towards City Airport.

'He really is leaving the country,' said Wendy.

Clive switched on the wipers as it began raining, and the red rear lights of the taxi disappeared in the haze. Wendy implored him to put his foot down. Moments later, the road veered sharply to the left, bringing the red lights into imminent view.

'They've stopped!'

Clive slammed on the brakes. The cab pulled away.

'Go, go, go!' cried Wendy, but before Clive could oblige there was a tapping on his window. He wound down the glass.

'Which flight are you here for?' asked the guard.

'That cab,' said Wendy. 'A friend of ours is inside. We've just been to the theatre, and he left his wallet in my handbag. He's not answering his phone, and we need to return it before he leaves.'

The guard peered into the vehicle. 'Very well.'

Clive accelerated. 'Why are we being stopped?'

Wendy read the passing sign. 'Because this is Charter Flights Only. The man really *is* on a top secret mission – with *our* samples as his cargo!'

They wound through a maze of lanes until two lights appeared in the rain. This time, however, they were white, not red.

'They're coming back,' said Wendy.

The cab passed close enough to reveal that the back seat was empty.

'But Sir Peter's gone!'

'Then let's find where he's been deposited,' said Clive, driving on until the road ballooned into a cul-de-sac, bordered by a high grass verge.

Wendy leapt out, striding up the grass as a mechanical din pierced the soggy night air. Looking down, she saw a small jet powering down the runway and soaring up, into the clouds.

'Hey!'

She leapt onto the tarmac and sprinted towards a runway marshal, dressed in luminous yellow and bearing a miscellany of plastic lollipops.

'You with the sticks!'

The marshal stopped as she reached him. 'What on earth?'

'I just need you to answer one question. That flight. Where was it headed?'

The man looked uncertain.

'Seriously, you don't know how much it matters.' She reached into her pocket and offered him a fifty pound note.

'Oh, I'm afraid I'm not one to divulge confidential information,' he frowned. 'And I certainly won't be bribed.'

He walked away, but stopped after a few paces, considering. Moments later, he turned back, grinning.

'Oddly enough, however,' he said, 'on this particular occasion, it just so happens I'm *itching* to tell you what you want to know. I'm itching to tell everyone!'

'You are?'

The marshal beamed back.

'So where was it going?'

He looked heavenwards. 'JoeTown, California. Home of my hero, Joe Seabright.'

Wendy thought she must have misheard. 'Joe *Rise of the Glozbacks* Seabright?'

The marshal nodded. 'And you know the best bit?'

'Tell me.'

'It had Emperor Tyron inside.'

Chapter 9

Taking the plastic bag from Grace, Joe whistled a medley of *Solix Chronicles* themes as he sliced it open with a miniature *Solix Chronicles* laser-sword.

'Such sweet music,' murmured Sir Peter.

The aged actor was slumped on a sofa, having turned his impromptu visit into a week-long holiday in between sets of *Hamlet* performances at the Globe Theatre in London.

'Excuse me, boss,' said Jerry, concluding a call on his cell phone. 'Apparently I'm needed at reception.' He headed out.

'So long,' sang Joe to the surging fervour of *Mark and Regina's Love Theme* as he peered into the plastic wrapping to see two tins awaiting his attention. 'So long . . . Oh I've waited so long for you . . .'

It was true. When Sir Peter came good four days previously, Grace had commandeered the WAC hair clippings to isolate the DNA, only for her purpose-built machine to fail. Naturally, she urged Joe to wait until she'd fixed the problem, but when Lester Howells offered to isolate the DNA instead, Joe couldn't resist. Typically, Grace then fixed the bug within hours – a software glitch, which for some reason hadn't affected previous isolations – leaving Joe feeling pretty dumb, having to wait three days for the clippings to be shipped to Pennsylvania, processed, then sent back to JoeTown.

Still, at least they'd returned intact. After laying aside the tin containing the original WAC hair samples, he opened the new one and impatiently checked off the ten test tubes: Francis Bacon, the Earl of Oxford, Christopher Marlowe, Walter Raleigh, Roger Manners, William Stanley, Mary Sidney, Tom Cobley, Queen Elizabeth I and Henry Neville – the ten leading authorship candidates, as identified by the affiliation of those currently serving on the WAC's organising committee.

Joe looked to Grace. 'Let's do it.'

'Only if you promise.'

Joe sighed. 'Please, Grace. Cut me some slack.'

'Ten days between each pill. Nothing less.'

'But that's gonna set us back months!'

'So be it.'

Joe let out a sulky groan. If not surprised, he was certainly deflated by Grace's circumspection – and worried too. With the delays they'd already endured, any more setbacks could mean pushing back the May 2024 release date by a whole year. That could prompt some awkward questions about what had delayed the production of Joe's much-improved, Oscar-winning masterpiece.

'I doubt very much you'll need months,' said Sir Peter. 'Heavens, you may not even need weeks. What if you strike gold immediately? The odds are one in ten. Better still, if you start with the most likely – Bacon, say – and work your way down.'

Joe shook his head. 'It can't work like that.'

'But surely you'll know when you have your man?'

'Perhaps, but we need to be certain. And that won't be possible until we've done all ten and compared. After all, Bacon, Marlowe . . . Some of these guys were pretty mean in their own right.'

'Quite,' said Grace. 'Which is all the more reason why you can't just take a pill, write a reel or two, then move on to the next without a break. It's not just that your nervous system will get disoriented. It's because a lot of these muses are so creative you're going to feel seriously drained after each, no matter how low the dosage. Don't forget how exhausted you were after swallowing Shakespeare – and he was totally inept.'

Joe shut the DNA tin and placed it in the top drawer of his

desk. Grace's caution was unshakeable. Even though he quite fancied taking the risk – it was the last movie, after all – deep down he knew it was too dangerous. His only realistic option was to take his time and then shave even more off the already-streamlined production schedule.

'What's wrong?' said Grace suddenly.

Joe looked up to see that Jerry had returned, looking tense and red-faced. He glanced nervously at Sir Peter before facing his boss. 'Bad news.'

'Bad news?'

'You've got some visitors.'

***

Wendy stared at the clock: nearly there. She bit her lip in a potent mix of anger and apprehension as the seconds ticked towards the point when she and her friends, stationed in the bloated hallway outside Seabright's office, would force their threatened entry.

In the end, she reflected, bringing the whole committee over had been a masterstroke. Despite her initial misgivings, there was little doubt that she and Clive alone would have struggled to command the attention all ten of them had just managed. Not for the first time, she was grateful for the inherent democracy of the group. With intrigue overflowing after the unfathomable oddness of Sir Peter's thievery, the entire committee had insisted on helping to discover what lay behind it. The flight tickets hadn't been cheap but, as their treasurer Pat observed, what were their financial reserves for, if not moments like these?

Hitherto, it had all gone to plan. As agreed on the plane over, they accessed JoeTown by taking a guided tour, posing as a bunch of *Solix Chronicles* geeks from across the pond. After an hour spent riding in helicopters and jeeps, enduring endless paeans praising JoeTown's scale when the only truly noteworthy feature was its soullessness, they finally arrived at Joe Seabright's mansion: a spectacular gothic residence which, they were nerdishly told, was off-limits for today's tour, being the place where Seabright was currently ensconced, working on the screenplay for the final *Chronicles* film.

All of which, naturally, was the cue for the committee to leap out of the jeep and sprint up the immaculately-lined front lawn. Easily outrunning the rotund guide who gave chase, they burst in through the gold-edged front doors, emblazoned with the *Solix Chronicles* logo, and strode up to the startled young receptionist.

'Get me Mr Seabright,' Wendy demanded.

Intimidated by their number, the woman lifted the receiver and summoned 'Jerry' for assistance. A tall, smart man duly appeared, introducing himself as Jerry Botstein, Producer of *The Solix Chronicles*, and asking what the problem was. They'd come to retrieve what was rightly theirs, Wendy explained, and weren't leaving until they had it.

Botstein had no choice but to relent. He led them to the hallway outside Seabright's office, where Wendy allowed him a minute – no longer – to prepare his boss for their arrival.

She looked again at the clock. The minute was up.

'Come on, men. We're going in.'

Clive and Pat opened the doors to Seabright's office, and Wendy stepped through.

'Mr Seabright.' She spoke as firmly as possible, but felt an unexpected pang of awe on seeing the squat, grey-haired, round-headed movie mogul sitting, arms folded, on the front of his desk. 'I believe you have something of ours.' The nine other committee members fanned out around her.

'I'm sorry,' replied Seabright, his famous west coast accent soft and slightly pinched. 'I'm not sure we've met?'

'You know who we are.'

Seabright's producer stepped up beside his boss. 'Remind us.'

Wendy introduced herself and her colleagues, who began searching the room for stolen goods.

'And what do you do?' asked Seabright.

'We are representatives of the Worldwide Authorship Circle,' declared Clive. 'We're the world's leading authorities on the question of who really wrote Shakespeare's plays – and we own these.' He held up a tin he'd found on Seabright's desk, opening it to reveal ten tiny plastic bags containing offcuts of the WAC's treasured hair samples.

Delighted by Clive's efficiency, Wendy fixed Seabright with an inquisitive stare.

'It's a pleasure to meet you all,' he smiled, eyes darting between them. 'Though surely what you mean is that you *used* to own the samples.'

Far from fearful, Seabright appeared genuinely confused.

'Come again?' said Wendy.

'Well, yes, they were yours originally...' He leaned to one side, nodding towards the corner of the room. 'But now, thanks to Sir Peter's kindness, they're mine.'

Wendy turned to see Sir Peter Heyward on the sofa, sporting the same suit he'd worn back in London. Above him was a shelf: curiously empty, as if waiting for something.

'It really was a fantastic gift, and I'm so grateful to Pete.' Seabright looked back to Wendy. 'Just recently, see, I've become totally fascinated by the authorship: and I mentioned as much to Pete on the phone, just last week.'

Sir Peter sat up on the edge of the sofa.

'And then a couple of days later, he shows up here with the hairs: a thanks for all the joy *Chronicles* has brought him.' Seabright chuckled. 'Just stunning. I can't imagine how much they cost.'

'*Cost?*' repeated Pat, his hair swinging from side to side.

'Well sure, they're only extracts, but still—'

'We didn't *sell* these,' interrupted Wendy, gradually clocking the true extent of Sir Peter's villainy. 'He stole them. Snatched them from under our noses.'

Seabright's mouth fell open, his eyes – like everyone's – travelling to land on the aged actor, whose face was a picture of alarm. Before he could protest, Joe summoned a lackey from his terrace, and ordered the actor's removal.

'What kind of a man gives as a gift something he's stolen?' he cried, as Sir Peter was manhandled out the room. 'Get out of my sight!' He slammed the door behind the actor and drew a deep breath, slowly turning back to the WAC. 'There are no words for how embarrassed I feel.'

Wendy couldn't think how to respond. She was flummoxed not just that Sir Peter had resorted to theft simply to obtain a gift for Seabright, but that Mr *Solix Chronicles* was at all interested in the authorship. If she'd been bowled over by Sir Peter's enthusiasm a few days before, Seabright's positively knocked her for six.

'I never had Sir Peter down as a thief,' lamented a red-haired woman, attired in a white laboratory coat.

'I knew it was an impulse thing,' said Seabright, 'something he saw and wanted me to have. But I never dreamed he'd have just cut bits off and taken them.' He grabbed the tin of hair clippings and offered it to Wendy. 'Here, take it back. And please accept my heartfelt apologies. Really, if there's anything I can do for any of you guys, just say. Some free merch for your kids, maybe?'

Struck by his good grace, Wendy took the tin. For a moment she wondered if she should let him keep it, but memory of Sir Peter's betrayal meant she swiftly thought better of such opportunism. Besides, if Seabright really was passionate about the authorship, there were plenty more considered means of courting him that could be employed in the weeks ahead.

'We'll be fine with these,' she said. 'But thank you for your kindness – and apologies for the intrusion.'

'Sure,' smiled Seabright, striding past and opening the doors. 'It's been a privilege meeting you all.' He peered into the hallway, then shook Wendy's hand. 'Really, I'm a huge admirer of all you've done for the authorship debate. I wish you well for the future, and apologise again for this terrible—'

The door flew back in his face, sending him tumbling into Wendy, who fell backwards into Clive, who collided with Pat, and so on until the entire committee had dominoed to the floor.

'Stop right there!' thundered Sir Peter, stepping out from behind the door, having seen off the guard, who peered round, clutching his neck.

'What the hell?' said Seabright, as Sir Peter stormed to his desk, yanked open a drawer and produced another silver tin, which he lobbed to Wendy.

'Careful!' cried the scientist as Wendy took the catch.

'Hello?' yelled Botstein into his mobile. 'We need an ambulance and security at the boss's mansion.'

Wendy looked at the tin. Outwardly it was identical to the one she'd just inadvertently dropped. Inside, too, it was the same, containing a velvet tray with ten spaces labelled with the names of the ten leading authorship candidates. But whereas the first tin held ten plastic bags, the second housed ten test tubes, each filled with a watery-looking liquid.

'DNA, ladies and gentleman,' announced Sir Peter. 'Isolated from the hair samples which Mr Seabright asked me to steal from you.'

'DNA?' Wendy looked at Seabright, who was wearing the fiercest scowl she'd ever seen.

'So close,' he muttered, letting out a bitter, defeated laugh. 'So *damn* close!'

'What could you possibly want with the DNA?' she asked, trembling with profound curiosity as six thick-set guards entered the room.

'Remove him!' ordered Seabright, pointing to Sir Peter. 'He, who shall be Emperor Tyron no more.'

Chapter 10

An hour later, Joe watched his ultimatum sink in. The faces of his guests were a real sight, their scattergun variety smothered as they huddled to confer, generating an excited murmur which confirmed he had judged it to perfection. Their minds were racing, and it was surely only time before they gave him the green light.

Puffing out his cheeks from the effort of it all, Joe grabbed a sneaky doughnut to munch while he waited. Having seen his project come so dangerously close to catastrophe, he needed all the sustenance he could get. Not that it should ever have got to this stage. Hell, he thought he'd cracked it with his *first* round of lightning thinking. By containing his horror, pretending the hair clippings were Heyward's gift, disaster had been averted with such dexterity the WAC could only give thanks and leave. Tough on Heyward, but also deserved, given how miserably he had failed to keep his mission secret.

Trouble was, if Joe had overestimated Heyward's criminal composure, he'd underestimated his physical strength – stupidly, since it was all the *Chronicles* training that enabled his eighty-year-old frame to overpower the guard with such chilling ease: a twist which left Joe not only needing a new Emperor Tyron for *Triumph of the Solix*, but facing the more pressing problem that the WAC knew about the DNA, and that Joe had lied in his desperation to keep it secret. Understandably, their curiosity was pricked, and they weren't going to leave without a full explanation.

All of which had dumped him in a near-impossible situation. On the one hand, he could no longer proceed without the WAC's permission. But on the other, he couldn't run the risk of the WAC – as they were likely to do – dishing the dirt on his activities and so destroying his Oscar hopes for good. What he needed was an agreement where the Brits not only allowed him to experiment with the DNA and use the winning muse to write his movie, but swore secrecy at all turns. And yet how could he possibly get their agreement without first explaining what he was up to?

It was then the brainwave struck. Despite the apparent weakness of his situation, there was still one thing he had very much on his side: mystery.

So it was, the moment Heyward left, Joe apologetically admitted that he had asked the actor to steal the hairs so he could isolate the DNA, but said nothing more, trusting that the ensuing speculation would make the WAC vulnerable. He parried a torrent of questions, regretting that the project's delicate nature prevented any further explanation, before finally suggesting that if the WAC really wanted to find out more, why not sign a pact? A pact, specifically, in which they granted him use of the WAC's clippings in whatever way and for as long as he wished, promising to keep the whole enterprise secret – in return for which Joe would happily tell them all they wanted to know. Alternatively, if they didn't want to make those concessions, they were free to take away both the samples and the DNA – which, naturally, was theirs by derivation – and return to normality, forever oblivious as to why he was at all interested in the authorship debate.

'What if we go to the police?' asked their frazzle-haired leader.

Joe chuckled. As Lester Howells had observed, this Wendy Preston was a real fighter.

'Seriously,' she pressed. 'You've given us your ultimatum, so here's ours: we go to the police and tell them you stole from us – unless you explain what you're up to.'

'I can't explain anything unless you agree.'

'So we'll have you arrested.'

'Fine. But I still won't tell a soul why I wanted your samples.'

'You'll go to jail, you know.'

'Perhaps. But don't forget you too will be imprisoned, and for life. Imprisoned by regret that you never found out exactly why I needed those bits of hair.'

'You can't blackmail us,' argued a man with a sharply-trimmed black goatee.

'Blackmail?' Joe laughed. 'How can it be blackmail when we both stand to gain?' He looked round at the ten bemused faces. 'Seriously, guys, I can't explain how, or why, until you agree to my terms. But I make you this pledge: you won't regret it.'

The WAC returned to their huddle: a forest of scratched and shaking heads.

'They're weak,' said Joe softly, finishing off his doughnut as Jerry stepped up beside him. 'At some level, however indistinct, they must know I'm offering them the truth – answers to questions they've been asking their whole lives. They've got to bite. Surely, they've *got* to bite.'

'And bite they will,' agreed Jerry, stepping in front of his boss and leaning in with a whisper. 'At which point, what say we keep them around a little longer?'

Joe wasn't sure he'd heard correctly. 'Are you serious?'

'At least for the duration of the experiment.'

'But why?'

'Isn't it obvious? Grace is insisting you leave ten days between testing the muse of each of the candidates – and yet here we have ten ready-made guinea pigs, each representing one of the candidates whose DNA we've derived.'

Joe smiled as he inferred his producer's meaning. 'Brilliant, Jerry.'

'Isn't it just?' grinned the producer. 'With a little planning, we can have this whole sideshow done, dusted and decided within the fortnight.'

A pointed cough from Preston signalled that they'd reached their decision.

'And your answer is?'

Preston coughed some more, and blinked, and squeezed her hands together, before looking Joe in the eye.

'We're in.'

***

The following morning, Wendy sat at Seabright's desk and read aloud the agreement which Jerry Botstein and JoeCo's legal team had devised overnight.

Twelve hours had passed since the extraordinary events of the previous evening, but though Seabright had kindly laid on ten luxury suites in JoeTown's residential district, none of the WAC were feeling especially fresh. They'd stayed up well past midnight – quite an achievement, given the jetlag – drinking vintage JoeTown Cabernet and speculating what their host could possibly be up to.

With his hyper-defensive attitude, Seabright's interest in the authorship was clearly more than passing. The way he sold it – the sense that the WAC themselves stood to gain – and the fact that he had already isolated the DNA suggested there was some strange forward momentum to his mystery project. And forward momentum where the authorship was concerned could mean only one thing: that Seabright, somehow, had found a way of –

'All sounds fine to me,' chirped Pat before Wendy had even finished reading.

'Yep, sign away,' said Clive, his traditional scrupulousness deserting him.

'Ok, ok,' muttered Wendy. Her hand shook as she signed both copies and handed them to Botstein, who nodded to his boss.

'Step this way, guys,' said Seabright, sipping fruit juice through a curly straw beside his swimming pool. 'Boy, have I got a tale for you.'

Wendy led the way onto the terrace, where ten empty deckchairs awaited them, each accompanied by a glass of juice and a selection of fruit – all freshly gathered, bragged Seabright, from

JoeTown's orchard. Even though it was only half nine, Wendy immediately felt the harsh Californian sun assaulting her dry, pasty skin, and made a beeline for one of the few deckchairs to be graced by a parasol.

'This is all very kind,' she said, taking her seat.

'Least I could do,' smiled Seabright, sitting alongside her at the end farthest from his office. 'Right now you guys are pretty damn special to me. You guys are the talent.'

'The talent?' repeated Wendy.

'Well . . .' Seabright winked at her. 'One of you is.'

'One of us?'

But Seabright would explain no more. 'Move your asses, people,' he said instead. 'We've got a busy few days ahead.'

While the others settled into position around the pool, Wendy surveyed the lawn that sloped down from the terrace – grass as green and lush as Seabright's teeth were white and shiny – to meet a copse two hundred yards away. She chuckled, marvelling at how surreal it all was: not simply the surroundings, but the sense, so vivid in each of them, that something extraordinary lay in wait – that impossibly, against all instinct and reason, and here in JoeTown, California of all places, their lives were about to be turned upside down.

'There's no easy way of explaining what's happened,' began Seabright, heaving himself out of the capacious deckchair into which he'd sunk. 'Whatever I say, it's gonna sound incredible. All I can do is talk, and ask you to believe what I say.'

He began walking round the pool, weaving between the deckchairs as he entranced them with the most mesmerising story Wendy had ever heard.

For as long as he could remember, Seabright explained – and they weren't to laugh when he said this – he had been hostage to an overwhelming desire to win the Academy Award for Best Picture. It was a lifelong thirst which, due to the failings of previous *Solix Chronicles* films, he now had only one more opportunity to quench. To do that, however, he knew he was going to have to improve his otherwise ghastly writing abilities, and fast.

In response, his ever-resourceful producer Jerry had commissioned a maverick Stanford geneticist to uncover the true nature of creativity. Working in the tightest secrecy, Grace Tremain had not only proceeded to identify the genetic muse, but had discovered how to emulate one person's muse in another's body – for which all that was required was a sample of the donor's DNA.

So it was, not being one to settle for second best, Seabright had visited Lester Howells – he whose obstinacy once worked such magic for the WAC – and borrowed Shakespeare's DNA, assuming that the resultant screenplay would not just be a runaway Oscar winner but the finest movie ever written.

Alas – and here Wendy's heart fairly stopped in a mix of jubilation and disbelief – it was not to be. The Shakespeare screenplay was, to put it mildly, crap: overblown, crass and clunky, flattering Seabright's own efforts with its awfulness. For a while, Seabright explained, they figured the system was at fault, or that Howells had provided them with the incorrect sample. But no. After double-checking every possible alternative, they were left with only one explanation: that William Shakespeare, the man, or rather the *moron*, from Stratford, was a talentless imbecile.

It was here that Seabright broke off and grinned, clearly expecting some kind of response, vocal or otherwise – but Wendy for one was frozen. All she could do was stare into the pool, mouth hanging open as she absorbed Seabright's story: staggering at every turn, but never more so than at the last.

'Am I dreaming?' she asked.

'Wide awake,' said Seabright.

'But that means . . .' She stopped and swallowed, whispering what followed. 'That means we were right.'

'You were.'

'Naturally,' wondered Clive, his voice ringing with awe.

'Never in doubt,' murmured Pat.

'We *knew* we were right all along . . .' began Keith. 'Didn't we?'

'Of course,' added Clive, with a diagonal jerk of the head, somewhere between a nod and a shake.

They were all experiencing the same shock, the gulf between

faith and fact, hunch and truth, suspicion and certainty – the gulf that had dominated their lives for so many years – having suddenly vanished. It didn't matter that each of them had spent the past twenty years insisting that Shakespeare was not, that he *couldn't be*, the true author, repeating well-worn arguments as they chipped away at the great granite monolith of received wisdom. No. Despite all those years of believing, the truth still came as an almighty surprise.

Wendy cupped her head in her hands and tried taking it in. So Shakespeare *wasn't* the real author. She let out a flustered laugh, startled by the hard, fast factness of the statement. Could this really be happening? It wasn't just the revelation that amazed her. It was that such a revelation was even possible. Though she had founded the WAC with the aim of at least trying to seek resolution, she realised now that she'd never really believed such a moment could actually come to pass.

For this didn't feel like growing up and learning Father Christmas doesn't exist. This was more spiritual, like being a lifelong atheist and learning unequivocally that God is a fiction. Deep down, she realised, doubting Shakespeare's claim had ultimately been a matter of faith – predicated on the knowledge it could be neither proved nor disproved; informed wholly by a trust which, at some bizarre, subconscious level, demanded the acceptance of that which you were fighting, if only in order to deny it.

And yet now here they were, discovering not only that certainty was possible, but that they were right: that the orthodoxy against which they'd positioned themselves, that had defined their lives, that they'd cherished inasmuch as they adored fighting it, was no more. And while of course that was the most fantastic thing imaginable, it was going to take a long while to get used to.

'I thought you guys would be psyched.'

Seabright sounded wounded that their celebrations were not more explosive.

'Oh, we are,' said Wendy. 'It's just a lot to take in.'

'Well you'd better hurry,' said Grace Tremain, appearing with a tray containing ten little brown bottles, each labelled with a small white sticker. 'Because Shakespeare is ancient history. Today we're moving on.'

'Assuming our research is correct,' said Jerry Botstein, following her with a clipboard and pen, 'there should be one of these each. So if you'd just identify yourselves as your name's read out.' He looked down. 'Francis Bacon?'

Wendy exchanged puzzled glances with Clive.

'Come on, guys,' urged Seabright. 'Who reckons Bacon did it?'

Zombie-like, Clive raised his hand. 'Here.'

Tremain handed him one of the bottles.

'Christopher Marlowe?' said Botstein.

Wendy answered and received a bottle of her own. Inside was a tiny white pill.

'Earl of Oxford?'

Pat identified himself and took his bottle, as did Colin, who gratefully received the one marked 'Henry Neville' – and so on until each of them held the bottle that belonged to their chosen candidate: Leonard for Queen Elizabeth I; Rob for Sir Walter Raleigh; Steve for Roger Manners, Earl of Rutland; Felix for William Stanley, Earl of Derby, John for Mary Sidney and, finally, Keith for Tom Cobley.

'Tom Cobley,' mused Seabright, back in his *Solix Chronicles* deckchair, toying with his spiral straw. 'Keith Cobley. You guys related?'

Keith beamed proudly. 'I'm a direct descendent.'

'Who is Tom Cobley?' asked Jerry. 'The others I all recognise. Him, I confess—'

'Cobley cobblers!' shouted Wendy, instinctively roused from her daze.

'Well said, that woman,' applauded Pat.

'Keith's theory,' explained Clive, with laudable restraint, 'is very much a minority view.'

'It's the only one with any supporting evidence,' returned Keith.

'We've got evidence,' said Pat.

'Conjecture. Inference, *circumstantial* evidence. Not proof.'

'I've got proof aplenty,' said Clive. 'Codes upon codes linking Bacon to Shakespeare. Hidden messages, deeply yet precisely embedded in the plays.'

'And me,' added Pat. 'I've got codes coming out of my ears. All manner of political allegory, symbolism, innuendo: you name it, it's there. And it all points to the Earl of Oxford as the only possible author!'

'Again, pure speculation,' scoffed Keith, directing his words at Seabright. 'Bacon, Marlowe, Oxford – all the usual suspects. Every one is mere fancy.'

'The fact is, Mr Seabright,' said Clive, 'the only scientific gauge for our different theories is the number of adherents. And whereas my beliefs, like Pat's, like Wendy's, are shared by hundreds of thousands – whereas Leonard's, Rob's and John's are shared by maybe tens of thousands – Keith's little theory is shared by . . .' He looked to Keith. 'How many at the last count? Ah, yes!' He turned back to Seabright. 'Precisely none.'

'Anyway,' started Grace. 'The bottles you are all holding contain—'

'I'm sorry, Miss Tremain,' interrupted Keith, 'I just can't let Clive's comments go. His prejudice is frankly primordial. Absurd, that in this day and age – .'

'It's not prejudice to say the Cobley diaries are fake,' said Pat.

'The Cobley diaries?' repeated Jerry.

'The only hard proof ever found in relation to the authorship,' declared Keith. 'Someone actually holding up their hand and saying they did it.'

'How so?' asked Seabright.

Keith sat up in his deckchair – or at least tried to – as he launched into his well-worn explanation: how, as a child clearing out his parents' attic, he found a chest of old family heirlooms. At the bottom was a dusty old diary written, allegedly, by a guy from Milton Keynes Village called Tom Cobley, who moved to London and became the manager of a London bear-baiting brigade. Strikingly enough, his year of death coincided with the year when, according to conventional chronologies, 'Shakespeare' wrote his last play.

'It was such a fat volume I didn't read it thoroughly at first,' explained Keith. 'But then I found a family tree from the early-20th century which listed Tom Cobley as having died in 1590, when in fact his diary went right up to 1613. So naturally I went back to the diary and, sure enough, it was the most mind-boggling thing. As well as being a bear-baiter, Tom was also a well-known street poet with a gift for concocting vulgar, yet brilliantly conceived rhymes of lusty low-lives and the like. One day, he encountered this ghastly actor who, wanting to be more than just a performer, yet lacking the ability to become the great creative artist he envisioned, read some of Cobley's masterful poetry and promptly kidnapped him. The actor, who's never named outright, but is obviously William Shakespeare, held Cobley captive in a basement in Borough for a full twenty-three years. He demanded play after play on pain of death, taking the credit for Cobley's genius, until Cobley, unable to bear it any longer, took his own life.'

'Whoa.' Seabright puffed out his cheeks. 'That's some yarn.'

'The dates all add up. 1590, the date Cobley was kidnapped, presumed dead, was the year that Shakespeare wrote his first play. And 1613 was the year he wrote his last, even though the Stratford Shakespeare lived on until 1626.'

'Sounds pretty watertight to me,' said Seabright. 'How come you other guys still argue?'

'Because it's patently a forgery!' laughed Clive. 'Probably by one of Keith's great, great, ancestors, in the early-20th century. That's when the authorship debate really kicked in, sparking the inevitable burst of hoaxes and fakes. Hence the family tree, which is dated 1925, being found so close to the diary.'

'The two go together?' asked Seabright.

Clive nodded. 'A little authorship pack.'

'It's all quite marvellously obvious,' chuckled Wendy. 'But we adore Keith nonetheless.'

Pat nodded agreement. 'Can't beat a bit of Cobley cobblers.'

'But you have no hard proof it's a fake?' asked Seabright.

'Well, no,' acknowledged Pat. 'Except the obvious.'

'The obvious?'

'Tom Cobley,' said Wendy. 'Get it?'

Seabright hesitated. 'Not sure I do.'

'Uncle Tom Cobley and all,' she explained. 'An old English phrase meaning "and anyone else you care to mention". It's clearly a joke. A comment on the sudden explosion of people being advanced as possible Shakespeares in the 1920s.'

'Surely if you have the diary, a little carbon dating would prove it?' asked Grace.

'Keith's never let us go near it,' said Wendy.

'Familial faith.' Keith tapped his heart. 'I don't need a machine to confirm it's genuine. As for the joke: coincidence, nothing more.'

Seabright laughed. 'You know, it's kinda sweet hearing you guys bicker like this. I guess it's almost healthy, getting it out of your systems one last time.'

Wendy felt a rush of goosebumps down her arms.

'You do realise, that was the last time you're ever going to have that argument?'

'How so?' asked Clive.

'Well, now we know Shakespeare didn't do it, it's time to find out who did.'

Wendy's heart skipped a beat.

'The bottles you are holding each contain a pill. A pill which will emulate in you the creativity of the individual whose name you see on the label.'

The WAC fell silent as they finally grasped Seabright's meaning. Although their first instinct, given the news about Shakespeare, had been to descend into good old-fashioned sniping about the alternative authors, plainly the time for traditional debate had passed. Clearly, the same methodology that proved Shakespeare *didn't* write the plays was about to be deployed again: this time, to discover who did.

'All you do is swallow the pill and you'll immediately acquire that person's creativity. You'll still be you: able to think your thoughts, write in today's language. It's just that your abilities will be . . .' Seabright grinned. 'Well, maybe enhanced, maybe diminished. Who knows? That's the fun.'

'The effects,' began Keith, his voice quivering. 'How long lasting will they be?'

'You've got a week each,' replied Jerry. 'Then your bodies will return to normal.'

'I'm sorry,' said Wendy. 'A week to do what?'

'To write!' proclaimed Seabright.

'Write what?'

'My film! Or at least the beginning. You each write the first reel of my movie, fuelled by the muse of the person you propose as the author. Then, once you're done, Grace will pre-visualise what you've written so I can sit down and judge them: work out which of these suckers was the real author and, more importantly, which I need to swallow to write the movie proper.'

Wendy stared at her bottle. So this was it: the moment they'd all been waiting for, even though they'd always assumed such a moment could never be. At long last, they were going to know the truth – at last, they were going to know who . . .

And then it hit her: the truth, quite literally, was in her hands. She was going to swallow that tiny pill, acquire the imagination of her hero, and in so doing prove to the world what she herself had known for so many years: that Christopher Marlowe was the real genius behind the 'Shakespeare' plays.

She glanced around. All her friends were either staring fixatedly at their bottle or gazing dreamily into space, lost in the same maze of emotions: a flush of delirious joy at the prospect of discovering the truth, followed by the spine-tingling realisation that their lifelong hunches were about to be put to the test and found to be joyously, gloriously . . . well, wrong, presumably, since Wendy, as her heart thumped ever quicker, was so certain *she* was right.

Goodness, she thought, breaking into a cold sweat, her hand

shaking such that the pill started rattling: she *was* right, wasn't she? What if she was wrong? What then? And even if she was right, what of the other nine, who'd then be wrong?

She clenched her fist and clamped it still with the other hand, trying to calm the scintillating upsurge of energy. For a start, she was definitely right about Marlowe, and so had absolutely nothing to fear. But even if she had her doubts, which of course she didn't, that wasn't the point. The real point, the issue of paramount concern, had already been tested in their favour: namely, that Shakespeare wasn't the real author. That was the only thing which ultimately mattered. That was the familial bond which had always brought them back together in the past, and which could surely be relied upon to do so again, no matter what the outcome of Seabright's experiment.

'You've already been assigned your apartments,' explained Jerry, handing out sheets of paper. 'You'll stay in those for the duration, monitored by your personal aides, who'll also cater for you and be your first point of contact for any queries.'

'What's this?' asked Keith, holding up his hand-out as Wendy took her own copy.

'A synopsis for the first reel of *Triumph of the Solix*,' revealed Seabright. 'Highly classified stuff.'

'I don't know,' murmured Wendy, 'I've never—'

'Doesn't matter,' said Grace. 'Doesn't matter if you've never written anything before, or if you don't know how to structure a screenplay. If the person whose muse you've swallowed is up to it, it'll all come naturally. If not, you'll spend the week banging your head against a brick wall.'

'What I actually meant,' continued Wendy tentatively, 'was that I'm not familiar with this whole thing.' She held up the paper. 'Who on earth are Greathen, Devras and Youtron? I mean, I take your point about letting the drug take its course, but surely we at least need to know that.'

Seabright was silent, staring aghast at Jerry.

'It's true,' said Keith. 'Who on earth is the Solix?'

'And the Spirit,' added Clive. 'What's that?'

Seabright was open-mouthed. 'You honestly don't know?'
Wendy shook her head in fearful ignorance.
Sighing, Seabright hauled himself out of his deckchair. 'Then I guess the truth will just have to wait that little bit longer.'

Chapter 11

After the intense brightness of the terrace, it was a relief to pass through Seabright's office into the darkness of his personal SolixScreen cinema. Seated four rows from the front, Wendy and her friends were accessorised with vast vats of JoeCola, great tubs of popcorn, and in-ear headphones to 'add spatiality' to the twenty-speaker surround sound mix.

Given Seabright's horror on learning that none of them had ever seen a *Solix Chronicles* film, it was probably just as well that she didn't mention never having experienced a SolixScreen cinema before. Not that she was unfamiliar with the concept, every cinema in the Western world having long been SolixScreen-enabled. It was just that she invariably saw movies which weren't SolixScreen compliant: arthouse films, typically filmed in three dimensions on traditional, digital film.

All of which meant that when the first of the four *Solix Chronicles* movies burst from the screen and speakers, Wendy was dazzled by the impact of the six separate projectors, each of which, through a complex network of mirrors, directed its rays onto one of three semi-transparent screens to give an amazingly immersive, wraparound 3D effect. It was fiendishly impressive, and for a moment Wendy understood how Seabright had become so involved in his fictional universe he'd never noticed the weakness of the dialogue. It really did feel like you were there, side by side with the characters as they fought on the bridge of some enormous spaceship, fearing that at any moment you might get hit by one of their big, bright laser swords.

Then, however, the characters started speaking, and the staggering visual spectacle succumbed to a script of such formidable awfulness that Wendy had to make a conscious effort not to scramble out of the cinema, owing it to herself *and* Marlowe to pay the closest possible attention.

The saga originally began life as a TV series, Seabright had explained in a prefatory talk. Made just over sixteen years ago – having brewed for decades in its creator's head – the show had been carefully structured both to stand alone and serve as a prologue to a hoped-for movie franchise. It was set in the distant future on the edge of the known universe, and focused on a mystical energy field called the Spirit – a force which, traditionally, had been harnessed by the Solix, a noble race from the planet Solus. Essentially, the Solix were an interstellar police force, maintaining galactic peace until, in death, each progressed to a nirvana called the Spirit Level, where they watched over their living comrades.

After acquiring cult status in its first series, the second season of *The Solix Chronicles* was a runaway hit, and it wasn't long before the TV network AmBro began talking about a silver screen transfer – whereupon Seabright ruthlessly went independent, producing the movies himself with the cash he'd amassed by retaining all merchandising rights. Three years later, *The Solix Chronicles 1: Birth of a Hero* was released worldwide – and popular culture was never the same again.

That was ten years ago, Seabright said as the lights in the auditorium dimmed: a decade during which every member of Wendy's committee *could* have got round to watching a little *Solix Chronicles*, but inexplicably, perhaps even uniquely, hadn't – a jibe which provoked another flurry of contrition from the WAC as the main titles burst into life on the screen.

Ten hours later, as the credits to *Rise of the Glozbacks* rolled, Wendy's overriding emotion was surprise. Even though the saga was a load of pseudo-epic, derivative dross, and even though the writing *was* abominable, she'd actually ended up enjoying it – even to the point of regretting her traditional snobbery on the subject. Everything *other* than the dialogue was executed with such care – the costumes, the score, the camerawork – she could very well envisage the Academy granting Seabright's wish, if only that one, rather crucial factor could be fixed.

All of which brought them to the task at hand – and what a fascinating, even fitting task it was. As the grand finale of the entire saga, resolving the unhappy events that concluded *Rise of the Glozbacks*, *Triumph of the Solix* was the obligatory happy ending – its cheerful endpoint manifest in the very title. In other words, everyone knew how the film began and ended. All that remained was to join the dots – to show *exactly* how the Solix's triumph was achieved. The focus of fans' anticipation, therefore, wasn't so much on the tale as on the telling; their hope not so much a good story as a good story well told.

And that was something which lent an unexpected legitimacy to Seabright's otherwise incongruous experiment. For not only was *Chronicles* authentically Shakespearean thematically, with its great battles, fractured families and flawed heroes, but the challenge of writing *Triumph of the Solix* was utterly Shakespearean in spirit: an exercise not in story-formulation, but in the far harder art of story*telling*. An apt undertaking, in other words, for a man whose special talent was re-telling stories – *Julius Caesar*, *Hamlet*, *Henry V* – already familiar to his audiences, but telling them so much more potently they somehow felt forever new. The parallels were such that had Shakespeare, or rather Marlowe, actually been alive, far from turning his nose up at the challenge ahead, he would surely have relished the task – a thought which, for Wendy, was more than a little reassuring, given that she was about to take the not inconsiderable liberty of bringing him back from the dead.

'It's eight pm, guys,' said Seabright, addressing them from below one of the giant SolixScreens. 'Getting late, but I don't want to lose today altogether.' Mouth twitching between a grin and a frown, he looked around at his new partners. 'What say you make a start right now? Get settled and maybe even get writing?'

'Most definitely!' replied Wendy, leaping to her feet, heart pounding with excitement. More than ever she was eager to become one with her beloved Marlowe. More than ever she wanted to experience the power of his creativity and stake his claim, once and for all, to the greatest plays ever written.

'Oh, yes indeed!' she cried. 'Bring it on.'

Chapter 12

Two weeks later, the silence outside Seabright's office was deafening. Eyes cast down at the ominous Cafillian carpet, Wendy led her friends in a slow, meditational dance, saying nothing, absorbed in their own thoughts and avoiding each other's trajectories as they awaited the summons to learn a truth that had laid buried for almost half a millennium. Wendy wiped a bead of sweat from her brow and tied her curly locks in a bob to stay cool. She reminded herself of their innate solidarity – the fact that, whoever was wrong, whoever was right, it mattered not a jot – even while reassuring herself that surely, without question, Marlowe was the man.

It was a shame that the mood had changed so drastically. At first, of course, after the experiment finished, it had been similarly awkward. The ten of them had emerged from solitary confinement utterly adamant that the emotional depth, poetic dialogue and comic timing of their respective scripts rendered the debate closed, and that Seabright needn't even bother judging the entries. But then Grace Tremain explained to them that their confidence was a side-effect of MET – that, with the alteration in their creative abilities came an associated change in their critical faculties, aligning them such that, no matter how awful one's screenplay, one would think it magnificent – and the atmosphere swiftly relaxed. Freed from divisive complacency, the ten friends launched themselves with gusto into JoeTown's manifold leisure activities, from swimming and shopping to walking on the JT hills. Uncertain when Seabright would declare a result, they unwound in the happy knowledge that, for the time being, all outcomes remained possible.

Desperate to shake the nervous energy from her limbs, Wendy jogged on the spot. How she wished they could return to that carefree atmosphere; the state of jovial, mutual expectancy which had prevailed right up until an hour before, when word came that Seabright had finally finished reviewing the entries and – heart-stoppingly – reached a definitive conclusion. As they proceeded across town, from the golf course to Seabright's mansion in a JoeTown people carrier, scarcely a word had been exchanged. The ten of them had sunk into a gloomy introspection which only deepened as they reached Seabright's mansion and assembled in the hallway outside his office, Wendy for one wishing he'd just get a bloody move on and let them in. All she wanted was to *know*, for heaven's sake. Was that too much to ask? She just wanted to know she was right.

'Joe's ready for you now,' said Jerry Botstein at last, appearing at the door. 'He's waiting in his theatre.'

Wendy looked to her colleagues, waiting for the stampede to begin. But rather than dashing in to discover the truth, everyone just stood stock still, staring blankly at one another. It was the same for Wendy. In a split second her body had lurched from restless anticipation to total numbness: heavy, weighed down and dead. She couldn't formulate a single thought, let alone a word. When she tried to move it was as if she was frozen. But frozen by what? Fear? Hope? Expectation? This was the moment she had spent her life wishing for, a moment she never dreamed possible yet towards which she had worked tirelessly for two whole decades. This was a moment for which she had made countless sacrifices – career, romance, motherhood – yet which, having finally arrived, she was finding shockingly hard to seize. It was as if her head was pulling her into Seabright's office while her heart was –

'Guys?' asked Seabright, looking puzzled in the entrance to his office. 'Is there a problem?'

'No,' said Wendy abruptly. 'No problem.' She shivered hot and cold as the blood rushed back round her body. 'Ready?' she asked, turning to the others.

'Of course,' Clive muttered, leading the way into Seabright's office.

Moments later, the WAC settled themselves in the front row of Seabright's cinema. Up on the screen were ten boxes, in each of which was frozen the *Solix Chronicles* logo from the opening credits, together with a number between 1 and 10.

'What we have behind me,' Seabright explained, standing in front of the screen, 'are the pre-vizzes based on your scripts. As planned, I waited until all ten were done before looking at any. That was early this morning, since when I've been sat in here watching and re-watching each individual effort.' He motioned to the screen. 'The numbers superimposed on each pre-viz were randomly picked as substitutes for the names themselves, making sure I wasn't prejudiced in any way.'

Wendy felt a nudge in the ribs – it was Clive, gesturing towards her knee, which was shaking twenty to the dozen. 'It's putting me off.'

'So anyway,' resumed Seabright, 'I guess what you all want to know is: how did you do?'

Wendy glanced down the line. The profiles of her friends' faces were illuminated by the light from the screen, every one a study in breathless anxiety.

'Well, the short answer,' Seabright went on, 'is that all of your efforts were good. A damn sight better than William Shakespeare's.'

A nervous chuckling trickled down the line, gathering in loudness until Wendy, at the end, snorted with demented laughter, delighted and reassured by the fact that *all ten* candidates were better than that thick-as-a-plank glover's son from Stratford. There are no losers, she told herself, clasping the arms of her chair to try to stop shaking: today, we're all winners.

'Indeed,' continued Seabright, 'after viewing three or four, two of which were just superb, I feared I had a tricky call ahead: that no single one would stand out in such a quality field.'

'But?' prompted Pat.

'There is a "but", isn't there?' echoed Clive.

Seabright grinned, and Wendy knew: indeed there was a 'but' – the biggest 'but' of all.

'It was entry number five. Just awesome. Everything about it. The phrasing, the pacing, the poetry...' He smiled. 'It just blew me away. Immediately, I got the script and started reading. Even the descriptions moved me. The whole vision was so clear, so economical yet so insightful, the characters drawn so uniquely...'

He gave a wistful sigh.

'Of course, I made sure to go on, watching films six through ten with an open-mind, then re-watching all ten again, just in case I had somehow been deceived. But no. Nothing came close to number five.' He scanned along the line, making eye contact with each of them in turn. 'Seriously, guys: it was the best twenty minutes of *Chronicles* I've ever seen. It alone would win Best Picture.'

'But who?' muttered one of Wendy's colleagues, apparently too nervous to speak properly.

'Yes, who is it?' repeated another.

'Tell us!' screamed Clive. The strain in his voice, usually so calm, was a gauge of their collective impatience.

Seabright, however, said nothing. He just scratched his stubble and smiled, prompting Wendy's heart to quicken: fearful that, after all they'd been through, Seabright, at the last, was going to keep the truth to himself.

'The truth is,' he said, savouring the tension, 'I myself don't yet know who number five is.'

Wendy exhaled in relief as Seabright delved into the back pocket of his jeans and removed a sheet of paper.

'What I have here,' he explained, unfolding the paper, 'is the legend, matching up the numbers with the candidates themselves.' He smiled at the WAC. 'I thought it'd be nice if we found out together.'

Wendy shifted in her chair as a cacophony of throat-clearing broke out in the seats alongside: everyone preparing for the moment of truth. For her part, she just closed her eyes and prayed. Yes, she was a committed atheist, but these were desperate, life-changing times and frankly she couldn't leave anything to chance. If even the possibility of divine intervention existed, she had to have that base covered. Please let it be Marlowe, she pleaded, clenching together her quivering hands. Oh, God, *please* let it be Marlowe.

She looked up to see Seabright staring at the paper, running his finger down the page until, about half-way, it stopped. He prodded the point on the page and ran his fingertip along the paper's width to the opposite side, raising his eyebrows as it went. Wendy sensed a slight shake of the head and a playful smirk before, swaying onto his heels, he returned the paper to his back pocket.

'Well, well, well,' he mused, hands behind his back, rocking gently to and fro. 'Who'd have thought?'

Please let it be Marlowe, urged Wendy: in the name of all that's holy, *please* let it be Marlowe.

'The real William Shakespeare,' Seabright continued, 'at least according to this . . .' He tapped his back pocket and took a deep breath, ready to reveal all – only to say nothing, staring pensively into the middle distance.

'Joe?' prompted Wendy after a few seconds' silence.

'I'm sorry,' said Seabright, looking apologetically in her direction. 'The real William Shakespeare, according to our little experiment, was none other . . .'

Oh, God, thought Wendy. Seabright's gaze, which had been fixed on her, was straying down the line. It wasn't her! Who could it be? His eyes kept moving down, before, extraordinarily, returning to her, filling her once again with hope.

'None other,' repeated Seabright, 'than Tom Cobley.'

An icy chill coursed through Wendy's body. *Cobley cobblers.* Oh, God, she thought, a sickness starting to form in the pit of her stomach. What had he just said? Surely she had misheard? Surely she had imagined it? Surely this was some kind of joke?

- 127 -

Seabright's eyes snapped away from her and fixed on a subject further down the line.

'Congratulations,' he grinned. 'You're the man!'

Good grief, thought Wendy: Seabright was for real. Shakespeare was Tom Cobley. And Shakespeare, more to the point, *wasn't* Christopher Marlowe.

Shaking, she held onto the side of her chair. She was going to retch, she knew it. It felt as if someone had reached into her, wrenching her heart from its bearings and freeing her gut to lunge upwards and outwards. She tried holding her breath, breaking a sweat with the effort, as the words ricocheted round her brain, devoid of anything but the horrific truth: Keith had been right all along, and she, stupid, brainless fool that she was – *she* was wrong!

Slowly, she looked across at the others, every one of whom, Keith included, was staring blankly ahead, open-mouthed as the perspiration on their brows glistened in the muted light.

'Oh God,' blurted Keith, shattering the silence as he collapsed to his knees and screamed with joy. 'Oh, yes!' He thumped the floor with his fist. 'Yes, yes, yes!' Moments later, he rose and walked towards Seabright. 'Thank you so much,' he gushed into Seabright's shoulder. 'This is the best moment of my life. I can't express . . .' The words grew muffled as he started sobbing.

'It can't be,' said Clive.

'Impossible,' said Wendy.

'The diary's fake,' said Clive, shaking his head. 'I just *know* the diary's fake.'

'The diary is *not* fake, chaps,' sniffed Keith, lifting his head from Seabright's shoulder. 'And that's a fact.' He wiped away the tears and stretched out his arms. 'Bacon, Marlowe, Oxford: it's time to wave goodbye and just accept – Cobley is the man.'

'But . . .' Wendy trailed off. Her mind was flip-flopping uncontrollably between the realisation that the Marlovian theory to which she, along with so many others, had always subscribed, was actually a total fiction – and the fact that Keith's patently ludicrous alternative, predicated on a transparent forgery, was somehow, *nonsensically*, true.

'If you don't mind, Joe,' she said, suddenly galvanised. 'I need to ask a question.'

Seabright was wiping Keith's slobber from his shoulder with a handkerchief. 'Go on.'

'Are you sure? Are you absolutely, undoubtedly, *unquestionably* sure?'

'Oh, please,' laughed Keith.

Smiling contentedly to himself, Seabright produced the legend from his back pocket. 'Let me double-check . . .' He looked down at the paper, face suddenly crumpling in horror. 'Oh, God . . .'

Wendy's heart leapt. It couldn't be – could it?!

Seabright laughed. 'Only kidding.' He held up the paper so Wendy could see that film number five was, indeed, written by Keith's ancestor. 'But seriously, you guys have no reason to feel downhearted.' He studied the page again. 'If memory serves, Bacon, Oxford and Marlowe were all unbelievably good, too.'

'Then let's see them,' said Clive. 'Let's see them all. If they were all unbelievably good, surely there's a possibility your judgment is wrong?'

'Clutching at straws, people!' exclaimed Keith. 'Joe just told you: nothing came close to entry number five.'

'But this is a huge moment,' stressed Wendy, turning to Seabright, 'not just for us but for you. Yes you want to press on, but it'll only take a few hours to verify your findings. Better that, surely, than to waste three years, and your last chance of an Oscar, simply because you didn't bother getting a second opinion?'

Eyes focused firmly downwards, steadfastly avoiding contact with the WAC, who – with the exception of Keith – had crowded round him in a circle, Seabright groaned in impatient frustration and nodded his consent.

Chapter 13

Three hours later, the sickness in Wendy's stomach had not only returned but worsened, exponentially intensified by the protractedness of the confirmatory exercise. The tenth and final 'first reel', penned by Queen Elizabeth I, had just concluded with the heartbreaking scene between Mark and Regina – heartbreaking, that was, when it had appeared several reels before in Tom Cobley's version: a rendering which was, quite simply, in a different galaxy to its competitors, Christopher Marlowe included.

'Congratulations, Keith,' she said, wobbling to her feet and tottering along the line, determined to be a good loser. '*Many* congratulations.'

Keith rose and shook her outstretched hand. 'Why thank you, Wendy.'

'I can't say it isn't disappointing about Marlowe. I can't say it's not – well, a little tough to take – and I can't pretend there's not some regret.' Her voice was cracking. 'But it's important to see the bigger picture, and—'

She stopped, set upon by a tidal wave of emotion which suspended all speech and movement as the past two decades suddenly unravelled in her mind. All that wasted time – all that wasted passion. Year upon year, squandered in so-called research, when all she was really doing was twisting facts to delude herself: convincing herself of a watertight conspiracy which defied all sense and was every ounce as fanciful as the notion that Shakespeare himself was the author. And all because she thought she understood the plays in a way denied to others. All because she thought she knew the key to their innermost secrets.

Well, by goodness: what a frightful fool she had been. And what foolish sacrifices she had made. Here she was, forty-two years old, and all she had accomplished with the best years of her life was to demonstrate what a gullible old crow she was.

'Come, come,' said Keith, embracing her as she sniffled. 'You mustn't regret a moment. So you were wrong about Marlowe. Well, that's only part of the story: a minor footnote in the mighty tome of our collective endeavours. Far more important is that we've disproved Shakespeare's claim. That's what we were fighting for, above all else. And by golly, that's been worth the fight, has it not?'

Wendy lifted her head and smiled. This was the crucial point, and as the group's Founder and Chair, it scarcely became her to forget it quite so emotionally. She stepped back and scanned her colleagues' exhausted faces.

'Keith's right. It doesn't matter who was individually right; just that we were collectively correct about Shakespeare. Let's forget personal passions, chaps. Let's celebrate the greater good.'

The others murmured agreement – sincere enough, but painfully weak – and Wendy forced her thoughts towards reason, trying to do the reverse of what she'd so excelled at over the past twenty years. Rather than working up from fancy, she urged herself to think down from fact. To accept, purely and simply, that Cobley was the author.

It took a few moments to silence the hysterical objections but, sure enough, with this *given* in place, she soon began to see some sense in Cobley's victory after all. Convinced as she had been by Marlowe, deep down she'd always known that all their theories, aside from Cobley, were predicated more on theory than proof. And she'd also known that, in sharing a lack of hard evidence, they tended to be over-complicated and, worse, mutually destructive: so many theories that they were each undermined simply by coexisting.

Whereas with Cobley it was straightforward. Here wasn't an elaborate piece of theorising or fanciful textual study. Here, in Cobley's diary, was a chap just telling the truth: a blow-me-down *extraordinary* truth, admittedly, but one which existed fully formed, in which the dates and detail fitted perfectly. And while once that very neatness seemed fiendishly suspicious, now, without the Marlowe blinkers on, Wendy wondered if the obviousness wasn't so much a case of 'Cobley cobblers' as 'Cobley – of course'.

'You're an angel, Mr Cobley,' she said, realising it was her turn to embrace Keith. 'So kind for tolerating us. You fought a good fight against impossible odds, and we were wrong to mock you. You deserve this. In a way, you deserve it more than any of us.'

'*Please*,' sniffed Keith. 'We *all* deserve this, like I keep saying. This victory belongs to us all.'

Oh gosh, thought Wendy, and off she went again: sobbing, overwhelmed by Keith's generosity and, by extension, the strength of these magnificent people. For all the spats and divisions, they had always been there for her, throughout the hardest times. Like the family she'd never had, the group – and the energy-giving mystery of who really wrote Shakespeare's plays – was the rock to which she could always return.

So it would be again. For this was a blow like few others, but as long as they were there for her, and she could revert to that wonderful old routine of debating the blissfully unanswerable –

She looked up, suddenly arrested as her thoughts shifted towards the future, which she had instinctively assumed would be just as it always was. But now the world was altered, the future not only unfamiliar but irreparably reduced: the staple succulence of speculation – all outcomes still possible – obliterated by cold, hard fact.

'The mystery's lost,' she whispered. 'There's nothing left.'

She looked at Clive, who nodded solemnly in agreement.

'What is this blather?' exclaimed Keith. 'Now's not a time to be lamenting what's lost. Now's the time to celebrate what we've *gained*. Now more than ever, the future is *alive* with possibility:

the possibility, real and irresistible, of putting right the greatest crime ever committed in the history of art!' He turned to Seabright. 'How about it, Joe? Where do we start?'

Where do we start? Wendy felt a renewed buzz of excitement. Yes, the disappointment about Marlowe was acute, as was the destabilising realisation that the authorship mystery was a thing of the past. But Keith was right. Amid the charred remains of their *nine* incorrect theories, there now arose a gleaming new future. It had crept upon them unawares, but here it was, against all odds, and the task they never dared dream of was suddenly uppermost on their 'to do' list: revealing to the world that Shakespeare didn't write Shakespeare – that *Tom Cobley* was the man – and so setting right this most criminal of historical wrongs.

'I'm sorry,' said Seabright. '*Where do we start?*'

'What happens now?'

Seabright shrugged. 'I start work and you guys head home.'

'You don't want in?' asked Wendy.

Seabright frowned.

'That's fine.' She looked to her colleagues. 'Right chaps? It's our show. We'll do it ourselves.'

'Do what yourselves?' asked Seabright.

'Make the announcement.'

'The announcement?'

'You know: Shakespeare out; Cobley in . . .'

'Whoa!' Seabright held up his hands. 'I'm sorry, but there is no announcement to be made. The whole thing stays secret, just as we agreed.'

Wendy's mind recoiled to the time, two weeks before, when Seabright first proposed his agreement, complete with its confidentiality clause – something which, at the time, hadn't really registered, since they had no firm idea of what he was up to, and which had long since been eclipsed by the excitement of the experiment.

'You do remember,' said Seabright. 'I can see it in your eyes.'

'If we'd known what was at stake,' said Keith, 'we'd never have agreed to keep it secret.'

Seabright scoffed. 'You had your suspicions.'

'You forced us into agreeing.'

'I forced you into nothing. I've been honest from start to finish. And you had the choice to walk away.'

'Balderdash!' cried Wendy.

'Quite so,' agreed Clive. 'Disingenuous balderdash, at that.'

Seabright looked round the group, obviously sensing they weren't going to be easily allayed. 'Listen, my friends. You have to understand that MET was a personal gift to help me win the Oscar. Now in principle, of *course* I don't have a problem letting people know that, and all the cool stuff that's followed—'

'But?' asked Wendy.

'But there are problems.'

'Problems?'

'Practicalities.'

'What, like embarrassment at admitting you took such desperate measures to feed your vanity?'

'Damn it, no,' answered Seabright, his measured tone fraying at the edges. 'I just mean the Academy would never give Best Picture to a movie whose screenplay had been, y'know... genetically-enhanced.'

Wendy had to stop herself shrieking with laughter, such was the absurd narcissism of Seabright's reasoning.

'So you're prepared to keep the entire world in the dark about Shakespeare's true identity, just so you can win an Oscar? An Oscar which is ultimately meaningless on a personal level anyway, since you yourself won't have written the film?'

Seabright stared into space, cowardly determination writ large across his face: the look of a man aware that his position was deeply dubious, yet whose spinelessness prevented him from acting otherwise.

'You can't just use other people's DNA without giving them credit,' said Pat.

'Can too,' snapped Seabright. 'It's not like Shakespeare or Cobley has done any work. Not like they've gone out of their way to help me.'

'But even if you don't owe Cobley a debt for using his DNA,' said Wendy, 'that's not the point.'

'And why's that?'

'Because this is bigger. This is about a discovery which fundamentally alters our understanding of the most pivotal figure in global culture.'

'It was just an accident!'

'And that means you shouldn't take responsibility?'

'I reckon so!'

'You reckon wrong! The fact is, the moment you started toying with Shakespeare's DNA, you were meddling with the fabric of history itself. There was always a risk you were going to make a bigger discovery than you intended.'

'But I didn't *know* that, did I? Hell, I hardly even knew about the authorship issue 'til Lester Howells brought it up.'

'That still doesn't excuse you from the moral obligation that comes with having discovered the truth.'

'Does it *really* matter?' returned Seabright, fists clenched. 'Would it really change the world *that* much?'

'Yes!' chorused the WAC.

'But is that a *good* thing?' Seabright was quaking. 'We've had four hundred years thinking Shakespeare did it, and everything's cool. His plays still get staged. They still teach them in high school. Why rock the boat?'

Wendy shook her head, amazed at Seabright's moral bankruptcy.

'I'm serious, people,' he persisted. 'The responsible thing to do is to keep this our little secret. Shakespeare's name is woven into history: part of who we are, part of our DNA, four hundred years in the making. You'd be out of your mind to tamper with that. The chaos it'd cause . . .'

Wendy opened her mouth to retort – only for Keith to raise his hand.

'Joe has a point,' he said. 'Or rather, he *would* have a point were we talking about any other candidate: Bacon, say, or Marlowe, or even Queen Elizabeth I – people who are already famous, who aren't owed anything by history and who, had they been the true author, would have been unknown because they *chose* not to identify themselves. Trouble is, Tom Cobley's different. He was, and remains, a man wronged. Wronged by Shakespeare for enslaving him, and wronged by four centuries of history which have bought into the Shakespeare fraud. If he were here now, today, I dare say he would *want* his name broadcast. He would want justice to be done!'

Rocking forward on his feet, Seabright ran his hands over his face. Wendy felt a faint rush of triumph. Sensing imminent capitulation, she began to think that under that leathery Hollywood skin lay a kind and decent man, more than capable of doing the honourable thing.

'Please don't get me wrong,' he sighed. 'I know it's a crime, and I totally get your passion. But what the authorship is to you, that Oscar is to me. And yes, it's selfish, but the same way you've spent twenty years debating, I've spent sixteen years giving the world *Chronicles*, enriching millions of lives. Curse me as much as you like, but I reckon I'm owed one final stab at an Oscar – and I deserve not to have it jeopardised by a sideshow I never even saw coming.'

'So you understand it's a crime,' said Wendy, 'yet you're happy to perpetuate it?'

'I'm not perpetuating it!' roared Seabright, erupting with fury.

'But you are!' pressed Keith. 'If you don't do the noble thing. If you use Cobley's DNA to help write your screenplay without telling anyone what you're doing, you'll be every bit as guilty as William Shakespeare himself: enslaving another to your will, then taking the credit for his genius.'

A hush descended as Seabright, trembling, stared into space. Seconds later, he strode fiercely up the aisle towards his office.

'The deal is done, people,' he boomed, 'and I have had my fill of being insulted in my very own theatre.' He turned to face them, silhouetted in his office entrance. 'I was gonna take this chance to say thanks for your help and patience, but since you're all so ungrateful I'll just say "so long" – and ask that you do the same.'

He stepped into his office and slammed the door behind him.

'Taxi for ten,' came a voice.

Wendy turned. The Fire Escape was open, framing one of Joe's lackeys.

'We're ready for you out on the lawn. If you'd just step this way.'

Stunned by the swiftness of Seabright's exit, and seeing no option but to comply, Wendy led them out, towards the waiting car.

***

'God damn it!' screamed Joe, flinging open the door to his writing room, where Jerry and Grace were preparing for his residency. 'I cannot believe the ingratitude! There I am, giving them what they've always wanted – what they never even knew was *possible* – and all they do is fling it straight back in my face.'

'How come?' asked Jerry.

'They want to tell the world. Even though I've said all along the whole thing has gotta stay secret, they wouldn't stop. Not enough that they now know who really wrote Shakespeare—'

'Which is?' interrupted Grace.

Joe hesitated, thinking back. 'Tom Cobley?' he answered uncertainly. 'Yes, Tom Cobley.'

Grace left the room to make up the pill.

'Oh, no,' raged Joe. 'It's not enough for me to give them the truth. They have to insist we then tell everyone else. And if we don't, I'm a criminal!'

'You pointed out that they'd signed an agreement?'

'Course I did.'

'Then what's the problem?' Jerry looked him deep in the eye. 'The agreement is watertight. They can't go against it otherwise we'll strip them of all they've got – not just the group but each of them individually. Right?'

Joe managed a nod. 'Right.'

'So why the anger? Are you worried they might have a point?'

'Of course not.'

'Then what is it?'

'I dunno,' sighed Joe. 'I guess it's just – I mean, why does it have to be so goddamn *difficult*?'

He sat on the side of his bed, toying with the *Glozbacks* duvet. Truth was, he couldn't tell what had left him so shaken up. Perhaps Jerry was right. Perhaps part of him really did wonder if keeping it silent was the right thing to do?

But no. As much as he could, possibly, just *begin* to understand where the Brits were coming from, he was surer still of his own ground. This was his discovery, made for personal reasons. There was no moral obligation to broadcast his accidental findings. Even if there were, it was far from certain that it would be in the world's best interests.

Besides, it wasn't like his secrecy was inherently amoral. He'd given the world so much, and soon he'd be giving it some more, this time with added Cobley goodness. He didn't owe 'world culture' anything. If anything world culture owed *him*, and he'd be damned if it wasn't going to pay up in the form of a Best Picture Oscar three years down the line.

It wasn't the dilemma, then, because there *was* no dilemma. But still there was a distant worry, darting round the recesses of his mind: a complication, or an opportunity, or *something*, which made him uncertain and afraid, like he was in danger of being caught out. What the hell it was, however, was impossible to identify with so much else crowding his thoughts.

'I dunno,' he repeated. 'I guess it's just *them*. Something about their determination. I remember what Lester said, and I worry that the same way they turned the tables on him, they're gonna defy me. I know it's crazy to think they might go against our contract, but—'

'You think we should keep an eye on them?'

Joe hadn't seen this far ahead, but now the suggestion came, he welcomed it. Not that he liked being bullied, but such were the stakes – especially now he finally had his Shakespeare, or his Cobley, or whoever the goddamn hell it was – it was just too risky to be left to chance.

'All we need do is station someone in their hotel,' said Jerry. 'Keep track on them, see how they're reacting. Just make sure there's nothing we've missed, that they really are screwed, then you can go into confinement without a care in the world.'

'But who do we ask?'

'Well it needs to be someone we can trust, but also someone *they* won't suspect.'

'Then there's only one man for the job.'

Joe reached across to his bedside table and picked up one of the action figures, screwing its head round to face him.

'One last chance, Emperor Tyron. One last chance to redeem yourself.'

Chapter 14

There was so much else to digest, it was unsurprising that they hadn't touched the tapas they'd ordered from their hotel restaurant in downtown Hollywood. None of them had much of an appetite while they still languished in the crazy limbo conjured by Seabright's outrageous insistence that their world-changing discovery had to stay secret.

'We can't leave without a fight,' insisted Keith, seated round one end of the table with Wendy, Pat and Clive. 'We have to go back. Make him see how much it matters.'

'He knows exactly how much it matters,' fumed Wendy, pouring herself a large glass of sangria which, in contrast to the food, was disappearing with indecent haste. 'Trouble is, his wretched Oscar matters more.'

'Then we make him see past his vanity,' pressed Pat.

'But how,' sighed Wendy, 'short of holding a gun to his head?'

'So we just swallow it?' snapped Clive. 'Is that what you're saying? Head home and carry on as if we still don't know the truth?'

Wendy took a big gulp of sangria. 'Our hands are tied.'

'The pretence would be too much to bear.'

'Then the ten of us will have to leave!' exclaimed Wendy. 'Bequeath the group to the ignorant masses!'

Struck dumb by the impasse, they lapsed into a tense, contemplative silence which was only broken when a familiar voice echoed across the room.

'May I join you?'

Wendy turned.

'I appreciate you may never want to see hide nor hair of me again,' said Sir Peter Heyward, looking and sounding less than well. 'But I'm staying here while I have meetings to fill the void left by my *Solix Chronicles* sacking. I spotted you from the lounge and wondered if you mightn't entertain an apology?'

Wendy looked at her friends. There appeared to be no objections, and since she'd long ago accepted Heyward was only guilty inasmuch as the devil drove him to it, she gestured for the old man to join them.

'There is no excuse,' he sighed, sitting down, 'except to say that Joe Seabright has – or rather *had* – a peculiar hold over me. Even though I detest *Chronicles*, I owe my living to it, and to some extent a man must do as his boss says.' He looked round and smiled. 'But having now experienced first-hand the man's appalling dishonesty, all I can do is apologise and hope that, somewhere in your hearts, you can forgive me.'

He gestured to a nearby waiter to bring another three jugs of sangria, but in truth the WAC needed no such inducement. As Wendy explained, they and Sir Peter were now very much at one where Seabright was concerned: disgusted by the man's vanity – by the crimes he was prepared to commit, the lives he was prepared to ruin – all in pursuit of his blasted Oscar.

'Why don't we just do it anyway?' suggested Keith with a sharp, straightforward suddenness after the first of Sir Peter's three jugs had been consumed. 'Ignore Seabright and go public regardless?'

Automatically, Wendy shook her head. 'We'll lose everything. Both personally, and—'

'I don't care how much I lose. Tom matters more than money. It's a sacrifice we should all be willing to make.'

'Yes,' conceded Wendy, 'but the group, Keith: he'd destroy the group.'

'So?' interjected Clive. 'What good is the group now? If we *were* to go public, then surely the group – by definition – is at an end? The truth established; no more to discuss. I say we've got nothing to lose.'

'Nothing to lose?' exclaimed Keith. 'At an end?' He looked round the table. 'Really, people. How long before you finally get your heads round what is happening here? Clearly, this should be only the *start*.'

'The start of what?' wondered Pat.

'Of changing the world. Re-writing history.'

'But do we need the *group* for that? Won't it happen automatically?'

'To an extent, maybe. When the news first breaks, say, when the shock's still raw. But Shakespeare is so embedded in our culture it's going to need campaigning once things die down. More campaigning, if anything, than the authorship debate itself.'

Wendy cupped her head in her hands and stared at her plate. Keith's point was well-made, and he was spot-on to admonish them for not keeping up. The impossibility of definitive proof had been so well-established for so long that the intricacies of this brave new post-Shakespeare world were proving distinctly hard to untangle.

'Because mark my words, it won't be easy,' continued Keith. 'As Seabright said, this is massively ingrained in every aspect of our culture. Someone's got to be there to steer the changes – to get inside people's minds and ensure Shakespeare no longer has a look-in, whether at school, in theatres or elsewhere. Mere facts aren't enough. Tom's going to need supporters at every turn, reminding the world that Shakespeare is no longer Shakespeare as incessantly as possible. And *that* job . . .' He took a sip of sangria. 'Surely, that job falls to us. Not only have we already got the educational infrastructure in place, but we made the discovery. We were the seekers of the truth. It's only right we become its guardians.'

'So we need the group to stay strong,' said Clive.

'Correct.'

'In which case, our hands are indeed tied. The moment we go public, Seabright sues and destroys us. There'll be no point having made the announcement because we won't have any means of following it up!'

'That's not strictly true.' Wendy spoke slowly but her mind was racing ahead. 'Like Keith says, this is a new reality, and everything has changed. Yes, we've lost that which used to make the group strong – purpose, and unparalleled expertise regarding the authorship debate – but think what we have *gained*.'

Keith frowned from across the table. 'You've lost me.'

Wendy smiled. Suddenly, she was ahead of the man himself. 'What we've gained is certain knowledge of a new author: one whose plays are universally acknowledged as the greatest ever written. Now that knowledge, in itself, is of no value. But what if we could find some way of formalising it? And what if, in so doing, we acquired an asset that would insure us against anything Seabright could throw our way?'

She caught Clive's eye. 'She means copyright,' he whispered, breaking out in a smile. 'The Cobley copyright.'

Wendy sat forward and planted her hands on the table. 'Think about it, chaps. If we secure the copyright *before* going public, we'll be invincible. The amount of money we'll make, owning the rights to the greatest plays the world has ever known . . .' She gave a cheeky laugh. 'Well, let's just say the *Solix Chronicles* profits will pale in comparison.'

One by one the others lit up in realisation of the ingenuity of her plan – all, that was, except Sir Peter, who had been following their discussion intently.

'Can you get copyright over such ancient plays?' he asked.

'Of course,' said Wendy. 'Yes, the plays are public domain now, but the discovery of a new author changes everything. They'll have to be republished and reclassified, just as if they had been written today, and that enables us to stake our claim – seize the rights as deserving guardians of Cobley's legacy: deserving not just because of our two decades' toil, but because of Keith's direct links to Tom.'

There was a dazed, delighted silence, interrupted only by short bursts of incredulous laughter, as they each thrilled to Wendy's untouchable plan.

'How about it, people?' She raised her glass. 'So many years spent championing our candidates, all because we wanted to feel that little bit closer to the mystery man.' She couldn't help but grin. 'Well, no more make-believe. Now he'll be ours for real. We'll own him, love him, and serve him as only we know how. Agreed?'

'Agreed!' chorused the others, clinking their glasses together.

'Very good.' She glugged down her sangria and summoned the bill. 'Then let's get back to Blighty and buy ourselves the Bard!'

Chapter 15

'You're a genius, Miss Tremain,' declared Joe, as Grace joined him on his patio to deliver the bottle of Tom Cobley pills. 'You do know how grateful I am, don't you?' He stepped towards her, breathing in the crisp midnight air. 'The Shakespeare thing has thrown me off course a little, but I'm always in your debt.'

Grace smiled as she passed him the pills, and Joe leaned in towards her. For a tremulous moment, he thought she reciprocated. But as their lips were about to meet, she pulled away.

'I'm sorry,' she whispered. 'But I can't ignore it.'

'Ignore what?'

'It was going so well. Everything felt so right. You gave me all I ever wanted; I gave you the same. And you're so sweet and all, even – in fact, *especially* – in your single-mindedness.' She folded her arms. 'But this stuff about Shakespeare, and now Tom Cobley. I just . . . I understand your obsession, I really do, but I deal in facts, evidence, truth. It's just not within my DNA to be able to ignore something so important.'

'I respect that,' said Joe. 'Of course I do.'

'Good.'

There was a lingering silence.

'So what are you going to do?' asked Joe finally. 'Break our cover?'

'No, of course not. But I can't continue to be party to keeping it secret. I just need to get back to Stanford. Forget any of this ever happened.' She tried a stoical smile. 'Which is fine, right? My work here is done.'

Joe felt his heart quicken. Grace's work was indeed done, but that wasn't the real focus for either of them. Truth was, the discovery about Shakespeare was forcing them apart, just as he believed they were coming together.

And yet what could he do? The temptation to appease Grace, while intense, faded next to the goal of winning his Oscar. It was for that lifelong dream that he had sacrificed relationships in the past. It made no sense that now, on the cusp of attaining it, he should suddenly do the reverse.

'Can I have my job back please?'

Peter Heyward stepped out of Joe's office, followed by Jerry.

'Well?'

'I found them,' confirmed Heyward, settling into a deckchair, illuminated by the multicoloured lanterns that bordered the pool. 'In fact, I joined them for dinner.'

'You did what?'

Heyward shrugged. 'I just thought it would be easier to reveal myself rather risk them finding me. And it really wasn't hard to win their trust. I simply joined in their moaning about you.'

'What were they saying about Cobley?' asked Jerry.

Heyward held his hands behind his back. 'It's not good news.'

'They're not actually gonna fight us?' said Joe.

There was no reply.

'You're kidding! They're actually gonna go public?'

Still, no response.

'But don't they realise the damage I'll do to them?' Joe clenched his fist. 'Don't they understand JoeCo's power?!'

'They know all about JoeCo's power,' said Heyward.

'And yet they're still prepared to take me on?' Joe stalked round the periphery of the pool, blood boiling at the audacity of it. To think that after all the challenges he'd surmounted, a bunch of bored British eccentrics genuinely had the guts to take him on. 'Are they really so stupid they'll risk everything for something so trivial?'

'They're not stupid at all.'

Joe stopped.

'They're ingenious. They have the whole thing planned out.'
Joe gazed through the luminous air at the aged actor.

'Copyright, Joe. They've realised that your discovery means the Cobley copyright is up for grabs: ownership of the greatest plays ever written. All they need do is seize it – and with it, the brand itself – and overnight they'll be ten times more powerful than JoeCo.'

Joe looked into the water of his pool. More powerful than JoeCo? The idea alone turned his body numb with fear. Surely nothing could be more lucrative than *Chronicles* – or could it? Shivering, he thought back through Shakespeare's – damn it, Cobley's – plays. *Hamlet, Macbeth, King Lear, Twelfth Night, Romeo and Juliet, Julius Caesar, Othello, Much Ado About Nothing* . . . Every one a masterpiece and every one etched into the culture and history of the world with an indelibility that *Chronicles*, despite its gargantuan popularity, could only envy. Here was a franchise, four hundred years in the making, which was not only bigger output-wise, but which had entwined itself so completely into the fabric of the planet that everyone, rich and poor, young and old, black and white, carried its essence within them.

He sat in a deckchair and massaged his brow, disgusted at his failure to foresee the opportunities of a post-Shakespeare world. Copyright? Branding? Intellectual property? These were the tools of his trade, yet not for a second had he considered the implications of his discovery in those terms. Looking back, he had sensed it sure enough – a looming spectre, earlier in the day – but in his crowded, defensive mind, he had failed to make sense of his instincts.

His mind whizzed ahead to a world where the WAC carried out their plan: a world where, days later, they brought his discovery to light. Insured by the greatest plays of all time, they'd be at liberty to humiliate him with tales of his egomania. Even worse, they'd be fully entitled to seize all JoeCo's Cobley chemicals and end his Oscar-quest once and for all.

'What can I do?' He looked despairingly at Jerry and Grace.

'There's literally nothing I can do. It's over. No pill. No Oscar. Quite possibly no movie, once they've destroyed my reputation!'

'I'm afraid it's true,' said Grace, her voice calm, clear and bright – quite at odds with the despair consuming Joe. 'Unless you do the obvious.'

'How so?' asked Jerry.

'I agree the copyright is the ultimate weapon. Whoever gets it wields absolute power. But why should that be the WAC?'

Joe climbed out of his deckchair. 'You're suggesting we register the copyright first?'

'I'm suggesting it's your only option.'

'What business would I have with Tom Cobley?'

'What business *wouldn't* you have?'

Joe looked doubtfully at Jerry.

'This is what I've been trying to tell you,' said Grace. 'It's a big discovery, not just in itself but in its implications. You've been so consumed by the Oscar, and your desperation to make it happen, you haven't thought through what we've uncovered. But give it a moment's thought, and you'll see that this is right up your street: an incredible story to tell – the imprisoned genius – and a ready-made series of great, epic masterpieces to *sell*. It's a marketer's dream. The most lucrative rights package there's ever been, but also unsurpassably high-brow. Seriously, if you really want the intelligentsia to realise you're one of them, nothing could be better than acquiring that copyright.'

Grace's words made more sense with every passing second, and Joe's mind began to fill with dizzying merchandising possibilities. This was indeed his specialism, and since the discovery was his by right – morally, he already owned the Cobley brand by virtue of having made the discovery – he was damned if the WAC were going to reap all the benefits.

'You're right,' he said. 'We *have* to get there first.'

'What?' exclaimed Jerry.

'It's too good an opportunity to pass up.' Joe winked at Grace. There was a spark in her eyes that urged him on.

'But there must be some other way of disarming the Brits.'

'This isn't about disarming the Brits, Jerry. This is about doing what's right – what falls to me naturally, as the discoverer of the truth – and, in the process, seizing the rights to an unprecedented treasure trove of goodies.'

'But the *Oscar*, boss. You can't capitalise on the truth about Shakespeare without revealing how you reached that discovery. And once you confess about MET, the Oscar's history. There's just no way those things can co-exist.'

'Really?' said Joe, answering his producer with a defiant smile. All of a sudden, he was not to be so easily deterred. Failure to spot Cobley's patent potential before the Brits was a timely reminder to always think one step ahead. Besides, talk of copyright had got him thinking brand-dimensionally, and when Joe was thinking brand-dimensionally, very few things were genuinely impossible.

The key was Cobley's story.

'Got it,' he declared.

'Got what?' asked Jerry.

'The way to make it work.'

For the first time in ages, he was back in his element. As Grace said, he had a story to tell, and what a story it was: a penniless prisoner, his genius abused by a master villain whose sensational fraud had held good for over four hundred years. But more than that, Joe had a profound *spiritual* connection with the main character – a kinship which made immaculate sense of the Oscar conundrum. This was neither compromise nor expediency. This was poetry. In a blazing revelation, he realised that the two of them, Joe Seabright and Tom Cobley, were one of a kind – flipsides of the same coin – and it was their destiny to walk onwards, hand in hand, gene to gene.

'So sure,' he explained. 'I admit it started selfishly. I wanted an Oscar, so I brought in Shakespeare. But then, amazingly, I discovered that Tom Cobley – Shakespeare's slave – was the true author of all those plays. Suddenly, my eyes were opened. In the course of my selfish secrecy, I'd discovered a terrible crime that's been concealed for four hundred years, and being the big-hearted guy I am, nothing – not even my Oscar lust, tempting me to make Cobley *my* slave – could stop me exposing the unbelievable truth. Why? Because I *understood* Cobley's pain. The pain of neglect; of a life lived without receiving due credit for your achievements.'

'So far, so good,' said Jerry. 'But what about the Oscar?'

'The Oscar will follow, just so long as I stay on track: so long as, having exposed Tom Cobley's suffering, I take the natural next step.'

'Which is?'

'Win him justice. Surfing the wave of support as the man who exposed this terrible crime, I vow to restore Tom's name in the most fitting way possible.'

'Oh boy . . .'

'Isn't it perfect?' Joe took Grace's hand. 'I declare that no longer do I want an Oscar purely for myself – I want to win it for Tom too: the two of us, overlooked geniuses both, our fates inextricably entwined! No one will care how I've achieved it. No one, the Academy included, will worry that I used MET. Why? Because the aims are so noble. Everyone will *want* me to succeed.'

He felt Grace's arm reach around him.

'Just think of it. A watershed in the history of culture: the day when Tom Cobley is formally accepted as the real Shakespeare, and the day when Joe Seabright – the bringer of justice, the visionary who discovered the truth behind the greatest plays the world has ever seen – finally gets the recognition he and his films deserve!'

Chapter 16

What a blessed relief it was to be back. Unlocking the door to her beloved cottage in Camberwell, it was with a tired but profoundly hopeful heart that Wendy dumped her luggage in the lounge and wandered into her kitchen, flicking on the kettle for a cheeky late-night cocoa before heading to bed for what would surely – and deservedly – be the most contented night's sleep she'd ever known.

As the kettle rumbled away, she leaned on the side and smiled, struggling to believe what had happened in the three weeks she'd been gone – and, indeed, what the future now held. Looking round her kitchen, and for want of any cats to chat to – she'd collect Molly and Polly from the cattery the following day – she felt an odd compulsion to report back to her doors, floors, carpets and cupboards on what had transpired since they were last acquainted.

So many ups, so many downs. First, the ludicrous business of signing into Seabright's confidence, then the swift, decisive news about Shakespeare – specifically the fact that Shakespeare really *wasn't* Shakespeare, even if the truth of it took some repeating to get used to.

Then there was the terrible discovery about Marlowe – who, despite Wendy's years of ranting, *was* merely Marlowe after all – and the equally shocking revelation that Tom Cobley, of all people, was the real author. Yes, they heard her right: *Tom Cobley*, imprisoned by the demon Shakespeare! It was just absurd – though arguably not as absurd as the battiness which then ensued, with Joe Seabright insisting that the whole amazing business be kept secret, for fear he'd lose face and, with it, his cherished hopes for an Oscar.

Well, they'd soon see about that, she chortled inwardly as the kettle boiled and she prepared her cocoa. Seabright might have an entire civilisation at his disposal – he might be friends with the President, he might very well boast a personal fortune greater than they could even imagine – but they, born fighters, had a weapon Seabright could only dream of: brains. Mere hours after his insane show of defiance, the ten of them concocted the perfect way to prick the big man's balloon. If they could only seize the copyright to Tom Cobley's *oeuvre*, they realised, they'd not only be immune from anything Seabright could throw at them, but ideally equipped to fulfil the WAC's destiny: ousting the impostor Shakespeare from the collective consciousness, and installing the incomparable Cobley, sometime bear baiter and playwright *par excellence*, in his place.

Wendy chuckled as she went to the living room, clutching her cocoa to guard against the cold. What a splendid couple of days they'd had since realising their strength, she told her bookcases as she sat on the sofa, grabbing a cushion and drawing her legs up close. Never mind the ins-and-outs of the paperwork – that could wait 'til they were back in London. Instead, their minds had been occupied imagining the amazement with which their mind-boggling news would be greeted, and the exhilaration that would follow: so much work, it was tricky to know where to begin.

It wasn't just a case of libraries re-stocking and publishers working overtime to reissue correctly-accredited versions. Goodness no! There would need to be a complete scholarly re-evaluation of the plays' merits, both on the page and on the stage, which would have to be co-ordinated by those with the greatest expertise. On top of which, there was the even more daunting task of weeding Shakespeare's name and image from the popular psyche, etched so forcefully into everything from banknotes to school textbooks. The Stratfordian orthodoxy was like an enormous skyscraper, every last storey of which needed demolishing, even as the Cobleian edifice rose alongside it.

In short, it was a gigantic challenge, but one whose appeal, as Wendy's eyes skipped along her rows of books dedicated to the Marlovian conspiracy, neutered any lingering disappointment. All she could feel was the future: hope, anticipation and honour that, after four hundred years, she should be the one to preside over the most significant cultural revolution the world had ever undergone.

But all that was to come. For now, she needed to get a good night's sleep so that tomorrow she'd be fresh for the first of their confabs with their lawyers. Taking a sip of cocoa, she switched on her TV, hoping a little late-night news might turn her brain off. Yawning, she flicked through the channels, gladly welcoming the first tentative advances of sleep as the midnight trash came and went, eventually reaching the BBC News channel which, oddly and irritatingly enough, was reporting live from JoeTown, California.

Wendy lifted her mug to take another sip of cocoa, only suddenly to check herself.

JoeTown, California?

Seized by a hideous terror, she lowered the mug to reveal the devil himself. Wearing the most gigantic grin, he was standing behind a jungle of microphones and waving at an assembled crowd several hundred strong, every last one on their feet, cheering and whistling vociferous approval. Trembling, scarcely daring even to breathe, Wendy dropped her mug even further so the rotating straplines at the bottom of the screen were finally exposed to view:

Mystery of Shakespeare authorship solved by Joe Seabright

Tom Cobley revealed as true author of plays and poems, Seabright asserts copyright

Seabright initiates 'Time for Tom' campaign, aims for Oscar glory

Strength failing, Wendy's mug fell on its side, sending cocoa all over her skirt.

The bottom had just fallen out of her world.

***

'Here goes!'

Joe took a beaker of JoeCola from Jerry and held up the pill he was about to swallow.

'For four hundred years he has languished in unjust obscurity. But now, on American soil, the truth is known at last. So long, Shakespeare – and *hello* Tom Cobley!' He glugged down the pill and raised the empty beaker aloft. 'Cobley is risen!' He stretched out the other arm, crucifixion style, just for the hell of it. 'He is risen, and justice will be done!'

For over a minute, Joe stood there, the rapture crashing down upon him – or rather, on the *truth*, on Tom Cobley, God rest his soul – before finally leaping down from the stage and high-fiving his producer.

'Hell, I'm pumped!'

'You did great, boss,' said Jerry. 'They totally loved you.'

'Outstanding work,' enthused Grace. 'You've just become a legend in your own lifetime.'

'You too,' grinned Joe, raising his arms in a victory salute as the three of them marched out of the Earloser Atrium – JoeTown's premier conference space – and left the hollering hordes behind.

'I can't tell you how good that felt,' he beamed, striding down the corridor. 'When I started saying what I'd been up to, I wondered what the hell I was doing. But then, the moment I told them what I'd discovered – boom! They just erupted! And then the Time for Tom stuff – they bought it wholesale! They went wild for me!' He checked himself. 'I mean, they went wild for *Tom*.' He checked himself again. 'No, they went wild for me *and* Tom – for I am Tom, Tom is me. Together, we are the great neglected geniuses of world culture, and boy are we ever diggin' it!'

'Didn't I tell you?' laughed Grace as they climbed into the awaiting taxi. 'This is such a big discovery; no way can the discoverer be anything other than a hero.'

'And that was just the media,' said Jerry, his scepticism banished at last. 'If *they're* loving it, imagine how the wider world's going to react!'

Joe trembled, delirious with unforeseen joy. He couldn't believe how virtuous he felt! If the Brits' scheming had forced him into a corner, he had more than merely stolen their thunder. He'd launched himself through a gigantic interstellar wormhole which turned threat into opportunity and left his enemies licking their wounds on the other side of the universe.

Ok, so he'd have preferred not to admit seeking help to try and win an Oscar. But since he'd always known he'd be sharing the credit, was it really that big a deal? Besides, Grace was right. The reason he craved the Oscar so bad was to show the establishment that, despite appearances, they and he were cut from the same cloth. And what could be more perfect for that than this? It was the perfect leveller; the ideal means of bridging the void, cutting through their snobbery and proving to them that he belonged.

Above all, there was the revelatory power of the Cobley rights, unfurling every second with amazing new possibilities. Foremost among these was the dawning realisation that, inadvertently, he had helped Cobley across the pond: no longer a stuffy old Brit, but legally adopted as a new, improved national poet for the greatest country on earth. The opportunities were endless.

'So here's what we do,' he said, as they drove through the streets towards his mansion. 'While I'm locked up, Jerry, get a stranglehold of the plays. A month's amnesty for any productions that are already out there – but after that, no more Shakespeare. All permissions to perform or publish those plays have to go through us.'

'Do we charge?'

'Sure we charge. This isn't just about protecting Tom's legacy, remember, but defining it. We need to make it a privilege to perform his stuff – he deserves that respect – and above all we need to guarantee quality control. From now on, anyone wanting to perform his plays needs to display two things. First, that they're committed. Second, that they understand their responsibility.'

'Which is?'

'The same as ours. Namely, to ensure that Cobley the man – the tortured, unacknowledged genius – is always there, right at the heart of everything.'

'So we take control of the plays,' said Grace. 'And then what?'

'Then it's over to our guys to organise the re-brand: the biggest the world has ever known – Shakespeare, vile English bully, *becoming* Cobley, wronged American everyman. I want them to spend the next fortnight brainstorming ideas, then fast-track the best into production without delay. Once I'm back out with the screenplay complete, we'll have a massive party and launch the whole thing: The Cobley Crusade!'

Jerry's cell phone rang. He answered, and promptly passed the handset to Joe. 'For you.'

Joe took the handset, figuring the interview requests would flood in thick and fast now the announcement had been made. Everyone would want a piece of him!

'How's it going?'

'What the hell do you think you're doing?'

Joe looked to Jerry in horror. It was *Lester Howells*. In his rush to sew up the Cobley copyright and go public, he'd totally forgotten to ask the big man.

'Damn it Joe, I thought we agreed to keep this secret.' Howells sounded furious, his frenetic voice a distant cousin of the relaxed, east-coast drawl that normally so distinguished him. 'Wasn't that the only way it could possibly work? For me *and* for you?'

'Oh God, Lester,' said Joe. 'I am *so* sorry. But really: the Brits left me with no choice. They saw the copyright loophole, and the only way to keep control was for me to beat them to it.'

'So it was just expediency?'

'You could call it that.'

'Because you looked to me like you were enjoying it up there.' The cab lurched to a halt outside Joe's mansion.

'Well, y'know . . . I've come to realise: it *is* fairly momentous.'

'You didn't think to consult me?'

'It all happened so fast.' Joe climbed out of the cab and headed into his mansion. 'Seriously, Lester. All I can do is apologise.'

'But don't you realise what this does to my reputation? Being seen to have deceived my clients? To have struck a Faustian pact with someone like you?'

'I resent that!' Joe was no longer willing to take Howells' throwaway insults on the chin. 'As for as your reputation, show me the man stupid enough to accuse either you *or* me, given what we've achieved.'

Howells fell silent.

'Seriously Lester, this is *monumental* news. You should be proud, not ashamed. To be a part of this—'

A steady tone indicated that the call was at an end. Joe returned the handset to Jerry.

'I refuse to feel guilty. Sure, I should've called him. But if the guy really wants to reinvigorate culture, what better than rebooting the Bard? This is a seminal moment for world culture. If Howells is too pompous to see that, he's an even bigger snob than I thought.'

'Quite right,' agreed Jerry, swinging open the door to Joe's writing room.

As before, it was immaculately prepared. There was freshly cleaned linen, a complete set of costumes, and a fridge bursting with supplies. Among the latter were several dozen doughnuts and, more importantly still, the six remaining Cobley Pills, to be consumed weekly until the end of the allotted period, or the completion of the screenplay – whichever came first.

'So I guess this is goodbye.'

Joe turned to his brilliant associates, aware of an all-new energy in his veins: the creative fission of a man whose genius had lain dormant, unacknowledged and untapped, for upwards of four hundred years.

'Well, come on,' he said, ushering them over for the necessary farewells, keen to channel the adrenalin from the press conference into his first session of Cobley-inspired creation. 'The guy's waited an age for this. The creative juices are ready to burst!'

He shook hands with Jerry, and then – with the producer stepping out discreetly – took Grace in his arms and kissed her on the lips.

'Congratulations,' he said. 'Your moment has arrived. Go back to Stanford, and don't rest until you've confronted every last person who doubted you.'

'I will.'

Joe waited, hoping desperately she would say something more. 'And then?'

'Then what?'

'Then where will you go?'

Grace took his hand. 'Why, then I'll come back here. Here, where anything is possible – and where I now know I belong.'

Joe couldn't believe this was happening: everything he had ever dreamed of, plus that which he hadn't, coming together in unintelligible symmetry.

'You'll have everything you need,' he assured her. 'Anything you require to pursue your studies – no matter how outlandish.'

She raised her finger to his lips. 'Get to work, boss.'

Joe watched as she left the room with a lingering smile, then headed for his desk. Closing his eyes, he transported his mind back to that familiar place – the place of infinite possibilities – which, for the first time in years, felt genuinely fresh. Fresh, because his imagination now boasted a reach unlike anything he'd known before, and also because he was no longer writing for himself, but Tom as well – the pair of them, unacknowledged geniuses both, striving together to win the recognition they deserved.

The Tortured Artist III

Until two months before, he had been relatively content.

Relations between him and the old man had thawed in the wake of the breakfast episode. Quite unexpectedly, those five simple sentences resulted in the old man requesting something very specific; and it was the one thing, astonishingly, which the young man was not only happy but supremely well-equipped to supply.

It was an elegant arrangement. The old man derived satisfaction from the belief that this would trigger further, greater acts of independent creation. The young man found consolation in his work, at last able to summon inspiration with some reliability.

For over half a year, he existed in untroubled equilibrium, his stability rewarded by no further alterations to the pills, which in turn only strengthened his sense of balance. He wasn't especially prolific. His exhausting standards of quality control – layer upon layer of centuries-old, chemical circumspection – meant that only the very finest dialogue made it onto the page, and only the cream of that was copied across to show the old man. But it didn't matter. He was assured there was no rush. Getting it right was more important than getting it quick.

Had it continued in that mould, the script would have long since been finished. As it was, however, the old man's meddling got in the way before even a formal first draft had appeared. Given time to contemplate completed passages, he started interfering once more with the make-up of the doses. Not that the young man's work lacked anything. But the better it became, the better the old man believe it could be. Indulging the elastic timescale, he added and removed ingredients in line with what he believed could be achieved with certain sections, which the young man then had to keep polishing, sometimes daily, to see what changes were having what effect.

The net impact was simply to scupper his hard-won contentment, returning him to psychological slumps that incapacitated him for weeks at a time. Now, just a few days before, he had been told that the deadline was suddenly imminent; the final draft was required, and he still hadn't got to the end of the first.

The door came ajar. A rim of light from the outside world shone briefly before the old man strode through.

The young man was at his desk, pen over paper. Yet again, his mind was paralysed by self-doubt. No sooner did one idea suggest itself, than a contrary voice shouted it down.

The old man peered over his shoulder.

'Nothing? Another day gone – and not a single word?'

'I can't disentangle . . .'

'The deadline is the day after tomorrow! How hard can it be to finish from here? The quality will take care of itself. You just need to write.'

'But the doses are cancelling each other out. I can't think straight.'

'Have you tried what I suggested?'

The young man couldn't remember what this was, but the answer was no.

'I swear son, distract yourself. Some composition, maybe, or a nice watercolour. Just for fun. I won't mind, if it helps you get it done.'

'It won't.' The young man put down his pen.

'How can you know if you don't try?'

'Right now, I need singularity. One voice inside my head, one task, one goal.'

'Damn it!' The old man slammed his fist on the desk. 'Why can't you pull yourself together?'

'Because you keep tearing me apart!'

The old man struck him round the head with the back of his hand. 'After all I've given you!'

The young man was shaking.

'You just need to get it done. And then . . .'

'Then what?'

'We move on.' The old man turned away. 'Something different. A sculpture, maybe.'

The young man nodded, more in agreement with himself than acknowledgement of the old man. Suddenly, it was clear. The pills were clotting his creativity, but he was so near the end of the script, with such detailed knowledge of the subject, he could surely overcome them if he wanted. The real truth was that he couldn't finish because finishing would be futile. Because now he knew for certain that the old man was mad — and there would be no end until it claimed one or other of them.

He looked back at the page, seeking inspiration not in the job at hand, but in formulating what he now knew he needed: an escape plan. As the pain from the old man's blow subsided, he ran through everything he knew about his predicament, and how it might be communicable to the outside world.

'My apologies,' said the old man.

'It's ok.' The young man sat up straight. 'You're right to chastise me.' He lifted his pen. 'I'll have it for you by this time tomorrow. And then, when I'm done, I'll set to work on whatever else you suggest.'

The old man looked a little taken aback, but thought better than to question the young man's resolution. 'I'll be back in the morning with your pills.'

The old man left; the young man set to work.

Chapter 17

Not one to dwell on what was past – at least, doing her damndest not to – it was with stoic determination that, six weeks after returning from the States, Wendy marched downstairs from the WAC's offices. Carting decades of cherished research to the skip outside, she tried desperately not to think about the wasted effort: the years spent fighting Marlowe's corner, battling Stratfordians and campaigning for truth, just to suffer the indignity not only of discovering she was half-wrong, but looking on helpless as a dastardly Hollywood hoodlum exploited the bit of her that had been half-right.

Tossing three lever-arch files into the skip – the first three drafts of an unpublished novel detailing the drama of the Marlovian conspiracy – Wendy urged her mind towards oft-repeated platitudes and returned indoors.

They'd had fun while it lasted. What did it matter that, at the last, at the hour of their greatest triumph, at the culmination of all they'd fought for and the dawn of a new age – an age which would have brought the group unparalleled wealth and adulation – what did it matter that they'd had their thunder stolen by a trumped-up little squirt from across the pond? The sun still shone, the birds still sang, and the wind still blew through the trees. Life went on – so why couldn't she?

'Oh, for heaven's sake, you silly old bag,' she cursed, climbing the stairs and slapping her forehead to stop the negative thoughts clogging her brain. Whatever the regrets, whatever the might-have-beens, there was but one simple fact: thanks to Sir

Peter's insidious intervention, Seabright had the whole thing sewn up. The WAC was kaput.

'Hey chaps!' she chirped, peering into the morgueish first floor meeting room. For the first fortnight or so, the whole committee had come in on a daily basis to brood over what had happened. Then the numbers had begun to dwindle, until finally plateauing out a week before with the three inevitable last men standing: Clive, Keith and Pat.

'How's it going?'

A trio of non-descript grunts, combined with the airless stench of stale alcohol, confirmed that 'it' was going precisely nowhere. Each man was slumped gracelessly on some hunk of dilapidated furniture, staring mindlessly at the muted TV. Wendy marvelled at how the three of them, once so vibrantly different in their eccentricities, had congealed in vegetative self-pity.

'You can't just sit around,' she said, 'expecting me to do everything.'

There was a synchronous shrug of the shoulders.

'There are things you each need to sort through. I can't take unilateral decisions. I only know about Marlowe.'

'Bin all the Bacon stuff,' said Clive.

'Same for Oxford,' said Pat.

Wendy sighed. 'Well even so, I could use a hand. It's tiring, traipsing up and down.'

'What's the rush?' asked Keith.

'The rush is to empty the place before we hand it back to the Globe,' said Wendy, aware that the real hurry was to clear her mind and forget the whole wretched business.

'I still don't understand,' sighed Pat. 'What use do the Globe have for it now?'

'I told you yesterday. They're going to carry on. It's all they can do. The theatre will keep staging the plays – albeit at a price – and the education team will keep teaching them; trying to add a modicum of respectability to the JoeCo onslaught.'

'Seabright won't allow it,' remarked Keith bitterly. 'His grip is too tight.'

'Well, they can only try. Besides, if the Globe *might* be done for, then we *certainly* are. So if you'd please just give me a hand.'

'We've still got a month,' said Pat. 'It'll get done.'

'Oh, I know it will,' replied Wendy, clearing up some more debris. 'By me!'

'Ok, ok,' said Clive – dear old redoubtable Clive – wobbling as he stood up. 'I'll give you a hand.' He swayed some more before collapsing straight back into his armchair. 'Oh bother. I will help, Wendy, I promise. Just not today. Today, I just need to gather my thoughts.'

'You've been gathering your thoughts for six weeks!' Wendy balanced a mountain of pizza boxes in her arms. 'If only you did some clearing out you might feel better about the whole situation.'

'Now come, come,' said Keith. 'This whole thing's been hard to swallow. Everyone copes in different ways. You're up on your feet, working away, we . . .' He paused, considering. 'We're drinking.'

Wendy tutted as she strode into the adjoining kitchenette, dumping the rubbish in a black bag. 'I just want to move on.'

'Move on to what?'

'Anything!' She grabbed a pile of unopened post from the side. 'Anything but this.' She opened the first of the envelopes, plucking out yet another complaint: one more to add to the pile of members' missives moaning that the committee let Seabright use their precious hair samples – many claiming they never actually *wanted* to solve the puzzle in the first place – as well as blaming the WAC for the disaster of JoeCo beating them to the copyright. That was an allegation Wendy refused to countenance, even while understanding the force of feeling. After all, it wasn't just the committee whose lives had changed. There were tens of thousands of members whose favourite hobby was no more; for whom the revelations, coming all at once, must have been devastating. First, the authorship discovery itself. Then, the realisation that, thanks to Seabright's unspeakable betrayal, the WAC had no role in the aftermath.

'Here we go!' proclaimed Pat, followed by the sound of the TV.

Wendy looked at the screen, groaning as she read the words 'Tom Cobley Day', plus the legend 'TM JoeCo', strapped unashamedly across the bottom of the screen. Blissfully, she had almost managed to forget that today marked the formal launch of the Cobley Crusade, and it was with a mix of irritation, envy and spiteful curiosity – willing the whole thing to go bottom-up – that she was reminded of it now, donning her glasses to watch the horror unfold.

'But seriously, ladies and gentlemen . . .'

Dwayne McAllister, US President and MC for the day, was speaking from a sunlit stage in one of JoeTown's several parks.

'Being here is an amazing privilege, reminding me once again that my first inspiration – the spark which first ignited my passion for politics – was the sight of Greathen Earloser and his heroic crew fighting the evil Emperor Tyron in the *Solix Chronicles* TV series.'

'Idiot,' snapped Clive, with some accuracy – although one had to remember that McAllister's famed candour about his *Chronicles* fandom, first exhibited while running for the Republican nomination two years previously, was widely credited with having earned him the keys to the White House. Though derided by some, his vow to model his Presidency on the leadership skills of Greathen Earloser had been admired by many more.

'But of course,' the leader of the free world went on, his tone as gruff as his build was bear-like, 'Greathen Earloser wasn't really my inspiration at all. My real inspiration was our host here today: a man of unparalleled vision who has never ceased to push back the bounds of what's possible.'

'It's a circus,' observed Keith – poor Keith, who in his own way was suffering more than anyone. So yes, he didn't endure the additional regret of having been wrong about the real author, but in a way that only made it worse, for he had to bear the anguish of watching Joe Seabright bask in the glory of *his* having been right – and about his beloved ancestor, no less.

'It's crazy,' Wendy concurred, sitting beside Clive. 'A total disgrace.'

McAllister continued wittering. 'Time and again, Joe Seabright has mesmerised us with his magic, and I know I wasn't alone in looking ahead to *Triumph of the Solix* with a tear in my eye, saddened that it was to mark the end of this great journey.' He used his sleeve to wipe away the imagined waterworks.

'But then!' he boomed. 'Just as we were getting ready to mourn, he and Grace Tremain – two of America's boldest pioneers – achieve the impossible. Not just an incredible scientific creation, but a world-changing discovery, transforming past, present and future, and giving JoeCo a whole new mission to wow us with: wiping Shakespeare's name from the record books, and filling them with the glory of Tom Cobley. Or, to put it another way, welcoming the greatest genius of all time, wronged by successive generations in the UK, into the cradle of American justice.' He nodded sagely. 'It is, to put it mildly, a great task. A great and *noble* task, for which there is no better man than Joe Seabright: a hero whose courage, vision and sheer humanity render him perfectly-equipped for this most momentous challenge.'

The crowd howled its approval; Wendy held her head in her hands. The tone was unmistakeable. The Yanks were not only stealing her thunder, but stripping England of its greatest ever artistic asset. Worse still, they were totally unashamed in saying so.

'It's with great humility that I endorse the Time for Tom campaign, and ask you to welcome the man who, having changed so many of our lives, is now changing history itself: the man I am honoured to call my friend, Mr Joe Seabright!'

As the squat little so-and-so emerged, Wendy glanced at the others, all blank in bewilderment, sharing the same speechless despair.

'Thank you so much,' grinned Seabright. 'May I welcome you all to sunny California on this day of days, as we set in motion the long, challenging task of avenging a deception that has plagued the world for over four centuries. A deception which has its roots in the villainous imprisonment of one man by another, and which has poisoned our culture so completely that it will take years, and every ounce of strength we have, to suck out its venom and heal it with the truth.'

'Ludicrous!' exclaimed Pat. 'Utterly ludicrous!'

'This, ladies and gentlemen, is The Cobley Crusade. It begins today with this . . .' The camera zoomed in to show Seabright holding aloft the completed *Triumph of the Solix* screenplay. 'And it shall end on that special day, two and a half years hence, when I, carrying the spirit of Tom Cobley within me, raise aloft the Best Picture Oscar in his name, knowing that I'll have done my bit to ensure, at long, long last, that justice is done for Tom!'

The assembled crowd leapt to its feet.

'Justice for Tom!' they screamed. 'Justice for Tom! Justice for Tom NOW!'

Calming the crowd with a warning not to get complacent, Seabright introduced the first of the day's Time for Tom events: a co-ordinated global book burning of Shakespeare plays and anthologies. Backed by a giant screen, he counted down the seconds until the annihilation began, whereupon the news channel cut away from JoeTown to show pyres lighting up in cities and towns across the world: piles and piles of Shakespeare editions, thrown into furnaces by men, women and children of all colours and creeds.

The stunt had been meticulously planned, and while it was doubtful that every single Shakespeare book in existence was currently being incinerated, the JoeCo propaganda machine had certainly had an astonishing effect. According to the strapline, it was estimated that over 99% of the world's Complete Shakespeares were going up in flames at that one moment, together with around 82% of individual Shakespeare volumes – statistics which should have warmed the heart of any self-respecting anti-Stratfordian but which, for Wendy, meant nothing but envy. So what if she'd dreamed of such a day for twenty years? There was no pleasure seeing it unfold like this: not when it so plainly should have been them, and not some two-faced rotter from the States, leading the charge.

'And now . . .' Seabright pronounced, having moved to a secondary stage, where he stood before a cloth-covered table. 'Now our errors have gone up in smoke, let us begin re-writing history!'

Stepping forward, he removed the shroud to reveal a giant mock-up of a book – 'The Collected Plays and Poems of Tom Cobley' – surrounded by hundreds of actual editions. As before, the coverage lingered on the scene for a moment before cutting to a montage chronicling the scenes both at the book-burning pyres and in supermarkets the world over, where the Collected Cobley, a JoeCo publication, was just that second going on sale.

'Look at them,' said Clive, 'they're clamouring for it.'

And indeed they were. All around the globe, people were fighting to be the first to buy a slice of corrected history.

'So the dough pours in,' said Keith.

'Well you do get a discount,' said Pat. 'Twenty per cent, if you have a ticket proving your Shakespeare's gone up in smoke.'

'Look!' cried Wendy, sitting forward as the TV displayed the covers of the Collected Cobley. In classic JoeCo fashion, the new tome came in three editions: a Basic, an Academic, and a Legacy. All were hardback, but whereas the Basic contained just the works themselves, the Academic featured supplementary notes shedding new light on the plays in relation to Cobley's traumatic life. These notes were then spurned by the Legacy, which favoured luxurious presentation ahead of detail: hand-bound and gilded, with a 3D cover, and limited to just ten million copies worldwide. The official line was that the editions were tailored to different requirements, but the intention was plainly to appeal to people's completism in the hope fans would collect all three versions – after which, JoeCo would presumably release 'Collector's', 'Definitive' and then 'Ultimate' editions to tie in with coming milestones like the release of *Triumph of the Solix*.

'I can't believe he's got his face on it,' said Wendy, wincing at the cover art. All three editions featured the already-familiar

Tom Cobley logo – italicised script, in a horrid luminous orange – together with an artist's rendering of Cobley. Drawn by *Chronicles'* chief conceptual artist, Larry Jones, the latter featured Tom at work in a murky cell with a shadowy figure lurking outside: impressively executed, but brain-stuntingly crass, not to mention completely spoilt by Seabright's face grinning away in the top corner with the words 'Time for Tom' emblazoned beneath it.

'So it begins,' nodded Seabright approvingly, as the coverage returned to JoeTown, 'All that remains is to give you a little teaser of what we have planned in the upcoming months.'

And off he went again, unveiling the first raft of Cobley merchandise: clothes, stationery and toys galore, including dolls of both the genius Tom and the dastardly Shakespeare – who, despite Seabright's rhetoric to the contrary, clearly still had a future as the villain of the piece – together with plans for the widely-rumoured Cobley Camp. Located in Milton Keynes – the town, built in the mid-twentieth century, which grew out of Tom Cobley's birthplace, Milton Keynes Village – construction work was to begin within the month. Seabright himself was to pay a personal visit to lay the first stone, and the park would open in July 2023, housing a host of attractions that would include a medley of rollercoasters and ghost rides based on Cobley's most famous plays, plus a museum taking guests interactively through Cobley's miserable life.

'And finally,' Seabright concluded, 'a declaration I never thought I'd make.' He took a moment to compose himself. 'Contrary to what I've previously said, *Triumph of the Solix* will no longer mark the end of JoeCo's filmmaking exploits. While *The Solix Chronicles* itself will cease to be, the movie-making will continue.'

The camera zoomed in as Seabright held up a book – instantly recognisable as Tom Cobley's diary, seized from Keith a month before by its 'rightful' copyright-holder.

'It's with huge pleasure that I announce my next project: an all-new JoeCo saga dramatising the *Cobley Chronicles* – films depicting the excruciating trauma Tom suffered at Shakespeare's hand, to be scripted through me by the great man himself.'

As the cheers went up yet again, Seabright gestured for Grace Tremain and the President to join him on stage, and there the three of them stood, saluting the hysterical masses, plus the millions of TV viewers, grins smeared across their faces like the almightiest taunts Wendy had ever experienced.

The President stepped up to the microphone, ready to bring proceedings to a close, only for the WAC's TV to turn suddenly black.

'What on earth?' exclaimed Wendy, looking across at the rest of the group.

'Come on.'

A hand reached over her shoulder and chucked the remote control into her lap.

'Let's go.'

Wendy stood and turned. It was Jim Withers.

'What do you mean, *go*?' she asked. 'Go where?'

'Where do you think?' said Jim. 'To the pub!'

Chapter 18

As they trailed through the Borough backstreets towards Jim's chosen destination – The Globe, naturally enough – Wendy had her work cut out keeping pace with her former nemesis, who strode ahead with a purpose quite unlike the aimless lethargy afflicting her colleagues in the WAC.

'I don't understand,' she said, trotting awkwardly alongside the mathematician. 'Why are you here? Surely you want to slaughter us for helping to expose the truth?'

'Well I *did*,' replied Jim, cheeks red and eyes gleaming. 'At first I wanted you all strung up: you, Lester Howells, Joe Seabright. At *first* I couldn't leave the house for shame, embarrassed at my own delusion. Heavens, I was even worried I'd be picked on. Duffed up for advocating the demon Shakespeare. With the man himself no longer here to answer for his crimes, what better target for revenge than those who defended his claim for so long?'

'But?'

'But, soon enough, I found solace in the fact that I wasn't the only one left high and dry.' Grinning, he glanced at Wendy. 'And also, that I wasn't the only one who was wrong.'

Wendy met his smile with a hint of her own. 'So yes, I was wrong too. About Marlowe. But please note, and note well: I *wasn't* wrong about Shakespeare.'

Jim fixed his eyes straight ahead, the tufts of hair on either side of his head flapping like elephantine ears in the early evening chill.

'No you weren't,' he said. 'Shakespeare wasn't Shakespeare,

and for that you have my heartfelt apologies. I see now that I was a bit of an arse twenty years ago – and that occasionally I've been a bit of an arse since.'

Wendy froze, astonished. Even though she'd long ago accepted the reality of Shakespeare *not* being Shakespeare, there was something about hearing Jim accept the new orthodoxy – embrace it, indeed, so openly, humbly and regretfully – which brought her up short.

'I was an arse too,' she replied automatically.

Jim stopped.

'Well, sometimes.'

Jim smiled. 'I'm not saying I regret it – except, maybe . . .' He broke off as the other three fanned out around the one-time couple. Wendy wanted him to continue, but Jim was blushing. 'Anyway, the point is: science is science. I of all people have to acknowledge that. And there's no comeback after what Seabright discovered. One must just face facts. Apart from Keith here, we've all squandered enough years, and endured enough emotional turmoil, to waste any more time worrying what might have been. Neither you nor I must let ourselves get bogged down. Not when there's such a terrible injustice to attend to.'

'Injustice?' repeated Wendy.

Jim made a beeline for the pub entrance.

'What injustice?'

'You mean Tom?' wondered Keith.

'No, I don't mean Tom.' Jim held the door open as they all shuffled in. 'At least, not directly.'

Once inside, Jim bought the drinks before returning to join the others round a rickety old table, the conversation having quickly reverted from the oddity of his reappearance to the dreaded Cobley Crusade – or rather the Cobblers Crusade, as it was quickly dubbed.

'I know I'm biased,' said Keith, taking his drink, 'but surely he could at the very least *thank* me for bringing Tom's story to light. You know? In lieu of any guilt he might feel, just *acknowledge* that I, like the group as a whole, played some part in exposing this. But is he human? Is he decent? No, he is not!' He lifted up his pint and drank almost half of it in one go.

'I just can't believe people are buying it,' growled Clive. 'Can't they see the egotism? He wouldn't be doing it if we hadn't forced him into a corner. *Plainly*, the Oscar isn't for Tom but for Joe. It's just that, to save face, he's having to pretend. I mean, if he *really* wants to do justice by Tom, then why's he so busy demeaning him by turning him and, God knows, *Shakespeare* into dolls!'

'You don't think you'd have been tempted to do the same?' asked Jim.

A surprised silence fell over the table.

'Well, I don't know,' stuttered Wendy. Thanks to Sir Peter Heyward's latest act of treachery, they'd never got round to planning the detail of what they'd do.

'I wouldn't have blamed you if you had,' smiled Jim. His conciliatory tone was both welcome and unsettling.

'Perhaps we'd have been tempted,' conceded Keith. 'But unquestionably, we'd have acted more responsibly. Put the truth out there on its own terms, a thing of inherent value. We'd have gone through the right channels: government, academia, schools – channels through which the truth could have spread thoroughly and respectably. We'd have kept the plays free to stage, not requiring a thousand dollars a time every time someone wanted to stage something that's been public domain for four hundred years!' He broke off and sighed. 'And then, yes, with all that in place, with the ground rules established, I suppose one could have had a little fun. Made a bob or two, even. What's for certain, though, is that there's no point giving kids Tom Cobley lunchboxes unless the infrastructure's there for them to learn what really went on.'

Nodding, huffing and puffing as one, they lifted up their glasses and drank an anti-toast to Seabright.

'Wouldn't you just love to stop him in his tracks?' wondered Jim, as the glasses returned to the table.

Wendy eyed him quizzically. It wasn't his meaning. It was the determination with which he spoke.

'Seriously. Wouldn't it be great to wipe that smug smile off his face and make him pay for stealing your thunder?'

'Stealing our thunder?' repeated Wendy.

'Leading the revolution. By rights that's your job, not his. Correct?'

'Correct, but . . .' Wendy hesitated.

'But why should you care?' wondered Clive on her behalf.

'Why should I care?' returned Jim in astonishment, as if the question scarcely needed asking. 'Because that's the deal. That's what's fair. That, surely, was always the arrangement.' He looked round and saw four puzzled expressions. 'Ok, so for twenty years we were at loggerheads – I couldn't tolerate what you stood for, and likewise you me. But ultimately there was a good deal of mutual respect, was there not?'

Wendy looked awkwardly to Clive.

'I mean it. In our own ways we kept each other going. We needed each other to keep the debate alive. And though that reliance frequently manifested itself as animosity, in the end we were on the same side: arguing because we *cared*. We cared about the plays so unusually much we were prepared to sacrifice everything to discover who really wrote them.'

Jim lifted his pint to his lips and took another sip. Wendy, in common with her colleagues, stared at the table.

'The day Seabright broke the news . . .' Jim's voice was just beginning to crack. 'The day he first broke the news, my first thought wasn't "God, so Shakespeare didn't write Shakespeare after all" . . .' He turned towards Wendy. 'My first thought was "why the hell isn't it you up there making the announcement?"'

Wendy looked up. A tear fell into her pint.

'In time, I knew I'd cope with the Shakespeare thing. But what I couldn't stomach was that after all the energy we invested, this *disgusting* man should just swan in and snatch the whole lot away, taking credit for something we all, *me included*, fought so hard to achieve.'

Wendy dried her eyes with her sleeve.

'This is why we have to make him pay.' Jim laid his clenched fist on the table. 'This is why we have to get revenge.'

'But how?' asked Keith. 'I concur with everything you say. Alas, Seabright is invincible. Not only has he got all the Cobley rights sewn up, he's established himself as the bringer and guardian of truth. He's the virtuous one. It's impossible to bring him down.'

'Not so.' Jim adjusted his pint on its beermat. 'Think about it. His Achilles' heel is so obvious when you just *think* about it. It seems like his greatest strength – the thing which gives the Cobblers Crusade currency and purpose – but it's actually his fatal flaw. Why? Because it's the only thing he *genuinely* cares about.'

'The Oscar,' whispered Wendy.

Jim nodded.

'You're suggesting we find some way of denying him the Oscar?' asked Pat.

'Precisely that.'

'But he has the Oscar sewn up,' countered Keith.

'How so?'

'Because Tom Cobley is the greatest writer who ever lived!'

'Is he?'

'Yes!'

'Really?'

'Of course!'

'How can you be sure?'

Keith was silent. Though the answer remained obvious – 'Because he *is*' – it felt suddenly unsatisfactory.

Jim sat forward in his chair, elbows planted on the table, hands clasped in determination. 'The moment I realised what perfect revenge it would be to beat Joe to the Oscar, my mind was drawn back to something I heard at college.'

He turned to Wendy, who felt a sudden rush of goosebumps.

'Do you recall? In the good old days, before you had the cheek to question me; before you got hung up on Shakespeare's identity? How we'd sit in the sun, wondering idly why no one, but no one, could compete with Shakespeare: why no one had ever come close? And you insisting that Shakespeare wasn't – that he couldn't possibly have been – some unique messianic miracle, but that surely *every* generation had similar geniuses, equal or even superior, lurking beneath the surface?'

Wendy shivered. She hadn't considered it for over twenty years, so preoccupied had she become with unmasking the *actual* Shakespeare, but Jim was right. Once upon a time she had indeed believed there must be other Shakespeares walking among them, their genius just waiting to make itself known, if only they picked up a pen.

'I don't mean to puncture the mood, Jim,' said Keith. 'But your implication is gibberish. If the whole of history hasn't found anyone better than Shakespeare, how on earth can we? There's certainly no one out there at the moment.'

'How so sure?' said Jim. 'Just because they haven't made themselves known—'

'But *really*. If anyone of Tom's calibre was alive, they'd already be writing.'

'Why?'

'Because true genius is uncontainable – impossible to ignore.'

'What rot!' laughed Wendy, joining Jim on the offensive and spontaneously rediscovering the conviction of her youth. 'You speak like there's a law, stipulating that everyone tries, at some stage, to write fiction. Yes of course, school and college *should* enable you to identify any talents you may have, but are they really that thorough?' She took a quick swig of her pint. 'Think of the statistics. In the same way it's inconceivable Cobley was a one-off, it's absurd to think that there isn't someone alive today capable of similar achievements – if only they'd think to try.' She grabbed Jim's hand. 'I've always believed this. Every generation must have its Mozart, its Leonardo – its Tom Cobley.'

A silence fell over the table, offset only by the clatter and chatter of other drinkers.

'So what's your suggestion?' asked Keith. 'That we go out into the world . . .'

'Correct,' said Jim encouragingly.

'Find a writer *superior* to Tom Cobley . . .'

'Right.'

'Have him *write a screenplay* . . .'

'Right again.'

'And then . . .' Keith hesitated. 'Then what?'

Jim frowned as if the answer was obvious. 'Why, then we make his film. We make his film, and we win the Oscar.' He sat forward and thumped his fist on the table. 'Think of it, my friends! We'll have something worth fighting for again – a genius in whose talent to believe – and can look on proudly as, in the wake of our victory, the Cobblers Crusade deflates and Seabright's passion is exposed as the narcissism it really is. Who knows? Perhaps he'll even return Cobley's copyright to its rightful owner, disgusted that the great man has let him down?'

For several seconds, no one said a thing. They were all too dazed to respond.

'Hold on,' said Wendy. 'Rewind a little. *Who* did you say should make this film?'

'You should. We all should.'

Wendy glanced at the others. As their eyes met, each broke into laughter.

'But why not?!' exclaimed Jim. 'Have any of us got anything better planned? All you need is manpower, money and motivation: the WAC's got all three in abundance. Don't forget that the vast majority of your members are artists of one kind or another: actors, writers, directors, designers, producers, technicians – you've got the full spectrum, already covered. All you need to do is rally them, and how difficult can that be, given what Seabright has done to you all? Simply channel their anger. Tantalise them with the prospect of sweet revenge!'

He smiled at Wendy, his discoloured teeth misaligned in well-meant sincerity, and Wendy stared into her pint. Certainly, Jim was right about the members. Almost all of them were artists of some description, many well-known and influential, and every last one doubtless simmering with the same slighted anger at Seabright having galloped off on their beloved hobby-horse. And it was also true, not only that money wasn't an issue – the group was fantastically well-off after two decades of generous donations – but that, in this post-Shakespeare age, none of the WAC's employees had anything better to do, either with their time or the organisation's funds. Indeed, by offering the members the olive branch of vengeance, perhaps she and the organising committee could make amends to those who felt the business with Seabright had been mishandled.

So no: the film-making practicalities were far from insurmountable. What was, however, truly daunting – to the point of hopelessness – was how in heaven's name they should find their Shakespeare.

'It can't be done,' she concluded. 'Even if there is a potential Shakespeare out there, it's simply impossible to search the population thoroughly or accurately enough to identify them.'

'Is it?' Jim had a twinkle in his eye. 'You really think it's *impossible*?'

There was silence around the table.

'Finish your drinks,' he urged. 'It's time to get to work.'

***

Having seen the President off aboard Air Force One, blood still pumping from the launch party, Joe collapsed into a poolside deckchair, ready to enjoy the fruits of his intensive labour.

He should really have checked the screenplay before the launch of the Cobley Crusade – just to make sure it really kicked, that nothing catastrophic had gone wrong with MET. But such was his enthusiasm to initiate the Cobleian revolution, he'd happily deferred reading *Triumph of the Solix* by a couple of days: hungry, after his confinement, to let off some steam by changing the world.

And boy, had the party rocked. From the President himself to the thousands who'd gathered in JoeTown, plus the millions who'd shown up at satellite parties around the world, the launch had gone down a total storm. Already, JoeCo's retail outlets were boasting record sales, surpassing even those registered at the dawn of a new *Solix Chronicles* movie. Everyone, everywhere wanted a slice of the Cobley pie.

'Joe?'

Grace appeared at the far end of the pool.

'Can I interrupt?' she asked.

Joe laid the screenplay on his belly. 'What's up?'

'It's Lester.'

'Oh really? What is it now?'

'He's dead.'

Joe had been all set to deliver a withering riposte. Instead, his mouth just hung limply open. 'Dead?'

'Unbelievable, I know,' said Grace. 'But there's been a fire at the DNA bank. All the assets are destroyed, along with Lester himself – and his son.'

'A fire?' said Joe. 'What kind of fire?'

'A big one,' said Grace. 'And it's pretty remote out there, so I guess—'

'But was it accidental – or arson?'

'Neither. Worse.'

Joe started in his deckchair, only to flop back down. *Worse than arson?*

'Suicide.'

Suicide? He felt faint. 'You're joking me.'

Grace took his hand, as Jerry strode onto the terrace, brandishing a piece of paper.

'Here . . .' he said. 'Lester posted a message on the web just before it started – coinciding with the Cobley Crusade launch.' He looked down. 'It says he can't bear to watch. That he's been driven mad by the shame of having conspired with us. That he feels like he's betrayed his late wife, and all the two of them stood for. "Quite simply, I can't tolerate the prospect of living to see the Cobley Crusade play out, overseen by . . ."' Jerry swallowed hard. '"Overseen by a God-forsaken philistine like Joe Seabright."'

Joe's numbness alchemised swiftly and irrevocably into anger. He released Grace's hand and slammed his fists into the plastic arms of his deckchair. Damn it all, not *once* had Howells treated him with the respect he deserved! Ever since their collaboration began, it had been insult after insult. Even now, as Joe embraced his responsibilities towards Tom Cobley and tried to right a grave historical injustice, Howells *still* failed to acknowledge his essential decency. Well, he was sorry, but as much as he grieved for Howells' *Chronicles*-loving son, no way was he going to waste a second of his precious time mourning such an incorrigibly pompous prig.

'Ok,' he said. 'Fine.' He picked up the screenplay.

'It is?' asked Grace.

'I refuse to weep for that condescending old bastard.'

'But what about the damage it might do to the project?'

'Damage? What damage? People are behind us every step of the way. The discovery has made us untouchable, and rightly so. Everyone wants us to win that Oscar, and Howells' actions only go to show what an impossible snob he always was.' He placed a cursory kiss on Grace's cheek. 'Seriously: it's no big deal.'

Grace looked uncertainly at Jerry.

'You're sure there's nothing we should do?' asked the producer.

Joe considered for a moment. 'Issue a brief statement,' he decided. 'Say we're grateful for the role he played in uncovering the truth about Shakespeare, and we're sorry his imagination didn't permit him to see that an everyday guy like me is exactly the type of fella who *should* be championing Cobley's cause.' He smiled. 'Regrets, JoeCo.'

'I'll put it out,' agreed Jerry. 'Then we'll take a first look at the pre-viz.'

Grace and Jerry headed indoors. Left alone, Joe munched on a doughnut as he read the first words on the page:

The Solix Chronicles V: Triumph of the Solix
by Joe Seabright

Third Draft, 2nd September, 2022

He turned over, returning his mind to the blank, black screen, place of infinite possibilities. Within moments, his eyes were skipping delightedly down the page, awed first by the opening crawl – exactly what he'd wanted all these months: punchy, poetic and tantalising – and then the first scene of Greathen conferring with the Solix Masters. At last, the sequence lived up to its epic billing. The twists were expertly dispatched, and the dialogue positively frothed with grandeur, leaving no doubt as to the universal power of the story at hand.

Line by unforgettable line, Joe forgot all extraneous concerns as Cobley's tremendous writing reeled him in. It didn't matter that he had already written the same story twice, or that he'd known the narrative for so many years before. This was a totally new experience. With teenage joy he abandoned himself to his beloved fantasy land for two whole hours until, tears streaming down his face as the Solix prevailed, he shut the script and burst out sobbing. Not a word, not the single tiniest detail, needed changing. Here was a movie as powerful, and as perfect, as it could possibly be.

There was no way he could fail.

Chapter 19

'I'm sure I needn't remind you of the details of my most recent presentation?'

Jim was speaking from the stage of the Globe's conference hall, to which a kind security guard had allowed them entry. The auditorium was empty but for Wendy, Keith, Clive and Pat in the front row.

'Anyone care to remind us?' he asked.

'It was piffle!' barked Pat. 'Utter codswallop!'

'Well . . .' Jim looked down at his computer, which was once again hooked up to the screen at the back of the stage. 'That's certainly what you claimed at the time.'

'And we stand by it now!' barracked Keith. 'All the more so, since we now know Shakespeare wasn't the author.'

'Ah!' Jim wagged his finger at Keith. 'Wrong. While most, if not all my other theories have indeed now been rendered redundant, this year's was different. This year's didn't seek to *prove* Shakespeare's claim. Rather, it sought to *discount* the alternatives.'

The details returned to Wendy: a ridiculously intricate numerical analysis of language, deployed in an elaborate game of authorial snap, comparing the mathematical imprint of different authorship candidates with that of the author of 'Shakespeare's' plays.

'I tried Bacon, Marlowe and Oxford,' recalled Jim. 'Ruled each of them out. Which tallies, yes? Which is in fact accurate.'

Wendy nodded on their collective behalf.

'What I never did, however, was test Cobley's diaries. If I had done, or indeed if I could do now...' He glanced sympathetically towards Keith. 'Then doubtless, according to my system, they would match.'

'You still have faith?' asked Keith.

A reflective frown crept across Jim's face as he glossed his hands over his head, smoothing the furry balls on either side.

'Well...' he replied. 'Initially, after my humiliation at conference, I shan't deny having my doubts. I feared that even though the method was different, my maths were just as fantastical as in previous years. As you rightly protested, not even the matches between Shakespeare extracts were exact and besides, who was I to claim authors couldn't change their skins? What proof had I that creativity was some kind of genetic absolute?'

Jim's words hung on the chilly air. *Genetic absolute*? Wendy had heard such talk elsewhere of late.

In a flurry of exchanged glances, the group realised what he was talking about.

'Grace Tremain!' yelled Clive.

'The Creativity Gene!' cried Keith.

'The Muse!' shouted Pat.

'Precisely!' Jim was grinning again. 'The discovery of the creative gene. Proof, I realised, that I *had* been on to something after all. Proof, indeed, that Grace Tremain and I discovered the muse simultaneously. Our only difference was coming at it in different ways. Whereas she mapped the muse's *biological* manifestation, its *cause*, I examined its effect – the mathematical, artistic imprint which, as proven by my comparisons between Cobley's plays, is every bit as constant as the muse's biological origins.'

Wendy was speechless, dazed not just that Jim, using his mathematical expertise alone, had matched the mighty Stanford geneticist in discovering the muse, but that her own anti-Stratfordian cynicism had stopped her making the connection sooner.

'Believing anew in my maths,' he resumed, 'I remembered Wendy's dream about finding a new Shakespeare, and returned to my old breakdowns. If only I could find some qualitative trend – some way of expressing mathematically that Tom Cobley's muse is more effective *per se* than, for example, Joe Seabright's – I would find the key to identifying a writer who can help us take our revenge.'

He dug into his bag and produced a pad of paper, which he passed to Wendy.

'I focused on reworking Shakespeare's – I mean *Cobley's* – data. Inventing new equations, combining, comparing, inverting... You name it, I tried the lot. All in the hope of paring the figures down, of finding some recurrent pattern whose constancy would identify it as the fingerprint of Cobley's muse.'

Wendy flicked through Jim's pad. Every page was plastered in obscure formulae and symbols.

'I knew it had to be there. I was convinced that if Grace Tremain could compact the chemical effects into a pill, I could distil its artistic imprint in a similar manner.' He took back the papers and plucked out the final sheet, waving it aloft. 'A week in, I uncovered it.'

Wendy sat forward. 'Uncovered what?'

'A ratio. A mysterious constant, which kept occurring in each of the various categories. Imagery, vocabulary, structure: this proportion was everywhere, whether in relative use of metaphor versus simile, dental versus plosive word sounds, or even the comparative length of speeches. Shot through it all was this *internal rhythm*, this *creative heartbeat*. Occasionally variable, but omnipresent as the nucleus round which everything else orbited.'

'And specific to him?' enquired Keith.

'That was the next challenge. I updated my old program so as well as gleaning the raw figures it would automatically calculate the formulas that yielded the constant ratios. I inputted some chunks of Chekhov and sure enough, the same constancy was evident. But, and a big but it is too, the ratio around which everything tended was *different* to Cobley's.'

There was an urgent, intrigued murmur from the onlookers.

'I did it again with Marlowe, then Miller, then Wilde, and the same thing happened. Every time a roughly constant ratio, but differing from one writer to the next.'

'Good Lord,' said Wendy. It was like the mysteries of the universe had just resolved themselves. 'But that's mind-blowing.'

'It was a start,' shrugged Jim. 'But it still wasn't what I was after: that qualitative expression of different writers' abilities. So then I calculated each writer's average ratio – the most accurate singular expression of their creative centre – and sought parity between it and their perceived quality.'

He tapped at his computer and the screen behind him came alive. On it was a list entitled 'Muse Ratios', with the names of several authors down the left, mirrored on the right by a column of ratios, each running to several decimal places.

'I figured the best way to discern any qualitative contrasts was to order them by reputation. So you have Cobley at the top, then Goethe, and so on – there's twenty in total – until you get to the utter dross, for which I downloaded a copy of *Rise of the Glozbacks*.'

Wendy laughed as she sought a pattern in the right-hand column. The hope was obviously to find a steady rise or fall, as in the points column of a league table, but she could see no recognisable trend.

'Hopeless, isn't it?' said Jim. 'However much you look, there's just no correlation.'

'So?' wondered Wendy.

'So taste *is* subjective after all. There's actually no scientific truth in saying Cobley is a better writer than Joe Seabright.' He smiled wryly. 'Except, of course, we all know that's not true.' Returning to his computer, the list disappeared from the screen. 'I went back and persisted, asking myself what other variables there could be – and before long I had my answer.'

'Which is?'

'The variations themselves. The variations *around* the mean muse ratio. The fact that, once I went beyond three or four decimal points, the constancy I derived from an author's figures was never absolute; that, though obviously trending towards a central point, the ratios for each aspect of their writing were all different – hence needing to calculate the average.' Jim was beaming now. 'What I should've realised earlier was that one average wasn't enough. What I needed was *another* average, this time representing how *much* a writer tended to diverge from his mean muse ratio.'

Wendy felt her cheeks reddening. 'And?'

'Bingo.' Jim hit a key and another list appeared on screen.

As before, the authors' names were listed on the left, with Cobley at the top and Joe Seabright at the bottom. But this time, on the right, were percentages: percentages which grew larger further down the list, from 0.008187% next to Cobley down to 0.142931% alongside Joe Seabright. The point being that the lower the number, the better the writer; the less his or her writing strayed from their mean muse ratio, the more *centred* they were, the more profound their work.

All of which, Wendy dizzily realised as she turned the thought on its head, offered a scientifically exact way of gauging any given author's abilities, just by inputting some of their writing into Jim's program. Precisely what was needed, in other words, to discover a new, living Shakespeare.

Overwhelmed, she climbed on stage and looked again at the screen, double checking the pattern. As the rest of the group gathered round, awestruck by the figures, she turned to Jim.

Bless his heart! They had mocked and maligned him for so long that she'd quite forgotten what a kind and clever man he really was. Here, however, was a reminder of such ingenuity and promise that she was already overflowing with regret for the disagreements of the past. Having understood the muse even more profoundly than Grace Tremain, Jim was not only giving them the means to wreak revenge on Seabright but, with it, the possibility of a new dramatic genius for them all to adore as they had done Shakespeare.

'You've bowled me over, Mr Withers,' she whispered in his ear. 'Well and truly bowled me over.'

Jim smiled back at her, eyes aflame with determination.

'This really is possible, isn't it?' she said. 'We really can do this.'

'Oh, yes,' came the reply. 'Oh, yes we bloody well can.'

Chapter 20

The sky was full of drizzle and, from the motion of the trees outside, he knew the wind was blowing a gale. But as Joe surveyed the soon-to-be-transformed green field on which his chopper was coming in to land, even the cruddy English weather couldn't dampen his spirits. If anything, indeed, the bleakness only made him more excited. The contrast between how it was now, and how it would be once JoeCo had completed its heroic act of empire-building, added yet further spice to his already pioneering relish.

The chopper touched ground and Joe lifted up his hood. Pulling the lever to release the door, he jumped onto the soggy ground, where three men awaited his arrival under a trio of JoeCo umbrellas.

'Mr Seabright!' bellowed one of the greeting-party, hand outstretched. 'A hundred welcomes. I'm Bob Price, Mayor of Milton Keynes. A delight to meet you.' He gestured into the distance. 'If you'd just follow me: the site is a short walk away.'

Gazing towards the Milton Keynes skyline, rising modestly on the horizon, Joe spotted the great cranes and floodlights towering over the Cobley Camp-to-be and set off over the squelchy ground, flanked by the Mayor's umbrella-wielding stooges.

'Apologies for our dismal English weather,' said the Mayor. 'Hand on heart, it's not always like this.'

'Fear not, my friend. The Park will soon bring with it some Californian sunshine to brighten your gloom.'

'I'm sure it will. And really, a million thank yous for all your wonderful work.'

Joe laughed. 'Don't thank me. Thank *Tom*. Really, it's a great story all on its own. I'm just the lucky guy who gets to tell it.'

'But you're telling it so *well*,' blushed the Mayor. 'And we really are grateful. For so long we here in Milton Keynes have struggled for respectability: a new town mocked for its newness.'

They scaled a small incline and the site came fully into view: as yet, nothing more spectacular than a 500-acre wasteland, with a few temporary structures at the centre, but full of promise nonetheless.

'Thanks to you, that snobbery is no more.' The Mayor led them towards the perimeter fence. 'What you've done, see, is given us *history*. And that's all we ever needed, a dash of history. Something to make people realise that the village from which we grew has much proud history to its name: the proudest of all, indeed. The Bard in our very blood.'

'That's good to hear.' Joe's insides were glowing as once again he heard how his discovery was improving others' lives. This really was *the* biggest-hearted thing he'd ever done. Sure, *Chronicles* had been mighty successful, but its purpose was mainly to entertain. It had given a few people jobs, and made a lot of people happy, but even Joe knew it was ultimately more about enjoyment than enrichment.

With the Cobley Crusade, however, it was different. Outwardly it was still a leisure industry based on folks having a good time, from babies toying with their *Romeo and Juliet* dolls, to kids making mischief in a Malvolio play cell, and adults relaxing with Cobley Canon Top Trumps. But what distinguished it was the overriding goal of correcting history: of good old-fashioned American justice coming in to sort out someone else's mess. However big or small a customer's investment in the Cobley cause – whether purchasing a Cobley Pencil in their local stationery store, starting a new job at a Cobley attraction, or handing over a thousand bucks to buy the rights to stage one of Cobley's plays – they knew, as they made that commitment, they were also doing something more: contributing to a global revolution, headed inexorably towards the 2025 Oscars, to overturn the greatest cultural crime the world had ever known.

And as that contagious virtue made people feel good – *so* good that the Cobley Crusade had *already* earned more merch money than the entire *Rise of the Glozbacks* campaign – it made Joe feel even better. The intoxicating righteousness had grown exponentially to the point where now, as he stepped through the open gate and stood atop the stairs, surveying the scene below, he could scarcely believe the magnitude of his achievement. How supremely beautiful it would look once his dream was realised, with lakes, parks and exhibition tents surrounding the massive Cobley Dome, home to the museum and all its component rides.

'Wow,' he murmured proudly to himself. 'Tom Cobley, you really *are* the man.'

'If you'd just follow me . . .' The Mayor was trotting ahead. 'The people are all ready and waiting.'

Lifted from his philanthropic reverie, Joe followed the Mayor. One of the flunkies placed a hard hat on his head as they crossed the excavated earth to the specially-erected stage that stood between four grandstands, packed with a mix of *Chronicles* fanatics, Tom Cobley obsessives – for such there were already – and passionate locals.

'Ladies and gentlemen . . .'

The cheers echoed round the makeshift arena – 'Time for Tom!' 'We love you Joe!' – and Joe had to step back a moment to let the enthusiasm subside.

'Ladies and gentlemen,' he resumed finally. 'I just don't know what to say.'

That was a bit of a lie. He most certainly did know what to say, and proceeded to say it over the course of an entire hour. First, he reported back on how amazingly the first phase of Cobley merchandise had been received, promising that JoeCo's finest were working overtime to satisfy the demands of their Cobley-crazed public. Then, he proudly unveiled the next round of goodies, the highlight of which was the much-requested Cobley video game: a virtual reality, puzzle-platform escapade in which one could play either Shakespeare or Cobley in a dash across Elizabethan London, the bittersweet premise being that Cobley had escaped from Shakespeare's clutches, and was trying to convince a disbelieving world of his crazy story. Finally, Joe talked more about the Cobley Camp – what it would contain, and how determined he was to bring happiness and prosperity to a town whose true worth, like Cobley himself, had been so unjustly overlooked.

Speech over, he alighted from the stage and waded into the trenches. Steps heavy amid the mud, strides short from turning, every few seconds, to acknowledge the ongoing ovation – 'We want Justice for Tom, Justice for Tom, NOW!' – it was a good few minutes before he arrived at the enclosure where a small portion of wall had already been constructed.

'And here it is!' he smiled, watching a small yellow crane chug into position, inching the cornerstone forward until it hovered above the appointed gap in the brickwork.

Joe steadied the stone and examined the inscription. 'Cobley Camp Foundation Stone,' he read. 'Laid on the 24th September 2022 by Joe Seabright, creator of *The Solix Chronicles* and discoverer of the Shakespeare Fraud, in loving memory of the great Tom Cobley. "May the Park be testament to your living memory, so that justice be done, and you no longer languish in deceitful oblivion. With love and respect, Joe Seabright."'

Joe lowered the stone into position, heart swelling with pride as the applause resounded. He took a trowel from Jake Walker, the JoeCo stalwart he'd sent over to run the Cobley Camp, and smoothed the cement. Job done, he stepped back and bowed in reverence, keen to show this wasn't about him: that the real star was the genius, late of this Parish, who gave such wonders to the world.

As the cameras flashed and the tears flowed freely – tears of a town finally coming to recognise its greatness, and of a man finally achieving the acclaim he deserved – it felt like a fitting sequel to the more funereal events of the day before. Then, Joe had visited Westminster Abbey to see the Memorial Statue of William Shakespeare in Poets' Corner ousted by a statue of Tom Cobley: one which, sculpted by JoeCo model-makers, depicted the great man at work in his cell. Overhanging the sculpture was an American flag; hidden beneath were Tom Cobley's remains, freshly exhumed the day before in Milton Keynes.

It had all been stirring enough, but very much about the past: an apologetic setting-right of the dual crimes of Shakespeare's villainy and history's neglect. Today's events, on the other hand, were all about the *future*; about helping to resuscitate the great man's living memory, and ensuring it was sustained, via the Cobley Camp, into the years, decades and centuries to come.

'Shakespeare is dead!' shouted Joe, raising his hands as the clouds overhead dispersed to reveal a radiant sun. 'Long live Tom Cobley!'

'Three cheers for Joe Seabright!' cried a voice in response, to which the crowd hip-hip-hoorayed their lungs out.

Joe laughed, pointing at the foundation stone. 'Really, it was all him.'

'Sir,' said the Mayor, 'a zillion apologies, but Jake says we need to press on.'

Waving at the crowds, Joe headed towards a makeshift gazebo that had been assembled a short distance away. It was here that he was to spend the rest of the day, signing copies of the *Complete Cobley* and meeting Cobley's fans.

'Do please let us know when you've had enough,' said the Mayor. 'We'll happily make your excuses for you.'

'Had enough?!' laughed Joe. 'Mister Mayor, you have *no* idea.'

It was true. While others might have viewed such a marathon signing session as a chore, Joe knew that Tom would want him to soak up as much love as possible, drinking down the fervour of the British intelligentsia, the most discerning critics there were, in recompense for all those years his genius went unrecognised.

And yet scarcely had he got halfway to the gazebo than a scuffle in one of the grandstands distracted him. Focusing on the commotion, he saw a raincoated figure leap over the security barricades, brush aside the guards' resistance, and make directly for him.

'I shouldn't worry, sir,' said the Mayor. 'Just an over-zealous autograph-hunter.'

But Joe knew the Mayor was wrong. 'Trust me,' he muttered. 'The last thing this woman wants is an autograph.'

***

'Delightful to see you again!' chirped Wendy.

'Good to see you too,' said Seabright, looking immediately vulnerable.

'No need to fret.' Wendy cracked an enigmatic smile, then offered her hand in peace. 'I just wanted to say well done on all you've achieved.'

Seabright glanced around as if seeking confirmation of her sincerity. With none forthcoming, he could only accept the surprise rapprochement.

'Well, I wasn't expecting this,' he began, shaking Wendy's hand. 'But hey: I guess I was wrong about you—'

He broke off as Wendy tightened her grip, morphing her smile into a scowl.

'Step this way.' She dragged the lumbering Yank back towards the podium. 'And before you think about calling your flunkeys to restrain me, know that any such attempt will only play into my hands.'

Seabright took her at her word. As she stepped onto stage unopposed, the gasps in the stands went off like muted fireworks, ignited in quick, quivering succession. To think that this interloper should be stealing Seabright's thunder with such audacity: well, imagine! It was a timely taste of his own medicine, with plenty more still to come.

She deposited Seabright by her side. With the world's media watching, she trusted he would never dare run away, either physically or indeed from the challenge she was about to issue.

'First, my apologies for interrupting the day's events,' she began, settling at the microphone. 'I'm sorry it muddles the day's itinerary . . .' She stared into one of the several cameras trained on the podium. 'And I regret, too, if it upsets any TV schedules.'

She took a deep breath, trying to conquer the adrenalin that surged through her.

'My name is Wendy Preston. I am the founder of the Worldwide Authorship Circle: an international charity, based in the UK, which has spent twenty years debating the authorship of Shakespeare's plays. It was one of our members – a relative of the man himself, no less – who first uncovered the evidence suggesting Tom Cobley wrote "Shakespeare's" plays. It was us who gathered hair samples from the leading candidates, Cobley included. And it was also us who helped Mr Seabright prove that Tom Cobley wrote the plays.' She smiled down the camera. 'But then you presumably knew all that already.' She frowned. 'Or did you? Actually, now I think of it, you probably didn't. Why? Because not only is Mr Seabright cheerfully reaping the fruits that were ours by rights, he has failed to give us any credit *whatsoever*: neither for keeping the debate alive over all these years, nor for helping him discover the truth.'

She glanced at Seabright, busy sulking by her side, and then into the crowds. There was the odd angry expression, but on the whole people looked engaged and intrigued.

'But we are not here to cry over what's past. We are not here to derail the Cobley Crusade. We recognise that JoeCo, and through JoeCo the United States of America, owns the Cobley rights, and despite his being English by origin, despite having a direct descendent in our ranks in the shape of Keith Cobley . . .' She gestured to Keith, watching from the stands. 'There is no earthly way we're going to wrest them back.' She peered bullet-straight at a camera. 'But what we do intend to do – what is only fair – is to offer Seabright and Cobley a challenge.'

A murmur broke out in the grandstands.

'For want of any stake in the Cobleian revolution we brought about, we propose to find our own, present-day Tom Cobley.

The best author currently alive in this country: a brand new genius for us to champion, and a replacement national poet for the one we've lost to the Yanks. Then, once we have found him or her, we shall have them write a film to go head-to-head with Tom Cobley at the Oscars – doing all we can to deny him victory.'

The grandstands fell silent. Many cupped their hands to their mouths as all eyes fell on Joe Seabright, his gaze cast down at the rubbly earth. The big oaf was plainly boiling with anger, but recognised that answering back would only work in her favour.

'Now I know that, from a certain perspective, it seems shocking, insensitive even, to try to deny Cobley his moment of glory after all this time. But even if you've been mad enough to buy in to JoeCo's cultural vandalism – if you're American, say, or a resident of Milton Keynes – then you must see it's best that someone offers Tom worthy competition. After all, what good the Oscar, how meaningful the *justice*, if that victory is a mere coronation?'

She glanced again at Seabright, who was glowing scarlet. Evidently, an uncontested coronation was exactly what he wanted.

'Far better to have a clean, close fight,' she said. 'That way, when – or rather *if* – Tom Cobley wins, the victory will really mean something.'

The hum from the stands intensified, evolving into a sound of unmistakable approval. Encouraged, Wendy kicked on, eyes flitting from one camera to the next.

'Now I'm sure you're all wondering why we felt it necessary to come and announce this now. After all, if we want to challenge Tom and Joe, why not just get on with it? We don't need anyone's permission, so why sabotage Mr Seabright's – I mean, Mr *Cobley's* – special day?'

She rubbed her hands together in anticipation.

'Well, let me explain. For this to happen as it should, it is vital that in judging our respective writers, the Academy are comparing like with like. Otherwise, the very essence of our head-to-head "challenge" is undermined. And where would be the fun in that?'

Seabright managed a reluctant nod of agreement.

'It's therefore only appropriate that our film should tell exactly the same story as Tom's own: that is, the finale of *The Solix Chronicles.*'

'What?' exclaimed Seabright.

'I know it sounds batty,' continued Wendy calmly. 'But not only is it the obvious option, the very nature of this film makes it a perfect test: two films, both starting in the same place and concluding with the required happy ending. Two films, in other words, to be judged on storytelling alone.'

The crowd was growing ever more vociferous. The sci-fi geeks in particular were roaring with glee: two *Chronicles* films for the price of one!

'I'm glad you approve, but as you'll appreciate, for this to happen we do in fact need permission after all: specifically, permission to use all the *Solix Chronicles* trademarks – places, characters, spaceships . . .' She turned to Seabright. 'What do you say? Will you allow us the liberty? Do you accept the challenge?'

Seabright gazed round, his measured expression twitching as the incandescence fought through the veneer. Fully exposed before a bank of cameras and journos, he was vulnerable to her every whim and had no choice. He forced a smile and shook her hand, eliciting a huge cheer from the grandstands.

She spun back to face the cameras. 'And so it is decided. So the hunt begins. For this to work we're going to need the assistance of every grown man and woman in the UK.'

Gesturing for silence – conscious that now she really *was* hijacking Seabright's party – she assumed her best wartime pose and stared soberly into the camera.

'What we ask is perfectly straightforward. All you need do is visit our website at any point within the next two months and tell us what you had for breakfast in no fewer than five, fully-formed sentences. Don't make any special effort. Just hammer it out, and click submit.'

An intense, curious silence gripped the building site and, Wendy imagined with excitement, the nation as a whole. Everyone was marvelling how on earth they could judge so much based on so little. Heavens, even Seabright seemed uncharacteristically numbed by the weird, wonderful mystery of it all.

'I can't explain any more at the moment,' she teased, 'but rest assured our methods are judicious in the extreme. If there is someone out there as good as or *better* than Cobley – if that person is you...' She pointed, Churchill-like, at the camera marked 'BBC'. 'Then we *will* uncover your genius. We *will* win you that Oscar.'

***

Joe couldn't believe his ears as Preston stepped back from the microphone and soaked up a burst of applause as loud, if not louder, than that lavished on him just before. People were so goddamn fickle! Gritting his teeth, he only just managed the requisite grin as the photographers shouted their requests from the foot of the stage, forcing the two of them to adopt a sparring stance in readiness for the fight ahead.

How had this been allowed to happen? How had Preston even been allowed into the confines of the Cobley Camp? It had been one of Joe's specific requests that eyes be kept open for an embittered old spinster wanting revenge. And yet still the morons running the Cobley Camp had managed to screw up. Boy, oh, boy – someone was going to pay for this.

'Smile,' whispered Preston, alerting Joe to the grimace that had smothered his grin. He rediscovered the latter just as the barrage of photography subsided and the two of them relaxed their stupid pose to exchange one final handshake.

'May the best film win,' said Preston.

Mustering more grace than she deserved, Joe reciprocated her best wishes before leaving the stage, heading without pause to the awaiting gazebo. He was determined to get his head straight back in the game, doing right by Cobley by fulfilling his signing commitments as thoroughly as he'd originally planned.

But even as he took his seat, his focus was not on the adoring queue snaked out in front, but on the equally busy huddle round Preston: a scrum which included photographers, TV reporters and notepad-wielding journalists by the dozen.

Thumping his fist on the table, Joe barked for his pen and, without looking up, took the first *Complete Cobley* and scrawled 'Best wishes, Joe Seabright / Much love, Tom Cobley' on the title page. He let the ink dry, then turned to the contents and read the list of Cobley's plays in an effort to calm his ...

His what, exactly? Anger? Fear? Embarrassment? His eyes flicked down the page: *Hamlet, Macbeth, King Lear, Othello* ...

Why the hell was he letting her get to him? Sure, it was shameful of Preston to pull that stunt in public. Yes, her persistence was *really* beginning to irritate him. And boy, how he wished he hadn't had to accept their crazy challenge. But in terms of their actual aim, he told himself, continuing down the list – *Twelfth Night, Romeo and Juliet, A Midsummer Night's Dream* – *surely* he had nothing to fear.

'Cobley is the pinnacle, right?' he said aloud, handing the book to its proud new owner. 'Cobley *is* perfection?'

'Don't you doubt it for a second, Mr Seabright,' grinned the sweaty, bespectacled nerd, clad in a *Glozbacks* raincoat. 'Nobody else comes close.'

Chapter 21

'Oh my,' said Jim, appearing at the door to Wendy's office. 'You look dazzling.'

'Hah!' chortled Wendy. 'Chance would be a fine thing!'

Securing her earrings, she headed to the mirror, adjusted the top of her dress, and peered down at the heels she'd bought especially for the occasion. It was a curse how they cramped her toenails but, hey-ho, to hell with it. With the eyes of the world on them, she had to make the effort – at least this once.

Grabbing her handbag and switching off the light, she took Jim's proffered arm and stepped into the open plan office which, while quiet tonight, had been a dizzying whirl of activity since they moved in two months previously.

'Can I just say,' began Wendy, stopping by the window that looked out across the moonlit park. 'Can I just . . .'

Jim stared back in puzzlement. He was himself something of a picture in his newly-purchased DJ – a replacement for the one he'd had ever since college.

'Go on,' he smiled, oblivious to any awkwardness. 'Can you just?'

'I just realised . . .' The nerves and tiredness made it hard to speak coherently. 'All I mean is, it occurred to me earlier when we were rehearsing that I hadn't ever thanked you. Not properly. For coming back and giving us purpose.'

Jim swatted away her gratitude. 'You don't need to thank me. I'm as chuffed as anyone about what we're up to. Besides, the last few weeks have been far too hectic to let sentiment interfere.

There'll be time enough for that once we've won the blasted Oscar.'

And with that he was off, striding out of the office while Wendy, trying not to trip, followed him down the stairs to the ground floor.

He was right to ward off premature self-congratulation. Today marked the climax to only the first phase of their project, and the real toil – to make, market and release a *Solix Chronicles* movie – was still ahead. But even so, Wendy couldn't help feeling a smidgen of pride at how tremendously it had gone so far. From the second they sabotaged Seabright at Milton Keynes, it was clear that their gamble stood a decent chance of paying off; that the challenge of finding an all-new Shakespeare, fused with the chance that 'it could be you', even if 'you' had never written a word before, had ignited people's imaginations.

In part it was thanks to the sheer simplicity of their invitation – just write five unadorned sentences and, with unprecedented mathematical accuracy, the WAC would identify the best there was. But soon that elementary appeal was reinforced by the even more powerful incentive of national pride. By pitching their rhetoric as patriotically as possible, the WAC's sob story grew seamlessly into a sense of countrywide injustice. Before long, their angry determination was shared by people throughout the land.

The media helped. Seizing on the group's status as a bunch of wronged underdogs – just as badly treated as the enslaved Tom Cobley himself – the press both depicted and defined the unfolding cultural war. The atmosphere turned almost warlike in its defiance. The Prime Minister decreed it every citizen's duty to describe what they had for breakfast, and encourage those around them to do the same. As entries poured in through the WAC's new website, the resistance gathered pace, and commentators called for a nationwide boycott of the Cobley Crusade: a defiance splendidly exemplified by the Bank of England, who reversed their decision to reprint all Shakespeare-branded banknotes in Cobley's image, declaring that to do so would legitimise the Yanks' unsporting act of misappropriation. Instead, they'd wait until the WAC had declared a winner, and do him or her the honour instead.

The whole thing thrived because it so clearly occupied the moral high ground. Not for them unsavoury legal wrangling over the rightful ownership of Tom Cobley. Rather, a more mature approach, responding to the loss by seeking something better to take its place. The nation, as a whole, just 'got' it. As people turned their backs on Seabright's tat, some refusing even to stage Cobley's plays lest it be misconstrued as surrender, only Milton Keynes exempted itself from the nationalistic fervour: a lonely outpost of pro-Seabright Americana; a 51st state with the Cobley Camp as its capital.

Having worked hard to establish this supportive backdrop, it was with real self-belief that the WAC had set about meeting the logistical challenges of their plan. First, the question of staffing: how to assemble a fully-fledged film production company in a matter of months? It was a petrifying task, but rendered significantly easier after over a thousand WAC members offered to leave their existing jobs and dedicate themselves full-time to the mission: confirmation that a huge majority of authorship sceptics were indeed artists by trade, and that their smouldering anger at Seabright's behaviour – both his betrayal, and the crassness with which he was selling Cobley to the world – was a powerful motivation.

All Wendy had to do was hire the most experienced of the four film producers who applied, and invite them to begin building the rest of the team. From there, the main difficulty was a welcome one, with the sheer wealth of talent meaning many ended up disappointed, unable to play a paid role in the production.

The next step had been to purchase the property that formerly belonged to the Royal Shakespeare Company in Stratford. While the Globe struggled on in London, grudgingly co-operating with JoeCo, the one-mighty RSC had crumbled within days of Seabright's seizing the Cobley copyright, unable to stage any more productions without JoeCo's consent – permission which would never be forthcoming, since Seabright saw it as the Cobley Crusade's duty to reduce Shakespeare and Stratford to the status of reviled historical footnotes.

All of which made Stratford a shoo-in as the WAC's new HQ. Not only was the RSC's deserted property cheap enough to afford – its warehouses and principal playing space, the Royal Shakespeare Theatre, providing all the studio room they needed – but there was also a profound spiritual connection. For just as Seabright had stolen the WAC's soul, he had ripped the heart out of Stratford: a town whose dependence on the Shakespeare industry had been so all-consuming that its shops, cafés and hotels had rapidly followed the RSC into closure. Any simmering resentment that the WAC had contributed to the town's demise was comfortably outweighed by solidarity. As the Mayor had remarked on welcoming them to their new premises, the town was united in hoping their arrival would restore its purpose and prosperity.

As the weeks went by, and they began planning the structural changes required to create a viable film-making centre, the WAC's new premises began to feel ever more like home. There was much left to do, but the progress already made meant they'd be able to start pre-production before the screenplay was even complete – crucial, if they were going to have their film released in time for the 2025 Oscars.

And yet, for all the giant strides they'd strode, nothing quite compared to what lay ahead this evening. In front of a worldwide audience of millions, they were about to take the 49,648,324 responses received before that morning's deadline – a mind-boggling total, representing over 95% of the adult population – and ask Jim's amazing program to analyse each one, until finally revealing the name of the greatest writer currently alive in the UK.

Stepping into the cold Stratford night, Wendy and Jim were met by a huddle of well-wishers who accompanied them on the short walk to the stage door of the Royal Shakespeare Theatre. As the expectant chatter flowed back and forth, Wendy's nerves flared up like never before, even while reminding herself that tonight was far from an *actual* be-all-and-end-all. Yes, the all-important selection was about to be made, but nothing more. After tonight the world would be no wiser as to the ultimate wisdom of their plan: whether their winner was worse than, as good as or, heaven knows, *better* than Tom Cobley. That wouldn't be established until the 2025 Oscars, when the Academy would decide whether Tom Cobley's *Triumph of the Solix* confirmed his standing as the greatest writer ever known – or if the WAC's equivalent effort, penned by TBC, did in fact prove that comparable geniuses were out there, just waiting to make themselves heard, if only one bothered to look.

It didn't have to be so, of course. If desired, they could have used today's ceremony not just to unveil a winner, but to disclose whether his or her Divergence Percentage was higher or lower, better or worse, than Tom Cobley's DP of 0.008187%. But since their mission was aimed squarely at the Oscars, it was only right that the Academy be allowed to make its judgement unrestrained by knowledge of the maths. Besides which, Wendy for one was having such a ball she didn't want to run the risk of discovering, this early on, that even the best writer alive couldn't come close to Tom Cobley.

Shivering from cold and anxiety, she and Jim approached the harsh bright light of the stage door.

'Hurry up!' urged Clive, appearing out of the shadows to guide her into the bowels of the famous old theatre. 'We've less than a minute to go.'

Crikey, she thought, gesturing for Jim to keep up. She'd wanted to cut her arrival fine so the nerves didn't multiply to the point where she did something buffoonish. But less than a minute? That was fine indeed.

They arrived in the wings, the crowd's murmur filling the air with anticipation. Wendy looked round for reassurance. Amid the backstage gloom, she just made out the rest of the committee. As ragtag a mix as ever, they were scattered on stools, chairs and flight cases. Each looked terrifically concentrated.

She peered at the stage. A pool of white light illuminated a table, telephone, microphone and computer.

'All set, Miss Preston,' declared a runner, arriving at her side and hastily applying some make-up for the TV cameras. 'Going live in ten, nine, eight, seven . . .'

Wendy felt Jim arrive by her side.

'Six, five, four . . .'

She took a deep breath.

'Three, two, one.'

'Go get 'em,' whispered Jim in her ear, following through with a tingly little kiss.

***

'Love it,' said Joe, somehow managing to sound glum and gleeful at once. 'As much as I hate it, I kind of love it too.'

Sitting in the lounge of his mansion, sipping a cold beer as events unfolded on his 70-inch TV, Joe couldn't deny the power of the spectacle. Sure, there wasn't quite enough glitz for his taste – it lacked the frenzied operatic thunder he'd have favoured – but glitz was nothing without good drama, and the WAC had drama in abundance. As Wendy Preston stood on the stage, backed by a giant screen which, at the press of a key, would shortly throw up the name of the finest writer currently alive in the UK, Joe was man enough to admit he felt a pang of envy at the theatre of it all.

It was just a pang, however. Though there was fun in the fight, the novelty of the WAC's leech-like persistence had long since faded. Their outrageous decision to challenge Cobley had not only dented the Crusade in *the* key overseas market – albeit prompting a converse rise in US business – but there did exist a chance of their actually finding a writer superior to Tom Cobley. Statistically, it was massively unlikely – if the whole of time hadn't thrown up a better writer, the likelihood of one being alive, right now, in the UK, was negligible – but if those odds ever could be overturned, then Jim Withers' fearsomely exact math meant the Brits were well-placed to do so.

'Oh, baby.' Grace squeezed onto the couch beside him. 'Keep calm. Have faith in the old man Tom.'

'With the 49,648,324 responses loaded into the system,' said Wendy Preston on screen, 'it's time for the test to begin. When I hit return, Jim Withers' groundbreaking maths will get to work, deducing every person's Mean Muse Ratio, and then calculating the degree to which, on average, the different aspects of their writing vary from that central ratio. The one with the lowest average variance will then be revealed as our winner.'

She reached out towards her computer. 'Here we go . . .'

'Look at her shaking!' cried Jerry, perched on the arm of the couch.

Preston's hand was indeed quivering. Even though today's events had been designed only to reveal the winning writer, and not how he compared to Cobley, you could see the pressure in her eyes: the knowledge that, for all the challenges still ahead, this was the moment in which their fate would be sealed.

Suddenly galvanised, grinning at the camera like a deranged granny, Preston thumped the button. Behind her, on the plain white screen, a number appeared, quickly rising to 100,000.

Joe watched in silent fascination. The climb of the number was interspersed with cutaways of anxious faces in the crowd, suggesting the tension in the Royal Shakespeare Theatre matched the mood in Joe's lounge. Not a word was said as the number crept past 1,000,000, then on towards 10,000,000, before a minute or so later reaching 40,000,000.

Joe put down his beer and sat forward on the couch. The total hit home at last.

'This is it!' He grabbed Grace's knee as the number disappeared.

'And the winner is . . .' said Preston.

For about ten seconds there was nothing. Then, finally, a name appeared: one which was both familiar, apt – and yet heart-stoppingly strange.

'William Shakespeare.'

***

Wendy stared at the screen.

William Shakespeare. The name rattled round her head, making no sense. She turned to the computer, half expecting it to display something different, but there again were the words.

'William Shakespeare.'

A collective gasp worked its way round the audience, followed by a murmur, gathering itself like a wave. She looked into the wings for assistance.

'It must be a mistake,' she said.

Jim came running out. 'A ghost in the machine,' he agreed.

Killing the screen so only they could see what he was doing, Jim cross-referred data between several windows, before rewinding the process and regenerating the result.

'William Shakespeare.'

He looked up at Wendy. 'Everything has worked perfectly.'

'But what does it mean?'

'What does it mean?'

'William Shakespeare.'

Jim turned back to the screen, as if struck anew by the absurdity of it. No sooner had Joe Seabright rid the world of one genius named William Shakespeare than another appeared in his wake!

'That's our result,' he said simply. 'William Shakespeare: the best adult writer currently living in the UK.'

If Jim said it, it must be true. Wendy turned to the microphone.

'The winner is: William Shakespeare.'

There was a short burst of applause, stubbornly refusing to take off into a proper ovation.

'A pseudonym!' exclaimed Jim suddenly. 'That must be it. Some wag who thought it'd be fun to put a fake name in.'

It was as good a suggestion as any. Wendy retrieved the winner's phone number and grabbed the phone. It still seemed coincidental that this particular joker had won, but there were presumably thousands who'd had the same idea.

'Just calling him now,' she said into the microphone. 'First question: what is your real name?!'

There was a roar of relieved laughter as the audience acknowledged the likely solution to what had initially seemed so spooky.

She waited for an answer, but no ringing tone sounded. Instead, there was an ascending beep, followed by an error message.

'The number you have dialled does not exist.'

She hung up. 'It seems,' she sighed, 'the number given by our William Shakespeare was in fact a fake.'

There was a communal groan inside the theatre, amplified in her head as she imagined the millions watching on TV. This really *was* a balls-up. Such a sophisticated system, yet no way of double-checking the phone numbers people were supplying.

'Second best,' whispered Jim.

'What?'

'If we can't reach the best, we'll have to use the second best.'

It was unsatisfactory, but they had no choice. She stepped aside, allowing Jim access to the computer, and was about to announce their new plan when Clive ran on from the wings, brandishing her mobile phone.

'Call for you!'

'What?' Wendy glared at him, embarrassment pressing upon her from all sides. 'Can't you see I'm busy?'

'Everyone knows you're busy,' said Clive. 'That's why any call, right now, must be important.'

She grabbed the telephone.

'Hello?'

'This is William Shakespeare.'

The blood rushed to her cheeks.

'Mr Shakespeare,' she blurted out.

Jim looked up. The noise in the room died.

'Put me on speaker,' said the voice: soft, deep, urgent and English. 'Hold me up to the microphone, so everyone can hear.'

Wendy did as she was told. 'Thank you for phoning.'

'It's my pleasure.'

'Perhaps you might begin by telling us your real name?'

There was a moment's silence. 'Why do you think I gave a fake number? Why do you think *I'm* calling *you*?'

Wendy looked at the screen of her mobile. The number was withheld.

'I assumed your name was a joke,' she said. 'You can't actually mean you don't want to be known?'

'That's exactly what I mean.'

Wendy couldn't think quick enough. Of all the things that could have gone wrong...

'May I ask why?'

'Of course,' came the courteous response. 'I am, I regret to say, rather shy. I detest being the subject of scrutiny, and though I greatly enjoy writing – which I have done for many years privately – I do not wish to be invaded by sudden celebrity.'

'You don't want to write our film?'

'I would be honoured to write your film.'

'But you won't do us the politeness of saying who you really are?'

'Under no circumstances.'

Amid Wendy's confusion, an impatient anger was starting to focus her thoughts.

'What if I said the invitation to write our film is entirely contingent on you revealing your true identity?'

'In that case, with regret, I'd have to decline.'

'Even if we'd promise to look after you?'

'Even then.'

'There'd be no pressure to do anything embarrassing. No pressure to do anything but write our script.'

'Perhaps not,' said Shakespeare. 'But why then do you need to know who I am at all?'

Wendy had argued herself into a corner. 'Because, I think, people are curious.'

'And that's why it frightens me. It's hard to contain curiosity nowadays. I appreciate your assurances, but privacy is not something you can guarantee. There would always be the risk of it turning into something more than I am comfortable with, and neither I – nor my family – want to risk that kind of intrusion.'

In keeping with his ranking as the best writer in the land, Shakespeare was clearly a smart cookie. With the 'family' thrown into the mix, Wendy had no reasonable comeback. But then again, her curiosity wasn't a question of reason. He could argue all he liked, but there was something illogical in her that needed to know who she was dealing with; that could no more live with his anonymity than he could live without it. Furthermore, given their history together, she believed that others in the group would share her convictions.

'I'm afraid I must stick by my guns, Mr Shakespeare,' she said. 'We haven't organised this – and the other 49 million people haven't submitted their entries – just to have their curiosity denied by your timidity.' She looked to Jim, who nodded back, endorsing her conviction. 'If you're not interested in helping us, then we are fully prepared to look elsewhere.'

There was hesitation at the end of the line. Shakespeare hadn't expected her to dig in.

'Are you sure that's sensible?' he asked.

'It may not be sensible, but that's the way it has to be. Call us weak-minded, but we've waited a long time for this. We all want to know who you are, and if you won't tell us—'

'You don't think your endeavours will be undermined by settling for second best?'

'Perhaps. But not as much as by your remaining anonymous.'

'But it's such an honourable undertaking . . .' persisted Shakespeare. Wendy sensed he was arguing more with himself than her. 'What you're seeking to achieve. Avenging Joe Seabright for what he stole . . .'

'You don't need to tell us, Mr Shakespeare. We're all on the same page. It's only you who is throwing a spanner in the works.'

Shakespeare sighed, and Wendy knew her defiance was paying off. He prized his anonymity highly, but he prized participation higher still.

'Wendy – may I call you Wendy?'

'May I call you Will?'

'Of course.' He laughed, a little unconvincingly. 'Wendy: may I speak frankly?'

'Please do.'

'My shyness, as I call it. I don't think it's an entirely selfish thing. I think it's also prudent. For you, I mean, as much as for me.'

'How so?'

'Because I worry the quality of writing would suffer as a result of all the attention.'

'That needn't be true.'

Shakespeare sighed. 'Well, all I can do is say how I feel. Already I find myself a little – what's the word? – *burdened* by this knowledge that I'm the best writer in the land. I worry the weight of expectation will stop me reaching my full potential. And I can only imagine how that pressure would increase if I was constantly being watched.'

Wendy no longer felt so sure-footed.

'I can't speak for others, of course. But my worry would be that anyone – second best, third best, fourth best – would suffer in the same way, no matter how outgoing they think they are. The pressure's going to be intense.'

Wendy turned to Jim. 'Is he right? Could it really make a difference?'

Jim looked unsure. 'Even the greatest artists sometimes succumb to pressure.'

'But isn't creativity a constant?'

'The *potential*, yes. But there may be other things that interfere in its actual delivery.'

'So how about a compromise?' continued Shakespeare. 'I stay anonymous while I write the script and you make the film. Then, if together we do in fact win the Oscar, I promise – on my son's life – that I will express my gratitude by revealing my true identity, there and then, on the night of the ceremony.'

Wendy stared into the blackness of the auditorium. 'I'm not sure . . .'

'What's not to like? I get time to prepare for life in the spotlight; you get the best possible script – the best possible chance of beating Joe Seabright – as well as finding out who I really am.'

Wendy looked to Jim, who whispered in her ear.

'He's the best there is, and he wants us to win. We should do as he says.'

'It's a deal,' said Wendy.

A burst of applause from the audience confirmed that they were happy too: that it was more important to recruit the best writer, and guarantee themselves the best script, than to satisfy their short-term curiosity.

'We look forward to working with you,' she said.

'Likewise,' said Shakespeare. 'When do you need the screenplay by?'

'Four months' time.'

'Very good. You'll have it in three.'

He hung up, and was gone.

***

Joe stood up and switched off the TV.

'So that's our guy,' he said, looking at Grace and Jerry, both of whom appeared spent, exhausted from the drama of it all. 'Tom Cobley versus William Shakespeare. Round two.'

He grabbed a doughnut, cracked open another beer, and paced up and down the *Chronicles* carpet. Joe didn't much like a coward. He'd have far preferred to know who he was fighting.

'William Shakespeare,' he reflected, in between mouthfuls. 'You've got to think pretty highly of yourself—'

'It was a joke, honey,' said Grace.

'He said so himself,' agreed Jerry.

Joe took a long swig of beer. 'The greatest writer alive in the UK today.'

He looked out at his pool, tummy tense with worry. There was something about this man Shakespeare – his manner, his mystery, perhaps even something he'd said – that, in Joe's fearful imagination, seemed to tip the otherwise unfavourable odds in his favour.

'You don't seriously think he might—'

'No!' cried Grace. 'Cobley *is* the greatest!'

'Right,' said Joe, remembering those plays – *Hamlet, King Lear, Macbeth, Romeo and Juliet, The Merchant of Venice, Henry V* . . . 'Cobley is the greatest. Cobley is a class apart.'

The Tortured Artist IV

'An incredible effort, son.'

The old man touched the young man's shoulder as the final notes died away.

'So moving. So redolent of the past, yet still so fully realised in its own right. This is all I ever wanted. I'm hugely proud.'

'Sorry my playing is so inaccurate,' said the young man, lifting his hands from the keyboard. 'The pills don't help much with performance.'

'Your playing was just fine.' The old man lifted the score from the stand and took it under his arm. 'I'll bring a curry tonight in celebration.'

'That would be great,' smiled the young man, lying down on his bed, exhausted both from the day's travails, and the cumulative impact of his efforts over the past year.

None of it had been easy. Though the doses had remained fairly constant, the depression and mental cramps had never gone away. Their impact was tempered only by his determination to weave a constant thread through the paintings, sculpture and symphony that came after the script – and fathoming how to achieve that without the old man noticing.

Now, the job was done.

'Don't rest on your laurels,' said the old man, oblivious to the subtexts and symbols that had sustained the young man for so long. 'Remember how you used to be. Slovenliness is the enemy. Only in creating will you find the impulse to create more.'

'I understand.' Reluctantly, the young man rose in answer to the old man's advice, and took his place at his desk. 'I won't forget the lessons of the past few months.'

'What's next?'

'I was thinking a stage play,' replied the young man, though in truth he was thinking no such thing. 'I have an idea, but I'd rather not discuss it yet.'

It was all a lie, but the old man didn't notice. After the increased productivity of recent times, he was entirely amenable, and would doubtless remain so for a while: continuing to trust the young man for want of any reason to think that things had changed.

Even so, there would come a point when the old impatience crept back in, and the young man was under no illusion regarding what would follow. There would be changes to the pills, anger, and mounting violence.

What there wouldn't be was any more co-operation. The young man had made himself a promise, and he fully intended to keep it. Once there was no more for him to relay, he would create no more. The old man could try to persuade him with whatever he could muster, physically or chemically. But unless more useful information presented itself – and he struggled to imagine how that could possibly occur – then his life as an artist was done. After so long spent channelling others, all for the sake of a selfish old tyrant, he owed it to himself to stop.

He wanted silence and empty space. A blank stave, a blank page, a blank canvas.

'See you later, son.' The old man opened the door. A shaft of daylight fell fleetingly into the room as he left.

They had entered the endgame, and with that knowledge came a kind of peace. The young man had done all he could. Now, he could only hope. Either they would come, or his life in the room would play out to its inevitable conclusion.

A train rumbled overhead. The young man looked up as the light swung from side to side, burning itself into his eyes. The clues had been placed, the clock had been started.

He turned his mind to waiting.

Chapter 22

Arm in arm with Jerry and Grace, Joe felt like he was about to explode with delight. After two years' tireless labour filming, editing and marketing *Triumph of the Solix*, they had finally arrived on the red carpet.

Having lurked in his limo down the street for several minutes, watching the Brits arrive via the crew who were documenting events for the last of the *Cobley Chronicles* movies – filming for the first of which, *The Man from Milton Keynes*, was to begin within the month – Joe's fashionably late appearance sparked a deafening cheer from the grandstands. It sounded especially sweet in contrast to the jeers with which the American crowd, decked out in Tom Cobley memorabilia, had greeted his rivals moments before.

Energised by the acclaim, Joe broke free and approached the crowd.

'Let me hear you sing!' he cried, willing from them the words that had defined the last two and a half years of his life. 'We want Justice for Tom!'

'Justice for Tom NOW!' came the cry back. 'We want Justice for Tom, Justice for Tom NOW!'

'Alright!' grinned Joe, punching the air. 'Let's do it!'

He re-joined his fiancée and producer, and together they continued down the carpet, stopping to express their confidence to various showbiz reporters along the way.

'Cobley is the pinnacle,' Joe said, time and again. 'Cobley is perfection. This is his time. This is his place. Justice will be done tonight!'

With the fervour still ringing out, they reached the entrance to the theatre, and scaled the scarlet steps. Joe's heart was bursting with pride, joy – and just a little trepidation.

The latter was understandable. Although he was confident that JoeCo's *Triumph of the Solix* trumped the WAC's version in almost every way, he'd had to have been a robot not to feel his stomach churn at the momentousness of what was about to happen. Contrary to what others claimed, he really did believe, and believe more with each passing day, that the Cobley Crusade was the defining achievement of his whole life. William Shakespeare – or at least the original, villainous William Shakespeare – had been deftly and irrevocably demonised in the popular imagination. In his place, Tom Cobley had arisen as a far superior cultural icon: an inspirational everyman who gave the world so much, under the most oppressive circumstances, and without receiving a single shred of credit until now. Those who complained that his plays had somehow suffered in the process needed their heads seeing to. The artist, not the art, had to come first, and any knock-on effects were simply part of the corrective process. The justice justified everything.

All of which made the Oscar more massive than ever. Yes, they'd accomplished much, but everything still hung on attaining the seal. Without it, their good work might yet be undermined. But with it, the Crusade's legacy would be immortalised, and Tom's name etched indelibly into history.

The three of them followed their guide into the back of the auditorium. But for them, the house was already full. With a satisfied grin, Joe followed the lead given by a camera crew towards the front. As the TV feed confirmed their arrival on monitors above the seats, the audience rose to applaud – and Joe wiped away a tear, so touching was this show of solidarity from his fellow filmmakers: the great and good of Hollywood, united in reverence for the incomparable Tom Cobley.

A cymbal crash heralded the start of the ceremony, and he took his place beside the Brits – who, adding to the delicious drama of it all, had failed to stand during his arrival.

'Good to see you again,' he said, nestling next to Wendy Preston.

'You too.' Her eyes were fixed resolutely ahead, sweat twinkling on her brow.

Up on the giant SolixScreen, a montage of the year's best movie clips, the majority from the two competing *Chronicles* movies, was accompanied from below the stage by a heart-pounding orchestra.

'What do you say?' Joe nudged her in the ribs. 'Excited?'

'All I say,' whispered Preston, 'is let the best film win.'

***

Oh, for heaven's sake, thought Wendy. Why had they been seated together? She was tense enough without the added distraction – never mind discomfort – of having Seabright right next door.

The introductory montage gave way to the evening's host, a Hollywood has-been comic whose spiel commenced with a barrage of dreadful puns conflating the evening's several focuses – *Triumph of the Solix*; the UK versus America; Tom Cobley versus William Shakespeare the First; Tom Cobley versus William Shakespeare the Second.

Wendy and Jim took turns to whisper reassurances into the other's ear, the cumulative effect being only to heighten their mutual anxiety. It was clear that both *Triumphs of the Solix* were fairly evenly matched. Theirs was more old-fashioned, priding itself on in-camera stunts and effects, plenty of model work, and even a more formal, classical script from the mystery man William Shakespeare, as opposed to the contemporary language deployed by Seabright as Tom Cobley. But in terms of overall impact, the two contrasting films – Seabright's sleek and computerised, Wendy's rough and authentic – were alike courtesy of transcendent scripts which were never less than moving, lyrical and immaculately paced.

Such, at least, was the objective view. Critical opinion had split firmly along national boundaries. Back home, reviewers favoured theirs. Over here, in the Californian cauldron, the response was precisely the reverse. Such had been the recent crescendo of patriotic passion, indeed, the Academy had been forced repeatedly to re-state their neutrality – insisting that their focus was on honouring the best film, pure and simple, and not assuming some pre-appointed role in Seabright's ridiculous fairytale.

Wendy peered down the row, to where the rest of her committee colleagues were seated: every face a study in nerves. She reached into her handbag and sought a tissue with which to wipe away the forthcoming waterworks, be they of joy or disappointment, all the while insisting to herself that it didn't really matter. So much had happened since Seabright's original betrayal that it was silly to get hung up on this one act of vengeance.

There was the film itself, for a start. Even if it didn't go on to win the Oscar, their *Triumph of the Solix* was a work of art of which they could all be proud. Its script was so powerful that Wendy's main battle throughout production had been fighting the urge to hunt down its enigmatic author and discover the personal secrets that lay behind its heart-wrenching impact. At two hours and 22 minutes long, the film was an instant classic, destined forever to speak well of their grand experiment, and proving – even more than the JoeCo version – that sweeping, operatic sci-fi was indeed the natural descendent of the epic histories and tragedies that occupied the geniuses of centuries gone by, Cobley chief among them.

Then there was the impact of the film on those who made it. The British film industry had long since been decimated by Hollywood's dominance, with the unstoppable rise of computer technology putting an end to the art and craft of film technicians. The WAC's membership turned out to include many of these former filmmakers, who rediscovered their artistic purpose in making *Triumph of the Solix*. They were matched by numerous designers, actors and technicians, each revelling in the group's hands-on, analogue approach. Together, they savoured the thrill of collaborating with a living genius to fight a genetically-revived bard whose skills were being ruthlessly misused by a company so technologically advanced that their entire film, bar the actors, was realised using computers.

The mission, then, had achieved much, even before one considered the secondary impact of how they'd found their author. Bowing to overwhelming public pressure, the WAC had revealed the full results of their groundbreaking experiment two months after crowning Shakespeare the winner. No matter that they still didn't disclose people's absolute abilities; the relative rankings alone created a whole new artistic orthodoxy. Key benchmarks quickly established themselves – anyone in the top one per cent, ranked roughly in the top 500,000, was highly proficient, while the top 100,000 or so were outright geniuses – and the consequences were extraordinary. In the wake of its work with William Shakespeare, the WAC was bombarded with people desperate to start writing now they knew how good they were, and the entire literary life of the country was transformed.

The WAC itself, of course, couldn't represent everyone, so comparable agencies were founded to meet the demand. But Wendy nonetheless took hundreds of writers onto their books – screenwriters, novelists, poets and playwrights by the dozen – and the Stratford campus grew to include a brand new set of theatres, plus a publishing house and printing works. The idea was to produce the cream of their writers' work themselves, then strike deals with third parties for the rest.

It had been an amazing odyssey. They hadn't always acted as strategically as they might have done, but it didn't matter. All those employed or represented by the WAC were financially secure, since the certain knowledge of writers' abilities meant there was no longer any risk attached to artistic endeavour. Films could be given the go-ahead, plays staged, novels published, with direct reference to the authors' relative rating. Money was funnelled into the written word knowing just how much of a hit, bestseller, or box office smash everything would be.

Flops were a thing of the past. Buoyed by a certain return on investment, the arts were well on course to become the UK's single strongest industry.

Inadvertently, Wendy and Jim had initiated a golden age of writing so efficient it had already given rise to a dozen of the most life-affirming cinematic and literary masterpieces of this or any other era. And given the progress Jim was making in analysing the genetic hallmarks of the muse in music and the visual arts – such that they'd soon be able to identify the country's best composers, songwriters, sculptors and painters – the future was brighter still. Even those bereft of artistic flair were happy. No longer hampered by the fancy that they might have a novel 'in them', people stuck with what suited them, finding fulfilment in pursuits at which they excelled rather than those in which they were destined to fall short.

In the grand scheme, then, a Seabright Oscar victory would scarcely dent their morale, let alone their achievements. And even if they hadn't had all the other stuff to fall back on, there remained no shame in losing to Cobley. The trick was simply to overlook how wretchedly Seabright had demeaned the man and devalued his plays, recalling instead Cobley's original, irreducible masterpieces as the standards by which one was being judged.

And yet, as the plump little beast fidgeted beside her, Wendy simply couldn't detach Cobley from the man who had misappropriated his muse. There might well be no shame in losing to Tom Cobley *as was*, but she'd be ashamed indeed to lose to Joe Seabright. For all that she cared about those writers whose talent they now represented, nothing since had mattered as much as the authorship question. Lacking any great writerly flair herself – she had been ranked somewhere in the mid-29,400,000s – she'd come to realise that the authorship debate had been her *magnum opus*: the thing by which she had best expressed who she was.

That Seabright had not only stolen this but made such a ghastly wreck of Cobley's canon – the plays irreparably cheapened, the dissemination of truth dominated by meaningless, money-grabbing gimmicks – made her angrier than even William Shakespeare's words could describe. Very occasionally, she managed to focus solely on the future. But deep down, she knew only one thing: that she would cheerfully sacrifice everything that had happened to go back in time and be allowed to reveal the truth about Shakespeare herself.

'Oh boy,' exclaimed Seabright, giving her another hard poke in the ribs. 'This is it!'

There was indeed no further ado. The host had concluded his tiresome spiel and summoned on stage some famous Hollywood thespian, whose face Wendy recognised but whose name she couldn't place.

'And the Oscar for Best Visual Effects goes to . . .'

She hadn't even heard the nominations read out. As the actor untucked the golden envelope, she glanced to the end of the row. A cameraman had his lens trained on her and Seabright, ready to relay their reactions to billions worldwide. She glanced up at the TV monitors, the camera zooming in first on Seabright's face, then hers, then back out to frame them both. She adjusted her specs, the tension absurd and frankly unbearable. It was only Visual Effects, but it could still be a crucial indicator of where the Academy's sympathies lay.

The TV feed cut back to the onstage announcer, permitting him to complete his distended sentence: the Oscar for Best Visual Effects goes to . . .

'*Triumph of the Solix*,' he said, sponging every last drop of drama from the moment. 'A WAC production.'

***

Joe grinned inanely as Preston shuffled past and made for the stage, where she launched into a patronising lecture about the superiority of authentic special effects over JoeCo's automated approach, and how grateful she was for the award, hoping it set the tone for the evening as a whole.

'Don't let them rile you,' cautioned Jerry.

Joe realised he had started frowning.

'This is a good sign,' the producer assured him. 'We both know – we know all too *well* – that Visual Effects is just a booby prize.'

Joe sought his customary Oscar grin, locating it just in time as Preston left the stage.

'You realise that's just consolation, right?' he murmured as she passed. 'They're saving the serious awards for us.'

Preston stopped directly in front. Without lowering her head, she peered at him beneath the rim of her glasses, considering her reply. Then, violently yet inconspicuously, she stamped on his foot.

'I do apologise,' she chuckled, returning to her seat.

Struggling to retain his toothy smile amid the pain, Joe refocused on the stage. A young Hollywood starlet was reading out the nominations for the next award.

'And the award for Best Sound Design goes to . . .'

She sliced open the golden envelope. With clockwork precision the aisle camera returned to gaze upon Joe and Preston's faces.

'*Triumph of the Solix*,' came the announcement. 'A JoeCo production!'

Wow, he thought, as a cheer lifted him from his seat. The early indications had been that the Brits were getting the token gongs, but no. Fact was, JoeCo and the WAC were *sharing* the early spoils. It was proof – surprise proof – that the Academy were sticking to their word. They were dishing out the statuettes on merit alone, determined not to make this a coronation.

'Oh boy,' whispered Joe as he took the statuette in his hands. 'Oh boy, oh boy.'

The rivalry with the WAC was real. The fight to the finish was well and truly on.

Chapter 23

'And so, whatever happens in the coming minutes,' declaimed Sir Peter Heyward, three hours after the ceremony began, 'I simply *must* dedicate this award to the two magnificent men, without whom tonight's extraordinary drama wouldn't be unfolding. To the inspirational Joe Seabright. And of course...' He gazed heavenwards. 'To the masterful Tom Cobley.' He held up his Best Actor Oscar. 'Tom, this is for you.'

'Dear God, have mercy!' shrieked Wendy, as a standing ovation shot up around her. She'd felt poorly enough before Sir Peter's speech, but now, having held her stoic smile throughout, she was truly on the brink of retching.

'Can you believe this idiot?' she raged at Jim. 'It's not Tom Cobley he should be thanking – it's us! We're the ones he betrayed to win his job back!'

'Come on, people,' said Seabright. 'Get on your feet and show a little respect!'

Conscious of booing amid the cheering, Wendy looked up at the monitors, where an aerial shot showed her and her friends still seated. Seeing no alternative, she rose and forced her face towards a smile, silently applauding as Sir Peter posed – and by goodness could he pose – with his statuette. For over a minute he stood there sobbing, before finally ceding the spotlight in a flurry of dismissive, hand-waving modesty.

All evening, the two *Solix Chronicles* films had matched each other blow-by-blow, garnering an equal number of minor awards. Some murmured that the even-handedness was contrived to build the drama of the evening, but Wendy believed the Academy had been judging objectively. Big enough to accept where the WAC had deservedly lost out – Best Score correctly went to Seabright's veteran old-school composer – and proud enough to know where they rightly prevailed – it was a delight to see their army of brilliant costume designers and dressers rewarded – she felt that every one of the evening's awards was pretty much justified. Heavens, even the dreaded Sir Peter *probably* merited his.

As they settled in their seats for the climactic announcement, then, the Academy's message was simple: there was no favouritism, only fairness. The best film would win it, fair and square, meaning Wendy hadn't the foggiest idea which way the dice would tumble.

'And so, ladies and gentlemen,' began the Academy President, 'we reach the moment of truth: the Oscars for Best Screenplay and Best Picture. Such are the unique circumstances surrounding this year's ceremony, these two awards, usually dispensed separately and to different films, are this year being given out simultaneously and to the same film. For this, above all, is a *celebration*. A celebration of the role played by the *writer*, not only in our craft, but in our culture, our history, our language – our sense, quite simply, of self.'

Wendy met Jim's glistening eyes. His hand was outstretched. Smiling, she took it in hers: the two of them, united in intolerable tension.

'There are only two nominees. *The Solix Chronicles: Triumph of the Solix,* a JoeCo production, screenplay by Joe Seabright and Tom Cobley; and *The Solix Chronicles: Triumph of the Solix*, a WAC production, screenplay by William Shakespeare.'

Wendy squeezed Jim's hand as the President opened the winner's envelope. Breathless, she glanced to Seabright, only to find him staring straight back. The anxiety on his face mirrored that in her mind. Exchanging the faintest of amicable nods, they turned back to the stage.

'And the winner is . . .'

Wendy leaned forward.

'*The Solix Chronicles.*'

Silence.

'*Triumph of the Solix.*'

More silence.

'A WAC Production.'

Still more silence. Wendy waited for the decision, so overwrought she only noticed it had, in fact, just been announced when Seabright gave a despairing sigh on her left – and Jim leapt to his feet on her right.

'Written by William Shakespeare,' concluded the President.

A WAC Production. Written by William Shakespeare. That was them, she thought. Ludicrously, incomprehensibly, wonderfully, that was them. She looked up at Jim as a wave of applause – warm, but not ecstatic – washed through the auditorium.

'Congratulations!' he grinned.

'We did it!' yelled Clive. He and the others were on their feet, hugging and shaking hands. 'Victory is ours!'

'Come on,' urged Jim.

Wendy turned to shake Seabright's limp, sweaty, hand, then pushed herself up and into the aisle, beckoning for her friends to follow.

'How about that?' gushed Jim, taking her arm as they climbed on to the stage.

'How about that,' smiled Wendy, conscious of her elation but struggling to translate it into anything physical or verbal. She was mightily proud of their winning film, delighted for the group, and frankly overjoyed at having reduced Seabright – visible on the monitors – to an inconsolable wreck. But for all this, she knew the victory wasn't yet complete. There remained one key component to be put in place.

It wouldn't be long now. William Shakespeare had always pledged that he would unmask himself should they win the Oscar, and Wendy had arranged for him to call a special number in the event of a WAC victory.

She collected the two awards and said what was expected of

her – commiserations to Seabright and America, congratulations to *everyone* in the UK for their support and enthusiasm – while waiting for a signal that William Shakespeare was ready to speak.

A minute went by, then two, and still the call didn't come. On she droned, increasingly incoherent as the panic clogged up her brain. Why had she been so sure he'd keep his word? Was it just the certainty with which he'd spoken on the day of his selection? If so, she was a top-notch buffoon. The man was self-confessedly shy, yet had clearly wanted to write for them, so gave a promise which was as easy to break as it had been easy to make. With their mission accomplished, and without a clue who he was or where he lived, the WAC had no sanction. Shakespeare couldn't have been freer to disobey their gentlemen's agreement.

She should have seen it coming. The fact that he'd evaded the best efforts of a curious media underlined his determination to stay hidden, as did his insistence that he only spoke to Wendy when it was strictly necessary. She'd never been given his number, they'd never discussed anything save his writing – not even the weather! – and he'd not once shown the slightest interest in the WAC's other activities. Just what sort of fool was she to have believed his good intentions?

'He's ready, ma'am!' came a voice from off-stage.

Wendy stopped speaking, completely unaware of what she'd just been saying. She looked into the wings. 'He's on the line?'

'We're putting him through now.'

Hurriedly, she turned back to the audience. 'But that's quite enough of me. Time now to hear from the man to whom we're most indebted, who at long last is about to come out of the shadows.'

She stepped back, awash with relief, flanked by Jim and the rest of her redoubtable friends. She'd dreamt of this moment almost as much as the Oscar victory itself. Quite why it mattered so much she wasn't sure, but matter it unquestionably did.

'Ladies and gentlemen,' said Shakespeare, his voice echoing round the auditorium. 'May I begin by saying how delighted I am to be a part of this victory. It has been an honour to be the first of the WAC's legion of new, living geniuses, and a great privilege to have helped correct the appalling cultural crime committed by Joe Seabright.'

'In both those respects, the award of this Oscar is an act of the grandest justice. But there is another, equally important dimension to our victory.'

Wendy's stomach, already tense, tightened further.

'As everyone knows, I agreed to write the WAC's film on condition that I remain anonymous. I am by nature a shy man, and I feared that the attention I received – combined with the pressure wrought by knowledge of my talents – might inhibit my creativity.'

There was a pause. The crowd began murmuring. Wendy wished they would be quiet.

'With the film finally triumphant, however,' the disembodied voice continued, 'I feel that – true to my word – the time has come to be more open with you all.'

Wendy's tummy twisted some more.

'In particular, I want you to know my name.'

There was widespread shushing. Wendy could feel the crowd leaning forward in anticipation. Seabright, for one, was standing.

'My name,' continued the voice, 'is William Shakespeare...'

The silence was immaculate.

'...and so it shall remain.'

For several moments, nothing was said. People were taking time to digest Shakespeare's roundabout way of stating his intentions. As the truth slowly registered, Wendy took it upon herself to speak for them all.

'No!'

She rushed to the microphone and slammed the statuettes onto the lectern.

'Yes,' came the voice.

'But you promised!'

Her protests were promptly taken up by those in the audience

– Seabright included – jeering and gesticulating their displeasure.

'If everyone could just stay calm,' said Shakespeare, 'I'll happily explain myself.'

'But how can you not want to be known?' pleaded Wendy. 'Just come out of your shell and enjoy it! Nobody's going to hurt you!'

'They hurt Tom Cobley.'

The jeering stopped. Wendy saw Seabright return sheepishly to his seat.

'How do you mean?' she asked.

'The reasons I originally gave for wanting to stay anonymous,' came the reply, 'were only true to a degree.'

'To a *degree*?'

'Quite so.'

'To *what* degree?'

'To the degree that I feared unmasking me would diminish my work. But that fear had nothing to do with any shyness. It wasn't to do with me, as the artist. It was all to do with the audience.'

'The audience?'

'The audience, and the manner in which they would appreciate my work.'

'Explain.'

'Must I?'

'Yes you bloody must!'

'But hasn't it become unavoidably apparent, the extent to which an artist's work suffers when too much is known about the artist himself? Think back to before Tom Cobley: when the world coveted that shadowy genius William Shakespeare, that *idea* of a man rather than the man himself, his plays seeping with potential precisely because so little was known about their creator. For over four hundred years, we were denied any detail about his life, and what happened? As if by magic, his masterpieces multiplied a thousand fold: absorbing any number of interpretations and reinventions; never ceasing to surprise and astound.'

'But then the authorship mystery was solved, and the fixation on *fact* began gnawing away at the *fiction* of his plays. No longer was the author an anonymous mystery but a specific historical character – a *caricature*. Since Mr Seabright made his breakthrough, there hasn't been a single production that hasn't felt incalculably weaker for having had its endless possibilities bent by abridgement and meddlesome direction to those few readings that fit what we know about the man Tom Cobley. Every last play is now a treatise on imprisonment, exploitation or injustice – every great soliloquy now a coded longing for freedom – to the exclusion of everything else. Why else has the number of performances of his plays declined so drastically? Why else has the Globe in London closed? It's not because Seabright has been charging for the rights to stage the plays. It's not because you turned your countrymen against Cobley. It's because the genius we once worshipped has been irreversibly diminished; the power of his plays tragically diluted.'

'I agree!' cried Wendy. 'By goodness I agree!' She brandished one of the Oscars to help make her point. 'But it would have been different with us. It wasn't the truth that did what you describe. It was Seabright's attitude. If we'd have been left in charge—'

'Things might have been more tolerable, yes . . .' Shakespeare's voice resonated through the theatre with utter composure. 'But the truly corrosive factor was knowledge of the author in and of itself. No amount of prudence could have stopped that having a negative effect on the plays; denying us that universality of meaning, that relevance to each and every one of us, without which neither you nor I would have fallen for the plays to begin with.'

'Is that so?'

'Absolutely. Without those infinite interpretations to explore, you'd not have cared so much about the plays as to worry who wrote them. The perversity being that, in seeking an answer to that question, you were jeopardising the very quality that first drew you in.'

Wendy leant towards the microphone, but – whether because

of the pressure, or some other kind of change – found it impossible to offer any defence.

'So what of the future?' asked Shakespeare, sounding ever more like some beneficent, Godly authority. 'Well, as you must by now appreciate, Shakespeare – the original Shakespeare, about whom we knew so little – is my model and my inspiration. Dearly wanting to return to the time when *Hamlet, Lear* and *Othello* were as rich as ever, yet conscious that such a return is impossible, I have set myself the next best challenge: not only to bring new masterpieces into the world, but to remain anonymous in the hope that, for want of any knowledge of who I am, where I hail from, or what I believe, my art will prosper to its fullest potential.'

An intrigued whisper worked its way round the auditorium. This mystery man Shakespeare was undeniably captivating: his philosophy persuasive and his oratory inspiring – all the more so because they didn't know who he was.

'My victory today stands as a first step. A symbolic triumph for the potency of anonymity, which I trust will inspire other artists to follow my lead. As for the WAC – well, I dearly hope you will join me in my efforts.'

There was a pause. Belatedly, Wendy realised he was prompting her to speak.

'You do?' she asked.

'But of course. I propose that you continue disseminating my writing – whether plays, films or novels – as widely as you can. And I implore you to encourage your other writers to go undercover and disguise their true identities. For great though their talents are, the impact of their creations could yet be greater if we were denied knowledge of the creators themselves. If we can just achieve that, if we trust in the power of art for art's sake, then this second Renaissance you've initiated will not only match but surpass all that has gone before.'

Wendy hadn't a clue what to say. Moments before, she'd been all set to find some way of insisting Shakespeare disclose his true identity, adamant that their Oscar triumph meant nothing if she couldn't have her curiosity sated. But now she found herself hesitating, and not just because there was no obvious way of forcing the issue. The authority in Shakespeare's voice, combined with his consummate artistry, gave her pause for thought. She started to feel relieved that he hadn't disclosed his true identity after all; that she wouldn't have to tame the overpowering effect of their *Triumph of the Solix* with knowledge of its author.

Involuntarily, her mind cast the piercing light of the present back over the past. For the first time since her epiphany beside the Cam, she found herself open to the notion that perhaps it *was* wrong to have sought so earnestly an answer to the authorship question. Behind it all, like Shakespeare said, was this question of mystery: of disciplining oneself to embrace anonymity as the ally of great art, and recognise that the more closely one tried to know an artist, the more one chiselled away at the qualities that attracted one in the first place. That didn't mean one couldn't be curious – to wonder at leisure who might be responsible; to question lazy orthodoxies – but it did make it unwise to seek a definitive solution.

She let the logic linger, fully expecting one of her myriad traditional reactions: it being either a matter of fairness, entitlement or accountability that an artist be made to put his or her name to a work of art. But as she stood there, spotlit and scrutinised by millions, she no longer felt tied to her traditional opinions. With Seabright defeated at last, she was free to admit that nothing would ever make her happier than those times *before* the authorship mystery was solved.

The mystery itself had been her lifeblood – not the quest to solve it, but the joy of exploring those plays by speculating about different possible authors. Resolution had actually been anathema, the last thing any of them needed. Their specialism had been in pluralising the plays, not singularising them. Having found evidence to back up the claims of tens of authors, their very success was an expression of the plays' limitless meanings – their speculation, the ultimate celebration of the author's anonymity.

'Are you there?'

The voice brought Wendy back into the theatre.

'I'm here.'

'Well? Will you work with me?'

She straightened her back and took a deep breath. 'We will.'

'You won't come looking for me?'

Wendy shook her head. 'No.'

'You'll continue to air my work?'

'We will.'

'You'll encourage others to be similarly anonymous?'

'We will give them the option.'

'You'll insist?'

Wendy could hardly believe what she was saying. 'We'll insist.'

'And you promise you won't come looking for me?'

Wendy hesitated. Hadn't the question already been asked once?

'We pr—' she began, only to be cut off by a commotion in the audience: the sound of vacated seats, clattering to rest.

Squinting to see into the darkened auditorium, she made out three figures, hotfooting their way to the exit.

Seabright, it seemed, had left without saying goodbye.

Chapter 24

Unable to get comfortable in his chair, Joe perched on his desk, tossing the figures around his head as Jerry stood opposite. It was the end of Monday – just twenty-four hours after the Oscars – and the Cobley Crusade had hit the skids.

'Our projections might not be right, of course,' said Jerry. 'But if the signs from today are any gauge, the whole project is in big trouble.'

Joe grabbed a doughnut and took a big, grumpy bite. Just as he'd never realistically entertained the possibility of failure, so he'd never thought through its implications for the Cobley brand. Already, however, the consequences were clear. Folks weren't just apathetic but *angry*: wilfully rejecting the product, disappointed at being denied their fairytale ending; possibly even enflamed by William Shakespeare's implicit demonization of JoeCo.

'We need to start a new campaign, right away,' said Grace, seated on the sofa beside Joe's shelf – still empty, despite the best efforts of the greatest writer who ever lived.

'Some kind of fightback,' she urged. 'We still have the most powerful thing: the plays themselves. We just need to nudge the fans a little and they're sure to rally.'

Joe looked enquiringly at Jerry, who frowned back.

'It's a tough sell, boss. Whatever the reason, the plays aren't selling as well as when we first took them on. There's been a steady fall in rights revenues for over a year now. We can't rely on them to underwrite a full-scale re-boot. As for the merchandising: that was all fixed on the Oscar.'

'It was fixed on Cobley being the best,' said Joe. 'It was fixed on winning him justice!'

'Right,' agreed Jerry.

'But he's not the best is he?' Joe stared at his empty shelf. 'Not any longer.'

Inexorably, his thoughts returned to the crook whose cowardliness matched that of the man from whom he took his name: the faceless scoundrel who, like the original William Shakespeare, had overshadowed Cobley at his moment of greatest triumph, boasting talents which, against all odds, surpassed Cobley's own. Cobley, the peak, the pinnacle, perfection itself... No more.

'We have to at least try,' insisted Grace. 'After last night, Cobley needs justice more than ever. It's outrageous that after all these years, some other guy comes up on the rails and steals his glory. Even if he is in fact better – mathematically, genetically better – it's still deeply unfair that Cobley should be eclipsed, yet again.'

Joe nodded vaguely. It wasn't that he felt any malice towards Cobley. As far as anyone could tell, Cobley had done the best he could – JoeCo's *Triumph of the Solix* was exactly the masterpiece it should have been. But it was simply impossible to regain any enthusiasm for Cobley while the mystery man William Shakespeare was lurking in the shadows.

'I'm serious, honey,' persisted Grace. 'You can't just ditch him. Not after everything that's happened.'

'I'm not suggesting we ditch him.' Joe was struggling not to sound impatient. 'But I don't see how we can make him special again. If he's not the best, it's gonna be—'

'He's still pretty damn good!'

'But he's not the focus of people's fascination anymore. This other guy is. And that means Cobley... well, we just need to let him find his place in this brave new world, where William Shakespeare is the greatest. Let the brand sink or swim on its merits.'

'Which is fine for the merchandise,' said Jerry. 'And the plays. We'll see if the demand's there. But given these figures, we need to fix on a plan for the Cobley Camps – both the UK and US facilities – and the *Cobley Chronicles* right away. It's too risky, just letting them be.'

Joe deliberated for a moment. With a sharp intake of breath, he gave his producer the nod. 'Shut them down.'

'Both of them?'

'Both of them.'

'What?' exclaimed Grace.

'Just temporarily.'

'*Joe!*'

'I can't turn my mind to them. Not right now.'

'But the *movies*. So much work has already been done. We're due to start shooting—'

'We'll do them at some point!' Joe hesitated. 'Maybe. For now, I just need to think . . .'

Not wanting any more Cobley chit-chat, he strode onto his terrace and gazed across the lawns that swept down from the pool. He heard Grace follow him out.

'I needed that Oscar,' he sighed. 'Yes, I wanted it for Cobley, but I *needed* it for me.' He lifted up his head. 'I just can't believe we failed. I can't believe this other guy . . .'

He lapsed again, unable to stop thinking of the phantom author who had trampled on his dreams. This, at the end of it all, was the real injustice. It was all very well Grace arguing Tom's corner, but the same rationale applied to him – arguably even more so. He was the one who'd spent his life doing good by others, entertaining a global audience with the most popular films planet Earth had ever known. He was the one who'd conceived and built a creative paradise for the most brilliant artists alive, looking on selflessly as their flourishing talents were rewarded with countless Oscars and unceasing acclaim from their peers.

And yet what of him? The only thing he'd ever truly craved for himself was that Oscar. But now, having had MET, his last best hope, jeopardised first by the authorship confusion, then by the tenacity of the WAC – having even had the humility to fuse his search for vindication with that of another spurned genius – Joe had been denied yet again. Not, this time, by the stubborn snobbery of the Academy, but by a fate more sickening still. One which decreed that, after four hundred years, and helped along by those infernal Brits, history had chosen *that* moment – the moment when, surely, victory was his for the taking – to throw up a writer *better* than Tom Cobley.

It was almost too unlucky to believe.

In fact, come to think of it, it really *was* too unlucky to believe. And that was why he refused to believe it.

'Enough of this.' He marched indoors. 'I'm going.'

'Going where?' asked Grace.

Joe glanced back over his shoulder. 'To offer my congratulations to you-know-who.'

***

It had been a long night of partying, followed by a hard day of press. Having spent over eight hours in the dauntingly plush Chateau Marmont, busy doing her obligatory international interviews, Wendy was relieved to return to her own, rather more modest hotel to pack ahead of their midnight flight back to Blighty.

It wasn't just the exhaustion which gave her pause for a stiff sherry as she contemplated her cases, and the clothes that had to fit inside. There was, of course, no denying the surreal exhilaration that came with the attention, nor the profound satisfaction of having seen off Seabright – a triumph for her personally, and hard-won justice for the group. But with the victory came a refocused restlessness. For all the fun of it, she couldn't wait to get out of the Hollywood maelstrom, and back to work.

To an extent, this was expected. The Oscar race was over, but the WAC had long since been independently enriched by its emergence as a vessel for other, brilliantly talented writers. Win or lose to Seabright, Wendy had fully anticipated a keenness to get home and achieve ever greater things with their wonderful flock. What was new, however, was the clarity that had come with closure: the realisation that life, and art, were so much better with certain mysteries left intact.

Well, she wasn't going to make the same mistake again. Except, of course, that she already had, with all those writers to whom they had given voice. Every last one of the published and performed had been paraded in front of the media. Their biographies had been plastered over their work and memorable life stories aired *ad infinitum* as though the only possible prompt for enjoying their work was knowing every last detail about them. 'Write what you know' had been Wendy's best advice, and in marketing the resultant opuses she'd done all she could to demonstrate that her writers had, indeed, written what they knew – making it impossible to view their work in any other light.

So this was the urgency. To get home, and put a stop to all that. Tom Cobley had once been the man he was – and William Shakespeare was the man *he* was, whoever that might be – thanks to his anonymity, and the only way her brood of brilliant writers could fulfil *their* potential was by going similarly undercover. The work would start immediately, and she wouldn't rest until every last one was as anonymous as humanly possible.

There was a knock at the door. Quite obliviously, Wendy realised, she had not only polished off two whole glasses of sherry but got half way through her packing.

'Who is it?'

'Only me.'

She smiled and opened the door.

'Making progress?'

'Getting there, it seems.'

'The bus will be here in half an hour.' Jim breezed in and picked up the two Oscars from the dressing table. 'One for me, one for you?'

Wendy laughed. Letting the door fall to, she took the statuettes, tossed them casually into her case, then put her arms around his shoulders.

'Both of them,' she said, 'for both of us.'

Jim looked briefly nervous before breaking into a smile. The two of them had grown close – awkwardly so – in the time they'd been working together, the old wounds slowly healing as they hunted down their new, superior Shakespeare, and assembled their cohort of magnificent new writers to nurture and cherish. But something indefinable, that they'd never discussed, had stopped them acknowledging that the old resentment was a thing of the past.

Wendy didn't know what it was. Neither of them had anyone else. Clive was still happily married, and Jim was too guileless to be carrying on with anyone behind her back. There was just a sense that they had been waiting. Possibly for the Oscar, possibly for something more.

Whatever it was, Wendy knew now that the moment had come – and so did Jim. Responding to her touch, he put his arms round her waist and pulled her towards him.

'Let's get back,' he said. 'Make it all a mystery again.'

Wendy's heart leapt as he leant towards her, those wonky yellow teeth more alluring than ever; the tufts of hair flapping gaily above the ears, liberated from the pasted shackles of their recent public displays. She moved her head towards his. Their lips were on the brink of meeting when a voice piped up behind them.

'I'd offer to come back another time,' said Joe Seabright. 'But they tell me you're leaving within the hour.'

Letting go of Jim, whose features fell in disappointment, Wendy turned to find their sometime rival standing in the doorway.

'Do come in,' she said.

Seabright pushed the door shut.

'What can we do for you?' asked Jim.

'I wanted to say congratulations.'

'Thank you,' said Wendy. 'And the answer to your next question is: no.'

Joe looked disappointed. 'When you say no . . .'

'I mean no.'

'But is it—'

'No on both counts? Yes.'

'Yes?'

'No! No, we don't know who he is. And no, we wouldn't tell you even if we did.'

'You're going to try to find out, though. Right?'

Seabright was a good deal shorter than Wendy. Despite his aura, she'd always looked down on him one way or another. But now he appeared genuinely belittled: unshaven, sleep-deprived and broken-hearted. He cut a desperate figure, yet any pity she felt was quickly quelled by her brutal new professionalism.

'You heard what I said last night,' she said.

'You're actually gonna stand by that?'

'You sound surprised.'

'Can you blame me? Twenty years devoted to unmasking Tom Cobley, and yet now you're happy to let this new William Shakespeare go unidentified? This guy, whose anonymity means he has no accountability whatsoever? You're happy to take *his* preaching as some kind of divine authority?'

Seabright spoke with real passion, but Wendy wouldn't be swayed.

'I don't take anything he says as gospel,' she said. 'I feel what I feel regardless. He just opened my eyes to the folly of it.' She went to the fridge. 'But let's not argue anymore.' She pulled out a bottle of beer. 'Why not let's make up and have a drink together?'

Seabright took the beer and drank it down gratefully. Wendy poured herself and Jim a couple more glasses of sherry.

'You realise,' said Seabright, stroking the half-empty bottle. 'I don't really care who he is. Sure, I don't like losing to a coward. I'd like him to come out in the open, say what he's got to say to my face. But knowing who he is? It doesn't trouble me like it used to trouble you.'

'Then why do you ask?'

'Because I just don't buy it.' He took another giant swig. 'The greatest writer who ever lived. Greater even than Tom Cobley.

And yet he doesn't want to be known?'

'You think he's some kind of cheat?' asked Wendy.

Seabright held up his hands. 'I just want to know that the fight was fair.'

'But how could someone have *cheated* to write such a brilliant film?' said Jim. 'How could he have *cheated* to win our contest? It was an incorruptible mathematical experiment.'

'Who can say?' replied Seabright. 'But given the stakes, I feel I'm entitled to at least pose the question.'

'Of course,' said Wendy. 'But that doesn't mean it needs answering. This is the whole joy of it, see? The world is richer for these unanswered questions. We're all left dazed and enthralled. Trust me: our film will seem even greater now its author has compounded the mystery of his identity.'

Seabright finished his beer. 'What if I come out tomorrow; tell the world of my suspicions? That I refuse to accept defeat?'

'Do it,' encouraged Wendy. 'It'll only deepen the mystery further, ensuring that whatever he does next will be doubly successful.'

'And if I try to track him down?'

'Again, it'll only make the whole thing that much richer. Though don't forget what happened with The Cobley Crusade – if you do find him, I mean.'

This seemed to catch Seabright off-guard. Perhaps it was the beer; perhaps it was because Cobley had been found wanting, and their rivalry was in any case at an end. Either way, his customary defiance seemed to desert him, and he sank into a chair.

'May I have another beer?' he asked.

Jim went to the fridge and obliged.

'You're the experts, right?' Seabright took the bottle. 'All fighting aside, you know those plays pretty well. So let me ask you: was the Cobley Crusade as destructive as he says?'

'I think it probably was,' replied Wendy, as gently as she could. 'But don't think we'd have avoided the same fate. It may have happened slower, more stealthily. But as Shakespeare said, the root cause was the fact of Cobley's authorship, not how you handled it.'

Seabright lapsed into thought, eyes in shadow. Wendy couldn't decide if he was scheming, or genuinely heeding the lesson she herself had only just learned. Either way, it didn't matter. Even if he refused to be placated, there was something about this new William Shakespeare that felt truly undetectable.

'I'd better get packing,' said Jim, making for the door.

Wendy nodded. 'I'll be done in ten minutes.'

'Wait,' said Seabright.

Jim stopped.

Seabright sat up on the edge of the chair and gulped down his beer. 'Alright,' he said at last. 'You win. Let's give this man his anonymity. And let's all enjoy what comes of it.' He stood and offered Wendy his hand. 'Congratulations. And this time, I really mean it.'

Wendy couldn't believe the sudden show of magnanimity. She shook his hand, and looked on, dazed, as he bid farewell to Jim and opened the door to leave.

'Before I go,' he said, turning back. 'Just between us . . .'

'Yes?' asked Wendy.

'I feel I need to know. Did it really happen?'

'Did what really happen?'

'Your guy. Is he really better than Cobley? Mathematically, I mean.'

Wendy held up her hands. 'God's honest truth, we've never found out.'

Seabright seemed to find this extraordinary. 'You never pulled off the Divergence Percentages?'

'It's our policy,' explained Jim. 'For all our writers.'

'I know it's your policy.' Seabright shut the door. 'But I assumed you'd have had a sneaky look.'

Wendy resumed packing, taking out the two Oscars to make room for her high heels. 'We created the policy. Surely we'd be the last people to go against it?'

'We like to know they're good,' explained Jim. 'That seems to help people: both the talented and untalented. But exactly *how* good? That's best left unknown.' He smiled at Wendy. 'Just like the writers' identities.'

'Will you check for me?' asked Seabright.

Wendy had sensed this coming, but was still surprised by the desperation in his voice.

'We'll keep it between ourselves.'

'There's no merit in knowing,' she said. 'You're better off wondering.'

'Not when it matters as much as that Oscar did to me. I need to know just how unlucky I was.'

'Wendy won't be swayed,' advised Jim.

Seabright considered for a second. 'I'll give you Cobley back.'

Wendy looked up.

'Seriously. The international Cobley rights – the whole package – if you just tell me: is your guy better than Tom?'

Wendy stepped back, and Jim held her steady as a faintness came over her.

'Just think of it,' persisted Seabright. 'What you always wanted, but with a new mission: fixing all the things I screwed up.'

The names of the plays tumbled through her mind – *Hamlet*, *The Tempest*, *Richard II* – quickly chased by thought of what they had become under Seabright's corrosive stewardship. There was certainly lots of work to be done, and she'd dearly like to be the one to do it: to make Cobley mysterious again.

'But you've invested so much in the Crusade . . .' she began.

Seabright picked up the stray Oscars, one in each hand, and stared wistfully into their eyes.

'It didn't work out for Tom and me,' he said. 'I didn't get my Oscar, he didn't get his justice. Worse than that, I damaged him along the way.' He put the statuettes aside. 'It's time to straighten things out.'

Wendy looked at Jim. Half her brain was all set to offer manifold reasons why they couldn't grant Seabright's request. But the other half, still besotted by the memory of what Cobley's masterpieces once were, screamed down the first with unarguable volume.

'We'll do it,' she said. 'But only if you promise to keep Shakespeare's DP a secret – known only by the three of us.'

Seabright nodded. 'That's all I want.' He held out his hand. 'Shake?'

Wendy shook, and Jim went to retrieve his computer from the next-but-one room. She and Seabright passed an uncomfortable couple of minutes making small-talk, during which she tried desperately to think through the implications of discovering whether their Shakespeare was, scientifically, more or less of a genius than Tom Cobley. As long as it stayed secret, she figured, it didn't matter. Even if she ended up loving one more than the other by virtue of knowing the mathematical truth, it was of no object since, thrillingly, she now had the rights to both bodies of work.

'Right,' said Jim, returning. 'Joe, do you have your script with you?'

Seabright handed Jim a flash drive. 'Always.'

'Great. Ours is on the system already.'

Wendy and Seabright gathered round the screen as Jim brought his Muse Management software to life.

'Let's take this back to basics,' he said. 'Three scripts, for the avoidance of doubt.'

One by one, he submitted the scripts to be analysed: first, *Hamlet* by Tom Cobley, then *Triumph of the Solix*, by Joe Seabright and Tom Cobley, then finally *Triumph of the Solix*, by William Shakespeare. The results screen appeared, with three rows per script: 'Author', 'Screenplay', 'Divergence Percentage'.

'Any second now . . .' said Jim.

The first figure appeared on screen:

> Tom Cobley, *Hamlet*
> 0.008187%

Almost immediately, this was followed by the second:

> Joe Seabright, *Triumph of the Solix*

0. 008187%

'There it is,' said Jim. 'The first proper, mathematical proof that Tom Cobley was indeed the old William Shakespeare, author of *Hamlet*.'

'And the first proof, too,' reflected Seabright, 'that Grace's MET works to mathematical perfection.'

Wendy gave a muted laugh. It was astonishing indeed to see the fact of Cobley's authorship given hard, numerical form by Jim's analysis. But where was the third script? The one written by *their* William Shakespeare? The one whose DP would be either lower or higher — better or worse — than Cobley's?

'I've never known it take this long before,' said Jim. 'Perhaps I should re-start—'

The result appeared on screen:

William Shakespeare, Triumph of the Solix
0.000000%

'Zero per cent?' said Seabright. 'What does it mean, *zero per cent*?'

Jim, turning pale, ran his hands through his tufts of hair. 'Goodness,' he said.

'But what is that?' persisted Seabright. 'Some kind of perfection?'

'In theory, yes. Zero per cent divergence means this is as good as it can possibly get. I just don't see ...' Jim clicked back a couple of screens to re-analyse the scripts. Exactly the same thing happened. He bit his lip. 'It's mad. I mean, everyone must have *some* divergence — surely? I've always assumed perfection is impossible.'

'So what are you saying?' asked Seabright. 'The guy is some kind of robot?'

'Stay calm, Joe,' said Wendy. 'I'm sure it's something perfectly straightforward. Perhaps we just need a few more decimal points to see the variation.'

Jim seized her suggestion and changed the settings accordingly – but the outcome was more of the same:

> William Shakespeare, *Triumph of the Solix*
> 0.000000000000%

'It's impossible,' he said.

'Is it?' returned Wendy.

'Yes. So Shakespeare is better than Cobley – we can agree on that. But by such an enormous order of magnitude? To the point of absolute faultlessness? Heavens, even I can identify a few flaws in his screenplay.'

'Then what the hell is going on?' demanded Seabright. 'I thought this math of yours was infallible?'

Jim took a deep breath. 'Let's take it back one step.'

Wendy saw he had started sweating. She reached out to calm him, but he only trembled more, resistant to the strange equanimity she herself was experiencing: relief that, for whatever reason, this latest truth – like all the best truths – looked set to leave them baffled after all.

'Here we go,' said Jim, clicking into a new window. 'The Mean Muse Ratios themselves.'

> Tom Cobley, *Hamlet*
> 1.8934:1
>
> Joe Seabright, *Triumph of the Solix*
> 1.3741:1
>
> William Shakespeare, *Triumph of the Solix*
> ERROR

'Ah,' he said. 'There, you see? The Divergence Percentage is defaulting to zero because it can't establish a Mean Muse Ratio to begin with.'

'And?' asked Seabright. 'Why can't it do that?'

Jim frowned. 'I have no idea.'

'It's a mystery!' laughed Wendy.

'Right,' agreed Seabright, defying Wendy's levity. 'An *impossible* mystery.' He stared at Jim. 'I'm right, am I not? This is an impossible result. We've all got a Muse Ratio. That's the law of being human, same way we've all got a creative gene. Our unchanging signature?'

'Well, clearly, we were wrong,' said Wendy. 'Jim was wrong.' She patted him on the back. '*Honestly*. Just when you think you're certain of something . . .'

Jim looked at her doubtfully, then turned back to Seabright. 'You're right,' he said. 'That's the law. But clearly something in Shakespeare's writing is preventing my program from establishing what that signature ratio is. It's like he has no fixed centre. He's actually transcending the laws of the muse.'

'But isn't that thrilling?' asked Wendy. 'Can't we just be happy with that?'

Jim slumped onto the bed. 'It makes no sense.'

'It makes perfect sense,' roared Seabright. 'The man is some kind of cheat.'

'Really?' said Wendy. 'Then I ask you again: how exactly does one cheat in such circumstances?'

'Some kind of artificial intelligence?'

Wendy howled with laughter. 'Oh, *please*. You haven't got a clue.'

'It's not down to me to explain it!' protested Seabright. 'It's down to you!' He turned to Jim. 'It's down to him!'

Jim lifted his head. 'I can't fathom it.'

'Well I demand that you do.'

'You'll demand no such thing!' snapped Wendy.

'Then I'll go out, into the world,' said Seabright. 'Tell everyone about this error. Your whole victory will be undermined.'

'Nonsense!' exclaimed Wendy. 'You only see it as suspicious because you're clutching at straws. The wider world will plump for the far likelier option – that our Shakespeare is just too good to be analysed by Jim's maths. Human ingenuity outfoxes science. People will love it!' She sat beside Jim and held his hand in her lap. 'Isn't that right?'

Jim looked from Wendy to Seabright, then back again. 'Yes.' He managed a smile. 'You're quite right.'

There was a moment's silence. Seabright, standing over them, was breathing heavily, his fists clenched. Wendy braced herself for the next onslaught, wondering how they'd ever make their flight, given the intractability of the situation. But after a moment's consideration, their guest steadied himself and turned to exit.

'Well, if you two are certain,' he said. 'I guess I'll just have to suppress my curiosity after all.' He turned at the door. 'Apologies for roaring at you. I promise I'll keep the whole thing secret, errors and all, just as we agreed. And good luck with Cobley. I'll miss him, but it's good to know he's where he belongs at last.'

***

Joe stepped out of the room and shut the door softly. Smiling to himself, he walked down the corridor, turned the corner, and waited.

Although his plan offered no guarantees of explaining Shakespeare's mathematical erroneousness, he knew he'd found a way of at least giving it the best possible shot. And that, truthfully, was all he wanted. But for that one niggling question of Shakespeare's DP, he really had reconciled himself to the previous night's failure. His ruthless single-mindedness was a thing of the past, and he humbly accepted his part in the damage done to Cobley's plays. Had the result come out in any way normal – better or worse than Cobley – he'd have happily let the matter rest, turning his thoughts towards a happy, albeit Oscarless life together with Grace.

But that's not what had happened. There had been an error. And if he was willing to accept *his* errors, wasn't it only fair that others at least try to explain theirs? All he wanted was to know the fight had been fair.

A door in the corridor clicked open and shut, and Joe heard retreating footsteps. He peered round and saw Jim Withers, computer under his arm, walking to his room two down from Preston's. Joe followed on tiptoes, reaching the mathematician just as he entered.

'Don't say a word.'

Withers spun round in a fright.

'Just give me a hearing,' whispered Joe. 'Five minutes.'

The flappy-haired fellow looked him in the eye. A few seconds passed, and then, as expected, Withers ushered him in.

'I suggest we keep our voices down,' said Joe.

'What is it you want?'

'I saw your face just now. You can't bear not knowing what's wrong with your math.'

Withers shifted on his feet. 'Really, Joe, my first loyalty is to Wendy.'

'Your first loyalty is to yourself. And how do you express yourself if not through your work?'

The mathematician went to the wardrobe and pulled out a pile of clothes, throwing them on the bed. Joe took the silence as permission to continue.

'I know you can't betray her wishes,' he said. 'And I'm not suggesting you investigate the error yourself.'

'How else can it work?'

'I'll tell you how. You give me the full results – here and now – of the test you just ran. Then I take them back to JoeTown and invite Grace to take a look. If she finds the source of the error, you'll be the first to know.'

'And?' Withers was holding a pile of underpants. 'What if that points towards some kind of foul play?'

'Then, of course, between JoeCo and the WAC, we'd have to make some kind of announcement.'

'Well, there you go.' The Englishman stuffed the underpants into his case. 'Wendy would shoot me for passing on the results.'

'If it comes to that,' said Joe, 'then I promise I'll put all the blame on me. Say we stole the results. You know as well as me that she'll buy it.'

Withers nodded. 'That she certainly will.'

'Well, then? What have you got to lose?'

He looked down at his computer.

'Don't tell me you're not curious to know what lies behind it. Whether it's a problem with your math, or something else altogether. Don't let the anonymity stuff cloud the issue. This is different. For you, it's about getting the math right. For me, it's about fairness.'

This appeared to seal it. Withers reached for his computer and held out his hand. Joe gave him his flash drive and watched as the results were loaded on to it.

'Now leave,' said Withers. 'If I hear nothing, I'll assume you've found nothing.'

'You're a gentleman, Jim.' Joe took back his drive. 'A genius and a gentleman.'

Chapter 25

'And you asked for no money?'

Jerry was sitting opposite Joe, separated by the calming blue waters of his sunlit pool. Nominally, he was checking his tablet computer for press reports about Shakespeare – seeing if there were any clues about the mystery man's identity that had yet to be noticed. In actuality, however, his productivity was hamstrung by incredulity.

'What the hell did Grace say?'

'She agreed it's for the best,' replied Joe, reclining in his favoured deckchair. 'Cobley's back where he belongs. Where he should have been all along.'

'But for free?'

'It was the honourable thing to do.' Joe took a sip of milkshake. 'Besides, as we've discussed, the Cobley rights are of little intrinsic value now. Whoever the owner, they'll have to invest to get any meaningful return. As it is, that's no longer our problem.'

'But what do we actually do? *Chronicles* is at an end, The Cobley Crusade is no longer ours. What is JoeCo actually here for?'

'Right now?' replied Joe. 'To find the source of that error message.'

'And that's it?'

'Pretty much.'

'I don't know what you're expecting me to find,' said Grace, cradling a pile of printouts as she joined them on the terrace. 'My math is nothing like as strong as Jim Withers'.'

'Just see,' replied Joe, as she settled beside him and began sifting through the analysis. 'The DP error occurred because it couldn't obtain a Mean Muse Ratio. So somewhere in the results, there must be another error that led to that.'

'And another error that led to *that*.'

'Quite possibly,' said Joe. 'But in tracing it back, seeing where the errors occur, we may start to understand what it is about this Shakespeare that's defying the laws of creativity.'

'Here's a thing, boss,' said Jerry. 'Article in the *New York Times*, yesterday morning. *Shakespeare's Summons: Will the World Listen?* Apparently, the answer is: they might. "Even before Shakespeare's imploring Oscar speech," it says, "there were signs of a new hunger for anonymity among artists across different forms. Already, four separate works have come independently to prominence in central Europe, each hailed as a masterpiece." It goes on to list them – two paintings, a symphony and a sculpture, all submitted under pseudonyms by artists preferring to remain anonymous. "It is as if the mere fact of Shakespeare's anonymity, originally ascribed to shyness, hit an instinctive note with other artists, even before he espoused its benefits so memorably on Sunday night. With such an appetite latently in place, it is difficult to believe Shakespeare's summons will not have an explosive, anonymising impact on the face of world culture in the months to come."'

'Which is all very interesting,' said Joe. 'But what does it say about the man himself?'

'Ha!' exclaimed Grace, immersed in her papers.

'What's that?' asked Joe.

She looked up, smiling, and reflected for a moment. 'Oh, it's nothing.'

'Tell me.'

'Just a funny coincidence.' She looked back down and turned the page. 'But it's no kind of clue.'

'Tell me anyway.'

'It's not what caused the error.'

'*Grace* . . .'

She sighed and turned back. 'It's one of the simpler scans. The

Median Test, he calls it. Having totted up the total word count for a given scene, it then halves that and picks out the twenty middle words. It's all sub-conscious, of course, but across a whole work, you generally find there's a similarly-constructed sentence at the heart of every scene. One which, like so much else, bears out the author's Muse Ratio.'

'And in this case?' asked Joe. 'It doesn't, right?'

'I can't say,' said Grace. 'I'm only looking at the raw data. The calculations come later. What struck me wasn't any pattern, but the words themselves. Specifically . . .' She ran her finger down the page. 'The median passage in Scene Forty.'

She read aloud:

> 'To know who I am, look in my creations. They're all mine.
> Crack the code to uncover the real me.'

Joe gazed into the shifting water of his pool. He felt suddenly cold, despite the temperature pushing one hundred degrees.

'Weird, huh?' said Grace. 'And weirder still when you see that it shows up twice in the results.'

'How come?'

'Once, because it's the middle passage of scene forty. And then again, because it's the median passage of the screenplay as a whole.'

'Wow,' said Joe. 'That is extraordinary.'

'What do you mean, *extraordinary*?' laughed Jerry. 'It's Tyron, right? Telling Mark Earloser where he's come from; how he's achieved what he's achieved. His creations are the Glozbacks, and cracking the code means understanding their chemical make-up – tracing back the origins of the distorted Spirit.'

'Sure,' said Joe. 'It makes sense in context. But still, you've got to admit . . .'

'Admit what? That the author is addressing us directly? The author, who notoriously doesn't want to be found, is telling us how to find him?'

'But what if it's subliminal? Grace said this Median Word thing is another expression of the writer's sub-conscious. Perhaps, despite his surface efforts to remain anonymous, he can't silence his inner voice. Or maybe his vanity means he secretly wants someone to find him after all – his ego bursting through his faceless façade!'

Jerry put down his tablet. 'You seriously think this is a clue to his true identity?'

'I'm just putting it out there.'

'It only feels like that because of its placement,' said Grace.

'But that's what I mean. What are the chances of something like this being right at the centre of the screenplay?'

'Slim,' agreed Grace. 'But far from impossible.'

'The point being,' said Jerry, 'if Shakespeare *did* want to lead us on, wouldn't he make it just a little more accessible? As it is, we've only noticed it because of Jim Withers' analysis.'

Between them, Grace and Jerry made a convincing case. But as they each returned to their respective labours, Joe couldn't put the sentence from his mind.

'Humour me for a second,' he said, rising and prowling round the pool. 'Let's break it down. "Crack the code", sure, makes no sense. But what of the other bits? "Look in my creations."'

He stopped, immediately deuced.

'So far, there is only one,' said Grace. 'If we have to wait for the others, we're going to be here some time.'

'There is only one,' repeated Joe, '*as far as we know*. What if he's used a different name in writing other things? That would make sense of the qualification: "They're all mine."'

'Why use a different name?' asked Jerry. 'The guy's anonymity is bullet-proof. All the more so, now he's persuaded Wendy Preston of its merits.'

'Right, but then I ask again: why the qualifier? Why might he suppose there to be some doubt that they're all his? What could be so unlikely as to require that clarification?'

Grace and Jerry stared back blankly, but it didn't matter. Joe already knew where he was headed.

'Let's take the suppositions at face value. Let's imagine there are other "creations" out there at the moment – not all carrying his name, but all somehow anonymous . . .'

'In which case,' said Jerry, 'they'd have been mentioned in the *Times*. But according to that, the only anonymous artworks created so far are two paintings, one sculpture, and one . . .'

Joe grinned. Jerry had walked straight into his trap.

'Oh, come on. You're not seriously suggesting that the same guy who wrote the WAC's *Triumph of the Solix* is also a genius painter, sculptor and composer?'

'It's just a hypothesis,' said Joe, pausing briefly before adding: 'But it's the only one we have.'

He set off towards his office.

'Where are you going?'

'Just now, Jerry, you were asking what JoeCo is for. Well, now you have your answer.'

'Which is?'

'Cracking the code!'

Within minutes, he had ordered full-size digital prints of the two paintings, plus a detailed photograph of the award-winning sculpture and a full-score manuscript of the symphony. An hour later, the items arrived, and he assigned each to a different JoeCo department.

Larry Jones and his conceptual artists looked at the two paintings – one an abstract called *Revival*, the other a sweeping landscape entitled *Omniscience* – while their esteemed *Chronicles* composer, flanked by his copyists and orchestrators, took away the *Sinfonia Rinascente*. Lastly, the few staff that remained of JoeCo's modelling team agreed to focus on the abstract iron sculpture, called *Polymath*. In each case, the brief was simple: look for anything which might pass for a code, and try to crack it.

Joe re-joined Grace and Jerry on the terrace, the two of them still engrossed in their detective work.

'Well?' said Jerry. 'What's your gut feeling? Could the same person be responsible for each?'

Joe took a deep breath. 'We did notice that the word *Revival* is a bit like *Rinascente* – which means rebirth. So there's some kind of theme.' He went to sit by Grace, and sighed. 'But other than that, the three visual pieces couldn't be more different.'

'I tried telling you, boss,' said Jerry. 'I did say.'

'How's it going, honey?'

Grace looked up from the paperwork. 'Well, I'm yet to light upon any outright errors. But I'm now into the calculations – where the math is trying to derive the all-important ratios. And what's obvious is that in every single aspect of Shakespeare's writing, there just *is* no recurrence. Every instance of every subconscious ratio is at variance with the next. That's why it's creating an error. But the source isn't an error as such; it's just the way he is.'

'Which is what? What is he like?'

She removed her glasses. 'Inconstant. From one sentence to the next, it's like he's a different writer. As an artist, his inherent style is always shifting.'

'Which backs up what I'm saying, right?' Joe felt suddenly encouraged. 'He's indefinable. So it's no wonder those four artworks are all so different from one another.'

'I don't know . . .' said Grace. 'There's a big gulf from being a schizoid writer to an artist who can be schizoid across different art forms. Sure, these results are arresting, but—'

'Boss!'

The cry came from indoors.

'It's me! Larry!'

Joe moved towards his office, but before he got there Larry strode onto the terrace, holding aloft the full-sized print of Philip Lake's *Revival*.

'You were right, boss.' He draped the abstract painting over a pair of deckchairs.

'I was?' Joe glanced at Jerry, but found himself too surprised to gloat. Being right was nice, but it raised as many questions as it answered. 'Are you certain?'

'One hundred per cent,' said Larry, donning his glasses. 'And here's why.'

***

'Chop chop, people,' said Wendy, sitting at the head of the desk in the WAC's main meeting room, back to the door. It was the first time she'd seen the rest of the team since leaving the last of the Oscar parties four days before. While she and Jim had stayed in Tinseltown to meet the press, the others had trooped back to Warwickshire and returned to work. There was a lot to catch up on.

'First things first,' she began. 'How's the response been to Sunday?'

'Tremendous,' replied Clive, emerging from the line of people on Wendy's left. 'Hundreds of messages of congratulation.'

'Lovely,' she smiled, though this wasn't quite what she meant. 'And the other thing?'

'Likewise tremendous.'

This time it was Pat, leaning forward on her right.

'We emailed everyone as soon as we returned, and the response has been 100% positive. All our publications, plays, films, to be henceforward anonymous with immediate effect.'

'And people really believe it?' asked Jim, from the opposite end. 'They're not just scared of losing their contract?'

'It seems they are speaking from the heart.' Pat smiled at Wendy. 'You judged the mood of the group – and the nation, dare I say it – to perfection.'

'Well thank goodness for that,' she said. Truthfully, she hadn't been thinking about anyone other than herself when agreeing with Shakespeare on Sunday night.

'Best of all,' said Clive, 'the press coverage has been hugely complimentary. No sign of any movement to unmask Shakespeare.'

'Wow,' said Wendy, genuinely moved to hear this. Despite everything she'd said to Seabright, part of her had still feared a popular desire to hunt down Shakespeare. She'd worried that the modern world, with its inability to keep a secret, would be unwilling to indulge the pleasure of simply marvelling at something fantastic without requiring the additional gratification of finding out what lay behind it.

'We have some news of our own,' said Jim.

'Ah, yes,' said Wendy. 'Do you want to, or—'

Jim smiled back. 'It's all yours, Miss Preston.'

Wendy felt her cheeks reddening. 'The night following the ceremony,' she explained, 'we had a visit from you-know-who. I shan't bore you with the details. Suffice it to say, he left feeling ever so penitent about how he treated Tom Cobley.'

'And?' asked Keith. 'A little late in the day to make amends, surely?'

'Perhaps.'

'There's no undoing the damage he did.'

'Really?' Wendy winked at Jim. 'Well, in that case I guess we shouldn't bother.'

Keith sat forward. 'Say that again?'

'No, no. You're right. There's nothing to be done.'

'Tell us!' demanded Pat.

Wendy grinned. 'The Worldwide Authorship Circle — I'm so happy to say — is now the proud owner of the full international rights to Tom Cobley. Kindly offered to us for zero pence by Joe Seabright, with the only proviso that we do our best to mop up the mess he left behind.'

She took in the gallery of dazed expressions — none more disbelieving than Keith.

'After all this time.' Cobley's descendent stood and raised his arms aloft. 'Finally, justice is done!'

There was a spontaneous round of cheering, table-tapping and applause. Now the moment was upon them, this felt like an even greater reward for the group than the Oscar itself. Revenge had been sweet, but nothing matched the simple righting of the wrong that had so enraged them in the first place.

'There's still much to decide,' cautioned Jim, 'but the challenge couldn't be more timely. Re-anonymising Cobley will embody everything we now stand for: doing away with his biography, making people forget the detail of his life, so his plays can once again be judged on their own terms. If we can do it for him, we can do it for anyone!'

'We should start with the merchandise,' said Keith, marching round the table. 'Discontinue everything Seabright ever created, from the dolls to the video games. Destroy it all!'

'What about the plays?' asked Clive.

'Ban them,' said Wendy.

'Really?'

'*Absolutely*. A moratorium on Cobley. Quarantine the plays for six months, and then drip-feed them back into the world, right here in Stratford: one-by-one, unabridged and in the most literal productions possible – freed from the shackles of Seabrightified Cobley biography!' She looked round. The others stared back blankly. 'What? Don't you think that's a tremendous idea? Don't you think it's exactly—'

A cough from behind made her realise that her colleagues were looking over her head.

'I'm sorry to interrupt.'

Wendy turned. It was Joe Seabright.

'I wouldn't have come if I didn't think it was the right thing to do.' He scanned round the table, eyes landing on Jim. 'But I think you'll want to know what I've discovered.'

***

Having briefed Preston's colleagues on their encounter in the hotel – and on the error message in particular – Joe stepped back as the fuse caught light.

'You did what?' Preston slammed her fists on the table and glared at Withers.

'I was powerless,' said the hapless mathematician. 'I couldn't resist my curiosity. He promised me . . .' He turned to Joe. '*You* promised me. It was meant to be between us. And if somehow it got out, you were meant to say you stole the data!'

'Oh, this is great,' laughed Preston bitterly. 'I can't trust you, you can't trust him . . .' She pointed, finger trembling, at Joe.

'And he can't accept that he lost fair and square!'

'Please guys . . .' Joe held up his hands. 'You're the first people outside JoeTown I've come to. You'll understand everything once I tell you what I've discovered.'

'I don't want to know what you've discovered!' shrieked Preston, jumping to her feet and bearing down on him. 'Didn't I make myself clear the other day? I don't mind questions – the more questions the better – but I'm not in the market for answers!'

'Let the man speak, Wendy,' said a bearded, tweed-jacketed fellow. Joe remembered his name as Clive. 'He's come all this way to see us. Let's at least give him a hearing.' He turned to the group. 'Those in favour?'

Nine hands went up. Only Preston and Withers kept theirs lowered: one stubborn, Joe figured, the other simply frightened.

Preston took a deep breath and sat back down.

'Go on,' she said to Joe. 'Tell us what you've discovered – but nothing specific. No spoilers.'

'Don't worry,' said Joe. 'Only you can supply the spoilers.'

***

Wendy glared unremittingly at Jim as Seabright prattled on, sickened not only by his betrayal, but by the group's curiosity to hear what the Hollywood man had to say. For her, Shakespeare's erroneous Muse Ratio had been seamlessly assimilated into the rich tapestry of questions that lay behind his identity: questions to which she desired no answers. Why couldn't they do the same? Had they learned nothing? Democracy, once their lifeblood, now threatened to be their undoing; the end of this brave new era, even before it had begun.

Quite frankly, she felt like leaving the room in disgust – and would have done so, had it not been for fear of what other, even worse nonsense might unfold in her absence.

'And there,' Seabright said, 'at the mathematical centre of your screenplay, was this one, mysterious sentence: *"To know who I am, look in my creations. They're all mine. Crack the code to uncover the real me.'*'

Opposite Wendy, Jim remained scrupulously expressionless, while the others hesitated, then leant inwards, exchanging words of intrigue.

'Stop it!' she snapped. 'All of you, stop it now!' She turned to Seabright. 'How dare you come in and prey on their weakness?'

'Weakness?'

'Nonsensical speculation. Hidden codes. Cryptic messages. For years, it was the fuel that kept us going, but we – *I've* – moved on, and my colleagues are trying their hardest to kick the habit. The cheek of you coming in to exploit their vulnerability, just so you can exact some freakish revenge on the man who denied you the Oscar!' She tossed back her head and tutted.

'I agree,' said Seabright calmly. 'The placement of the sentence need be nothing more than coincidence. The line makes sense in context; far more, certainly, than the idea of Mister Anonymous leaving clues to his true identity. And hey, if he *did* want to do that, wouldn't he find a simpler way? The line would never have been flagged up without Jim's analytics.'

Seabright's inflection placed a strange emphasis on this last point. But before it grew into anything more, he continued with his story: stressing the idea of multiple 'creations', the clarification that 'they're all mine', and the fact that four other magnificent artworks had appeared in central Europe – all anonymous, and all created *before* Shakespeare's call to arms.

'It seemed a long shot,' he admitted, 'but I figured it was worth a go, so we distributed copies of the artworks among our specialists. Nothing so far has come back from the landscape, sculpture or symphony – not even the faintest sign of any code – but this time yesterday, Larry, our conceptual artist, spotted something in the abstract.'

He delved into his rucksack and produced a print-out of the painting. '*Revival*,' he said. 'By a guy calling himself Philip Lake.'

Wendy studied the inchoate scramble of wavy, multi-coloured, thickly-layered and overlapping coloured lines – no masterpiece to her eyes, but then she wasn't much in the mood for art criticism.

'What are you on about?' she sighed. 'You can find anything you like in abstract—'

'Go on Joe,' said Clive. 'Tell us what Larry found.'

Seabright placed the painting face-up on the table, then retrieved a set of smaller prints from his bag.

'Larry focused on the overlapping elements. Twenty are visible in total, some occupying only part of the canvas, others much larger. But what's really striking, he noticed, is the layout. However little of each layer is visible, there are enough crucial turns and twists to be able to infer the rest.'

Seabright began arranging the smaller posters. Each one roughly resembled a letter.

'Obviously, wanting the utmost accuracy and speed, Larry didn't do it manually. He scanned the image into a computer and asked it to unpick the layers. The genius being that, with the sensitivity of our 3D scanners, the computer was also able to calculate the order in which each layer had been added. And guess what? From the bottom up . . .'

Wendy watched Seabright assemble the individual layers in sequence. She was conscious of an advancing sense that, despite her hard-won wisdom and valiant efforts to prevent it, the richness of her Shakespeare's art was about to be . . . if not destroyed, then definitely weakened by firmer knowledge of the man himself.

The first letters were now in place:

I A M T H E N E W T C

'I am the new TC,' read Clive.

'I am the new Tom Cobley,' said Keith.

Wendy fell into her chair. 'Which is to say, I am the new greatest writer in the world. I am William Shakespeare.'

'This was the moment we knew,' explained Seabright. 'Not only that the artist called Philip Lake is also the writer called William Shakespeare, but that Tyron's words *were* significant.'

'What kind of polymath is this man?' wondered Clive. 'Not only a genius writer but a genius artist and – apparently – sculptor and composer. How is that even possible?'

'It's all very odd,' said Wendy, her head beginning to spin as she tried to counter Seabright's momentum. 'But this new clue tells us nothing of who he really is. The screenplay message suggested that cracking the code would unmask him.'

Seabright began arranging the remaining letters.

'Besides which,' she continued, 'I maintain that the screenplay message could still be mere coincidence. The only thing distinguishing it is being right in the middle – and we've only noticed that because . . .'

The first three remaining letters were now in place:

W A C

Wendy said no more. Seized by befuddlement, and a strange kind of fright, she felt Jim's gaze fall upon her as Seabright positioned the final layers:

H E L P M E

Seabright folded his arms. 'Now, do you accept the message in the screenplay? Left there deliberately so you – and *only* you – would find it. He's appealing directly to the WAC. Hence why I had to hand this over. He wants you to help him by finding out who he really is.'

Wendy leant forwards, pressing her fingers into her brow. 'But why?'

'Because, as you just said, you guys are well-known as code-crackers. It was virtually your specialism, when you were arguing over Shakespeare.'

'But why not just contact us directly? Why leave codes? And why does he even want to be unmasked in the first place?'

'And why, more to the point,' said Jim, joining them at the top of the table, 'is there no actual useful information to be decoded from the painting – apart from confirmation that we're on the right lines?'

The questions themselves seemed impossible, so it was unsurprising that no answers were forthcoming. The entire lot of them, Seabright included, said nothing for almost a minute, as the contradictions swirled silently round the room, obscured further by the eerie overtones of Shakespeare's plea: 'WAC HELP ME.'

And yet, for all that Wendy wished the questions would just disappear – that the Error message had never sparked Seabright's suspicions; that they'd never capitulated to his demands in the first place – there was no longer any denying that they had been meant to reach this point: that, in some unfathomable way, their assistance was not only being summoned but was *needed*.

Her phone rang. Desperate for distraction, she answered immediately.

'Hello, WAC?'

'It's Shakespeare.'

She jumped to her feet.

'How are you?' she asked, waving to ensure continued silence from the others.

'I'm well. Many congratulations on Sunday.'

'Likewise,' said Wendy, speaking more quickly than her brain would have liked. What on earth was she meant to say to him?

'So glad we agreed on the anonymity issue,' continued Shakespeare. 'It's a huge weight off my mind, knowing we'll be able to continue our fruitful relationship . . .'

Wendy stopped listening. She had to think instead. What was she to ask of this man who, despite everything he said about wanting to remain hidden, actually wanted to be found – and was supposedly leaving clues to that effect in other artistic achievements of which he'd never made the faintest mention?

The tangle of questions was too knotty for her to unpick. Besides, why should she? He was the one who'd left them all so vexed.

'What's going on?' she demanded.

There was a moment's silence. 'I'm phoning to let you know about a stage play I might be—'

'We know what you've been up to on the side.' Wendy looked towards Seabright, who wrote down the names so she could read them out. 'Philip Lake . . . Harold Sharp . . . Friedrich Helm . . . Janos Gáspár. Two painters, a sculptor and a symphonist. All of them you.'

There was silence on the line. 'What are you talking about?'

'You don't recognise the names?'

'Oh, I recognise the names alright. They're pseudonyms for other artists, inspired by my precedent.' Despite the conviction of his words, he sounded oddly uncertain. 'All wonderful artists, I'm sure.'

There was another pause. Wendy let it linger.

'But I'm intrigued,' continued Shakespeare. 'Why on earth would you think . . . ?'

'The messages.'

'Messages?'

'Messages addressed to us. Asking us to help you. To crack some kind of code to find out who you really are.'

'Oh, *please* . . .' Shakespeare paused. 'I mean, *really*? Are you out of your mind?'

'I honestly thought we were.' Wendy looked again at Seabright. 'But it's all tallying up.'

'You're crazy.' The words were coming in bursts. 'You're imagining things.'

Wendy stopped herself replying, struck anew by Shakespeare's discomfort. He sounded both shocked and fearful.

'It must be your sub-conscious,' he said. 'Or maybe my sub-conscious.'

'There's no sub-conscious about it. Trust me. After everything that's happened, I desperately didn't want to believe it. But the evidence is impossible to—'

There was a click. Shakespeare was gone.

Wendy turned to the others. 'Terrified. Clearly. Not only surprised at the messages, but panicked by their presence. And now he's hung up like his secret is out . . .' She reflected again. 'He sounded almost angry.'

'Angry at what?' asked Clive.

'Or . . .' Jim was surveying the letters once again. 'Angry at who?'

'What do you mean?'

'"I am the new Tom Cobley". Why frame it at one remove? Why not "I am WS" – meaning our author, William Shakespeare? Why make us jump through that hoop to understand him?'

'It makes no sense,' said Wendy, a sickness starting to squeeze her throat as she caught up with Jim's thinking. 'It makes no sense because that's not how he intends it. "I am the new Tom Cobley." He's not talking about his writing abilities. Heavens, no. For he knows full well he's *better* than Tom Cobley. He's talking about his situation: an imprisoned genius, doing the will of another. That's why Shakespeare knows nothing. Because he's only the master. There's another person, the Tom Cobley of the outfit, actually doing the creating. And it's that Cobley who intends to embed codes in his work without Shakespeare's knowledge. "Crack the code to uncover the real me." He's talking about us finding him. The codes are intended as clues as to where he is.'

'So why is there no meaningful clue in the abstract?' asked Clive.

Wendy smiled. There could be only one answer. 'Because he doesn't have any. Not yet.'

'Not yet,' repeated Pat. 'Operative words.'

'Right,' said Jim, standing.

'How so?' asked Wendy.

'You just blew the cover of this new Tom Cobley. Shakespeare now knows about the clues, and is most likely less than impressed. If there are any pointers to his location in those other artworks, they won't be useful much longer.'

'Then we'll have to work quickly.' Wendy looked to Seabright. 'Your chaps are still working on the other artworks?'

The Hollywood man nodded. 'But Larry aside, they've made no progress.'

'No matter,' said Wendy. 'We're the experts, right chaps? Cobley's asked us to do a job, so let's get to it.'

***

It was time for Joe to step back. As Cobley had correctly observed, this was the WAC's forte, honed during years of uncovering codified evidence supporting different authors' claims to the plays of the original William Shakespeare. Never mind that most of that evidence had proved to be wrong. The skills by which it had been amassed were what mattered, as this 'new' Tom Cobley recognised – and as Joe now saw for himself.

Within half an hour, they'd sourced pristine copies of the three artworks – a fifth-sized model of *Polymath*, by Friedrich Helm; an A1 print of *Omniscience*, by Harold Sharp; and a full score copy of the *Sinfonia Rinascente* by Janos Gáspár. No one had any special expertise in any of the particular art forms – these were all literary types – but that didn't deter Preston and Withers. Having divided the others into threes, they worked the room as dual overlords, skipping from group to group, sparking new lines of inquiry.

Just forty minutes after starting, the first answer came, and it seemed watertight. Of the three visual pieces, *Polymath* was the closest in spirit to the senselessness of *Revival*: a complex network of plastic tubes, each a different thickness, colour and material, interlacing to form an upright alien figure, gazing towards the heavens. But what at first seemed irresolvably complex, containing nothing that could possibly be whittled down into a clue, in fact possessed a remarkable symmetry: the twists and turns of every tube occurred in exactly the same relative proportions across the piece. The varying lengths meant that each tube looked either stretched or compressed beside the next, but they all followed the same series of undulations. And when the length of each was standardised – as was easy to envisage once the model had been dismantled, and the different tubes laid side by side – the nature of the uniformity was self-evident, even to Joe.

'It's the Thames!' he exclaimed. 'The Thames, winding through central London.'

So their hunch was confirmed. They were indeed looking for place-based clues, pointing to the prison where this new Tom Cobley resided – and the first piece of the jigsaw was in place. The artist, himself something of a polymath, was in London.

'Over here,' shouted Clive, who was working with two others on Friedrich Helm's *Omniscience*. 'I've just seen it.'

'Seen what?' asked Joe, peering over his shoulder.

'Hidden in the stars. Ignore the planets. Just see the stars.'

Joe looked at the print. Even to his untrained eye, it was an impressive piece. The focus was a man at work in his study, seated with his back to the viewer. Balding, wizened and clad in unglamorous rags, he looked like a painter, with screwed-up paper strewn around, a forest of pens, pencils and brushes cluttering his desk, and a large canvas in front of him. But more striking than his circumstances was his posture: arms held out wide, as if embracing the vista that opened out before him, through a pair of French windows.

And what a view it was. The anonymous artist had made his home at the top of a hill in a generally Italianate landscape. Beyond the base of the hill, however, the land fell abruptly away, subverting perspective until – at the line of the horizon – the curve of the earth bulged from one side of the canvas to the other. Above it a thin, glowing blueness underscored the black mass of space, its vastness punctuated by a haphazard assembly of planets, stars and galaxies.

Except that now, it appeared, there was method to it after all. As Joe's eyes lingered on the night sky, he remembered Clive's advice and saw through the planets to discern a tailing-off in the density of stars in particular places. Stepping back, the impression was of the darkened shadow of an archway. Flat-topped and positioned directly above the artist, its sides curved down to the point where, if they continued below the horizon, they would be precisely enveloping the artist himself.

'Bit far-fetched?' asked Preston.

'But you agree it's there,' said Clive, 'a definite feature.'

'There for all to see,' agreed Preston. 'And that's my problem. Surely it's just part of the surface meaning?'

'Really?' said Pat. 'Something this subtle, when everything else is so forthright? And anyway, what *would* it mean, on a superficial level?'

'Never mind that,' said Joe. 'The only question that counts is: what *could* it mean for us? Famous arches in London. What have you got?'

'Marble Arch,' replied Preston. 'Admiralty Arch. Charing Cross Station. He could be near any of them.'

'But how would he know that?' asked Withers. 'Our guess is that he's trapped, unsure of his location. Assuming he's working purely by sound or instinct, how could he be so specific?'

'It looks like the archway is enclosing him,' observed Joe.

'It's all too vague,' muttered Withers, heading to the last trio of investigators, who were flicking through the score to the *Sinfonia Rinascente*. 'Any joy, chaps?'

Keith shook his head. 'This is phenomenally complex. None of us are musicologists, but even if we were, we'd struggle. I mean, how do you bury a clue in notation?'

'But Cobley must know you guys aren't musical, right?' said Joe. 'He must've made allowances.'

'Even so . . .' Keith turned a page. 'It's just so hard looking when you don't know what you're looking *for*.'

'There must be something that lets you in,' asserted Joe. 'A clue to the clue.'

'There!' exclaimed Withers, pointing at the score. 'What's that? *Rome's Legend*.'

'The symphony's in five movements,' explained Keith. 'We're in the middle of the third, which has this little trio section, subtitled *Rome's Legend.'*

'Do any other bits have subtitles?' asked Preston.

'Not that I've seen,' replied Keith.

'Then perhaps it's a clue!'

'No perhaps about it,' smiled Withers. *'Rome's Legend.* The music itself – I can see from here – is all pizzicato strings.'

He half-hummed, half-sang a tune consisting exclusively of oddly clipped phrases: regular to the point of banality.

'Peculiar, eh?'

'Most unremarkable,' agreed Keith. 'Certainly compared to the rest.'

'So why pick it out for subtitling?' asked Preston.

'Why indeed?' said Withers. 'And why, more to the point, pick a subtitle so inappropriate? *Rome's Legend* sounds heroic. You expect something mighty but this is reticent. More mechanical than melodic; reminiscent of something else altogether – something unmusical.'

He gazed around, urging the others to see it – to *hear* it – for themselves.

'Morse Code!' cried Preston. *'Rome's Legend.* "Legend" is key, is code; Rome's is an anagram of Morse.'

'The music *is* Morse code?' asked Joe.

Withers nodded. 'The notes are exclusively crotchets and minims – dots and dashes. That's why it's so brief; so lacklustre.'

'But what does it say?' asked Preston.

'Two secs . . .'

Withers retrieved his laptop and inputted the code to a Morse decryption program. Seconds later, he read out their answer:

AVERAGE UP
1154 1201 1209 1217 1220 1224
1231 1237 1241 1246 1254 1301

'Random ascending numbers,' said Keith.

'Not random,' said Withers. 'Averages.'

'But averages of what?' asked Joe.

'Times,' said Wendy. 'The last two digits are never higher than 59.'

'Average *Up* . . .' mused Clive. 'What could that mean?'

'Wait!' exclaimed Withers, turning the page of the score. 'There's more. This repeat, at first glance it looks identical, but it's very slightly different.'

He processed the data and read out the second part of the clue:

AVERAGE DOWN
1154 1202 1207 1216 1220 1229
1235 1241 1245 1250 1254 1303

'Average Up, Average Down,' he said. 'Up times, down times.' He smiled at the rest of them. 'We're talking trains, people. This is a timetable. Up trains to London, down trains out of London.'

'But what use is that in finding his location?' asked Preston.

'Co-ordinates,' said Joe, seized by inspiration as he looked again at *Omniscience*. 'These aren't departure times or arrival times. These are times the trains pass over our man Cobley – on average; calculated over several days, to allow for variations.'

'What do you mean, *pass over* him?' asked Clive.

Joe nodded at the painting. 'See the archway, hidden in the stars?'

There was a moment's silence as everyone studied the print.

'Of course,' murmured Preston. 'A railway arch.'

'Right,' grinned Joe. 'A railway arch, somewhere in London – and it's where our man is trapped right now.'

Chapter 26

They were just round the corner from the Globe – in Shakespeare's London, as it was, in Cobley's London, as it had become, and in heaven-knew-who's London, as it now was.

In the end, Cobley's clues had returned them to the area in which they had begun, and indeed been based for so many years. They weren't quite on the riverside, next to the dear old Wooden O, but Union Street was a five minute walk away at most.

'So this must be it,' said Jim, once he, Wendy and Seabright had checked the adjacent arches and found them occupied by legitimate businesses: a theatre, café, printworks and removal company.

Of the many railway arches in London, only five had fitted the bill, according to the nifty program Jim knocked up to cross-refer Cobley's timings with published timetables, thereby deducing the places at which up and down trains passed in the manner described. All five were side by side and now, they knew, there could be only one: damp, boarded-up and graffiti-ridden, with a wooden door which, though padlocked, looked eminently destructible.

'Do we go in?' asked Seabright. 'Or do we wait for someone to come out?'

Wendy smiled. 'First, we do what you always do when invited.' She knocked loudly on the wooden board. There was no answer. 'Well, politeness is over-rated anyway, particularly when you're on a rescue mission. Joe: please assume your position.'

Seabright stepped back a few paces, ready to launch the attack.

It was a full six hours since Wendy had alerted Shakespeare to their activities. There was no time for dithering.

Hurling himself at the door with abandon, Seabright smashed through it at once, throwing the wood back on its hinges as he tumbled into the dark. Wendy dashed in and scrambled around for a light switch, soon sensing the worst. The place felt, sounded and smelt deserted – and proved to be just that as she flicked on a pair of faltering fluorescent tubes.

'Gone,' she said, staring at the bare brick walls, coated in grime, crumbling cement, and decades-old traces of paint. 'Well and truly gone.'

Seabright rose to his feet, caressing the shoulder with which he'd forced their entry. 'But were they even here?' he wondered. 'It's not just the emptiness. It's the staleness in the air. It doesn't feel recently occupied.'

'The damp is vile,' agreed Jim, touching the walls. 'Not much of a secret hideout – at least not if you want to keep you and your prisoner healthy.'

Wendy probed round, checking the dark corners for any signs of habitation, and scouring the walls for clues as to where Cobley had been taken, if indeed this was his former prison. But it wasn't to be. After no more than a couple of minutes inside, she led the way back out.

'I know the Morse Code is irrefutable, Jim,' she said, flicking off the light and pulling the door to. 'But what if your program missed other timetable matches?'

Jim looked doubtful.

'Or what if the clock by which Cobley was tracking the train times was inaccurate?'

They turned left onto Union Street and began walking towards London Bridge.

'Perhaps you could recalibrate it, so the program focuses on the spacings between trains, and throws up any arches in London where that particular pattern occurs, regardless of the specific times.'

'Wait,' said Seabright.

Wendy and Jim stopped.

'No!' said Seabright. 'Keep walking.'

'What is it?' asked Wendy.

Seabright glanced back over his shoulder; Wendy followed suit. His focus seemed to be a white van on the opposite side of the road, facing the direction from which they'd just come.

'The driver,' he explained. 'Crazy, I know – but there was something about him. I couldn't see any detail, but his profile . . .'

'You recognised him?' Wendy looked again. The driver was now fully out of sight.

'Not recognised as such,' said Seabright. 'But there was something familiar. And then, the way he began to turn his head as we passed.'

They arrived at a crossing. Seabright veered sharply to the left, down Great Guildford Street, where he stopped and pressed himself against the wall, shuffling back to peer round the corner.

'I knew it!' he said.

'What?' asked Wendy, looking over Seabright's shoulder to see the driver step out of his van and look up the road towards them, then back the other way, and then again in their direction. The road was clearly free of other vehicles, making his deliberation deeply suspect. Bedecked in a hat and full-length overcoat, he set off across the street, hurrying as he went. 'You recognise him?'

'Kind of,' said Seabright. 'Something about his frame: tall, spindly. Wait a second.' He leaned further forward. 'He's headed for the arch.'

Wendy could no longer see the man.

'He's stopping,' said Seabright. 'Checking again. And now – yes, he's going in!'

The three of them stepped out and ran back up the street. Arriving at the arch, they found the door was still pushed to, but a thin crack revealed that the lights were on inside. Seabright gestured for Wendy to go first.

'He summoned you.'

Wendy took Jim by the hand. Without a sound, she pulled the doorway open. The man they'd seen enter was standing on the right, and appeared to be placing a key into the brickwork of the opposite wall. They heard a click, and a door opened: a door disguised immaculately with a deeply textured painting of brickwork. A dim light came from the inner room.

'Mr Shakespeare?' said Wendy.

The man froze, with the door half-opened. There was a brief pause, then his shoulders dropped, he lowered his head, and he cursed under his breath. Pushing the door closed, he took off his hat to reveal a few wisps of silvery grey hair – and then, ever so slowly, he turned to face them.

***

Joe couldn't believe it. Lester Howells, a dead man walking? Lester Howells, William Shakespeare, the man who had snatched the Oscar from his clasp? Lester Howells, the man who was keeping the new Tom Cobley prisoner?

'What have you got in there?' demanded Preston. '*Who* have you got in there?'

Howells cast his frail, narrow eyes to the ground. The answer, Joe realised, was obvious. Pulse accelerating, he stepped towards the camouflaged door.

'Stand guard, guys,' he said. 'Ensure Mr Howells doesn't leave the premises.'

Braced for the worst, he pulled open the brick door and peered into the gloomy interior.

'Oh boy . . .' he whispered. Whereas the fluorescent tubes ensured the outer room was at least bright in places, this inner chamber was a black box, a solitary overhead lightbulb struggling to assert itself as the walls swallowed up its energy. And whereas the outer space was empty, this hidden domain was overflowing with junk. The walls were plastered with maps, charts and faint reproductions of great paintings and sculptures, all crammed around bulky bookcases, sagging under the weight of more oversized volumes than they could bear. In the corner to Joe's left stood an easel with a half-completed canvas on it, while on the opposite side was a music stand with tonnes of instruments littered around – brass, strings, woodwind, you name it. Next to them, an upright piano was just visible beneath swathes of sheet music smothered on its lid, stool and keys – a chaos matched by hundreds of paper notes covering the gigantic pinboard just beyond.

But it was only as Joe's gaze drifted further on that, with a chill, he realised what he was actually seeing. For there, amid a heap of rancid pots and pans, stood various units that together compromised a kitchen. Beside them was a half-open door, through which was the outline of a toilet and shower, and beside that was a single bed whose sheets had been strewn restlessly about. Up on the ceiling, a painted starscape looked almost scientific in its detail.

Joe lowered his gaze and focused on the foreground. The centre of the room was dominated by a large desk, occupied by towers of paper: sheets of all shapes and sizes which seemed to serve different purposes – some covered in pencil sketching, others crammed with tiny handwriting.

And then, finally, he saw it. Raising his eyes from the floor, Joe looked beneath the desk and observed four sturdy wooden legs surrounding a pair of thin, practically skeletal *human* legs, rising from two bare feet and obscured from the knees up by a ragged black bathrobe.

Rushing forward, Joe brushed aside the piles of paper to reveal Casey Howells, slumped asleep on the desk, his right hand holding pen to paper next to a nearly-extinguished candle. It was three years since they had first met, but such was the boy's wasted, angular frame, he hadn't so much grown in the interim as shrunk. Diminished by the ravages of his strange imprisonment.

'*Casey*?' whispered Joe. There was no reaction. He walked round and crouched beside the boy. 'It's Joe Seabright here, son. Your pal, Joe Seabright?'

Roused by the name, the kid twitched. Then, blinking to regain focus, he lifted his head and looked at Joe.

'Mr Seabright?' His pale, sunken face turned from blankness into bewilderment. 'What are you doing here?'

'I've come to rescue you, son.' He nodded toward Preston, who stood in front of the desk. 'We both have.'

***

Ever so slowly, Casey looked up and smiled. 'You got my messages?'

'We did,' said Wendy, voice cracking as she stepped round to comfort the poor child.

'I was relying on you,' smiled Casey, the tears escaping at last. 'I knew you'd run tests on my screenplay. I just hoped you would notice.'

'We didn't,' said Wendy. 'We totally fell for your dad's trap. Your friend Mr Seabright, on the other hand . . . he was a little more persistent.'

Casey grinned incredulously at Seabright. There was obviously a connection between them – Casey, presumably, a gigantic *Solix Chronicles* fan – which set the seal on the young man's rescue.

'How could you do it, son?'

Wendy looked up. Howells was standing in the doorway. His native Bostonian accent came as almost as much of a shock as his actions, so convincing was his English while posing as the publicity-shy, anonymity-adoring Shakespeare.

'After all I've given you. How could you deceive me? If you had problems, you should have—'

'What have you been doing to him?' demanded Wendy.

'I . . .' Howells hesitated. 'It's just a little . . .'

'Tell us!' yelled Seabright.

'Alright!' Howells took a deep breath. 'Casey is *Homo Universalis*. A Renaissance man. A Leonardo for our age. A master of all arts and all sciences.'

Wendy looked at the young man. Though plainly the source of

multifarious masterworks, his fragility was quite at odds with the superman evoked by Howells' heroic rhetoric.

'How?' asked Seabright.

'What do you mean, *how*? This is who Casey is. A young man of supreme talents.'

'Garbage! Casey wasn't like this first time we met. He was bright, sure, but he was also happy and healthy. A perfectly ordinary American kid, obsessed by *Chronicles* and not much else.'

Howells stared, trance-like, at his son. Wendy could see him planning the punishment in his eyes, and was determined to deny him the pleasure.

'Why won't you say what you've done to him?' persisted Seabright.

'Me?' said Howells, feigning surprise. 'Really, Mr Seabright, it's not me at all. It's you. Or rather: you and your fiancée.'

'My fiancée? You mean Grace?'

'Extraordinary,' chuckled Howells. 'Even at the last, your naiveté astonishes me. I waited years for the right person to come along, but not once did I imagine I'd have the good fortune to get someone so unspeakably dumb.'

Seabright stepped forwards. 'Excuse me?'

'You really were the perfect associate. A man so consumed by his own megalomania he not only offered me what I needed but was prepared to believe anything in the process.'

'Believe what?'

'The whole thing! Your unflinching credulity made it easy – particularly when you teamed up with the authorship lunatics.' He smirked at Wendy. 'It was sublime. The lot of you, reinforcing each other's gullibility.' He looked again at Casey and sighed. 'It's just a shame how that selfsame trait now has you thinking my son is genuinely unhappy. Sure, he left you those messages, but we all have off days – especially if you're as creative as Casey. Most of the time, I assure you, he's buzzing. Wildly elated by the work he's creating. Don't let the angst trick you into thinking—'

'Explain what you've done,' demanded Wendy. 'Or we're calling the police.'

Howells considered for a moment. 'Very well,' he said finally. 'As you know, I have, for many years, been preoccupied by the state of world culture: how, since the second half of the last century, art has regressed into degenerative, populist trash, epitomised by *The Solix Chronicles*.'

'You're right,' returned Seabright. 'We know this.'

Howells smiled. 'What's rather less well-known is that in the decades before founding the DNA bank, I sought to address this directly. Film after film, I wrote. Book after book, hoping each would resuscitate world culture and trigger a second Renaissance.' He gazed at the stars on the ceiling. 'Alas, I had not been blessed with the necessary talent.'

Howells went to stand behind the desk, where he placed his hands on his son's shoulders. Casey didn't look uncomfortable so much as vacant – not all there, somehow.

'It was shortly after resigning myself to my failings that Ruth and I decided to have a child. Like me, she adored great art – it gave her life purpose and meaning – and, like me, she lacked the ability to spark the revolution herself.'

'Hence Casey?' said Wendy.

Howells patted his son on the head. 'Casey, who gave us hope. Hope that he might be the one we dreamed of – the redeemer of world culture.' He looked around the study. 'We did our damndest. Had him listen to Mozart from his earliest days. Filled his nursery with the great Impressionists. Read him Shakespeare and Dostoyevsky from the second he could understand either . . .' He resumed pacing. 'But then, at the age of six, they showed him *Birth of a Hero* at school, and what do you know? Suddenly he couldn't give a damn for high art. All he ever wanted was *The Solix Chronicles*: to watch the films over and over, collect the plastic figures, buy the stickers, play the games, sleep in the goddamn bedclothes!' He rammed his shaking fist into the palm of his hand. 'The boy had been contaminated, and it destroyed us. Just two years later, Ruth died, driven to despair by Casey's fall. It was over her deathbed that I made my pledge.'

'Your pledge?' said Seabright.

'I vowed that Casey *would* become a universal man.'

'So you founded the DNA bank,' said Wendy.

Howells nodded. 'In my determination to honour Ruth, I asked what I was *actually* trying to achieve. At root, I realised, my wish was for Casey to be akin to the great masters I idolised from bygone eras. And since Casey was failing to match my aspirations of his own accord, why not force the issue? Delve into the past to acquire the talents I valued and then, instead of training Casey to be *like* them, simply do the more direct thing, and turn Casey *into* them.'

'Oh boy . . .' muttered Seabright.

'At the time, of course, most said cloning creativity was impossible. But I knew it wouldn't be long. All I needed was to gather the DNA of the great artists of centuries past, spin some half-truths about why I was doing it, then sit back and wait – safe in the knowledge that, when the day dawned that somebody discovered how to clone creativity, they'd have to come to me first.' He grinned at Joe. 'To this day I still can't believe the poetry. The fact that, of all people, it turned out to be you. The man who destroyed my Casey.'

***

'Hold on a second,' said Preston. 'You're saying you stole MET from Joe?'

'To say I stole does me a disservice. I stole it, and then I *improved* it.'

'How did you steal it?' asked Joe.

'That's where Shakespeare came in handy. My greatest challenge had always been how to acquire the technology once its exponent came knocking. I figured it was far more likely to be secretive, high-security stuff than an off-the-shelf product, and so it proved. How was I meant to penetrate the JoeTown fortress? I had a decent enough geneticist working for me in Pennsylvania, but he was hardly cutting edge. Certainly not up there with Grace Tremain.'

These last words were aimed squarely at Joe, who sensed with a shiver where Howells was headed.

'But why Shakespeare?' asked Preston.

'Shakespeare gave me the window of opportunity I needed to sneak in and snatch MET. Had it been anyone else, I'd have been reduced to something cruder: a break-in, or computer hacking. But thanks to Shakespeare, and the authorship question in particular, I was able to achieve something far more elegant: using MET to inspire my resident geneticist with its inventor's genius.'

Joe shuddered. 'You turned your man into Grace?'

Howells nodded.

'But how?'

'It was right at the start. Don't you recall? The first time we met, back in Pennsylvania, we were celebrating our little deal and I gave your fiancée a great big jubilant hug. At which point I plucked a loose lock of hair from her shoulder and had my man isolate the DNA before bringing it over to JoeTown, claiming it was Shakespeare's.'

'So the DNA you gave us at the start, *Shakespeare's* DNA, was in fact—'

'Grace's?' asked Howells. 'Precisely.'

'And the Shakespeare Prescription we made up in JoeTown – the formula *you* took back to Pennsylvania for safekeeping—'

'One hundred per cent Grace Tremain.'

Howells couldn't stop grinning – unable to stifle his self-satisfaction, despite his precarious predicament.

'Of course,' he continued, 'it was just a hunch that art and science would be connected. I couldn't be sure that my guy ingesting Grace's muse would give him her scientific prowess. Thankfully, fortune favoured my bravery. The moment he swallowed the pill his mind ignited. Within hours he'd inferred everything he needed from studying the prescription alone, and set about building his own MET Surveyor.'

'So that first screenplay,' said Joe, still catching up. 'The really bad one. That was written by Grace?'

'Afraid so. But hey: did *I* care that it was terrible? That was the joy of the authorship. It meant I was perfectly prepared when you came back, complaining how terrible it was. One mention of the authorship controversy, and my tracks were covered. All that remained was to sabotage the DNA Isolator in JoeTown, which my guy – fuelled by Grace – was able to do remotely. I knew your impatience would then prompt you to ask me to isolate the DNA of the alternative candidates – whereupon, my only decision was which of the candidates' DNA to swap with Shakespeare's.'

'And you chose Tom Cobley?' said Preston.

Howells bared his teeth in a grin. 'Well, you know what they say: the bigger the lie, the more people will believe it. As long as people went for it at first – and who could ever resist such nonsense? – Cobley provided the perfect cover.'

***

'So Shakespeare really was Shakespeare,' said Jim, who had been listening in the doorway.

Amid all the hideousness, Wendy found a strange solace in the simplicity of this statement. 'Shakespeare really was Shakespeare,' she repeated.

'But is that right?' asked Seabright.

'Without question,' said Jim. 'Your screenplay – written with Shakespeare's muse – matched perfectly with *Hamlet*. The two authors are the same man.'

Mention of Jim's experiment reminded Wendy of the anomaly which first set them on Casey's trail.

'So who wrote our *Triumph of the Solix*?' she asked. 'Who inspired Casey?'

Howells smiled. 'Who, you mean, can possibly be greater than the first, best and indeed *only* William Shakespeare? Well, it was a team effort.'

Wendy felt the perspiration building on her brow. 'A team effort?'

'Quite literally. Your screenplay was written by Schiller, Goethe, Chekhov, Beckett and Wilde. Not forgetting, naturally, a bit of Shakespeare himself.'

'You're seriously claiming that Casey's body is emulating different people's muses *at the same time*?' asked Seabright.

Head held high, Howells nodded. 'A universal man.'

'But MET can only emulate one muse at a time.'

'As I said: I stole Grace's work, and then my guy improved it – inspired by her miraculous creativity, of course. Credit where credit's due.'

'You're insane,' said Seabright.

'Perhaps. But it just seemed so much simpler than turning him into a universal man one genius, one muse, one pill at a time. This way, he was not only able to create stuff head and shoulders above everyone else – Shakespeare included – but he could create across different forms simultaneously. So we made *Polymath* – didn't we, son? – which was mainly Rodin, with a hint of Dali. And *Revival*, fifty-fifty the work of Kandinsky and Mondrian; followed by *Omniscience*, a cocktail of Picasso, Monet, and Constable. Then finally the symphony, which mixed up Mahler, Beethoven, Brahms, Bach, Schubert – even a little Wagner, for good measure!'

Casey said nothing. He looked awake, but only just, staring emptily ahead.

'Are you with us?' asked Wendy, kneeling beside him, but getting no response. Whether it was other people's muses or yet more sinister substances, the poor lad was virtually comatose on some kind of drugs.

'He goes through phases like this, don't you son?' asked Howells. 'Like I say, a few dark nights of the soul are to be expected, given some of the geniuses whose creativity he's been channelling. But for every depression, every day like this, every hidden message—'

'Do you have any idea what you've been meddling with?'

roared Seabright, obviously as sick of Howells' psychotic self-justification as Wendy. 'How little we actually know about the muse? Yes, MET worked ok for me, but that was over a short, controlled period, with a clear purpose and just one muse. To inspire Casey with so many, bending him to your will for so long . . .'

'But it's not my will,' pleaded Howells. 'This isn't something I wanted to do. The second Renaissance I've always craved isn't some decadent luxury. It's a necessity for the good of civilisation. Just ask Casey. Casey knows the selflessness of my intentions.'

Wendy needed no second invitation. 'Casey? You asked us here. Are you happy with this? Are you content, martyring yourself to your father's cause? Because if you are, then fine: we'll be on our way.'

Casey kept staring into the distance.

'I'm calling the police,' said Jim. 'And I'll tell them to bring an ambulance—'

'Wait!' cried Howells.

Jim stopped as the old man strode up to his son.

'God damn it, Casey, why won't you tell them? For your dear mother's sake, just tell them you're ok!'

Still there was nothing from Casey.

'*Son*. Tell them they're wrong. Tell them what you've always told me. That you care as much as your dear old father.'

Casey turned away. 'You're no kind of a father.'

Howells pulled Casey towards him. 'Please, son . . .' His voice was finally giving up. The tears were streaming down his worn, wrinkled face. 'Please tell them you're happy. Tell them you're not suffering.'

Casey pushed his father violently away. Then, gathering the strength to stand, he shuffled over to Seabright, who took the young man in his arms as Jim left to call the police.

Nothing more was said until the sirens sounded, and Howells – eyes averted from his son and his son's one, true hero – staggered out to give himself up.

Chapter 27

It was hot under the spotlight, but Joe didn't care. He was so psyched for what was to follow – the culmination of a life's work, under circumstances which made it more fulfilling than even he could have expected – that no degree of discomfort could quell his enthusiasm.

He grinned into the wings, loving every second, only to see Preston frantically signalling for him to start. He faced the audience and waved down the standing ovation.

'Please,' he said. 'I'm under strict orders. There's a lot to pack in tonight – that Shakespeare, for all his strengths, wasn't the most concise of fellas – so if you don't mind . . .'

The obedient Stratford crowd took their seats, even taking the trouble to shush each other on Joe's behalf. It was his first time back in the UK since exposing Howells six months previously, and his first time in Stratford full stop. While the glitter of the surroundings, both inside the theatre and out, didn't quite rival his and Grace's special day a month before, the whole place possessed an irresistible, old world charm which he loved just as much.

'Before we get down to the performance,' he continued, 'there's a little housekeeping to attend to.'

He winked at Grace, who stood beside him in front of the dark blue curtain. Her red hair was gathered in a bob above a bejewelled golden dress.

'Ladies and gentlemen, please welcome on stage the young man who – as of last week – my wife and I are proud to call our son. Casey Seabright!'

He stepped to one side and applauded, roaring encouragement in the knowledge that Casey would be feeling the pressure as he took to the stage. Not that he had any inherent cause to be nervous. He had long since overcome the psychological turmoil caused by simultaneously ingesting so many powerful muses, and was looking fully fit in his top-of-the-range tuxedo. It was more the context: speaking publicly about his imprisonment for the first time, and announcing a brave decision that had the potential, albeit remote, of upsetting the very people to whom he was announcing it.

'Thank you,' said Casey, taking his place as the microphone. 'I don't want to keep people long, so I'll cut to the chase. Oh, and before anyone protests: please know that I have Wendy Preston's full blessing for what I'm about to say.'

Preston nodded approvingly from the wings, and Joe rubbed the sweat from his palms on the back of his jacket. If anything, he was more nervous than his son.

'As you all know,' Casey explained, 'I've not had it easy these past few years. Despite my old father's claims to the contrary, I never once consented for the MET drugs to be used on me. It was only because of his threats, and for want of any means of escape, that I remained incarcerated for so long. But there's no point dwelling on what I endured. Let's just say that if great artists have a reputation for being bi-polar, then those extremities are only exacerbated further when inspired by the muses of several geniuses at a time. Oh, and before anyone suggests that the highs balance out the lows, let it be known that for every day of exultant creativity, I had whole fortnights where I failed to conjure any kind of positive energy whatsoever.'

Tears were working their way into Joe's eyes. He wondered if Howells was watching in his prison cell. Was it possible that, even now, faced with such courageous honesty from his onetime son, he still believed in the wisdom of what he did? Just how deep did the old man's madness go?

'So here is the first of my justifications,' continued Casey. 'I created five works of art while imprisoned, and it is simply wrong that any good should come from them; still less that they should be officially acclaimed. However powerful each may be, I cannot separate them from the circumstances in which they were created, and I do not want the world to make this distinction either. If it's not quite possible to erase them from existence, then I at least ask everyone to do their best to forget them.'

Joe and Grace initiated a round of applause which was swiftly taken up by the audience. Comforted by the crowd's empathy, Casey smiled at his parents. He knew now it was going to be ok.

'My second justification balances the first. For if my old father ruined my life, then my new father wasted no time in undoing the damage.'

'Oh jeez...' Joe reached for his handkerchief, abandoning any attempt to disguise his surging emotion.

'I am here to tell you, ladies and gentlemen, that the man you see before you tonight is as fine a specimen as this planet has to offer. It's not always been obvious to everyone, but I've known it since my earliest days. *The Solix Chronicles* have been a constant companion to me, and never more so than during my confinement in London. The vision, humanity and joy of his storytelling helped me through the darkest times, and I was overwhelmed to learn it was him, not the WAC, who uncovered the first of the clues that led to my rescue.'

Casey cleared his throat. The trembling emotion in his voice was sending Joe over the edge.

'Since then,' the young man resumed, 'he has been as kind a father to me as he once was an inspiration, and JoeTown has provided the finest possible setting for my convalescence. The place is everything it claims to be: a genuine haven, full of the warmest, smartest, most amazing people I've ever met. Truly, I am indebted to all who have dedicated their lives to *The Solix Chronicles* – my father, the great Joe Seabright, foremost among them.'

A rapturous cheer went up. Joe stepped briefly back into the spotlight, acknowledging the adulation, while Wendy Preston walked onto stage, a golden statuette in each hand.

'I therefore have no choice,' concluded Casey. 'This is what I want. It's what my dad deserves; and, above all, it's justice.' He took the awards from Preston, who scurried back into the shadows. 'With the Academy's permission, I hereby transfer this year's Oscars for Best Screenplay and Best Picture – won by me, via the WAC – to Joe Seabright and JoeCo for their *Triumph of the Solix.*'

The applause rang out once more as Joe and Grace stepped forward. Taking an award each, they raised the golden statuettes in celebration.

'Thank you Casey,' said Joe into the microphone. 'Thank you to everyone here in Stratford for your magnanimity, and thanks above all to the great, the original, the one and only William Shakespeare, for his crucial part in helping me achieve this lifelong dream.' Trying not to sob, he smiled at Preston. 'It's good to know that, through him, this victory ultimately belongs to us all.'

***

Wendy whooped back her approval. It was indeed delightful that in the end, after all the betrayals, reversals and misfortunes, she and Seabright were sharing the plaudits. For while the American's film was now the official Oscar-winner, it was their writer, reclaimed at last, who had helped the Hollywood man pen it.

Amid all the hullabaloo backstage – actors rushing to and fro, making final adjustments to costumes and make-up – it had been hard to keep track of what was being said on stage. But Wendy didn't mind. She was in her element, at the centre of it all, doing little of substance but overseeing everything, knowing that the great man and his works belonged to her at last, and that she'd do everything in her power to ensure his reputation was not only restored but gloriously, eternally enhanced.

Barnardo, Francisco and Marcellus arrived beside her in the darkness, puffing out their lips and rolling their tongues in preparation, while Seabright set about announcing the end of MET.

'It's a no-brainer,' he declared. 'Not only is Casey a living reminder of the danger when that kind of technology falls into the wrong hands, but you at the WAC have removed the need to resort to the past by uncovering abundant talent in the present. If our knowledge of the muse is to be channelled at all, let it be through Jim Withers' talent-spotting math, rather than anything more direct.'

Grace Seabright, as she now was, nodded her agreement, just as Horatio appeared alongside Wendy, offering a word of advice to the trio of starters. Moments later, a flurry of activity among the costumiers confirmed that Hamlet himself had arrived on the scene.

'We need to start in five,' said the stage manager.

Wendy gestured for Seabright to wind it up. The man had changed a good deal since they first met, but he could still rabbit on with the best of them.

'*The Solix Chronicles*, as you know, is at an end,' he was saying. 'But in chatting to Casey, I have rediscovered what it meant to write *Chronicles* in the first place, and desperately want to recapture the magic of making sci-fi for the simple thrill of taking others on a damn good ride. I therefore officially announce an all-new epic space trilogy, coming from JoeCo in three years' time, written not by me but my new apprentice: a man whose love of the genre cuts deeper than anyone's. My son, Casey Seabright!'

Wendy stepped on to the stage as yet more applause cascaded down upon the Seabright family. This time, it seemed, Seabright was indeed done, and off he went, arms around Grace and Casey, Oscars safely in harness, kissing Wendy on the way.

'And now,' she began, reaching the microphone, 'to the main business of the night – the main business, indeed, of a lot of our lives. As you know, we at the WAC own the rights to many great writers. Some prefer to remain anonymous, others are at liberty to hog the limelight as much as they please. Soon, once everyone in the States has told us what they had for breakfast, we will have even more. But even then, it is difficult – if not quite impossible – to believe we'll ever sign a writer greater than our most recent recruit: the man whose reputation, once unmatched, was systematically and unjustly destroyed three years ago under a cloud of deceit.'

'Now, following a six month moratorium – a ban on all performances and publications regarding him or his work – it is time to unveil the first in our complete cycle of his plays. Over the next year, in this wonderful old theatre, our collaborators at the reformed RSC will perform all 38 plays in straightforward, unabridged productions. The aim is to restore not only our national poet, but the depth of meaning which for so long was the hallmark of his masterpieces. Only once this is done, and the plays have re-established themselves in people's minds, will we begin the wider dissemination. But more of that, as they say, anon.'

She signalled to the stage manager to start the show.

'First, simply sit back and savour the return of one of the jewels in the WAC's crown.' The lights began to dim. 'Ladies and gentlemen . . .' She sensed the curtain rise behind her. 'I give you *Hamlet* – by our very own William Shakespeare.'

She strode off, taking the microphone with her. The opening exchange sounded on stage behind her.

'Who's there?'

'Nay, answer me. Stand and unfold yourself.'

'Long live the King!'

'Barnardo?'

'He.'

'You come most carefully upon your hour.'

She turned to watch, feeling a warm hand on her shoulder.

'Congratulations,' whispered Jim.

Wendy looked round. 'Where have you been? I haven't seen you for hours.'

Jim smiled, just as Horatio and Marcellus strode past.

'Stand ho! Who is there?'

'Friends to this ground.'

'*And liegemen to the Dane.*'

'Let's go and take our seats,' said Jim.

'No,' replied Wendy, fixated on the stage. 'I'm happier here. I like to feel it all going on around me.'

'We'll get in the way.'

'I don't care. Just for tonight, I want to be part of it.'

'Well in that case . . .' Jim stepped in front of her.

'Get out of the—'

Wendy saw what he was holding: a muted sparkle in the dim backstage light. She fell back onto a stool as Jim dropped to his knee – his teeth wonkier, his tufts of hair fluffier than ever.

'Well?' he mouthed.

The ghost of Hamlet's father strode past, on his way to the stage. Wendy's attention went with him.

'*Peace, break thee off. Look where it comes again.*'

'*In the same figure like the King that's dead.*'

'*Thou art a scholar. Speak to it, Horatio.*'

'*Looks it not like the King? Mark it, Horatio.*'

'*Most like. It harrows me with fear and wonder.*'

Wendy looked down at Jim, who had likewise got distracted. She gave him a poke with her foot, and he turned back to face her. Laughing, she held out her hand. Jim slipped the ring on and took his place on a stool beside her.

The ghost made his exit and Wendy followed him into the wings with her eyes, bringing into view Jim's face, close to hers. Quite involuntarily, she felt her head fall forward, drawn towards his like a magnet. Their lips touched.

'*'Tis gone and will not answer.*'

Resting her head on his shoulder, they joined hands and watched the action together.

'*How now, Horatio? You tremble and look pale. Is not this something more than fantasy?*'

Jim squeezed her hand. There was no need for any words, united as they were by the love of an eloquence more searching than anything they could conjure; an eloquence which once divided them but now, at long last, belonged to them both.

Printed in Great Britain
by Amazon.co.uk, Ltd.,
Marston Gate.